The Girl in the Tile

Publisher, Copyright, and Additional Information

The Girl in the Tile by Kevin E. Timm

Copyright © 2025 by Kevin E. Timm
All rights reserved. No part of this book may be reproduced or transmitted in any form or by any means, electronic or mechanical, including photocopying, recording, or by any information storage and retrieval system without the written permission of the author, except where permitted by law. For permissions contact: mail address.

This book is a work of fiction. Names, characters, places, incidents, and dialogue are products of the author's imagination or are used fictitiously and are not to be construed as real. Any resemblance to actual events or locales or persons, living or dead, is entirely coincidental.

ISBNs:
9798309674756 (Paperback)

Editing by Brett A. Savory
Author portrait by Alexander Slade
Cover design and typesetting by Rafael Andres

THE
GIRL
IN THE
TILE

By

KEVIN E. TIMM

This book is dedicated to my beautiful wife, Michelle, for all her support and patience over the years. Without her belief in me, this book would never have been finished. She was my first editor, sounding board, and best friend.

PART ONE

The Fisherman
Haarlem
The Dutch Republic of the Netherlands
Mid-Winter
1654

CHAPTER 1

For six days, Piscator sat in the foul cellar of the jail, slowly losing his sanity to the constant drip of water.

There was one small slit of a window high in the wall above him. Each day, he entertained himself by watching the rectangle of light gradually climbing the moldy wall opposite him as the sun lowered to the west.

The dungeon was cold, gloomy, and dark most of the day. Stinking water was mid-calf on the floor of his cell. The various forms of debris had clogged the drains, but he had found high ground on a pile of rotting straw piled against the wall opposite the heavy door that reeked of old vomit, urine, and excrement. The cell stank with the disgusting odor; he gagged at the smell when he tried to eat the bowl of thin gruel the guards handed him twice daily.

His guards laughed when he forced himself to drink water from the filth. He had held off drinking until his raging thirst forced him to his knees in the pool, lapping like a dog from a gutter and closing his eyes as he tried to strain the muck through his teeth. His toilet, an overflowing and filthy pot, was in the corner of the cell, as far from his mound of straw as his chained ankle would allow him to move.

He tried not to think of the many occupants who had left their mark in this cruel cistern.

When his Brotherhood called, when the very foundations of the world shook, he would take his vengeance. The people behind this mockery of justice? They would drink from the filth of this room and be left here to die.

The chilly evenings seeped into this cell. He pulled the reeking straw around him and tried to sleep, shivering until his body ached; mostly, he sat and trembled as the empty hours gorged on his heart.

He did have cellmates: long-tailed rats that crawled over him at night, little ruffians that nipped at him and scratched at his exposed flesh. When he could take it no longer, he would scream and flail until the flea-infested wretches flew off him to splash in the foul water.

He didn't know what had become of Johannes. Dead, he presumed. When he had asked the guards about his friend's fate, they had lashed out at him with fists and told him to hold his tongue if he wanted to stay alive.

Where *were* his Masters? They must know of his imprisonment. Why hadn't they come for him? Why was he still here in this cell filled with rats and stink? He had never been so miserable and lonely.

Could dying be worse than this?

CHAPTER 2

Six Days Earlier

Three days of constant rain had finally stopped earlier that afternoon, but the evening fog from the sea was dense and cold as it mounted the city's red brick and stone buildings. A dog was barking somewhere, but with the peculiar ability of fog to muffle and alter surroundings, the distance and location of the barking were spectral uncertainties.

The alley alongside their table outside the inn on the Grote Houtstraat exhaled the stench of refuse and human waste; the gutter in the passage ran black with the filthy bathwater of buildings scrubbed by the assault of rain, draining down to the canals and eventually to the sea. Ghostly voices and shouts flowed with the mist. Laughter and loud voices spilled from the closed door of the tavern beside their table.

Piscator watched Johannes draw his cloak tighter about himself and grumble about the insistent chill of the night.

"Can we at least go inside and sit by the fire?" Johannes asked, vainly trying to warm his fingers over the small lantern at the center of the scarred table. "My fingers feel like they're going to fall off!"

Piscator eyed his friend over the brim of his tankard, smiling to himself. Johannes had his wide-brimmed hat pulled down low over his blond hair, leaving his brown eyes in shadow. His blond mustache and pointed beard hung like icicles from his face.

Piscator had known Johannes since they were children wandering the streets of Haarlem and had grown accustomed to his complaining. He had already explained that sitting in the mist outside at the little table on the red brick-paved street was more private. The tavern was crowded and hot, with too many listening ears for their discussion. He took a large mouthful of excellent Haarlem beer and listened to his good friend.

"All you say sounds well and good, Pieter, but what of France and Spain?" Johannes asked. "And the English, what of them? They won't just lie down without a fight. And the Austrians won't allow it, either. And that isn't all!"

Johannes waggled a finger in Piscator's face. "Don't forget the Poles and the Swedes, and what about the Holy Roman Empire? This world is full of countries and armies just spoiling for a fight. Why do you think your little group can best all of them?"

Johannes was teetering along the fine line between clarity and drunkenness and pronounced each word slowly and carefully, with only occasional slurring of words. Another tankard might push him off that delicate edge, though. Piscator was also feeling the effects of the beer, a slight tingling in his brain. However, it endowed him with eloquence and courage.

Piscator drained his tankard and thumped it on the table.

"My dear friend, hasn't it occurred to you that my Masters have considered all these things? I am not the only one poised to do this thing. Others above us concern themselves with such issues. We are to wait for word from those who lead and do what they ask of us. And it is then when we small fish, we dainty minnows, will take our rightful place. Our Brotherhood has thousands of followers throughout Europe, waiting for the signal to move. And when we do move, it will forever change the face of the world."

The tavern door opened, flooding the alley with diffuse light. Piscator stopped talking as the tavern owner's wife brought out a pitcher and refilled their tankards. She pocketed the offered coins while eyeing the two men suspiciously before returning to the warmth of the tavern.

Piscator swallowed the fresh beer and let out a bubbling sigh. "We need only bide our time, and our reward will be greater than you can imagine."

Johannes looked at him oddly, chewing on the whiskers sprouting beneath his lower lip. "And another thing: Why are you calling yourself Piscator? What kind of name is that? You are, and always will be, Pieter Jacobszoon—at least to me."

Piscator sighed. The beer made Johannes childish and petulant, as it always had.

"It's Latin for 'The Fisherman,'" Piscator said coldly, "and the name my Masters gave me when I finished my training. I consider it a badge of honor and will not speak further of it here."

"But what of those who object to that name?" Johannes asked. "You're treading on dangerous ground, my friend! Hundreds have been tortured and executed for less than this! The Church doesn't take blasphemy lightly."

"The name has nothing to do with Christ, Peter, or the Church. There are other fish in the sea than those He seeks and other fishermen plying yet unknown waters. Leave it at that." He looked at Johannes flatly.

"Forgive me," said Johannes, shaking his head. "I don't understand any of this, Pieter, but I know *you* aren't a fisherman! What are the names of your Masters? *'Veel Ezels'?—'Many Donkeys'?*"

Johannes laughed uproariously as if this had been the most amusing thing ever uttered. But when Piscator did not join him in his playfulness and looked at him frostily, he stopped. "And you have also lost your sense of humor. Why are you so serious? You're not the Pieter I remember."

"This isn't a laughing matter, Johannes. Of course I'm not the man I was. I've seen and learned too much to find humor in anything. The world is suffering, Johannes. The poor are fodder for the wealthy, who grow ever wealthier, while the poor are used and cast aside like broken chamber pots. My Brotherhood can change that, but it won't be easy or quick. But change it, we will! I pray it won't be too late for you!"

Surprised by Pieter's solemnity, Johannes's smirk left his face. "Listen, Pieter," he said, "you've been gone for what? Four years now?"

"Barely three."

"Oh, very well, three. And yet, you can't tell me where you were in those three years or what you were doing. And here you come from God knows where telling me tales of a great secret army plotting to take over the world and expecting me to join this group of yours without explanation. Why should I listen to you? Things have changed in the past three years for me, as well! I have a new son now, little Willem, and I finally have a boat to carry trade up and down the river." He narrowed his eyes as he peered at Pieter. "Do you know how long it's taken me to get where I am today?"

"Of course I do, Johannes," Piscator said, his irritation rising. Johannes had always followed his lead, even as children. When had he become so independent? Piscator had been gone too long. "I stood with you when you married Katharina. I was there when you christened Sophiia and Jacobus. You've always been my closest friend and ally. That's why I came to you first."

Piscator thought he heard a sound from the darkness, a furtive scuffling down the alley next to their table. *Just a dammed rat!* Europe was crawling with the flea-ridden creatures.

"And you, Pieter? What of you?" Johannes continued, finding courage as he spoke. "You're an artist, a true Master. Even with your long absence, you'll still have patrons lining up outside the door of your fine house with bags of coins. Are you willing to give all that up if this grand plan fails? Because if it does fail, you'll be arrested for treason and executed in the town square like a common criminal. Is this thing worth all that?"

"Have you listened to nothing I've said? It won't fail, Johannes! That is what is so brilliant about the plan. It can't fail!" Piscator growled in frustration and slammed his tankard forcefully on the table, squinting at his friend over the lantern. "You don't understand that when this great revolution takes place, and the world is set on its ear, I'll gain everything I've ever desired. All of Haarlem will be at my feet, and not only Haarlem but all the great Dutch Republic of the Netherlands. My leaders will greatly reward me, as they will you, if you listen to me and put in with us. What have you to lose?"

"My wife," Johannes answered glumly, staring into his tankard, "and my children. Pieter, I don't know."

"Look, Johannes," Piscator said, vexation growing in him, "think of the elegant houses the Verenigde OostIndische Compagnie, the VOC, live in with all their servants and fine food. Don't you think Katharina deserves everything the Dutch East India Company has? Your children will wear the finest clothes and receive an education at the greatest universities, befitting their statures. When the VOC falls, as surely it will, everything it owns will be ours, Johannes. Everything! Think of that!"

"Yes," Johannes said, his brown eyes wistful. "Katharina does deserve that. *I* can never give it to her—not on my pitiful earnings, even with my boat."

"There, you said it yourself!" Piscator exclaimed. *I think I have finally gotten through to him!* "Of course you can't! When my Masters take control of the government and seize all the treasures of the wealthy, they'll shower us with all those things and more! No one can stop us. My Masters have planned too well. Their strategies have taken decades to grow to fruition, and soon we'll rule in the place of those squatting like fat hogs on the backs of us who serve them! I want you to be at my side as you've always been."

"But what of your father . . ." Johannes asked.

"Don't talk of my father," Piscator insisted, suddenly angry. He struggled to keep his composure, taking a deep breath, and closing his eyes. Piscator ground his teeth, thinking of the man. *Ah, the great Captain Jacob van de Kust: scourge of England and Spain.*

He was one of the few sea captains in the recent war who had done well against the better-equipped English fleet. Before and after the war, he had plied the seas, captain of the *'Verda.'* He had made the run 'round the Cape of Agulhas and on to the East Indies and back dozens of times, bearing spices and silk for a wealthy and ever-greedy populace.

Captain van de Kust was one of the wealthier captains of the Dutch East India Company. The VOC had rewarded him handsomely, but at a high cost to his family. He controlled his house like he commanded his ship, with brittle words cutting deep and scarring forever. He was seldom home, but he was belligerent, imposing, and usually drunk when he was. He was a hard man, Captain Jacob van de Kust, and he brooked no disrespect. Not even from his wife, who endured the worst of his anger and drunkenness. She had died a sad and lonely woman just before Piscator had left on his three-year journey to the mystics of the East.

His mother, the quiet woman she was, had yearned for a marriage of love, or at least one of care and concern for the well-being of herself and her son. Instead she had to follow orders like the lowliest of deckhands. Yes, his father had made sure they were fed and clothed, and he had been well educated, but that wasn't an indication of love, only responsibility.

Piscator learned at an early age to hold his tongue, to heave when he was to heave and ho when he was to ho. Great battles ensued between father and son when Pieter chose the peaceful world of painting rather than going to sea, as his father had. He had no fond memories of the man and doubted he had said more than a thousand words to him his whole life. He hadn't seen the captain for more than a decade.

"My father is dead to me," Piscator said flatly.

Startled by his friend's outburst, Johannes looked sheepish and nervously fingered his tankard. "I meant no harm, Pieter," he said. "Please accept my apology."

"See here, Johannes," Piscator said briskly, impatient at his friend's reluctance. "I risked a great deal to meet you here. I've lain this before you openly. I'm offering this to you as someone I consider my friend—no, my *brother*. Will you take it up with us or not? If not, I've wasted both my time and yours, and I'll never bother you again."

Seeing Johannes's indecision, Piscator judged the time was right for his next revelation.

One last incentive, then.

He leaned in carefully, the brims of their hats nearly touching. "I've met someone in the Brotherhood who has taught me . . . other things—skills you can't even imagine. There's more to this than I ever dreamed possible. And I have taken those teachings far beyond even what they could imagine."

Johannes looked at Piscator warily. "What sorts of things?" he asked hesitantly, not liking this sudden change of subject. A cold prickle crept down his neck, like a ghostly feather fingering him. It slithered down his back, and he shivered.

Pieter's eyes had taken on an even more fanatical gleam. He had known Pieter since childhood and had never seen him like this. When he had returned home one evening to find the letter from Pieter on the small table by the door asking to meet, he had gladly agreed, anxious to see his old friend. Now he wondered if he should have stayed home.

Quickly glancing suspiciously around them, Piscator said softly, "There are doors to *other* worlds, worlds beyond number. I know where the doors to these worlds are, and I've learned how to open them."

A harsh laugh from behind them cut the fog-shrouded night.

"Well, I think we've heard enough. Take the two traitors!" said a voice from the fog.

Dark figures rushed them as Piscator and Johannes leaped back, stumbling from their chairs, and drawing swords in a metallic hiss. Piscator jerked his blade back for a thrust but strong arms pinioned him. He fell in a chaotic mass of arms and legs to the ground. The onrushing figures overturned the table, sending lanterns and tankards dashing against the tavern wall and clattering to the street.

He heard Johannes growling to his right, the struggling men's curses, and panting breath.

"You scum! You dogs!" Piscator snarled, kicking and squirming. "Take us like thieves in the night, will you?"

But the roar of a pistol cut him off.

Piscator's ears rang, and the double flash of the wheel lock momentarily blinded him. He heard the grunt and crash of a body hitting a chair or the table and falling. Johannes's sword spun across the cobbled street.

"No!" Piscator shouted, struggling against the strong arms holding him. "Johannes!"

Piscator bit off a piece of the ear next to his face. The man screamed and blood filled Piscator's mouth, hot and coppery. He spat the blood and ear into another man's face, and then a fist struck him across the chin, knocking his head against the street's cobbles. Strong hands grasped his head and slammed it again onto the stones. Lightning filled his mind with starry brightness, and dazzling pain shrieked through his head as someone slammed it one last time. He saw a smirking face beneath a wide-brimmed hat before darkness engulfed him.

CHAPTER 3

Six Days Later

Piscator was dozing, dark dreams clouding his mind, when he heard the guards unlocking the door to his cell. The thick oak groaned heavily on rusted hinges as it swung ponderously open. The two guards stood on the stone steps leading down into his cell, with the shorter guard holding a lantern above his head. The sudden light stabbed shards of brightness into Piscator's eyes, nearly blinding him.

The larger of the two, Thijs, a great ox of a man with heavy-lidded eyes and fists of iron, cleared his throat. "Time to get up, Jacobszoon. The judge is waiting for you!"

Piscator stirred in his putrid nest. His little bedmates hissed at his movement.

"I don't want to get up. I've yet to eat my breakfast, and I haven't bathed. And my name is Piscator. I've told you that a thousand times, and still you don't learn. I'm concerned about the intelligence level of this jail's staff." He ran his tongue along the jagged line of his broken teeth, a gift bestowed upon him by his guards. "Please convey my misgivings to the judge, will you?"

The two men laughed and nudged one another.

"It makes no matter what you call yourself," Thijs said as he stepped down to the first stone tread. "The judge wants to see Pieter Jacobszoon, and it's Pieter Jacobszoon he'll see. Now, get yourself tidied up. We can't let the judge see you like this. He might think we've not taken care of you."

The shorter guard, Krellis, a scrawny scarecrow of a man who seemed as filthy as Piscator, snickered. "Master Pissy is a mess, Thijs. He's a nasty mess! Smelly, smelly Pissy!"

Piscator loathed this guard, with his incessant whiny voice and his sneaking hands. Whenever the two guards needed to beat him, Krellis always found a way to grab at him, giggling like an imbecile. He would be the first to die when his Brotherhood finally came.

He had this at least to say for the big guard: Thijs was honest in his beatings. There was no covert touching with Thijs, just straightforward mayhem. He liked that in a man.

"Please tell him I'm busy with other things," said Piscator. "I'm in no mood for the judge. He made me waste away in this hellhole for a week. Now let him wait."

Thijs laughed, exposing his remaining teeth like crumbling yellow gravestones.

"Maybe it's not us that's dumb, Pissy. How often do I have to beat you until you learn it makes no difference what you want? You'll do what I say, or we'll have to learn you some more, eh, Krellis?" He clapped Krellis heavily on the shoulder, and the little man stumbled forward, almost stepping into the filthy pool. He cringed back as though it was full of snakes.

CHAPTER 3

"Now get over here so we can unlock you and be off." Thijs rattled the keys in his beefy hand.

"No, I think not," said Piscator. "I'm amid my morning meditation. You two run along now and see to the needs of the other guests this fine establishment is hosting."

Thijs glowered at him with narrowed eyes. "We don't have time for this, Jacobszoon. Don't make me lose my patience."

"Come over here and get me," Piscator said, glaring at his jailers.

The two grew silent, their faces grim in the wan light of the lantern.

"Damn you, Jacobszoon! Stop this foolishness and get over here." The two guards stood clenching their fists.

"No. And my name is Piscator."

Thijs snarled, stepping into the pool as Krellis put down the lantern and followed. They splashed awkwardly through the filth, hands to their faces to ward against the foulness. When they reached Piscator, the two men grabbed him and dragged him to his feet.

As Krellis unlocked his chain, Thijs angrily took Piscator's greasy hair in one hand and laid a fist across his mouth. His head snapped back and struck the stone wall behind him. He groaned, slumping against the rough wall. Cursing, they dragged him headfirst into the stone corridor.

Piscator staggered to his feet, one arm against the wall for support, drenched and reeking, spitting blood and gamey water from his damaged mouth. The two men pushed him forward, and he fell to his knees on the stone floor. Krellis kicked him in the ribs, and he collapsed as pain lanced his body.

Thijs grasped his hair, thick with muck, and pulled him to his feet. "Come along now, Master Pissy!"

The guards half-pushed and half-dragged him up the stone steps of the cellar and out into the jail courtyard.

The brilliance of the cloudless sky dazzled him. After the rank gloom of his cell, it was like a new and fresh world. Piscator stood breathing the cold morning air before the guards forced him to stand by the wall near a water trough. The two guards roughly stripped him, then he stood naked as Krellis heaved a bucket of icy water on him. He gasped from the sudden cold, and then a stiff-bristled brush was scrubbing him, followed by a fresh bucket of water rinsing sludge and torn flesh from his body. Krellis threw a robe of rough cloth over his shoulders.

Thijs laughed nastily. "There, Master Pissy. All clean and shiny, eh?"

Iron shackles were locked on his wrists and connected to the shackles on his ankles by a short chain. The two men picked him up, carelessly throwing him into the back of a waiting wagon like a sack of turnips.

The wagon traveled over cobbled streets, each thump and jostle inflicting more pain. They pulled up behind the dark wall of the Stadhuis, the Town Hall, with its white tower basking in the richness of the morning sun. He grunted in pain as the guards hauled him from the wagon and shoved him up stone steps to a white wooden door, then down a long hallway and a flight of stairs.

Piscator stumbled twice when overcome with weakness or pain. Thijs was always there to prod him along with a rough shove. When they stood before an oaken door, Thijs knocked.

CHAPTER 3

"This is the judge's chamber, Pissy," grumbled Thijs. "Now you had better be on your best behavior if you know what's good for you. The judge has no mercy for louts and brigands."

CHAPTER 4

"Come," a voice came from inside.

"Good luck, Pissy!" Thijs whispered to Piscator, grinning. A swift jab with a rock-hard elbow to his injured ribs sent a lightning bolt of pain through him.

The leaden, diamond-shaped window panes facing onto the cobbled square below lit the room warmly. The paneled walls were dark-stained oak and lined the room rising to the oak ceilings. Bookcases filled the walls, heavily laden with various tomes of unequal size. The floor was a checkerboard of four-square-foot pieces of stone outlined with the dark wood of the walls, running diagonally through the room.

Above the blue-and-white tiles of the fireplace hung a large image of an older man dressed in official robes with a blue cap on his bushy, graying hair. The man gazed angrily from the painting, a look of disgust on his sallow face, his thin lips pursed like a slash below his nose. Other portraits of dour men hung on the walls, glaring at him like voyeurs through windows from a different time. The room was silent, except for Thijs' heavy breathing.

There were several chairs around the room, including two opposite the fireplace where a churchman and another man wearing a black robe sat, a simple sword with a red cross pommel hanging at his side. The minster's brow furrowed as he glowered at Piscator while the robed man merely stared, but it felt to Piscator that the man's gaze pierced his soul. He looked away from the armed man, unnerved by his gaze. Something about his clothes and the sword at his side tugged at his memory.

After taking in the room, Piscator looked at the old man in black robes seated at a table below the windows. He was frowning at a paper before him at which another younger, black-robed man was pointing. The younger man had looked up when the door opened and smiled broadly at Piscator. He had long, blond hair pulled back into a tail from his thin face. His head sat on a white starched collar covering his shoulders. He was clean-shaven and stared at Piscator. His eyes looked dead like fish eyes, cold and lifeless in a pallid face. Even from a distance those eyes bothered Piscator.

Ah!" the blond-haired man said, "here's the person we are speaking of, our honored guest Pieter Jacobszoon! Please, come and meet the men who will aid us in deciding your fate this day."

He took Piscator by the arm to escort him to the table where the old man sat, but Piscator jerked his arm away. Thijs growled behind him, poking Piscator in the back.

The smile on the younger man's face was false, as though it had been painted on. Yes, it looked real, but something was wrong with that smile; it was like something quickly applied, imperfectly, as though trying to cover up an earlier expression. Beneath it, you could still see the shadow of sneering lips in a mocking face. The man put an arm around Piscator's shoulder, wrinkling his nose in disgust.

CHAPTER 4

"My word, Jacobszoon," he said, "you should be more concerned about your hygiene. You know what they say: 'Cleanliness is a virtue.' I would say you're as far from that lofty goal as possible. Nevertheless, we must continue."

He turned away from Piscator. "Here is the man of the hour," he said brightly to the old man seated at the table, "the artist, Pieter Jacobszoon! Have you met these gentlemen, Pieter?" After nodding at the judge, he swept his hand toward the two men sitting along the wall.

Piscator shrugged the man's hand off his shoulder. "I am afraid you have me at a disadvantage," he said. "Not that I care."

"Come, now," said the blond man. "They'll decide what we must do with you and your awful business. Here, let me introduce you!"

He took Piscator's arm and tried to urge him toward the old man at the table. He stood firm, resisting the attempt at moving him. The blond man looked at Thijs and nodded briefly. Piscator felt the guard's massive hand on his upper back, followed by a none-too-gentle shove that made him stumble forward, clumsily stopping when his thighs painfully hit the table's edge. He threw his hands to the table to keep from smashing his face into it.

He looked from mere inches into the watery, red-rimmed eyes of the old man seated at the table. The man looked up at him, furrowed brow arching over a bulbous nose. His green eyes stirred as he stared at Piscator. The old man smelled of fish and cabbage.

"Gerben?" the old man whispered. "Gerben, is that you, my boy? Where have you been? Your mother's been looking for you."

The comment puzzled Piscator as he watched 'Gerben' walk to the old man, scowling.

"Your Honor," said the man who seemed to be named Gerben. "I've introduced this man to you as the renowned artist, Pieter Jacobszoon. You're here to judge him. Do you recall what I told you about him?" He bent down to whisper in the gray-tufted ear. "Father, please."

Piscator frowned. Was his father the judge? What was going on here? Despite his aching side, he was curious about what was happening in this office. And who were the two men sitting along the wall? Witnesses? He knew neither of them.

"This is the legendary Judge Henrik van de Groom," said Gerben, looking at the artist. "He's agreed to oversee your case, coming out of retirement and a sick bed just for you. He's honest and knowledgeable and will remain unbiased as he considers the testimony of our witnesses."

He frowned at Piscator.

So, the two men *were* witnesses. Since he didn't know and had never seen them, Piscator doubted the veracity of their testimony. The man with the sword stared at him, making his skin crawl.

"Are you listening to me, Pieter? It would seem to me you'd be concerned enough about this hearing that you'd at least want to hear what's going to happen to you," Gerben growled.

"Why should I?" Piscator sneered. "This is an unlawful proceeding since your father is the judge. And he's a mush-minded imbecile, at any rate. Given that, I think the decision of this so-called court is a forgone conclusion. After nearly a week in your hellhole, I've heard of no crimes I've committed. That alone is enough to free me."

CHAPTER 4

"Oh, I think once you hear the testimony of our witnesses," Gerben said, glaring at him, "you'll understand why you're here. And there's something you need to understand, Pieter." He took Piscator's face in his hand and squeezed. Piscator felt his face distort painfully.

"You will never be free." He roughly shoved Piscator back. Thijs stopped his fall with a large hand.

"Since you're so very concerned about your hearing, it's time we moved on with it so that these gentlemen can return to their day," Gerben said, gesturing at the witnesses. "I must tell you, I've spoken with them; their testimony is damning." He glanced sideways at Piscator. "You'll be lucky to have your head on your shoulders after today. If it were up to me, you'd be at the chopping block as we speak."

"Do what you will," Piscator said, wiping a hand across his mouth. "You can't do much worse than you already have. Anything would be better than listening to you. And I still don't know what my charges are."

Gerben stared briefly at Piscator, frowning, then turned to the judge, who gazed at him blankly. He'd slumped a bit in his chair. Gerben sighed and helped the old man straighten.

"You must pay attention, Father," he whispered. "This is important to me. Please."

The judge grasped his son's sleeve. "I'm hungry, Gerben. I think I missed my breakfast. Could I have it now?"

Gerben angrily brushed his father's hand away.

"You had breakfast. I watched you eat it." Gerben said, eyes blazing. "It is time now for me to read this man's charges. You will be quiet and listen or you won't get your midday meal, do you hear me?"

The old man recoiled. "Yes, Gerben, yes. I'll be quiet."

Someone coughed nervously behind Gerben. He whirled around, his robe swirling at his feet. His pale eyes took in the men in the room, looking at each person. Piscator smiled at his discomfort.

"You may smile now, Jacobszoon," Gerben said harshly, "but you won't once I've finished with you."

Turning to the table where his father sat, he picked up the paper he'd been looking at when Piscator had entered the room.

"As the *Schout* of Haarlem, it is my duty as both prosecutor and sheriff to read the charges today against Pieter Jacobszoon, a citizen of the city and the Dutch Republic of the Netherlands. Allegations against Jacobszoon were brought to my attention by these two good men," he looked at the witnesses, "concerning his actions after his return to Haarlem following a three-year absence to places unknown. After a period of investigation, I, along with several of the town's militia, took Jacobszoon into custody at a tavern on the Grote Houtstraat. He was taken to jail and locked in a cell, awaiting trial. During this action, his accomplice, Johannes Cornelissen, died while resisting the militia.

"After consulting with Judge van de Groom, the court brought the following charges against Jacobszoon: sedition, treason, blasphemy, ungodliness, taking the name of the Lord in vain, creating works of gross indecency, conspiring with others to overthrow the government of the Dutch Republic of the Netherlands, and being a member of a secret organization, The Brethren of the Endless Rose, whose purpose is to undermine the teachings of the Church with their ungodly works and devices, and working to bring the whole of Europe under the rule of the eight mystics that govern this mysterious organization."

He lowered the paper in the ensuing silence and looked at the judge.

"These are serious charges, Your Honor, and if it pleases the court, I'd like to proceed."

The judge stared blankly back at him.

Gerben shook his head lightly and looked at Piscator, who had listened quietly to the charges.

"How do you answer these charges, Jacobszoon?"

Piscator glared at the *schout*. "This is an illegitimate proceeding, and I refuse to participate."

A hand slapped the back of his head, and then, he was roughly seized and dragged to his feet.

"You'll be speaking respectfully to the judge, Pissy, or you'll regret it," hissed Thijs in his ear, foul spittle spraying his face.

Piscator shook dizzily. His head ached fiercely.

"I answer to no man," he muttered. "And my name is Piscator."

"Very well, then," said Gerben, looking at his father. "The judge has asked me to call our first witness."

Piscator bristled. "But—"

He was interrupted by Gerben's index finger held before his face.

Gerben turned his attention to the two men seated along the wall.

CHAPTER 5

"The court calls the Reverend Andries van Buskirk. Please stand."
Reverend Van Buskirk stood. His black Geneva gown covered the length of his body down to his black shoes, the white vestments contrasting the frock. A simple black cap topped his gray-haired head. He was thin to the point of emaciation, fingers like delicate twigs sprouting from the sleeves of his gown.

Piscator's distrust of Christian ministers boiled in him. He hadn't been in a church since he was ten years old. They did nothing to help his mother, despite her being a regular tithe payer who attended church regularly. The reverend was now looking at him with an arched brow. Piscator didn't know the man and couldn't see how he could testify about anything regarding him.

"Please, Reverend, can you tell us how you came to know Pieter Jacobszoon?" asked Gerben.

"I have known Pieter Jacobszoon and his evil ways for some time. He is well-known in Haarlem for his tawdry carousing and odious depravity. He first came to my attention one foggy night while taking my leisure time after supper and I happened by his house. There was a celebration going on, loud and intolerable. Standing behind a tree watching, I saw no one I knew except Jacobszoon. The people in his house were laughing and drinking freely, flaunting the calm of the evening.

"As I stood dumbfounded, I saw a great cloud of darkness descend on the house from the night like a fog thicker than I'd ever seen. It chilled me to the bones."

"It wouldn't take much to chill those bones," muttered Piscator, earning him another jab from Thijs.

"Within the fog," sniffed the reverend, "I saw shadow figures flitting about: people with horns on their heads and claws like a bear for hands dancing on cloven feet with those gathered at the shameful bacchanalia. Then a great door opened in the fog, lit within by fires, and a massive man emerged from the door, skin blackened from countless fires. He had bloody horns like a great ox, and I heard the wailing laments of tortured souls echoing up the fiery stairwell on which the door closed. Jacobszoon embraced the great horned figure and drew him somewhere deeper into his house that I could not see. The vision then closed to me, and I staggered home, weak and fainting from the presence of such evil."

The *schout* looked intently at Piscator while the reverend talked as though trying to gauge his thoughts.

Piscator made his bruised face expressionless as he stared back at him. He wouldn't allow the *schout* to control his behavior.

"And did you know whose dark presence entered Jacobszoon's house?" scowled the *schout*.

The reverend mopped his brow with a kerchief he pulled from a sleeve. "Yes, I did. It's not something you'd want to witness or forget. It

CHAPTER 5

was the devil himself, the very prince of darkness and author of all evil and carnal in our world of woe. I've seen his presence many times, and the vision of that wicked being always leaves me weak and exhausted. I quickly returned to my home and stoked my fire after making tea. I needed warmth and silence to reflect on the episode."

"Do you have anything you want to add to your testimony, Reverend?" asked the *schout*. "Just listening to you makes my bones shudder. Thank you for sharing that with us."

The minister looked at Piscator.

"Please, Pieter," he said quietly. "It's not too late to forsake your wicked ways. It would be best if you repented so that your soul can be free of the stain it bears. I'm always willing to help a supplicant find their way back to the path of righteousness." A single tear trickled down his cheek.

"I've never been on the path of righteousness," Piscator said. "My path is one of reformation, allowing the oppressed and poor to be free from the heavy hand of politics and the suppression of the Dutch East India Company. My Brotherhood will rule all of Europe when we succeed in our strategy. All men and women will be equal, able to draw on the mystic power of the ancient gods of Egypt to—"

"Enough!"

The shout rang in Piscator's ears as the black-robed witness stood and cast his cloak off. He'd drawn his sword hissing from its sheath. It glinted in a ray of sunlight streaming through the window. Then Piscator saw the emblem embroidered on the man's chest: a small, blood-colored square cross. He drew a quick breath.

His Masters had warned him of such men. But seeing one standing with a sword and glaring at him made his blood run cold.

"I will not listen to such blasphemy while I can still breathe," the man said through clenched teeth. "I will defend God and Holy men until the day my sword falls from my dead hands. You say one more word of such deviltry, and your head will be forfeit. Do you understand?" His eyes flashed angrily in the silent room.

Piscator let his breath out slowly. The sword and emblem the man bore had left him bereft of words. Sweat had broken out on him, dripping off his forehead and trickling down his back. It had been a close one. He would have no defense against a man like this out of legend and myth.

The man sheathed his sword but remained standing.

"But," Piscator said quietly, "how can you be here? Your brotherhood was broken and dispersed hundreds of years ago."

The man arched a brow. "Indeed?"

"There are no more Templars. . . ." Piscator whispered, his throat dry.

"Ah, I see your confusion. I am but a poor fellow-soldier of Christ, wandering this world of woe." He smiled briefly. "And that has led me to you."

"Gentlemen, gentlemen," the *schout* intervened. "Please, let's control ourselves so the judge can focus on the charges before him."

The judge had been watching the scene before him with eyes brighter than earlier. His mouth was moving as if chewing his words. His wrinkled hands on the tabletop twitched, his long fingernails scratching the wood.

CHAPTER 5

"Your Honor," said the *schout*, annoyed at the sound, "I'd like to call as our last witness Roland de Hastings."

The judge looked at the *schout* with imploring eyes.

"Pie, Gerben," he said, licking his lips. "I must have pie for my meal. Steak and kidney." The *schout* irritably rolled his eyes as he approached his father, bending to whisper in his ear.

"There will be no dinner if you ignore this trial. It's the last one you'll ever have to preside over. Then you can return to bed and live out your days in disgrace. You've embarrassed me enough for the rest of my life." He was squeezing the old man's shoulder tightly. "Pull yourself together for the next little while so we can finish this up."

The judge squirmed under his son's iron grip. "Yes, Gerben, yes," he breathed. "I'm sorry. Please forgive me."

Gerben straightened, loosening his grip on the judge as he turned back to the room.

"But I like pie . . ." the old man whispered.

The *schout* ignored his father, scowling. Would that the man had died along with his mother. It would save him so much energy. But he knew no other judge would go along with this sham of a trial. It would be best to shift attention to the Templar.

"Master de Hastings," the *schout* said. "Could you tell the court what you know of Pieter Jacobszoon and this nefarious 'Brotherhood' to which he claims to belong? I'm not sure I've ever heard of it."

"Certainly," said de Hastings, smiling. "It has been my duty—indeed, my honor—to seek after followers of the Endless Rose and rout them out wherever I find them."

"And have you found success with your endeavors?"

"Oh, indeed. It is difficult to dissuade members of this organization. Across Europe, even as we speak, nets are closing about enclaves of this vile organization. My brothers and I have found many members and named them. Long hours of sweat and danger have ensued, and I have put myself at significant personal risk many times to crush this insidious brotherhood, but it has not been easy. I bear many scars."

The *schout* was eyeing Piscator as de Hastings spoke.

"Does this group have any emblem to designate themselves?" asked the *schout*.

"Yes," replied the swordsman. "They use a white cross with a rose at the center—sometimes red, sometimes white."

"And can you explain this religion to the court, sir?"

"This is no religion," growled the swordsman.

"Not a religion, you say?" the *schout* said in mock surprise, a hand to his mouth. "But, indeed, they use the sign of the cross as a token of their fellowship, do they not?"

Piscator felt his heart quail within him. He hadn't sacrificed and studied relentlessly to have these things bantered about openly. There was no doubt the swordsman would reveal things best kept secret. Yet there was nothing he could do to stop him.

"This is not the sign of the cross as good men know it," the swordsman said, making the sign on himself. "This symbol is an ancient one from before the times of Pharaoh when men groveled like animals in the dirt. From the dust, yet again, it rises. It is a wicked sign—a phallic symbol, the badge of the devil, evil manifest in its basest form. They take the cross of our Savior and corrupt it to their gross needs, using the symbol of our Savior's blood, the rose, and pervert it to darkness.

"There are eight leaders, grasping like the tentacles of an octopus, who teach the heretical doctrine that man's intelligence is higher than God, who created the universe.

"The Brotherhood gathers under this repulsive emblem to perform rites of arcane deviltry and mystic rituals I will not speak of here. They claim to have the power of creation, the ability to transform God's creations and subvert them to their sinister aims, to rule the world in its entirety. They claim they can alter the natural substance, change the flow of days from their proper pattern, and summon dark beings from realms of shadow that have haunted and plagued men since before Christ walked the earth.

"I quake at the knowledge that this organization subjugates men of free will with the designs of the master of all evil, the very devil himself: Satan, the prince of darkness."

The *schout* wiped the sweat from his face and eyes with his handkerchief while, at the same time, Judge van de Groom wept shamelessly, muttering about pie. Thijs and Krellis, the two guards, had seated themselves in chairs, eyes down. Krellis was whispering a prayer.

Piscator had listened to all this with a blank face. He wasn't going to allow any emotion to show. Understanding from his Masters how to shield himself and his reactions by lightly tapping his thigh while taking deep breaths was one of many things he'd learned during his sabbatical. Simple as it seemed, it worked wonderfully.

"When you find these followers," asked the *schout*, "these adepts of the Endless Rose, what do you do?"

The swordsman smiled humorlessly, staring at Piscator. "We encourage them to escape the clutches of this Brotherhood and offer them the gentler hand of fellowship in the belief of Christ our Redeemer if they forsake all the heinous practices they've adhered to."

"And if they don't submit to your entreaties?"

"Why," said the swordsman, his teeth showing, "we assist them on their way to face the Judgment Seat of Christ, whose hands are pure and irrevocable."

"What do you know of Pieter Jacobszoon, accused of these things?"

"Pieter Jacobszoon is the organization's leader here in Haarlem and the Dutch Republic of the Netherlands. I have seen him welcome members from England, France, and Germany into his home."

The *schout* had walked to stand before Piscator.

"Can you tell us the purpose of these meetings?"

"We believe the meetings were to plan the orchestration of overthrowing all the continent's countries to replace them with their leaders and followers. With the ongoing arrests of the significant adepts of the Brotherhood, we have succeeded in smashing the conspiracy and scattering the organization. We will question all who've taken part in these treacherous dealings and, following a period of reflection and repentance, allow them to spend the remainder of their lives in seclusion, contemplating the redemptive power of Jesus Christ."

The *schout* moved to stand beside the judge, who looked up at his son with watery eyes.

"And if they do not forswear allegiance?" he asked.

"Then our trained interrogators will—persuade—them by other means. Either way, they are thwarted and can no longer contrive to pursue their evil avenues."

CHAPTER 5

"Thank you, sir," said the *schout*. "I know your work is of utmost importance. Please accept the gratitude of Haarlem for your time and efforts on behalf of the God-fearing men of Europe."

Roland de Hastings stood and smoothed his tunic, replacing his cloak. He stared at Piscator, who shuddered at the look in the man's eyes. A trace of a smile touched de Hastings's lips. This man had seen many deaths, most of which were undoubtedly executions of those he hunted.

Then he was gone from the room.

CHAPTER 6

"Now, then," said the *schout*, "after hearing the testimony of these good men, how do you plead to the charges made against you? In the eyes of this court, they are undeniable."

Piscator glared at the *schout*. If the time was right, he could've called down fire from heaven, winds from the north, or the sea to rise. But the time was not right yet. If the things the swordsman had said were true about crushing his Masters and the grand plans they'd conceived, it might be years before the planets aligned themselves again to allow such magnificent hopes and dreams to come to fruition. Yet in his bitter disappointment, he still had enough power to change some things for the better—if, beyond hope of being freed from the certainty of the days ahead, he could still use his knowledge to help others somehow, in whatever way he could.

"Lies," he said calmly. "Lies and calumny. This trial is a travesty of justice. You've construed everything to fit your outcome today. I plead innocent to the charges and ask to be released to go my way. I will leave Haarlem and this country forever."

"Would that it could be so easy, eh, Pieter? No, I will forever erase the stain of Pieter Jacobszoon from the city of Haarlem."

The *schout* turned to his father.

"There you have it, Your Honor," he sneered. "Pieter Jacobszoon pleads innocent to all the charges brought before you. As *schout* of the good city of Haarlem, I have proven he is dangerous to the citizens and the government. As a just punishment for his crimes, I call for his deliverance to the hands of our good executioner, where further questioning and reflection will allow him to be free from the guilt and deviltry that consumes him. Only then can we be sure he will no longer be the threat he is today.

"For the sake of our city and the cursed nature of his soul, I demand this happen today, as soon as we finish here, so that he may begin his repentance."

Piscator watched as the judge stared up at the *schout*. The old man was trembling, clutching at his robe. Then, suddenly, the judge began to transform. His eyes cleared of confusion, becoming bright and wise. The trembling in his body stopped as he raked a sleeved arm across his face. A sudden fire lit his eyes. He straightened in his chair, squaring his thin shoulders.

"No," he said.

The *schout* stared at the judge, shaken, watching in disbelief as the old juror stood slowly to his feet, bones creaking. The *schout* placed a hand on his father's shoulder. "Father," he said, "you forget yourself."

The judge backed away from the hand on his shoulder.

"It is you who forgets himself, Gerben. You are merely the *schout* of Haarlem. I am the judge in this city, having spent the last fifty years of my life in this office. You do not make demands in my office. It is neither your right, nor your duty. I will deliberate on this man's life circumstances and decide by tomorrow. I will retire now to my chambers." He turned from the *schout* and took a step away.

The *schout* looked quietly at his father's back, an eyebrow arched.

"Father," he said softly, "you have no chambers. This room is not your office but one borrowed for this occasion. You have not been an official judge since my mother died. You do remember *how* she died, do you not? That was a sad tragedy. No one knows how she fell from that window. But you know, Father, *you* know—as do I."

The old man stiffened, turning slowly to his son, his wrinkled face ashen.

"As the *schout* of this city, I was able to shield you from any investigation, as is my *duty* and *right*. You kept your home, your pension, and your reputation," his smile broadened, "because you are my father, and I am merely the *schout* of this city."

"Yes, Gerben," the old man whispered, trembling. "Yes, you are the *schout* of this city." He collapsed into his chair. As Piscator watched, he seemed to shrink in on himself, becoming a shadow of who he'd just been.

The old man looked at Piscator, defeated.

"Take him," he said, voice rustling from his mouth. "Take him to the executioner."

CHAPTER 7

Thijs and Krellis pushed and shoved him down the stairs to the lowest level of the Stadhuis, through another dark hallway, lit only by a few sconces hung from the stone walls. A door toward the end of the hallway stood open, light leaking into the hallway.

Piscator eyed the weak light nervously, knowing well what happened in that stone room. He had seen the survivors of this room and those in other cities. Most died during the torture and questioning. Those who survived were lost souls, blinded and broken. Despite the ache and the pain he felt from his beatings, he knew what lay waiting for him would be beyond anything he had ever experienced. For the first time in his life, he was genuinely terrified. He felt his legs collapsing from terror and dread. Thijs and Krellis ensured he stayed on his feet, although only his toes scraped the stone floor as they dragged him toward his inevitable fate.

They entered the room of stone.

The walls were damp, lit by one torch jutting from the wall to his right. There were no windows in the room. The straw covering the floor was fresh and sweet, masking the odor of death and pain that seemed almost tangible. How many lifeless bodies had these guards pulled from this dark chamber? How many broken spirits had endured this room?

Piscator only knew that when this day was over, the man and instruments in this room would change him for the worse, and forever, if he lived through the next few hours. He took a deep breath and closed his eyes, cleansing his thoughts as he'd been taught by his Master, seeking the inner peace and calm in the hidden part of his soul. He opened his eyes and felt a bit better.

A small brazier smoldered in a corner; wood-handled tools protruded from the fitfully glowing coals and cast strange shadows on the stone wall beside it.

The man in the chair warming his hands at the brazier stood when they entered the chamber, placing an open Bible on the small table next to him as he rose. He was of indeterminate age, but bulky with heavily muscled shoulders and arms. A substantial scar, puckered and white like an angry frown, arced across his face from the bottom edge of his grizzled jaw, climbing a broken nose before disappearing under a black eye patch and exploding out the other side to vanish in his close-cropped gray hair. He pulled a black robe from a peg in the wall, placed it over his tunic, and covered his head with a tight black cap.

"Ah," said the man as he approached the prosecutor. "Master *Schout*, how good of you to visit me here in my chamber. It's been lonely of late, I must say." Piscator was surprised by the man's soft and educated voice. The Inquisitor shifted his one-eyed gaze to Piscator. The eye gazed at him, pale green like pond scum. His smile was like a shattered plate, marked by broken and missing teeth.

"And who have we here, Master *Schout*?" he asked.

CHAPTER 7

Piscator stared at the unblinking eye, seeing no malice or evil in it but a well of patience and stillness. He knew that beneath that calm gaze laid a soul that took pleasure in the pain of others. Why else would such a man choose this ungodly trade?

"This is Pieter Jacobszoon, good executioner," said the *schout*, clapping Piscator on the back. "He has been dutifully questioned before the Honorable Judge Henrik van de Groom and requires further motivation to fully reflect on the error of his ways. The good judge has given me responsibility for his reclamation, and I, in turn, give him to you, knowing the efficacy with which you administer your craft. I have full confidence in your skills!"

He smiled that infuriatingly false smile at Piscator.

"Well, then," said the executioner, nodding. He indicated a set of rings bolted to a sheet of iron on the floor behind him. "Bring him over here, and let's get him ready."

The guards dragged Piscator to the rings. The executioner placed Piscator's bare feet through them so the rings rested lightly on his ankles. The coarse robe was stripped from Piscator's shoulders and cast aside. He stood shivering, naked, and weak with dread.

He watched the executioner take a stout rope from an iron peg in the stone wall. After tying Piscator's hands tightly behind his back, he tossed the other end of the rope through another ring bolted to the ceiling, then tied the dangling end to a vertical wheel mounted to a nearby table. He turned the crank on the wheel, taking slack from the line, and then cranked a few more times for good measure.

Piscator felt his shoulders distort as his arms pulled up stiffly behind him. Sharp pain lanced through his body, just on the finite edge of agony. He moaned as a string of saliva trailed from his lips.

The executioner went back to his table and removed his cloak, returning it to the peg in the wall. He placed his cap on the open Bible.

"Well, Master Pissy," said Thijs, "trussed up nicely, aren't we? You'll think fondly of your stinking wet cell now, won't you? Missing it already, I'm guessing!"

Piscator heard the horrible little Krellis giggling from somewhere behind Thijs.

"Here's something to remember us by!" Thijs roared. He struck Piscator across the face, snapping his head back. Blood filled his mouth, hot as the anger that roiled through him. Growling, Piscator spat the sour mixture of blood and saliva into the guard's ugly face, watching with satisfaction as it trickled down the man's stunned features. Thijs's eyes blazed white-hot. He drew an arm across his face, smearing the tincture of blood and saliva as he raised his fist again to strike Piscator.

"STOP!"

The shout filled the chamber, and Piscator was startled to see the executioner rush to his side, drawing a filthy piece of cloth from his tunic and wiping the blood from his chin. The guards stumbled back, seeming to shrink under the full anger of the man, their eyes round and fearful.

"We'll have none of that, do you hear?" the executioner snarled. "I'll not allow you to entertain yourselves at this man's expense! He's in my care now, and I take my responsibility seriously. I'm doing God's work here, and this poor man's soul is in enough torment without the two of you meddling. My craft is ancient and honorable, and before I allow you to touch him again, I'll have the two of you hanging here instead of him, as God is my witness. Do you understand?"

The pale-faced guards fled from the man to a far corner of the room and stood staring at the stone floor.

The executioner turned back to Piscator, and he was surprised to see tears in the man's eyes. "Please forgive me, Master Jacobszoon. Such a thing should not have happened."

Piscator could only stare at the executioner, dumbfounded. He felt a surge of hope, desperately wanting the man to untie him and let him lie on the cold stone floor, released from the coming terror. This man was the only person to show him kindness since he was locked in the stinking cellar.

Alas, it was not to be.

The executioner sighed deeply. "Well, then. Time we started." He took hold of the wheel to which the rope was attached and began to turn it slowly.

Piscator's arms pulled up farther behind him, forcing him to bend forward at the waist. He began whimpering as the pain increased.

When the joints of his shoulders separated, he began to scream.

CHAPTER 8

Sometime later—he wasn't sure how long—he was lying on a hard surface, shivering beneath a rough cloth. He smelled loathsome and guessed he'd fouled himself sometime during his torture. Something hard touched his lips, and wine poured down his throat, warm and bitter, choking him. A damp cloth dabbed at his chin. A cool hand felt his forehead. Slowly, with infinite care, he opened his eyes.

The executioner's scarred face was inches from his own. "He's awake," he said, through his gaping smile.

The *schout*'s face appeared in his vision. "Ah, Jacobszoon, back again, are we?"

Piscator tried to sit up, but the pain was too great, and for some reason, his body wouldn't obey the directions of his mind. Every small attempt at movement sent a searing bolt of agony the length of his body. The *schout* put a gentle hand on his chest.

"You might as well lie back and rest," he whispered in his ear. He pondered him with a furrowed brow.

"You are a very stubborn man, Jacobszoon—very obstinate. It does you no credit, I must say. You won't be going anywhere soon, at least not by yourself. Master Executioner had to turn the wheel more forcefully than usual, and all of us, even I, were forced to lend a hand in your—introspection—shall we say? It was nasty work. I am afraid all the joints in your body have been rent asunder: your arms, shoulders, hips, knees, every joint. Of course, we had to break some bones, as well. Your fingers were brittle when I broke them. They sounded a bit like dry twigs."

He snapped his fingers before Piscator's eyes. "Snap, snap . . ." he whispered. He smiled at someone beyond Piscator's vision.

"Let's get him cleaned up. Haarlem is waiting."

CHAPTER 9

The Grote Markt was alive with people of every age, called by the pealing of the Great Church's bell. The raucous clanging rolled about the Grote Markt square, echoing off the buildings and shops. A festive spirit enlivened the cobbled market. Vendors sold bread, meats, or pastries from small carts. Children ran laughing and screaming around the adults' legs, playing games while their parents chatted with friends and neighbors as they waited for the coming entertainment.

Thijs and Krellis carried Piscator's useless body from the *Stadhuis* through the white door with

ANNO
1630

carved in the stone lintel above it.

Every movement was more torment as they took him down the steps. The guards jostled him more than necessary, placing him on a wheeled cart at the bottom of the stairs. The two men raised the cart section below his torso and blocked it, so Piscator sat up. The watching crowd roared with laughter as he slumped to one side, helpless to stop.

Just before he fell off the cart's edge, Thijs grabbed his arm and pulled him back upright while Piscator gasped with pain.

The two guards tied ropes tightly around his chest and the back of the cart, holding him upright. Piscator's head lolled to one side, resting on his shoulder. A thin thread of saliva ran from the corner of his mouth onto his chest. His head was yanked upright by his hair, and a piece of cloth was wrapped around his forehead and tied off somewhere behind him.

The guards began to push the cart around the square, making sure it jostled and bumped over the worst sections of the cobbled surface. The *schout* walked beside him, a hand on the cart, smiling and nodding to those surrounding them.

Piscator saw many people he knew: old clients, fellow artists, including his main rival, the great Franz Hals, looking sadly at him from a doorway. The old artist looked down when Piscator noticed him, then walked away from the Grote Markt.

The doors of shops were closed and locked so the owners could watch Piscator's humiliating procession around the square. The mass of stinking people milled like sheep around the market square, laughing and pointing at Piscator, mocking his anguish. Several onlookers spat at him. Children threw small stones and sticks at him until one hit Thijs on his cheek. A growl and a heavy raised hand put an end to that.

Piscator smelled smoke and was surprised to see through a haze of pain a bonfire blazing in the middle of the square, a stack of dry wood piled nearby. Backed up to the fire stood a horse hitched to a canvas-covered wagon. Two men leaned against the back of the wagon, eyeing the approaching cart with unconcealed boredom. At a nod from the *schout*, they lowered the wagon's tailgate. One driver placed a small barrel near the gate for the *schout* to step onto the wagon while offering him a hand.

The clanging bells of the Grote Kerk ceased their infernal call, and the clamor about the square died a bit. The crowd gathered closer, the murmur of voices rising again.

"Quiet, please!" the *schout* spoke loudly from where he stood on the wagon. The jabbering masses on the outskirts of the mob obviously couldn't hear him and virtually ignored him. Impatient with the people's ignorance, Thijs stuck two fingers between his lips and whistled loudly. Mothers quickly quieted their children. The din slowly died to silence.

The *schout* held up his hands.

"Pieter Jacobszoon has been condemned this day by the good Judge Henrik van de Groom as a traitor and servant of the devil!" he shouted. "The court shall take Jacobszoon's home and possessions, and he will also lose all honors and accolades. Because of the seriousness of his charges, this penalty will take place immediately!"

The crowd cheered raucously, clapping and whistling.

"I want his food!" someone yelled from the crowd.

"I want his shoes!" an onlooker from the opposite side shouted.

The crowd hooted and clapped with amusement.

"*QUIET!*" bellowed Thijs.

The mob settled down, although a few children whimpered. The *schout* put a hand on the guard's shoulder and jumped to the ground, his black robe fluttering.

He slowly circled the wagon, tracing it with a delicate finger until he completed an entire circle. He gestured to the wagon drivers, who nodded and pulled the canvas off the wagon.

"Ah," said the *schout* as he peered into the back of the wagon. "What have we here?"

He pulled out a rectangular object, holding it closely and scrutinizing it silently.

"Oh my," he said softly. "This is just lovely...."

He smiled at Piscator and slowly carried the rectangular object to where Piscator sat strapped to the cart. Piscator watched the *schout* draw near, hating the grinning man with an unbridled passion.

"Do you recognize this, Jacobszoon?" he asked, holding it in Piscator's view.

Piscator's heart sank. "Damn you!" he whispered.

The *schout*'s blue eyes widened in mock surprise. "I am sorry," he said, leaning closer to him. "What was that you said?"

"Damn you to hell!" Piscator spat at him, teeth clenched against the pain of every movement he made.

"Well," the *schout* noted, "it appears he does recognize it!" He held the item up to examine it again. "Just lovely, Jacobszoon," he breathed. "Quite a work of art, I must say. One of your masterpieces, I presume?"

It was the last portrait Piscator finished before he'd left on his three-year sabbatical. It was a whimsical posing of a wealthy matriarch and her two children dressed in lace finery, sitting on a stone bench amongst a garden of flowers and stately trees. A lovely home stood in the background. The patron who had commissioned the portrait had hung it enthusiastically in the house's foyer. Piscator wondered how it came to be in the back of the wagon.

Suddenly, the *schout* swung the portrait and smashed it against the corner of the wagon, splintering the wood and breaking it into several pieces.

Piscator cried out.

"Pity," the *schout* said, casting the useless wood into the flames.

CHAPTER 10

The fire was like a living thing, greedy and insatiable, the flames leaping at the touch of each painting.

All forty-three of Piscator's works were smashed one after another, nourishing the ravenous blaze; oils and pigments were like spice for the terrible feast of wood, handmade brushes, and easels. The liberal hands of the *schout* fed everything from the wagon into the fire.

Sweat flew from the *schout* as he labored at the back of the wagon. His eyes, like twin stars, reflected the raging fire. His hoarse laugh was maniacal as it echoed off the brick faces of the buildings. Children holding hands circled the blaze, dancing and singing as a wavering black column of smoke creased the rosy light of the waning afternoon—a smudge on the blush the setting sun had displayed on the vast facade of the Great Church. Sparks cavorted about the square like little demons flittering on wings of destruction.

The mindless mob in the Grote Markt was celebratory, enjoying the distraction from their daily tasks provided by the humiliation of Piscator, who sat weeping at the obliteration of his life's work in the engorged belly of the flames. How many hours had he spent pondering, planning, and sweating over each painting? How many drops of his sweat and blood sizzled in the fire? How many tears had he shed before standing back and proclaiming a portrait finished?

The fire took the core of his life and expelled it as black smoke. It was like losing a child as each work flared, adding to the erasure of his life. He could only watch and weep, helpless as a babe strapped to the cart.

Why couldn't the *schout* have torn his beating heart out and cast it into the flames? It would have been more merciful.

But Piscator knew mercy didn't reign in this square.

* * *

Clouds had gathered as the afternoon progressed, and lightning traced the dark underbelly of the coming night with jagged brilliance. Thunder rumbled as the storm grew closer, echoing through the night. The crowd, eager for their evening meal and perhaps bored by the spectacle, had begun drifting off into the waning light. The two guards, Thijs and Krellis, wandered into a nearby tavern.

Ultimately, it was just Piscator and the *schout* alone in the Grote Markt as evening closed about them. The breeze that had been building sucked the last sparks of his life into the darkness. He heard the *schout* stir beside him and sigh.

"You know, Jacobszoon," he said quietly, "it didn't have to end this way. I tried—we all tried—to get you to see the error of your ways. We extended the hand of mercy to you time and time again, but you're a very stubborn man. You had only to confess, just a few easy words, and you would now be back in your cozy home, warming yourself before the hearth. Now, someone else will have your fine house...."

CHAPTER 10

The *schout* paused, looking at Piscator with a piercing eye. "Do you consider yourself a martyr, Jacobszoon? Do you think others of your ilk look to you for strength, even as they fall? This is not the only fire tonight, not by any means. England and Europe are ablaze this night! If your friend, Johannes, hadn't had such an unfortunate accident, he would be lying beside you. As it is, his wife and children are currently, shall we say, looking to better their situation. It really is a disgrace, you know. What shall she do, I wonder? Three children, one a mere babe in arms, left with no home, no food. And she's such a lovely woman."

Clouds surged against the pillars of the night, piling and heaving as they blossomed, flooding the sky with darkness.

"No, Jacobszoon," he said. "You're very much alone this night. No friends, no supporters. Ultimately, the Great Deceiver has forsaken you, as he does all his minions." The *schout* pulled his robe tighter as a chill wind slipped through the square, scattering the ashes of the fire.

"There's no place to lay your head, no refuge for such as you. You have wasted your vaunted talent; so much has been irretrievably lost for you. I genuinely pity you. I truly do.

"Well, no matter," the *schout* sighed. "Once the physicians get you in working order, you'll still have a shadow of that God-given talent you so took for granted, though I think fine portraits are beyond your abilities now. But perhaps we can find something to fill your time."

The *schout* looked up into the dark sky as he spoke, breathing deeply the sea-tinged air that had arrived with the storm.

The whole time, Piscator had remained silent, fighting the urge to scream obscenities at the *schout* for his part in destroying his life. He'd withheld his tongue, not only in fear of retribution from the man but also because the pain of his broken body was too intense to do more than suffer without losing the last shreds of his sanity. But he had one question to ask.

"Why?" Even to himself, his voice sounded grating. "Why are you doing this to me?"

The *schout* looked down at him, puzzled.

"Why?" the *schout* asked, his brows furrowing. "You truly do not know, do you?"

Piscator could do no more than stare at the man.

"Ah," said the *schout*. "You don't remember me, do you?"

Piscator tried his best to sneer at the man. "Should I?"

"You don't remember the young boy following you, Johannes, and your little band of miscreants around Haarlem, trying to join in as you stole bread and meats from merchants and fouled the canal with your trash and dead animals? You don't remember teasing that young boy you pushed into the canal with several dead rats?"

The *schout* was growing angrier as he spoke.

Piscator tried through his fog of pain to remember. So many years had passed. His pain was like a hammer pounding on his soul. It was so hard to think.

"I was that boy, Jacobszoon. I was the boy forced to swim and clean up your messes so you wouldn't get caught. I was just a lad, smaller than all of you, so badly wanting to be a part of your cohort. But I was treated as a useless boy that no one wanted. Beaten behind the shops and left outside the city walls as the gates were closed because you'd tied me to a tree as night fell."

CHAPTER 10

He stared at Piscator but no longer saw him, focusing on some distant day.

"Did you know my drunken lout of a father forced me to leave my home when I was just a child because he and my mother couldn't afford another mouth to feed and clothe, along with the endless amounts of wine they consumed? Did you know that I ate rotten fruit and worm-ridden meat to survive? I was rescued by an old man one day as I cowered in the shadow of an alleyway. He took me in and raised me as his own. He sent me to university so I could be more than I was, or could have been, had I remained with my family. But you don't care about any of that, do you? I was just a target for your cruelty and sport. Nothing more than an object to torture and tease. None of that means anything to you because you're the great Pieter Jacobszoon, the artist, the former ringleader of the little group of thugs and rascals haunting the streets of Haarlem."

The *schout* suddenly slapped Piscator across the face, spittle spraying as he shouted, "I wanted to be part of your band; I wanted to be *you*, for the love of God! But you could only disdain the miserable youth that worshipped you. I would have done anything to have you accept and trust me to be your friend."

Blood trickled down Piscator's chin.

"When I discovered you were back in Haarlem, I knew it was my opportunity to destroy you, to make you feel like nothing, as I had. No, less than that. I could take everything from you and leave you a wretched shadow of yourself. I did that. I did all of it!"

The *schout* stared at him with wild eyes. He stood like that momentarily until he pulled himself up straighter, wrapping his robe tightly around himself. Then it was like the *schout* was a completely different man, suddenly calm and smiling.

"Getting chilly, don't you think, Pieter? I'm ready for tulips and sunshine! I'll be glad when spring is fully here.

"Well, it's been a long and weary day, hasn't it? I think a warm fire and a hot drink will take off the crispness of the evening!"

He leaned down and kissed Piscator on the forehead.

"Good night, Pieter. Try not to be out late...." He walked away, chuckling.

Piscator was alone and bereft in the gloomy market square.

A raindrop struck him in the face.

And then another.

CHAPTER 11

De Bloem Grecian
(The Grecian Flower)
Pottery Factory
Delft
Nine Months Later

Piscator's crutches laid on the floor where he'd put them after returning from his visit to the small room. The tile factory was hot and dusty. Sweat ran down his face, leaving grimy rivulets on his work table. He wearily blew the dust off his table and resumed the careful tracing on the tile, his clawed and crablike fingers painfully grasping the brush. Broken hands and fingers had been allowed to heal crookedly because the physicians did not attempt to set them properly during his recovery.

The *platdraaiers*, the flat-potters, had left ten more tiles on his worktop in his absence, and regardless of how fast he worked, he was falling further behind. He dreaded the eventual visit of the Master Baker.

He carefully laid the *spons*—the stenciled, pricked paper—on the tile, still wet from the white tin glaze. He had pounced the charcoal-covered rag on it several times. When he pulled the stencil off, it left charcoal dust in tiny spots across the tile surface, and then he began the arduous tracing of the outline and filling in the empty spaces with paint.

The tile was whisked away and placed in the fiery kiln where the charcoal would evaporate and the tin glaze would melt onto the tile surface, cooling to the distinctive opaque blue-and-white colors so much in demand. Then the *vloerwerkers*, the floor workers, would paint the tile with a lead glaze that hardened to an unyielding, clear finish.

He would begin another tile immediately.

But he was too slow. With each tile, it became more evident.

The other painters, the *schilders*, kept pace with the grueling schedule of the factory. He heard them muttering behind his back about "special favors for the cripple" and how unfair it was that he could only do less than half of what they produced in a day's work.

The *Meester-plateelbakker*—the Master Baker—the Delftware master, and the factory's owner all rolled into one had already expressed concerns over the past several days as he had observed his work. He hovered over Piscator, covered with the fine dust of the factory. Short and stout, he had a balding head of white-streaked red hair, mustaches, and a goatee waxed and pointed like a dagger. His teeth were yellow and horse-like. He watched Piscator through narrowed eyes, chewing on his lip.

"This order has to be completed by next week, Pieter," he said. "The patron and his wife are coming in the morning to approve the designs for the kitchen tiles, and he'll be very disappointed if we are not on schedule. I can't begin to tell you how important this job is. He's using a tremendous amount of tiles to renovate his home. This order is the largest we've had this year."

The Master's eyes measured him. "I realize this is difficult for you, but we must maintain our standards and schedule. When they sent you to us, they assured us you could maintain the pace we set here. If you fall further behind, I'll have to bring in another *schilder* to help cover your backlog of tiles. Honestly, I can't afford to do that. You have to work faster, or I'll have to replace you."

Piscator stared at his gnarled hands, feeling eyes on him like spiders. The workroom had become silent.

"I'm doing the best I can," he whispered. "I'll stay late every night until the tiles are finished. I'm sorry to have disappointed you."

The Master noticed the silence in the room and glared at the other *schilders*.

"This does not concern any of you!" he growled. "I can hire other *schilders* to take your places, too!"

The other painters resumed their work, glancing covertly at one another.

"I know this is hard for you, Pieter," the Master sighed. "When I think of all you have lost, what you can never do again, it truly saddens me. Mine and my wife's heart goes out to you, Pieter. You were a Master artist, and now you struggle to do the simplest tasks. But you have a room and food to eat. We've taken care of you as best we can."

"Yes, I know. And thank you, Master. I don't know what I would do without your kindness. But I try, Master, although it doesn't appear that way."

To Pieter's shame, he felt a tear trickle down his cheek. *Damn!* He didn't like to show weakness and was embarrassed by it.

He felt the Master's hand, gentle on his shoulder. "I know that, Pieter, I know. And I'm sorry to be harsh with you, but this is a business. I have deadlines and patrons breathing down my neck." The hand squeezed his shoulder. "Just try harder, would you?"

Pieter nodded mutely as the Master walked back toward the *faience* shop at the front of the factory, where they displayed samples of their products for potential buyers, and where the Master's wife, Lena, reigned supreme.

These two people had been the only ones to show him kindness or charity over the past nine months since his trial. He had never received a kind word during the months in the physician's care. They were callous with him, and at times, it seemed as though they had gone out of their way to torment him further. They had rarely spoken to him, and if they did, it was only with cruel, biting words. He had been kept in a tiny cell which, while cleaner and drier than his previous cell, was still lonely and austere. The only visitor he received was the *schout*, who only came to smirk and demean him with false concern. Oh, yes, and to bend back his fingers or arms to inflict more needless pain.

"Looks like you're healing nicely, Pieter. Keep up the good work!"

Then he would leave his cell and laugh with the physicians.

His hatred of the *schout* was deep and all-consuming. The man had been the author of his destruction, a monster that deserved death but was unlikely to be undertaken by Pieter's gnarled hands. He had spent many hours thinking of various ways to kill the man, which were all academic now. He could barely dress himself, but pondering the death of the *schout* was something to fill the empty hours.

The Master Baker and his cheery wife had treated him kindly, allowing him a room off the factory floor that he shared with bags of charcoal and mice, and they fed him twice a day. The room was next to the kiln. It was a warm refuge during this cold winter, but it would be sweltering come summer.

The Master had brought in his personal physician, a kindly man with caring eyes and a gentle touch, hoping the doctor could help Pieter. There was nothing the physician could do but leave a potion that soothed the pain of his injuries and helped him sleep.

He would have to push himself much harder, though how he could do that, he didn't know. He would have to do whatever it took to help get this order done, even if it killed him. He owed them that much, at the very least.

He felt a touch on his shoulder and turned to see Bartal, the head *schilder*, standing by his worktop, looking at him with concern in his eyes. He was a thin, angular man with black hair. Bartal reached down and took two tiles from his table.

"I'll take a couple of those," he smiled. "I'm short on work today."

Piscator looked at Bartal's table. He had several tiles ready for sponsing. Before he could say anything, Bartal had taken the tiles back to his table.

Piscator stared at him, dumbfounded. None of the other *schilders* had ever said a word to him, let alone performed an act of kindness.

Arjan and Nico, the other two *schilders*, followed Bartal and took some of his tiles to their worktables, shyly smiling and patting his arm.

CHAPTER 12

After a few short hours of sleep, Piscator returned to his workbench, still exhausted from the previous day's work. It felt like a herculean effort, but he knew he fell short of the mark. Every muscle in his body ached. His gnarled hands felt like heavy boots had marched on them.

He was grateful to see his breakfast waiting for him: cheese, dark bread, dried herring, and a mug of small beer, the low alcohol brew that saved them from drinking the polluted water of the city. The Master's wife was as kind as her husband: a plump woman with eyes the color of a rainy sky and a face creased from a lifetime of laughter and tears. She always brought his meals with a smile and the scent of warm bread.

He was wiping the plate with the last bit of the bread when he heard the voice.

"Well, well, my dear! Look who we have here! It's our good friend Pieter Jacobszoon, the famous artist! Can you believe our luck?"

He sighed inwardly, opening his eyes to see the *schout* standing beside his work table. He closed his eyes and kept his head down, his blood running cold, fighting the urge to run screaming from the factory. But he knew he had no choice but to stay where he was and take what was coming: humiliation and defeat.

"What do you want?" he muttered.

The *schout* wore fine clothes with rings on his fingers and held a perfumed white handkerchief to his nose. A ridiculously pointed mustache had sprung below his nose. His ice-blue eyes gazed merrily down at him.

"My dear, Jacobszoon, how good it is to see you!" he said, and laughed. "I've missed our little visits these past months. Haarlem isn't the same without you, I must say. It's so dull, so much quieter. Still, we must make do, you know?"

He turned to someone behind him and extended his hand. "Katharina, my love, come closer. I believe you've missed our friend, Pieter, as well!"

Before Piscator saw her, the delicate scent of lavender filled his senses. His heart sank when he recognized Katharina, the wife of his good friend, Johannes. Staring at her, dumbfounded, he saw that she had changed much since last he saw her; she was thinner, her green eyes haunted and dull, lined with darkness and loss. A long gown the color of a forest hung from slender shoulders of bone. Her golden hair, once bright like the summer sun on a field of flowers, was now dull and listless, hanging from beneath the white cap on her head. But her eyes haunted Piscator the most, and his heart ached at the sight of them.

As he watched her, tears welled in her eyes. A single tear stole down the contours of her cheek. She hastily wiped it off with a shaking hand.

Katharina. The wife of his good friend, Johannes.

CHAPTER 12

Dear dead Johannes. Perhaps it was a blessing that he died without knowing what would become of his wife and children.

He opened his mouth to say something, but she briefly shook her head, panic widening her eyes.

"Come, my dear," the *schout* said, "don't be shy. You know Pieter very well, I believe. You spent many hours with him and your late, lamented husband. And now here we are all together, old and lasting friends. How delightful this reunion is! I've looked forward to this for these long months, and now it is here at last!"

He gave Piscator another of his smirking glances. "We're married now, Jacobszoon. Did you know that? She's my blushing bride, and I am the father of her children. Isn't that marvelous?"

Piscator stopped breathing. *No, dear Gods, no!*

The *schout*'s eyes widened in mock surprise at the confusion on Piscator's face.

"Don't tell me you didn't get an invitation? We certainly sent you one. Well, I must look into this. It's intolerable, I tell you! Heads will roll! You were to be the guest of honor!" He laughed as he held his handkerchief before his nose. "Of course, we would have made you bathe first. You have grown quite rank since last I saw you!"

The *schout*'s mocking attitude cut Pieter's nerves like a knife, swelling his heart with anger and hatred. He wanted to lash out and wipe that scorn off the *schout*'s face forever. Yet what could he do? Hit him with his crutch? No, he could do nothing but let the rage fester within him.

The *schout* put his arm around Katharina's shoulder and drew her close. She leaned away from him, but he pulled her tight, eliciting a gasp from her.

"Well, I must be off to visit the Master about the tiles for our home. Why not stay and visit our friend Pieter? I'm sure you have much to catch up on!" He bent and kissed her lightly on the lips. She stiffened and turned away. The *schout* smiled at her, showing his teeth like a dog. He turned to leave and then hesitated.

"By the way, Pieter, you'll be delighted to know the good judge was impressed with my prosecution of you. He rewarded me with your house, since you won't be spending much time there in the future. I own it now, just like other things of lasting beauty. You really should come to visit us, Jacobszoon. You'd love what we've done with it!"

The *schout* grinned at his wife and walked away.

His contemptuous laughter echoed off the factory walls, settling in Piscator's head like a loathsome weight.

Piscator felt a light hand on his shoulder and looked up to see Katharina, eyes awash with tears. He put his hand on hers.

"Oh, Pieter, I'm so sorry. What have they done to you?" She threw her arms around him and sank to her knees, sobbing. He gently caressed her hair while she buried her face in his chest. He breathed in her lavender scent deeply.

There had been times when he envied Johannes for his chosen life, one of love and family. But he knew that life would never be his. He had devoted his life to painting and learning mystic arts that would change the world. Now, that bold change would never come.

CHAPTER 12

The Brotherhood was broken and dispersed, or dead. What other reason kept them from coming to his aid when he had been imprisoned and Johannes needlessly killed? He was a broken and useless man, reduced to laboring for hours in a factory of dust and heat.

After a while, she stopped weeping. The front of Piscator's shirt and coat was wet with her tears.

He put a finger under her chin and lifted her eyes to his. Dark smudges laid like crescents under her eyes. A shadow filled them, sad and haunted. He looked into those green depths, trying to read the hidden thoughts behind them.

"Why?" he asked.

She stiffened and struggled to her feet, turning from him to stand with her arms wrapped around herself. The room felt suddenly colder, as though the kiln fire had died.

"How can you ask me why, Pieter?" Her voice was so quiet he could barely hear her. "What was I to do? After Johannes died, I was alone. Because of the accusations against him, I could turn to no one. My family, my friends—they all deserted me. They took our home from us, as well, Pieter. Did you know that? They came one night and took our clothes, food, everything, forcing us from our home with just what we were wearing. We slept on the streets or in alleyways, my children and I begging for food from anyone we saw, digging in refuse like dogs for small scraps of rotten fish or moldy bread. Living like animals." Her eyes seemed focused on distant, bitter memories that would plague her for the rest of her life.

"I'm so sorry," he whispered.

"My children were ill. We were cold and hungry," she continued as though she hadn't heard him. "No one would help us. No one. No one would hear my pleas. It was like we ceased to exist in the eyes of the city. When he found me, I stood on a bridge over a canal in a snowstorm, staring at the freezing water with my children huddled in rags at my feet. It was my last resort."

She looked at him with dead eyes. "Can you imagine what it is like to hear the children you had borne and raised crying for want of food, sleeping in trash-filled alleys, snatching bones from dogs to gnaw on? It was more than I could bear. I didn't want my children to suffer any longer. I didn't want to suffer, knowing I could do nothing to ease their suffering. There would be no more pain, no more hunger. I almost did it. I was bending to pick up little Willem when he stopped me. He found me there and offered me safety, a home. Warmth and food. Clean beds and clothing. I had to accept his offer, knowing he was the one behind all we had been through."

He sat helpless, watching her breathe.

"He hurts me and the children sometimes," her voice was muted and ghostly, like the murmur of a sea breeze across dunes. "He can be tender one minute, loving and attentive, and then the next explode in a rage over the simplest things. And he's very jealous of Johannes and the relationship we had shared. He constantly asks if he pleases me as much as Johannes when we're alone. I submit to him, or he forces himself on me. His touch sickens me. It burns like a brand. I don't dare say Johannes's name, even to the children. They can't speak of their father, or he punishes them cruelly. They must refer to him as 'father' at all times. It is a sad and lonely existence, Pieter, but we are fed and warm."

He listened to her silently, memories flooding his thoughts.

"Please don't judge me, Pieter. I will be lost if you do." She took his hand and held it to her cheek. It broke his heart to feel the dampness there.

"I can't judge you, Katrijn," he whispered. "How could I? It is my fault Johannes is dead, and you're in this situation."

She kissed his gnarled hand gently.

"And what have we here? Cozy, are we?" The *schout* had returned and stood over them, glaring with blazing eyes, nostrils flared. "Get up, Katharina. Stop groveling like a bitch in heat!"

The *schout* tore the cap from her head and grasped a handful of her hair, jerking her upright. She gasped in pain, struggling with him. Piscator tried to stand, anger flooding him. He grasped and lashed out with his crutch, catching the *schout* weakly on the shoulder. The *schout* tore the crutch from his hands and flung it across the room, where it hit the wall and clattered to the floor.

He backhanded Piscator, forcing him to fall heavily to the stone floor. Groaning, he saw Katharina grasping at the *schout*'s arms, trying to pull him away.

"Stop it!" she screamed, raking her nails across his cheeks and drawing blood. "You've done enough to him!"

He turned on her, eyes like a wild beast, and slapped her hard. She staggered back, eyes wide with fear.

"I knew if I left you alone with him, you'd fall into his arms!" he roared. He slapped Katharina again. She cried out in pain. "I should have let you and your filthy brats drown that night. Life would have been so much easier if I had." He seized her arm roughly and thrust her toward the front of the shop.

"Go wait in the carriage!" he screamed. "I'll deal with you later!" He kicked Katharina as she hitched her skirts and ran from him, sobbing. He saw that the other *schilders* had risen to their feet and watched his actions in horror. He glared at them, fists clenched.

"Do you want some of the same? I have more than enough to spare!"

The *schilders* stared at him anxiously, then sat back at their tables.

The *schout* turned back to Piscator, bent, grabbed him by the hair, and pulled him close to his face. His eyes blazed like lava from a volcano, spittle spraying.

Piscator smelled the *schout*'s breath, hot and stinking like rotten fish.

"She's mine, Jacobszoon," he hissed. "Your house is mine, your furniture is mine, your bedroom is mine! I've destroyed you and any hope you may have had of a glorious future. You no longer exist as far as the rest of the world is concerned. You have always been worthless scum, and now you're *less* than scum."

He spat a stinking mouthful of saliva into Piscator's face, thrusting him back so violently that his head struck the stone floor. Sparks burst at the edge of his vision as darkness crept over his mind.

"I'm going to leave you now, Jacobszoon," the *schout* grated through clenched teeth. "I will never see you again, or think of you again. I will take *my* wife home to *my* house and take care of her insolence and disloyalty. One way or another, she will be screaming tonight."

CHAPTER 12

The *schout* kicked him full in the face, and Piscator felt his nose shatter, blood gushing from his nostrils. For good measure, the *schout* kicked him in the ribs. Piscator screamed in pain as several ribs possibly broke, blood spluttering down the front of his shirt.

"Goodbye, Jacobszoon. Enjoy what's left of your pitiful life."

He spat on Piscator again and turned to leave him groaning and bleeding on the factory floor.

Piscator heard the carriage door slam and the rattle of hooves as the carriage pulled away, taking Katharina forever from him

CHAPTER 13

He rolled over painfully onto his stomach, letting the blood flow freely from his smashed nose and mouth. The pain was excruciating; it was all he could do to avoid vomiting. He struggled to reach his bench when he heard footsteps coming near. He cringed, afraid the *schout* had returned.

Strong hands gripped his shoulders and arms. Nico and Bartal, the two *schilders*, gently lifted and carried him to his bench. Momentarily confused, he saw the Master carefully place a basin of warm water and some cloth near him.

The Master's wife fretted over him, tenderly washing the blood from his face and cleaning his wounds. He couldn't help spitting blood as he breathed. The front of his shirt was covered in blood, though most of the bleeding had stopped.

"What an evil man," she said, clucking her tongue. "Oh, dear, what has he done to you? Terrible, terrible man." Her brows furrowed in a grave face, rain-colored eyes filled with tears. She turned, glaring at her husband.

"We should never have taken this order, Tuen!" she hissed at him. "We knew what he was like the first time we met him! He's a wicked man, make no mistake; look what he's done to our Pieter, the poor dear."

She rinsed the blood from the cloth in the basin and laid it back on Piscator's nose. Pain shot through his head.

"I know, I know," the Master said, "but what's done is done. We can't change that; we need to finish this order, and then we'll never see him again." He laid a hand on Piscator's shoulder. "I'm truly sorry for what happened, Pieter. You have suffered enough at that man's hands to go through more. If I'd known what he'd do, I'd have kept him from you, as God is my witness, or placed some of my stronger men between the two of you."

Piscator looked at his two friends and tried to smile.

"Please," he whispered through swollen lips. "I'll be fine. You needn't worry about me. I've been through worse, believe me, much worse. I need to work; that will be the best thing for me now." He struggled to sit. The Master helped him up as pain lanced his head and body. "Yes, that's fine. Thank you," he grated. Sweat broke out on his forehead as he fought back the dizziness and pain.

The Master watched him gravely.

"Are you well enough to work, Pieter? I'll have my physician look you over in a bit, but in the meantime, the evil man has approved the design for his kitchen. They're ready for the sponsing. Are you up to it?"

Piscator heard a squeak and the rustle of skirts behind him as the Master's wife jumped to her feet. She came into his view, eyes ablaze.

"For the love of God, Tuen! Is that all you can think? Work? Pieter is badly injured, yet you stand there pressing him to work? Can't you give him a moment to rest?"

CHAPTER 13

The Master looked abashed. Blood rushed to his face. He never liked getting tongue lashings from his wife, especially in front of his workers.

"Well, now, Lena, I know that, same as you. You don't have to get yourself in an uproar. I was asking, is all. I meant no harm by it."

"No, you're right, Master. I'll be fine. It would be better to get back to work," Piscator said. "It'll help to vent my frustrations. The Gods know I have enough of them."

Lena clucked her tongue, hovering over him like a mother hen. "Well, you take it slow, Pieter. Don't let this man push you faster than you can go. And if he does, you let me know."

With a final glare at her husband, she flounced off to the shop at the front of the factory, her skirts swirling.

"I'm sorry, Pieter," said the Master as he watched his wife march away. "I suppose she's right, though. I'll have the *vloerwerkers* start you out slowly until you feel better. Now, let's get you washed up and get clean clothes on you."

"No, Master. I'd rather get started. I can clean up later before I go to bed," he said as he began to get his worktop back into productive order. "I really will be fine."

The Master chewed his whiskers thoughtfully.

"If my wife finds out I failed to set you up right, I'll be boiled, make no mistake. You take it slow and don't work too late, do you hear me? The work will still be here in the morning."

The floor workers, Guert, Olfart, and Joost began leaving tiles on the *schilder*'s worktops. The Master laid out some pricked pieces of paper. "These are some patterns he wants: simple floral patterns in the corners and special pieces for the fireplace to represent his family, their dogs, cows, chickens, and his children outside playing. You are the most talented here, so I want you to do those."

"Very well, Master," he said, his throat slick with blood. "Thank you. I'll start immediately."

"Right, then, Pieter. You are a good man." The Master patted him on the shoulder and left the factory floor.

Piscator studied the empty tiles in front of him. They silently beckoned him, stirring memories of the years spent learning in the East. He recalled other days and experiences—then it was there, bursting into his mind like a bright flame. He thought he heard voices speaking. Looking around, he saw the *vloerwerkers* had left the production floor, and the other *schilders* sat working silently at their tables, doing their studying.

After all that had happened to him since his trial, the pain and humiliation he had endured, the lonely, cold nights filled with hopelessness, he suddenly knew.

I know, he silently exulted.

He could hurt the *schout*, after all. He realized he could not hurt him like an ordinary man, as he couldn't leave the factory, not to mention that his body was crippled. No, not in a physical way, but he knew how to inflict the most significant wound. And, after all, he was no ordinary man. He was an artist and a master of mystic arts capable of more damage than the *schout* could even imagine.

He would remember the name of Piscator for the rest of his miserable life.

CHAPTER 13

Smiling through the pain of his beating, he took the first tile and set it before him. He closed his eyes and began to hum quietly—a strange, tuneless sound filled with searching notes. He experimented with different tones, climbing and descending scales—half-tones mixed with strident sharps and dissonant flats—until he hit the Perfect Tone. His body vibrated as he hummed the Tone; the table vibrated at his touch, and he knew he was ready.

He spat a mixture of blood and saliva on his finger and dabbed the four corners of each tile. He watched as the saliva and blood swirled together and slowly disappeared into the tiles. He sent his mind into the darkness, seeking the path he needed, maintaining the tone as his Masters had taught him—circular breathing, so the tone remained whole with perfect precision. He sent his mind searching further into the vastness of space and time, his soul rushing free, unbound by his natural body, opening immense doors, one after another, after another, bending space and time to his will as thousands of universes sped past him.

CHAPTER 14

The day was warm and cloudless. He thought it would be hot with two suns in the sky, but he found it comfortable. The shadows cast by the double suns were intriguing, but he cast no shadow. The red brick path he created as he walked was flat and smooth. There was a noise like the buzz of insects, but he hadn't seen any around him. He felt lighter, as though he weighed a fraction of what he had back where his body was in the painting room of the tile factory. He felt diaphanous, like a spider-web glistening in the early morning sun (or suns in the case of this world). He felt himself walking, but there was no perception of touch from the weight of his feet on the brick path, almost like he was floating, an insubstantial thought moving along the way. His search had brought him here, drawn by the strength of someone or something that dwelled here.

He noticed the strange flora of the world, all the different colors of the rainbow on one tree, and the large flowers that drooped from the mass of stems and branches. The colors were a bizarre mixture of blue, red, purple, white, and black, glowing faintly. He stopped frequently to look in wonder and realized he was wasting time. Then, the pull of the Presence here in this world drew him on.

He sensed it ahead of him, quite close now.

He heard a river off to his left beyond the trees, and then he willed the path to fork that way. He followed that path until he reached an opening in the forest beside the river. The Presence was in the form of a man fishing the river, casting in and out of the water. After a cast, he would let the line float for a while, then pull it back to him, only to send it out again. The Presence (person?) gave no indication he knew Piscator was standing there.

"I've been expecting you," said the fisherman, still casting. "I won't go with you, you know. My place is here on this world, in this universe."

Piscator smiled with his ethereal mouth.

"Ah, but you must. I haven't traveled this far to go back empty-handed. You have no choice."

"No." The fisherman repeatedly cast while he spoke. "I am content here."

The fisherman turned to look at him. Piscator began to swell, growing taller and broader. Power surged into him from the universe, his body doubling and quadrupling as he grew past the trees and the mountains, reaching for the Presence, who had dropped his pole, and growling began to expand. Soon, they were in the atmosphere of the planet.

Piscator reached with arms of power, transforming them into slender ropes of light and casting them over the Presence, who shrank away from him.

"You must come with me now," Piscator said in a voice of thunder. "I have cast my net, and I have you."

CHAPTER 14

The Presence pulled from him, struggling against the net. He suddenly slashed with sword arms of light, cutting the bonds and almost breaking free. Piscator redoubled his strength as the cords again wrapped the Presence, whose vain struggles weakened him. Piscator held him tightly, and the power of the universe flowed into him. The Presence began to weep great tears like liquid sunlight.

"Please," he wailed, "let me return to my home. I'm frightened of you. I've never experienced such power."

"No," said Piscator. "I need you to come with me now. I'll return you to your home when your task is complete. It'll only be a short while, I promise. What is your name?"

"I have no name."

"You do now," Piscator said, pulling the two higher into space. "I name you the Fisherman."

And then they were gone, enveloped in a blanket of space and time, and Piscator rushed back to his body fast as thought.

CHAPTER 15

Haarlem
One Month Later

He woke with the sun stabbing into his eyes from the east window. *Damn!* he thought. *She forgot to pull the curtains last night, the foolish woman! Well, he would set her straight. It would not be the first time!*

He rolled over on his pillows in his new bed, his head throbbing with pain. His mouth was dry and tasted of sheep dung. It certainly smelled like sheep dung.

What a celebration *that* was last night! He smiled through the pain and winced at the light piercing his brain.

After months of exhaustive work and planning, they finally moved into the renovated home yesterday. It was a joy to watch the lowly workers hauling in the many pieces of new furniture and all the new clothes he'd ordered for himself. He was the *Schout* of the great city of Haarlem, after all. He deserved only the best of everything, and usually got it. Maybe when things settled down, he would have a dress or two made for Katharina and, perhaps, for her children.

The children. Oh, how he hated them.

Every time he looked at Jacobus, he saw the image of the precious Johannes—the same piercing blue eyes, the same face and blond hair. Someday, he would deal with him, but not yet; no, not yet. He was only seven, in any case. Once he was a little older, the torment would begin—when he could appreciate the attention. The mewling baby, little Willem, smelled of soiled diapers and sour milk. A subtle pinch now and then when no one was looking...

Oh, and of course, the daughter. The lovely Sophiia, the lovely, *young* Sophiia. Beautiful like her mother. At sixteen, she was flowering wonderfully. She was a bit rebellious right now, but with a little training, she would become submissive like her mother. He would make sure of that!

It would be a wonderful life!

Last night was the housewarming party. He had invited all the important people of Haarlem, and most came. Those who did not attend would have their names stricken from his book and not invited to future celebrations. But that did not matter to him because now he knew who supported him and who did not.

When it seemed like the party would be a dismal failure, he had ordered the doors flung wide, and hundreds of people had filtered in. The wine and food filled the tables, and laughter and music filled the house until the wee morning hours.

He remembered climbing the steep stairs to their bedroom, supported on Katharina's shoulder, although it all seemed foggy. He did remember taking her to the new bed. *Breaking it in*, he thought, and laughed. She had resisted initially, but a few slaps took care of that.

CHAPTER 15

Afterward, he had fallen asleep nestled on the downy softness of the feather bed while she wept into her pillow. He smiled at the memory.

He rose slowly from the bed when a wave of nausea hit him. He stood for a moment as the room surged around him, the floor heaving like the deck of a ship. The urge to vomit lessened, so he stumbled to the basin and splashed cold water on his face. Standing naked before the mirror, he smiled at his disheveled appearance, at the bulge developing in his belly. He was beginning to look like the wealthy man he was soon to be. But first, a warm bath and a hearty Dutch breakfast would set things right with his head and stomach.

The thought of a plate of greasy sausages, potatoes, and dried herring filled his mind, but his stomach revolted. He leaned over and vomited on the floor—once, then again.

He would have Katharina clean it up later, rather than the scullery maids; it would teach her obedience and duty to his needs. Maybe he would have Sophiia clean it up instead. Now that was an idea! He wiped his mouth with the back of his hand.

He drew on his robe and shouted down the stairs, "Katrijn! I need you to clean something up!"

No answer.

"Katharina, I need my breakfast!"

Only silence.

Damn the woman! Where was she?

He lurched down the hallway, stomach churning, and checked the children's sleeping chambers. Empty except for the unmade beds, clothing, and toys scattered about like the flotsam of a whirlwind.

I'll punish them for this! They must learn to keep their rooms tidy!

He carefully descended the steep stairwell, leaning against the wall for support, dizzy and fearful of falling.

Downstairs, he wandered the house shouting their names, but the place was silent as a tomb. The remnants of the banquet were lying about on tables and chairs, and scattered on the floor. Flies buzzed and crawled over half-eaten meals.

Where were the servants? The servants should have cleaned this up hours ago, long before he had risen. There would be punishment for this, as well. The lazy, insufferable peasants! Heads would roll!

He opened the front door and screamed his family's names in the bright sunlight. He whistled for the dog, Nico, expecting to see the creature come in a clatter of claws. But Nico didn't come.

He shut the door and leaned against it, rubbing his eyes.

Where was everyone? What was happening? Puzzled, he walked to the kitchen at the back of the house. He shouted the cook's name and stopped, shocked.

Now, this was unforgivable!

The kitchen was a disaster: soiled pots and pans were on the counters and table, and half-eaten food scraps littered the stone floor. Flies buzzed fat and lazy around the room and covered the remains of the banquet. The fireplace was cold, except for the few coals fitfully flaring here and there. Angrily, he stirred the flame back to life and added more peat.

It was apparent the servants would have to be dealt with severely. This type of carelessness was intolerable and disrespectful. This behavior in the servants and cook could not be allowed, and certainly not from his wife and children. His house would be a house of order and tidiness. It was the Dutch way. As the *schout* of the city, his home must be an example, as should his household. It would be a hard lesson, but he would teach them proper etiquette however he deemed necessary, no matter how painful.

Pulling a chair before the growing fire, he sat heavily on it, letting the warmth creep into his bones. Anger boiled in him, and he glared at the fireplace in disgust.

The cook and help must have all gone to the Grote Markt. That was the only reasonable explanation he could think of. The previous night's celebration must have depleted the food stocks. That did not explain his wife and children, however. They had servants for these duties; she was the wife of the *schout*, not some scullery maid!

He would sit here and wait for as long as he had to until someone came home so he could vent his anger and frustration. He would hold everyone responsible for this. The blue-and-white tiles around the fireplace caught his eye. It calmed him to study them. Then abruptly, he stared wide-eyed, his blood running cold, and he knew.

He *knew* ...

The sun had set, the sky purpling with approaching night, the house dark and silent around him as he brooded before the long-dead fire.

Jacobszoon ...

The name rolled like thunder through his thoughts.

His family was never coming back.

Never.

CHAPTER 16

Delft
Two Days Later
October 12, 1654

Piscator woke early, grateful for the new day. The mice had taken the few crumbs he had left for them, and he was grateful for that. He could never repay the Master and his wife for their kindness and goodwill, so this tiny thing for the lowest creatures was a small payment.

He had changed over the past few weeks, knowing his vengeance against the *schout* was complete. He had finally been able to release the anger and hatred that had consumed him for so long, allowing something purer and cleaner to fill him. He didn't believe in the Christian and Jewish desert god. His gods were the gods of the Egyptians: Ra, the great god of the Sun; Osiris and Isis; and Anubis, the god of the dead and the underworld. He hoped his difficult path through the gates and doors of the afterworld, the Duat—naming the forty-two guardians of the doors and then having his heart weighed against the feather of Maat—would be easy, given the sacrifices he'd made. If his heart balanced equally against the feather, he would be presented to Osiris, who would admit him to the Field of Reeds, where he would wait to be reborn. He was anxious for this lush region and the beauty of the waterfalls that would heal him as he floated through the reeds.

Turning his thoughts to those strange beings had created a new meaning within him. He knew his life would be a struggle, and it would make him stronger. Along with that realization, he felt a sort of contentment, gratitude for being alive—still able to create works of art, insignificant though they may be—gratitude for his food and room, and a purpose besides ruminating on hatred and revenge.

He worked hard every day, and the Master seldom questioned his efforts. The floor workers had begun treating him with politeness. The Master's wife seemed to find more reasons to come into the factory to chat with him, which was always welcome. Sometimes, it annoyed the Master, and he sent her back to the shop so Piscator could keep working. Piscator always smiled at the words between the two of them. They would sound angry, but he saw their eyes twinkling.

Mostly, he was glad that Katharina and her children were free from the cruelty and degradation of the *schout*. He could harm them no longer, and for that, he was thankful. They deserved much better than the life forced upon them.

Today, there was a fair in the Hague, and the Master and his wife had gone to visit it, having left the previous night. In an act of incredible generosity, the Master had given the day off to all the employees. From the talk amongst the other workers as they left after last night's shift, most were planning on staying home or going to the market in Schiedam.

CHAPTER 16

Only one worker had stayed; a young apprentice named Jan was busy sweeping up and preparing for tomorrow's workday. He was a capable young man and had brought Piscator his breakfast earlier.

So today was quiet, and he used his free time attempting to paint a small picture on a piece of wood: a portrait of the Master and his wife. He wanted to present it to them on their wedding anniversary within the fortnight. It was a clumsy rendition, but still, it was a beginning. The brush felt awkward in his hand, his crippled fingers trying to remember the feel of the wood, once such a huge part of his life. Maybe he'd regain some of his skills with practice and effort.

He heard someone enter the building from the rear entrance and saw that it was Corneli Soetens, the owner of the powder magazine and armory located in an old convent next to the factory. He was a dour man with a perpetually sour face and suspicious, rat-like eyes. He had a long, clay pipe clamped in his mouth, blue smoke encircling his head like fog. The times Piscator had seen him, the unpleasant man was always frowning as though he had swallowed sour wine.

"Where's your Master?" Soetens asked brusquely. "I need to speak with him."

"He's not here today," Piscator answered. "He and his wife have gone to the Hague. They won't be back until tomorrow. Is there something I can help you with?"

Soetens sneered, his rotten brown teeth exposed through thin lips. "I doubt it," he said. "What could *you* possibly do for me? If he gets back today, tell him I was here. I'll be next door in the armory."

Piscator opened his mouth to answer, but the man had already turned to leave, refilling his pipe as he walked away.

Imbecile, Piscator thought. He returned to the tedious painting effort, carefully adjusting the contour of the Master's face. The going was slow, but having a brush in his hand felt good, painting something besides tile. He wasn't going to let anyone ruin his good mood. He tried not to think of the past. All that did was bring upon him a melancholy so heavy it felt like it was crushing him. It was much better to be content with his life now.

He heard the sound of heavy footsteps coming in the back entrance again.

"I already told you the Master isn't here today," he said, not looking up. "I will let him know you were here."

"Oh, I think he'll know I was here."

A black-booted foot kicked him from his chair, and Piscator fell heavily to the floor, dread filling him. Pain lanced his side. Groaning, he looked into the *schout*'s rage-filled face glaring down at him.

"Where are they?" the *schout* shouted. "What have you done with them?"

Piscator laughed up at the *schout*.

"Far from you. You'll never find Katharina and her children, and you'll never hurt them again."

The *schout* took him by the front of his shirt and jerked him to his feet. He felt the fabric on his shoulders tear.

"I don't know what happened to them, but I know you took them. Tell me where they are, or I swear to God, I'll kill you!" Spittle sprayed on Piscator's face.

"Of course, it was me, you fool," Piscator smirked. "Did you think I was going to let *you* have them? They're far better off where they are,

CHAPTER 16

you spineless coward! Do what you will to me; kill me if you like. At least then, I'll never have to see your repulsive face again. And you'll still never get them back. Go back to *your* house and live out your miserable existence knowing the lowly Piscator crushed your dreams of dominance and cruelty."

The *schout* shoved him back against his worktable, upsetting it and sending Piscator and his painting face down in the dust.

Piscator stared at the ruined portrait of the Master and his wife, anger welling in him. He'd had enough of this man. He struggled painfully to his feet to face the *schout* across his worktable.

"Pieter, can I help you?'

Jan was standing in the doorway to the shop, a shovel in his hands, staring wide-eyed at the *schout*.

Piscator looked kindly at the boy. "No, Jan," he said. "I can manage this. You go get the watchman and bring him back." He knew the lad was no match for the *schout*, even with a shovel.

"But . . ." the boy said.

"Go, Jan," Piscator said, calmly watching the *schout*.

The boy dropped the shovel and ran from the factory.

"You will tell me," the *schout* said as he went to the door and picked up the shovel. "Or I'll use this on you. I have no qualms about it. It'll do me good to crush your skull in. Somehow, I'll find them. With or without you."

Piscator laughed. "Go ahead. Do your worst. I have nothing to live for now. Knowing you're defeated and Johannes's family is safe, I am at peace. And while you're at it, go to hell."

The *schout* roared wordlessly and raised the shovel as he rushed at Piscator. Piscator pulled himself straight, readying himself for the blow.

A loud *fwump* came from the armory next door, shaking the ground. Dust fell from the rafters.

There was a tremendous explosion in the building behind the *schout*, who had fallen to the floor. The *schout* scuttled back like a crab, staring horrified at the wall between the factory and the armory. Rocks, timbers, and flames erupted into the factory. An avalanche of stone and fire collapsed behind the stunned *schout*, covering him like a fiery landslide.

Piscator fell back, deafened as dust and flames roared from the jagged opening left in the wall. The floor around him was a heaped jumble of flaming ruin; thick dust and debris blanketed everything, filling his lungs. He painfully began crawling to the door, which had been to his left, he thought. He had become disoriented. He heard voices and screams from outside.

"The powder magazine is on fire!" he heard someone shout beyond this dying world.

"Help me!" he whispered, knowing he was going to die.

Then he remembered Katharina and her children.

Lieve Gods, he screamed in his thoughts. *Dear Gods, I need to get them back! They will be trapped forever if I don't! Dear Gods, help me get out!*

Suddenly, the world became a conflagration of fire and stone and wood, filling the already dense air and piercing him with shrapnel. He was suddenly in agony, and then the tremendous sound of a billion worlds colliding burst his eardrums, covering him with an inferno of

CHAPTER 16

flaming ash and wreckage. A great burning beam fell on him and he could not move. His hair and trousers were ablaze. He smelled himself sizzling.

NoNoNoNo!

A volcano erupted with the sound of an immense crash of thunder. It filled the world with a hideous firestorm.

Katharina, I'm sorry. I can't free you. . . . The words escaped his dying thought as the devouring flames freed him.

A door opened onto a chill, silent void, and he was beyond all pain and sorrow.

PART TWO

Salt Lake City, Utah
Present Day

CHAPTER 1

He was toweling off after his workout when he heard the phone ringing upstairs.

He'd set up the exercise room in a cramped, stuffy bedroom in the basement of their current home. Even with the fan running full blast, he still got overheated, especially when using the treadmill. The new house they were having built would take care of that problem, along with many others.

The new exercise room would be 1,200 square feet, larger than their first house. They consulted with an exercise specialist to order the latest machines. For the first month, they'd have in-home instruction with a certified trainer from the equipment company. They were both excited about this new aspect of their lives. There'd be plenty of room for them and their daughter, Sarah, to exercise together.

Annie entered as he tossed his towel in the hamper.

"You need to hurry, Cart," she said. "Scott called and moved our meeting with James up an hour. There's a huge problem with the fireplace tiles that came yesterday."

"You mean the antique ones from Holland? It's been almost a year since he ordered them, and now there's a screwup. Why doesn't that surprise me? It's not the first time something like this has happened. Maybe James is too busy to keep things straight."

"Scott didn't say what the problem was. The meeting is in an hour, and we still need to drop Maddy at Mom's, so get showered." She kissed his forehead.

"Man, you stink." She grimaced and left the room

"What do you expect?" he called after her. "It takes a lot of work to look like this!"

She laughed. "Just hurry, Adonis!"

He heard three-and-a-half-year-old Maddy calling for her in the background. "Mommy?"

He was amazed at Annie. He loved her more than ever and still felt the desire for her he'd had as a newlywed. She'd grown more beautiful as she matured, and motherhood did nothing to lessen her appeal. She'd developed incredible organizational skills, efficiently keeping the house and family running while he was at work, dealing with clients or in court. She was what he needed; and her confidence and love for him steadied him. So many other attorneys where he worked were on their second or third marriages, and seeing the selfishness and arrogance with how they lived their lives made him glad his own relationship was solid.

He'd met her in a senior class at the University of Utah, sitting behind her in the old folding desk chairs. He was immediately captivated by her smile and sense of humor, not to mention her long blonde hair and how she smelled: clean and fresh. Soon, they were meeting at the library to study or grab lunch at the student union building. As they say, "one thing led to another." Eight months later, they were married

CHAPTER 1

and living in cramped student housing, poor but happy, eating meals Annie had seemingly pulled out of thin air while still finishing her degree. He was proud to be her husband.

She was so excited about the new house, helping James, the designer, choose things to fill their home—everything from color options for the walls and furniture to kitchen finishes and bathroom tiles. Her mark would be indelible in every room.

Sure, the house was expensive. But he'd worked hard for years—sometimes at the expense of time with his family—to get where he was today: Carter Benson, a partner in one of the most elite law firms in the area. All the years in law school, interning, and taking the worst cases when he joined the firm were paying off wonderfully.

She'd stood beside him the whole time, despite the loneliness of his absent hours. When he'd come home exhausted, she'd meet him at the door with a hug and a kiss.

She deserved this house.

Meeting with the architect and Scott Young, the contractor, Cart watched Annie's excitement grow as every nuance of the house grew to fruition. She glowed with enthusiasm as the months passed and the house neared completion.

She went there two or three times a week, walking through each room to gauge the progress and greeting the workers, except for one man, Digger, who made her nervous with his admiring stares and comments. In his mid-fifties, pony-tailed and lean, he worked in short cut-off jeans and no shirt during the summer, his over-tanned skin dry and leathery. He obviously thought he was quite a ladies' man but came off buffoonish more than anything else.

Lately, he'd been commenting, "Hello, pretty lady!" and trying to converse with her. Cart had spoken to Scott about how it made Annie uncomfortable. Scott had promised to talk with Digger. It wasn't a big problem yet, and Cart intended to keep it that way. He was a hard worker, despite his openly flirtatious remarks.

Regardless of the man's presence, Annie managed the weekly meetings with the architect, builder, and designer, overseeing all aspects of construction. She seemed happier and more alive than at any time in their marriage.

He would have been happier with something smaller, but he was doing this for her. It symbolized his love for her and his appreciation for what she meant to him. She was his wife, the mother of their children, and, most importantly, his best friend.

CHAPTER 2

Surrounded by the snow-packed Wasatch Mountains, Salt Lake Valley was a veritable outdoor lover's delight. With several world-class ski resorts within an hour of the valley, one could ski in the morning and play golf in the afternoon, depending upon the season. The high mountain forests offered camping, hiking, biking, and a cool retreat from the summer heat, which made it a year-round delight.

Quiet farmland that had been the backbone of the state's economy disappeared under the explosive need for new subdivisions and houses. Desirable properties were becoming scarce. They'd opted for an existing lot in an established neighborhood. Thirty to forty years ago, it'd been a lovely area known as the Cottonwoods. The houses in the area were still nice, but very dated. Most of the yards were overgrown with trees and shrubs planted decades ago, the yards not nearly as well-groomed when younger families lived in them. The current trend was to buy one of these older homes and bulldoze it to build a new home with modern architecture and convenience.

They loved the stately trees lining and arching over the streets, providing shade in the summer and a multitude of color in the autumn. The lot they'd chosen was nearly an acre with mature trees in the front and back that Scott had been careful to save. The backyard was overgrown, and the concrete patios were cracked and crumbling. However, once the landscaping, pool, and tennis court were in place, it would be a pleasant refuge from the world. They felt lucky to have it. It would be only two blocks from Sarah's new high school, which she'd attend when September came.

And that was a huge problem.

Sarah was angry about the move, not wanting to leave close friendships cultivated since elementary school. Sixteen and pretty, she'd inherited her mother's charm and good looks. They'd had several arguments with her about the move, some of them pretty heated and usually ending with her running to her room and locking the door. Hopefully, they could figure things out to make the transition easier for her.

The existing house had come down quickly; heavy equipment smoothed out the lot and dug the hole for the foundation, then the foundation was poured. It was exciting to watch the progress, noting each step with pictures and comments in a journal that Annie kept.

The electrical, plumbing, insulation, and all the other systems within the house's walls had passed the city inspection with only a few adjustments, and the sheet rockers finished the drywall just last week.

The finish carpenters and tile contractors were busy doing their jobs, dusty and competent. Although sometimes it seemed the work had stalled, Scott explained that the careful craftsmanship necessitated the extra time. Quality was fundamental to them. The house was costing them a bundle; they wanted the best work possible and were

CHAPTER 2

getting it. The woodwork was excellent, all done by Scott's crew of six carpenters.

Scott Young, the general contractor, was honest and forthright, earnest in his desire to build the home exactly as the owners wanted. Using the same craftsmen in each house he built assured the quality of the finished product, and he was always more concerned about that level of workmanship than finding the lowest bid.

They were, indeed, happy with the house. At nearly 9,000 square feet, there was plenty of room for them. Annie enjoyed entertaining, and the home was perfect for that.

Although it was typical for people in an existing neighborhood to complain about noise and dust, the only person they'd had problems with was Luke Vincent, who lived in the house next to theirs to the east. He worked from home and found every excuse to be upset. A thin, rangy man in his mid-forties with a balding head and sulfurous eyes, he was all sharp angles and wiry muscles. He complained constantly about the noise and dust, about the workers parking in front of his house. He shouted at them for using backhoes and skid steers, and cursed as the men ate lunch on the house's front porch. He made a nuisance of himself.

Luke had a large shed on the property line painted a fluorescent green. He adorned it further with obnoxious, smiling ducks waddling across the whole thing, grinning at anyone who walked out the back door.

Large signs appeared in his front yard complaining about "these people that come in and build enormous houses" (never mind that he'd done the same thing a few years earlier), and he'd call the police any time someone showed up a few minutes before 7:30 a.m. Luke was a joke among the workers, who laughed among themselves at his childish antics.

The continuing hassle of dealing with Luke was the only tiresome thing about building the house. Cart had tried talking to Luke early in the project, hoping to appease him, but only faced increasing ire as the house evolved and time passed. Lately, he'd considered getting a restraining order against Luke to keep him from harassing the workers and his family.

The man's wife, Kate, a rail-thin woman with a sad face and haunted eyes, was humiliated by her husband's actions but appeared sufficiently cowed by his anger. She kept to herself, fearing angry reprisals from her husband as his alarming actions escalated. Whenever possible, usually when Luke wasn't home, she would venture out of their house to meekly apologize to Cart and Annie for his behavior. They assured her they felt no ill will toward her and offered support if she ever needed it. They felt sorry for her and the life of misery she lived.

Despite Luke's foolishness, the house proceeded at a steady pace.

Today was the usual weekly meeting with James and Scott. Though Cart generally didn't attend these meetings, this was the monthly budget meeting, and it was frequently tense as the house cost increased with change orders and James's customized interior designs. Cart had initially tried to rein Annie and James in but ultimately let them continue their plans.

Several cars and trucks were parked along the street by their house, including the dreaded Luke Vincent home. Cart and Annie had learned to gauge the progress of their home by the number of vehicles outside. Today, they'd counted fourteen along the street but no cops were there, so Luke must not have been home.

The heavy oak front door was from an old chateau in the Normandy countryside. Hand-applied custom stucco replicated the outside of a French manor, with darkened corners and carefully applied "cracks" that made the house look centuries old. The soffit, fascia, and the trim around doors and windows were painted pale yellow. The three-foot-high wainscotting along the bottom of the exterior was limestone imported from an old quarry in Burgundy, France, and reclaimed antique gray slate from Paris covered the roof. James assured them the slate came from a home built at least two hundred years ago.

Cart had to hand it to James. The man knew his stuff.

The bedrooms in the home each contained a bathroom with custom handmade tiles for the wainscot and tub surround. Their master suite alone was about 700 square feet. The bedroom's focal point was the large fireplace on the south wall. A custom-built mantle would surround the 400-year-old Delft tiles salvaged from an old house in Holland before its demolition. Annie had fallen in love with the distinctive blue-and-white tiles, handmade long ago.

Air compressors were cycling all through the house, along with the pop of nail guns. Cart paused to speak with one of the cement guys, a slightly built man from Mexico who spoke no English. Cart had spent a few years there in his early twenties and spoke Spanish fluently.

Walking upstairs, Cart noticed Digger standing on a scaffold installing crown moldings in the kitchen, staring at Annie. He glanced away when he saw Cart looking at him. Cart felt a slow burn in his gut as he stared at the man. Annie shook her head.

Scott and James were chatting quietly near the fireplace. With them was Ben Withers, the foreman for the job—a younger man in his late thirties with black hair and a quiet demeanor. Scott was in his fifties, of average build, his balding head shaved closely. James was younger, maybe in his late forties, sporting a thick, blond goatee and wearing his usual tie and vest. At their feet were several tiles laid in a row, along with a cardboard box overflowing with packing peanuts and plastic wrap.

These must be the old Dutch tiles, Cart thought.

James smiled as they entered the room.

"Annie, Cart! I'm glad to see you," he said, shaking their hands. "I haven't seen you since you got back. How was your trip?"

They'd gone to Phoenix to visit Annie's sister and her family earlier in the month.

"Hot!" Cart exclaimed. "Saturday was only a hundred and fifteen degrees. Thank goodness for air-conditioning. It was even too hot to golf!"

"It *must* have been hot, then," Scott smiled. "Annie told me you'd probably go golfing on the day of your own funeral."

"Yeah, but I'd only have time for the front nine if I got there early enough."

They all laughed. Annie knew if there were a way, he'd do it.

A tall, slender man walked out of the bathroom. He wore black jeans, a black tee shirt, and black shoes with no socks. His hair was silver, and he wore wire-rimmed glasses. James smiled as the man drew close to them.

CHAPTER 2

"Man, the work in this house is unbelievable!" he said, smiling at James. "When are you going to do this to our house?"

"I don't think you've met Ron yet," James said. "This is Cart and Annie Benson, Ron. You've heard me mention them."

"I sure have." Ron shook their hands. "I'm Ron Dalton. It's nice to finally meet you. It's been fun hearing James talk about what you're doing here, and I'm glad I got to see it and meet you. When do you plan on moving in?"

"That's what we're here to discuss, among other things," Scott said. He turned to his foreman, Ben. "Would you grab Karl so we can get his input?"

"Sure thing," Ben said, and left the room.

James knelt by the tiles on the floor and reached into the box, rustling the foam peanuts before drawing out a bubble-wrapped bundle; cautiously unwrapping it, he laid it next to the other tiles. The antique Delft tile, its handmade surface pitted and holding small hairline cracks, was a picture of a windmill with blades high against the sky and small flowers in front of it.

"Oh, wow!" Annie exclaimed as she knelt to touch it. "I love it! I love it! Did you end up getting them where you thought you would?"

Cart knelt beside her and picked it up, grinning.

"I have a contact who owns an antique store in Haarlem," said James. "I've worked with him several times, and he found them for me. Nice, aren't they?"

"Nice?" Cart carefully laid the tile back down. "They're remarkable. How old did you say they were?"

James took another bundle out and unwrapped it. The tile was a picture of a woman wearing wooden shoes, a white cap, and an apron over a fluffy dress hanging to the tops of her shoes. She was stirring a bowl with a large spoon.

"Well, we know they came from a house built in the early 1600s," he explained. "So that makes them nearly four hundred years old, give or take. The house's first owner was a city official, a judge, or a prosecutor and was quite wealthy. They're demolishing that house and a few more to make a parking lot, which I think is a travesty. The house has been vacant for several years, so we were lucky to get them. They are in such good shape." He unwrapped and laid out several more.

"The only problem is this one." He pulled a plastic sandwich bag out of his pocket and laid the contents on the floor.

It was a shattered tile. Blue and white pieces chipped and cracked.. Annie sucked in her breath.

"Oh, no," she whispered, touching the pieces. "What happened?"

James shook his head. "I don't know. Somewhere between here and Holland, it got broken. It made me physically ill when I first saw it."

Cart tried to assemble the pieces like a puzzle, reconstructing them as best he could, but small pieces were missing. It seemed to be a picture of a girl walking along a row of trees, a dog cavorting at her side. She wasn't a child but more like an older girl in her teens.

"Can we glue it back together?" he wondered aloud. "But that wouldn't look good with the other tiles in such excellent condition. What do you suggest we do?"

"I've got a call in to my friend in Haarlem," said James, "but I don't expect to hear from him today since it's nighttime over there, so hopefully in a day or two. He might have some suggestions. I've never had this happen before." He was frowning. "The tiles were insured, of course, but losing this one hurts. It was an extraordinary collection: a family at work and playing, images of their home and farm animals. The design is pretty unique."

They heard footsteps and turned to see Ben walk in with the tile contractor, Karl, the latter of whom wore a ball cap over close-cropped gray hair and white overalls spattered with cement.

He was also in his fifties, and Cart smiled as he approached them. Most of the craftsmen on the job were in their fifties, and he supposed their years of experience explained their exceptional workmanship.

James showed him the broken tile.

"Shoot," said Karl, wiping his dusty glasses on a white cloth pulled from his pocket. "That's really too bad. I know these things are expensive. I'm surprised they can get tiles from the wall without breaking them."

"They didn't use Portland cement back then," James explained. "They used a lime and sand mixture to set the tiles. Depending on the age of the mortar, they can come off quite easily."

"I didn't know that. I guess you learn something every day. What can I do for you?" Karl asked.

"We wanted your input on this," Scott said. "We need to figure this out today to keep the job moving. It's holding up the installation of the mantel, and that's holding up the painter. We can't afford the delay. Do you have any suggestions?"

Karl thought for a minute, chewing on his lower lip.

"Are you going to replace the whole set or just this tile?" he asked.

James shook his head. "We can't order another set; it would take too long. There's no way to replace this, anyway. It's very unique. We might be able to get a replica piece, though. I know a guy in Germany who specializes in reproduction tiles, so that might be an option, but I don't know how long it would take. He's usually quite a way out on his orders. I'd have to contact him tomorrow."

"Can you get another tile about this size? It doesn't have to match. I'd set it temporarily until the replacement comes. That way, you can get the mantle put in."

"That'd work, Karl," said Scott. "Can you get a piece like that, James?"

"I might have something at the office," James said. "I'll see what I have and let you know. When do you think you can start on this?"

"I was hoping tomorrow or the next day," Karl said. "The sooner, the better."

James and Annie began wrapping the tiles in bubble wrap to put in the box.

"I'll stick those in the shower, so nothing happens to them," Karl said, taking them into the bathroom.

James's partner, Ron, said goodbye and left.

Annie and James left to discuss paint samples for Sarah's bedroom, and Ben went to check on a supply order due the following day. Cart took the opportunity to speak alone with Scott.

"Did you ever get to talk to Digger about his actions?" he asked. "I noticed him staring at Annie when we came in. He looked away when he saw I was watching him, but he would have done the same thing

CHAPTER 2

if I wasn't here. I've got to tell you, it's making me angry and Annie uncomfortable. I'm wondering if we should get him off the job?"

"I hate to lose him. It'll slow us down, but this has to stop. I've talked with him a few times," Scott said, visibly angry. "I guess my discussions didn't do any good. I don't see an alternative, though. I guess he has to go. I'll take care of it after work today."

Cart shook his head. "I want you to do it now. I want him out of this house immediately."

"I'd like to avoid a scene if I can. He's going to be pretty upset."

"Too bad. The sooner Digger's out of here, the better it will be. Besides, I want to be there when you do it."

"Well, okay," Scott said, looking at the floor. "If that's what you want."

Cart was annoyed with Scott's waffling.

"Just do it, Scott. You should have done this months ago. I want my wife to feel safe here."

"You're right, Cart," Scott said, his ears red with embarrassment.

Cart watched him leave the bedroom and head downstairs.

He went into the bathroom to look at the shower Karl had finished a few days earlier. He heard shouting echoing up the stairs.

CHAPTER 3

Scott and Digger stood face-to-face when Cart walked into the kitchen. Digger was holding a hammer, his face florid with rage.

"You can't fire me like this!" he shouted. "I've worked for you for over a year, and you just fired me? I bought over two thousand dollars in tools to do your freaking work! What am I supposed to do now?"

"I've told you several times to knock it off," Scott said calmly. "I've given you plenty of chances. Now, do what I said and get out of here. You've got one hour to load your tools and leave. Trent and the guys will help you."

Cart was impressed with how Scott managed this, not allowing himself to play Digger's game.

Digger threw his hammer down and raised a fist, pushing Scott back against a cabinet. The other carpenters watched, numbed and surprised by Digger's words and actions. Trent and a carpenter named Kelly rushed to hold him back. Digger squirmed to free himself.

Spittle sprayed from his mouth as he shouted, "Damn you! Let me go!"

Digger freed one arm and grabbed Scott, who pushed his arm away.

"Don't do anything you'll regret, Digger," said Scott evenly. "If you do, the cops will be all over you. Get your stuff and get out of here. Now."

Digger shrugged off Trent and Kelly and then saw Cart standing near the door. His face grew cold, and his bushy brows furrowed like fists over his blazing eyes.

"Well, it looks like you got your way, huh?" he smirked. "I'm the best carpenter here, but you still got your way. What's the matter, rich boy? Afraid your woman will want a real man? She'd go for it, I can tell you. I've seen how she looks at me, all hot and all. I can show her what a real man can do!" He started walking toward Cart, but Scott put a restraining hand on his shoulder.

"Shut up, Digger!" he hissed. "Get out of here before you get dragged out!"

"Oh, let him go, Scott." Cart smiled. "What do you say, Digger? Do you think you can take me? Just because I work in an office doesn't make me a pushover. So go ahead, take a swing. Show me what a real man can do."

Digger shrank back, stumbling on his hammer, his face ashen. He stood looking at Cart with narrowed eyes, regaining some of his insolence. He spat on the floor at Cart's feet and sneered, lips thin around yellowed teeth.

"Shove it, pretty boy." He glared at Scott. "I don't need anyone's help. I can get my tools. I've been alone my whole life. I sure as hell don't need anybody now."

He started gathering his tools, jerking his nail gun off a compressor hose with a pop.

CHAPTER 3

Trent looked at Scott, who nodded imperceptibly. Trent, Kelly, and the other carpenters started hauling Digger's tools to the garage.

"Don't think I'll forget this," Digger growled, removing his tool belt and glaring at Cart. "I won't ever forget this."

Cart heard a sound behind him and saw Annie and James standing at the door from the stairway, appalled at what they'd seen. Digger stomped past them with an armload of tools.

"Bitch . . ." he muttered under his breath.

Cart started after him, but Annie put her hand on his arm. "Don't, Cart. He's not worth it. He got what he deserved. You can't do anything worse to him, so let it go."

He glared at Digger's retreating figure. "I don't have to put up with this in our own house. And I can think of a few worse things than what he got." A vein in his temple throbbed uncomfortably.

Annie touched his cheek with a soft hand. "He'll be gone soon, and then we won't have to worry about him," she whispered. "Come upstairs and look at the paint we picked for Sarah's room."

She went up the stairs with James, who looked pallid with shock.

She had miraculous power in her touch, an innate ability to calm Cart when he was angry and fuming like this. Through all their years together, she'd defused his anger and frustration with just a few words or a gentle touch, helping him look more clearly at things that should have been apparent. He shrugged his outrage off as best he could and followed them up the stairs.

He knew the paint color wasn't why she wanted him upstairs. Annie was removing him from a provocation he didn't need.

And he loved her for it.

CHAPTER 4

That night they had another quarrel with Sarah. When Annie mentioned during supper that Scott told them they might be able to move into the house in two or three months, Sarah expressed her opinions in no uncertain terms.

"This is so stupid!" she shouted. "I don't want to move! I'll finally go to prom this year, and now I can't because I have to go to the other stupid school! This is so unfair!"

Cart patiently explained she would still have friends at her old school, but attending the new school would allow her to make new friends. It seemed reasonable to him.

"I don't need new friends! I like the ones I have!" She jumped up from the table, knocking over her glass, drenching her plate and chair with milk.

"You don't understand!" she sobbed, tears flowing down her cheeks.

"Sarah . . ." Annie began, but Sarah ran from the room, going upstairs to her bedroom. The echo of the slamming door reverberated through the house. Maddy was upset at all the shouting, staring wide-eyed at her parents. A few minutes later, Sarah stomped down the stairs and out the front door, slamming that as well, and headed to her friend Emma's house for the night.

Annie sighed and put down her fork. "Well, that went nicely," she said.

Cart stared dumbly at his plate, pushing the food around with this fork.

One thing all his years of schooling hadn't prepared him for was the hormonal emotions of a sixteen-year-old girl running at feverish intensity. While he didn't allow disrespect in his home, he and Annie had decided not to overreact to this particular issue. That just made things worse with Sarah. They'd tried including her in decisions with her bedroom, such as the paint, carpet, and tile, but she'd answered their inclusions with stubborn sullenness. The disturbing arguments with her had grown more frequent as the house neared completion, and the coinciding bouts of pouting, brooding, and anger had increased in frequency and duration.

Cart had trouble understanding any of this. The new house would be like a palace compared to this one. Her bedroom would be twice as big; there'd be a game room, a media room with the latest high-tech home theater system, and a state-of-the-art exercise room. A swimming pool, tennis court, and pickleball court would be in the backyard. He hoped that as the completion date grew nearer, she'd relent and become enthused about the new house, or at least accept it. That didn't seem to be happening, and no amount of pleading or persuasion on their part affected her. He was at a loss as to what to do. He didn't like the tension in their home or Sarah's reaction to the inevitable. It was what it was, and it wouldn't change because she didn't like it.

CHAPTER 4

They discussed it further that night in bed, with Maddy fast asleep in the next room.

The bedroom windows were open, a respite from the August heat following an evening thunderstorm. The whisper of leaves outside lent an aspect of tranquility to the darkened room. The air was cool and fresh, and the scent of rain tinged the night air. Cart watched the dappled shadows of leaves and branches stirring on the walls and ceiling, savoring Annie's gentle breathing, her head nestled on his chest.

Her hair smelled faintly of shampoo and children, and her breath was moist on his skin. He felt soothed in the hush of the night and his closeness with Annie.

She looked up at him.

"What's wrong, sweetie?" he asked.

"Oh, I'm just worried about Sarah. It breaks my heart to see her like this, and I honestly don't know what to do."

"Yeah, me, too," Cart said. "I've tried to talk to her about it, but you saw what happened at dinner. No matter what I say, she either takes it wrong and yells or ignores me, which is frustrating. I want her to be happy about the house. I want her to love the new home, but it seems she's bound and determined to hate it all, no matter what we say or do." He shrugged. "Maybe we can figure out some kind of compromise. Dealing with her is worse than negotiating multimillion dollar contracts with the most stubborn people I've ever faced." He looked at her. "Were you this obstinate at this age? I'm pretty sure she didn't get it from me."

"Oh, I don't know," she scoffed. "I've seen you get your back up a few times. Mom said I went through some difficult times, but nothing this extreme. I'm sure I was hard to deal with at times."

"I just want her to be happy and accept this," he muttered.

"We both need to get some sleep." Annie leaned up to kiss him. "We'll figure it out." In less than a minute, she was sound asleep.

He'd always envied her ability to fall asleep quickly, even when troubled about things. He always struggled with falling asleep. Tonight was no different. He kept playing the earlier argument out in his mind, wondering what he could have done differently. He liked order and neatness in his life; his personality demanded it. He knew he was trying to impose his will on Sarah and she didn't like that. He knew forcing her was a mistake, but if she wasn't willing to listen or try to understand, it would only cause them all more grief.

Eventually, the quiet night lulled him to sleep.

* * *

Focusing on work at the office was nearly impossible, his mind roiling over thoughts of Sarah's troubled heart. Annie had already called this morning to tell him Sarah had come home from Emma's and had gone straight to her room without slamming the door, but hadn't come downstairs yet. Her mom had dropped Maddy off after her sleepover, and they'd discussed Sarah quietly. They hadn't come up with anything, but had given her a hug and sympathy. Later, Annie called to tell him Sarah had come down and tearfully apologized.

"She's so confused right now," Annie said. "I told her not to worry about it, and we'd work something out. She seemed happier after that

CHAPTER 4

and even took Maddy for a walk around the block. I love her so much, Cart. Let's figure this out as soon as possible." She told him she loved him and hung up.

He had several client files on his desk awaiting consideration, knowing he couldn't put them off for long. He was staring at his monitor, zoning into the Sarah world, when he suddenly sat up. Straightening the mess on his desk, he put on his jacket and told his secretary, Cora, he'd be gone for the rest of the day. Puzzled, she watched him leave.

Carter has left the building! he chuckled, feeling he'd come up with a solution to all their problems. Sometimes, he just had to let his mind work independently.

He called Annie on the way home to ensure Sarah was still home. He told her what his idea was and asked what she thought, and she loved it. Relief from their constant tension and strain finally seemed in sight for the first time in months.

It was so simple.

* * *

Annie waited for him in the kitchen, her blonde hair pulled into a ponytail. The kitchen smelled of the morning, the scent of toast and jam, pleasant and homey. She hugged him tightly.

"Sarah's up in her room," she whispered. "I didn't tell her you were coming home, so this will surprise her. You're not usually home this early!"

"This is too important to wait." He smiled, kissing the top of her head. "If she agrees with what I came up with, maybe we can go to the zoo or a movie after we get lunch. I've really got my fingers crossed."

Annie hugged him tighter. "I love you, Cart," she said.

Then Maddy was there, tugging his pant leg for attention, her small face looking up at him, smiling broadly.

"Daddy's home! Daddy's home!"

She was wearing her usual Disney Princess outfit—one of many, a strange mixture of a pink billowy dress with a picture of Belle from *Beauty and the Beast* on it. Gossamer wings from her Tinker Bell dress hung loosely from her shoulders, and dark glasses with one lens missing perched upside down on her tiny nose. She wore one plastic ruby-red Dorothy slipper and a lone sock on her other foot.

"Did you bring me a treat?" she asked earnestly, her little blue eyes drilling into his.

He laughed and picked her up. "No, but we can get one later. How's my little sweetie-pie today?"

He blew a raspberry on her exposed neck, and she giggled and squirmed, her three-and-a-half-year-old body amazingly strong and agile. Her joyful and robust disposition was a constant wonder to him. He threw her up a few times while they laughed. She disappeared into the family room like a puff of pink magic loosed on an unsuspecting world.

Though sometimes demanding like her big sister, she was, like Sarah, one of the best things to happen in their lives. After years of trying to conceive following Sarah's birth, Annie finally became pregnant, and nine months later, the little bundle of animation had been born.

CHAPTER 4

Annie laughed at the retreating blur of their daughter.

"She's so funny today. I think that's the twentieth ensemble she's come up with this morning. It gets more bizarre every time."

Cart got a Diet Coke from the fridge and took a long swig. He loved the cold bubbles in his throat.

"Let's get Sarah down here, and we'll tell her, okay?"

He munched on a cookie while Annie went to get Sarah.

I hope this works....

When Sarah saw Cart standing by the sink, her eyes widened in surprise, then she stiffened and stared at the floor. He walked over and put his arms around her. She stood rigid for a moment but slowly relaxed like a melting candle, and he felt her head rest softly on his chest.

"I'm sorry, Dad," she said.

He hugged her tighter and kissed the top of her head. *Man, I love this girl.*

"I know, sweetie," he said. "This has been hard on all of us, but mostly you, I think. We are building a house, Sarah; we can't change that. After you left last night, we decided we had to work something out, something that might help you be happy about the new house. Today I couldn't concentrate at work. I thought there must be a way to work this out. We'll probably be moving in by Thanksgiving."

Sarah stiffened and tried to pull away, but he was stronger and held her tight.

"So, here's what we came up with: School starts in two weeks, right? As we've said, you'll start the year at your old school. But instead of transferring you to the new school when we move, we'll let you finish the year at your old school. That way, you'll have the whole school year and summer to prepare for the change. You can go to your dances, have fun with your friends, and be ready for the new school next year."

Sarah looked up at him, her eyes shining and lighting his world. "Will that work?"

The clock ticked on the wall, and they heard Maddy singing about wanting to be human, not a mermaid.

"Oh, Dad, do you mean it? Really?"

"Yep." He smiled. "I can drop you off at school, and your mom can pick you up when school's over. I think it could work, don't you, Annie?"

"Of course it will. And if one of us can't be there, we'll get someone who can be, or trade with each other." Annie smiled as she came to hug both of them. "I knew we'd figure it out."

"I have to call Emma!" Sarah said as she pulled from the group hug. "Thank you, guys! She'll be so excited!" Then she was pounding up the stairs two at a time.

They were alone in the kitchen.

Maddy began singing, "Let it go! Let it goooo!" and stomping her foot.

Annie put her arms around Cart. "Well, that went over nicely." She laughed, using the exact phrase as last night after the explosion.

Annie was still chuckling while she got Maddy ready for lunch and the zoo. Maddy insisted on wearing her blue *Frozen* Elsa dress and pink rain boots.

Moving about the kitchen, Annie said James had called earlier and told her he found a tile that would function as a filler on the fireplace

CHAPTER 4

until his connection in Germany could make the replica tile. He would drop it off to the tile guy later that day.

CHAPTER 5

With Sarah no longer an impossible issue, life began to return to their normal around the house. Cart was busy dealing with various problems at the firm, and Annie ran the house perfectly.

They all seemed happy.

Sarah started school two weeks before Labor Day, and since they were still in their old home, driving her to school wouldn't be a daily thing until they moved into the new house. She was happy and engaged in the family again.

The new house progressed well.

A few problems arose, but nothing of dire circumstance. Scott managed everything professionally, his crew and subcontractors working like a well-oiled machine, familiar with one another's functions and methods, and accustomed to the flexibility that building a house required.

Karl, the tile guy, had installed the Delft tiles on the bedroom fireplace, including the blank one in place of the broken tile. Trent had installed the mantle, and the contrast between the blue-and-white tiles and the subtle yellow of the wood mantle was quite striking. There were twenty tiles in the surround, grouted in pale gray.

The keystone tile in the middle of the top row was a picture of a fisherman standing on the deck of a small boat, casting his net into the sea. His wife was in another tile wearing her cap and apron, stirring a blue bowl of something. There were a few windmills, various fishing boats, a baby sitting under a tree with a sleeping dog, and a boy running alongside a hoop while he rolled it. The blank tile stood out like an unfinished portrait, but James had assured them he was collaborating with his contacts to get a replacement.

Sarah became more involved with the home, helping Annie and James choose fabrics and fixtures. It was fun to indulge her in this because she seemed to enjoy it.

Luke Vincent, the neighbor from hell, had not been much of a problem lately, at least not like in the early days of construction. He mostly complained about parking in front of his house, but even these were minimal, as though he'd accepted there was nothing he could do to make it go away.

Scott said Digger had driven past a few times but hadn't stopped.

Summer had passed, abandoning the heat and humidity to memory, and autumn proclaimed its entrance with flair. The trees lining the street erupted with color. Leaves of gold and red hung like colorful ornaments from the branches; the lawns, sidewalks, and pavement were blanketed with crunching leaves that had fallen as the season progressed. Some mornings frost tinged the air, leaving a frozen mist on cars and earth, crusting windshields with diamond-like sparkle and hardness.

October settled in like a cloak of cold heralding the coming of winter. Witches and skeletons began appearing in windows, and ghosts

CHAPTER 5

and goblins peered from front lawns, haunting the night with the approach of Halloween.

On the afternoon of October 27th, the first shadow of darkness insinuated itself in their quiet lives.

Annie called and asked Cart to meet her at the house at 3:30 that afternoon. Things were under control at the office, so at 3:00, he left Cora in charge. Driving out of the parking garage onto State Street in downtown Salt Lake, he headed south, his Porsche growling like an untethered beast beneath him. The sun was shining, the sky a brilliant blue, though a few stubborn clouds clung like spider webs to the mountains south of the city. Early snow in the high mountains dusted the ring of peaks surrounding the valley.

He geared down as he approached his exit on 23rd East off I-80, stopping at the first convenience store to get a Diet Coke and a sucker for Maddy. Ten minutes later, he pulled into their subdivision. Two houses up, he saw the cars and trucks lined up outside their home. He saw two people talking together on the street. As he got closer, he noticed one of them was Sarah. Sucking in his breath, he saw Digger leaning lazily against the side of his truck, a cigarette dangling from his lips as he spoke to Sarah.

Infuriated, Cart drove past the two and parked a few houses up the street in the first open space. He gripped the steering wheel, trying to calm himself. Annie hadn't arrived yet, so her influence wasn't here to control the rage roiling through his mind. Sarah was his precious daughter, and Digger's audacity filled his veins with fire.

He *would* safeguard his family and damn the cost.

Climbing out of his car, he slammed the door forcefully, staring at Digger as he stomped toward the two of them. Sarah turned at the sound of his footsteps and smiled. When she saw the look on his face, though, she frowned in confusion. Digger saw Cart approaching and smirked, standing away from his truck.

Cart stared at Digger coldly. "Go wait inside for your mother," he said to Sarah, never taking his eyes off Digger.

"But, Dad—" she protested.

"Sarah. Go inside and wait for your mother. Now." His words were abrupt, cutting the cool air. She immediately turned and walked hurriedly to the house, pausing once to look back at her father.

"What the hell are you doing here?" Cart asked through clenched teeth. "Why were you speaking to my daughter?" He felt his stomach harden, his pulse quickening.

"Hey, man." Digger laughed. "I only stopped to see how the house was coming along. I invested a lot of time and sweat into this place and wanted to see how it looked. Somebody dropped your daughter off while I was standing here, and I was asking her how school was going. You got a problem with that?" He sneered at him with crooked teeth the color of old ivory. "There's no law against talking to a girl, right? Even yours," he said as he blew a stream of smoke into Cart's face.

Cart stepped closer to Digger, mere inches from his face. He smelled the man's breath, sour with cigarettes and coffee; his body odor nearly overwhelming. He jabbed a finger into Digger's chest, feeling the wiry tenseness coiled within.

"If I ever see you talking to anyone in my family again, if I see you within a mile of my house, there will be no one and nothing to stop

CHAPTER 5

me from taking you down. I'll file a restraining order against you, so if you ever show your ugly face here again, you'll find yourself cuddling up with the biggest, worst, ugliest creep in the jail. And believe me, I'm the man that can do it. Do I make myself clear?"

Digger knocked Cart's hand away and leaned back against his truck.

"Screw you, rich boy. Don't harass me. I'm not afraid of your stupid threats. I can stand on a public street and talk to whoever I want to. I could drop you like a bag of wet cement, anyway, so why don't you take yourself and your pretty boy suit and get the hell out of my face? I've got better things to do than stand here listening to your crap."

He dropped the cigarette at Cart's feet and ground it under his booted heel.

"Then I suggest you go find them because you have exactly thirty seconds to get your sorry butt out of here," Cart looked at his watch, "starting now." He smiled humorlessly, fighting back the desire to pummel the man within an inch of his life.

Digger glowered at him, fists clenched, breathing raggedly, but he turned and opened his truck door. "I don't have to listen to you," he growled as he climbed into his truck, slamming the door hard enough to loosen dirt and dust from the undercarriage.

Cart felt the ridged energy draining from his muscles as Digger started the engine and began to drive slowly away.

Then Digger stopped and rolled his window down. "You sure got a good lookin' girl," he said, and leered. "Just like her mom, ain't she? I bet she'd like a real man, too, just like her mom!"

145

Laughing, his middle finger jutting skyward, he stepped on the gas, spinning the rear wheels and throwing dirt and gravel in a cloud that enveloped Cart.

Choking, Cart walked into the street and watched the truck drive down the street, leaves swirling in its wake.

Cart thought about chasing him down with the Porsche, pulling him from his truck, and beating the daylights out of him, but he didn't need an assault charge today. He shook the dust from his clothes and entered the house to find Sarah.

She was sitting on the floor in her soon-to-be new bedroom, hugging her knees to her chest and looking frightened. She looked warily at him as he entered the room, then looked down at the floor. Cart sat next to her.

"I'm sorry I upset you, sweetheart," he said, putting an arm over her shoulder and pulling her close. "I would never do anything to worry you purposefully, but there are things you need to know. You know he worked in the house for a while. He was doing and saying things to your mom that were inappropriate, things that were suggestive and disquieting. Even after several warnings, Scott had to fire him because he wouldn't stop doing those things. He was furious when Scott made him leave and was very threatening. When I saw him talking to you, I guess I lost it. I'm sorry you had to see that. You have to understand, some people think they can do anything they want, regardless of how improper or intimidating it can be to another person. He's a bully and a disgusting man. You guys are too precious to allow anything or anybody to hurt or jeopardize you in any way. Sometimes, the world is a bad place, and it's my responsibility to ensure nothing happens to you. I couldn't live with myself if I didn't take that responsibility seriously, especially if something happened to you because I didn't. Okay?" He squeezed her arm.

She looked up at him and nodded. "Yeah, I understand. I remembered him working here, and I always thought he was nice because he always smiled and said 'Hi.' I guess he's not, though, huh? I'll be more careful about it. Mom asked Emma's mom to drop me off here after school, and he got out of his truck and started talking to me."

"Now that you know how Digger is, let me or your mom know if you see him anywhere around here, okay?"

She nodded again and stood up, brushing sawdust off her clothes. "Okay. I guess I better see if Mom is here. Thanks, Dad. I love you."

"I love you, too, sweetie," he said as he watched her leave the room.

She is so innocent and naïve and trusting, he thought. It sometimes frightened him when he considered the kinds of people lying in wait for such a girl. He would do anything in his power to protect her. He dusted himself off and followed her out the door.

After all the long months of waiting and stressing, the house was nearing completion. Most of the contractors were finished, except for a few touch-ups here and there. The plumbers and electricians had installed the fixtures, and the painter cleaned his things up. The carpet would be delivered, and the installation would start toward the end of the week. The cleaners would come in to make sure the house was spotless and ready for them.

Everything looked beautiful, and Annie was delighted, her excitement and joy filling the family with a giddy sense of euphoria.

In a week or so, they'd be in their new home.

* * *

The moving company had arrived the week before Thanksgiving and, with remarkable efficiency, had all their possessions boxed and on the moving truck. They spent a few days in a hotel waiting for the movers to unload and move everything into the house. James's furniture order was delivered earlier in the week, which would harmonize with the design and ambiance of the house. The installation of window coverings and appliances went smoothly. The home was ready for the sounds of a family to bring it to life.

CHAPTER 6

Saturday morning arrived, clear and cold, with a hint of snow in the chill air. The sky was crystal clear, cleansed by a storm earlier in the week.

They had plenty of help: Annie's mom and sisters, Becky and Josie—and Cart's brother, Sam, and his wife Cindy who brought fresh donuts, bagels, and drinks. Cart was surprised by the amount of stuff they'd accumulated over the years. Considering the number of boxes to put away, it was going remarkably well, but it would probably take a few weeks to get it all into its proper place. While everyone was busy setting up beds and furniture, Annie hugged him for a private moment in their bedroom.

"It's all so beautiful." She sighed. "It's so overwhelming, but we're here, aren't we? We're finally here."

He hugged her tightly. "Yep, we sure are. And tonight we'll sleep in our new home. It'll take time to get used to all this space. Is it too much, all of this?"

Annie laughed. "It's a little late now, Cart. It'll be fine. The kids are happy, we're happy. What more could we ask?"

Sarah's voice on the intercom interrupted them, announcing the pizza had arrived, so with a final embrace, they headed down to the kitchen. Sarah had the pizza spread out on the granite-topped kitchen island, alongside bottles of water, soda, paper plates, napkins, and plastic utensils. Cart popped open a can of Diet Coke, munching on a meat-lover's slice. Annie sent Sarah to find Maddy while the adults chatted around the island. After a few minutes, Sarah returned to the kitchen.

"Mom, did you say what room she was in?' Sarah asked, concerned. "I looked in the playroom and her bedroom, but couldn't find her."

"Did you look downstairs?" Annie asked.

"Yeah, everywhere—even the room with the furnace and all the pipes, but I didn't see her."

Cart wiped his mouth with a napkin. "Go ahead and eat, Sarah. I'll go downstairs and see if I can find her. She's probably playing hide-and-seek with you, and you don't know it."

Everyone laughed.

"You want help?" Sam called after him.

"Nah, go ahead and relax," he answered. "I'll just be a few minutes."

He spent a few minutes looking through all the rooms, checking the three bathrooms, showers, and vanities. All the closets and the mechanical room where Sarah had just looked were clear.

"Maddy, Maddy, come out, come out, wherever you are!" he called as he looked in the exercise room and behind all the machines. Assured he'd looked everywhere a nearly four-year-old could hide and coming up empty, he returned to the kitchen.

CHAPTER 6

"Well, she's not downstairs, that's for sure," he said to everyone. "Did you look in any other room besides her bedroom and playroom?" he asked Sarah.

She shook her head.

"The little stinker." He sighed. "She must have found a great hiding place. I'll go look around up there."

"I'll look on this floor," said Sam, putting down his pizza. "She's got to be here somewhere." He headed for Cart's and Annie's workroom and offices.

Maddy's room was empty except for furniture and some boxes. All the other rooms were in the same state. No Maddy.

He met Sam coming from the family and guest rooms. Sam saw Cart's face and stopped in his tracks.

"She's not up there, either?" he asked, furrowing his brow. "I looked everywhere, Cart. She's not here."

Annie and the others came from the kitchen. Cart turned to her, panic flooding his body, his mind racing. She saw his face and grew ashen. Cart's stomach clenched, and it felt like his heart was creeping up his throat.

"Cart," she whispered, "where could she be?"

"Let's not panic yet," he said, putting his arm around her. "Let's spread out and look outside. She might be on the swing set or the tennis court."

"She doesn't have her coat on. . . ." Annie whispered, her voice breaking.

He felt her trembling.

"Sam, you look out back," Cart said, pulling on his coat. "I'll check the front yard and sides of the house. Annie, why don't you and your mom go to the Hobarts' to see if she's there?"

The Hobarts lived across the street and had a boy about Maddy's age. She'd played with him a few times while they were at the house during construction. Everyone grabbed coats and headed out through various doors.

The wind had picked up during the day, and icy tentacles crawled down Cart's neck. It was getting colder, and the thought of Maddy out somewhere without a coat filled him with dread. The street before their house was empty, but for the dead leaves slithering across lawns in the wind. Tree branches stirred, and bushes danced. No Maddy anywhere. . . .

Dear God, where is she? Where is she, please, God, where is she? he prayed silently.

About a year ago, the city had been shocked by a series of kidnappings, usually children walking to or from school. He'd empathized with the shocked and weeping parents, the terrible sorrow etched like death on their faces. He couldn't imagine anything worse for a parent to endure. Now, he had a hint of the terror they felt. It had only been a few minutes but felt like an eternity.

Sam ran from behind the house and shook his head. Cart passed Annie and her mom returning with the Hobarts in tow, bundled in coats, their faces pale and worried. He turned from them, shouting her name, *"Maddy! Maddy!"* but no little voice answered him, only the mocking cold wind. He bolted down the street, calling her name: *"Maddy! Maddy!"*

CHAPTER 6

And then he saw her.

He was sprinting past the Vincent home, the air like ice in his lungs, when he saw the Vincents' front door open. Luke Vincent stepped out holding Maddy's hand. Cart stopped cold and fell to his knees on the frozen pavement.

"Maddy...." he whispered.

He stood on shaking legs and stumbled across the leaf-covered lawn, staggered up the front steps, and tore his precious little girl from Vincent. He hugged his daughter tightly against him, feeling the warmth from her little body. Annie, along with her mother and the rest ran up behind him. Annie sobbed as she reached the porch.

"Maddy, oh, Maddy . . ." She knelt beside Cart and hugged her daughter fiercely, weeping openly.

"Mommy?" Maddy saw her parents' faces and stared at everyone in confusion.

Cart stood weakly, wiping tears on his coat sleeve, his body tingling as the adrenaline ebbed from his veins. The cold wind enveloped him in its embrace.

Luke Vincent stood stiffly, glaring down at the group on his front lawn, his eyes like shards of glass, cold and stony marbles of green. His face was unshaven, hair tousled from sleep. He watched the reunion of the girl and his parents with detached indifference.

"We couldn't find her," Cart said, offering his right hand to Vincent, who ignored the outstretched hand, squinting at Cart.

"She opened the door and came in the house while I was sleeping," he growled. "Keep your brat away from my yard and out of my house."

He spat onto the weedy ground, then returned to the dark domain of his house, slamming the door tightly against the stunned faces around his porch.

The wind rattled the last few leaves clinging tenaciously to the trees in his yard, and turning the tears on their cheeks to icicles.

* * *

They feared the worst, as any parent would.

You can never be sure these days, Cart thought as he watched Annie bathe their little girl in a warm, bubbly bath. Vincent's attitude had been extremely disquieting, and they had been taking precautions.

Maddy was her usual happy self, chattering about Thanksgiving and whatever else popped into her head. She seemed fine.

But, still . . .

Cart toweled Maddy off while Annie drained the tub and wiped it down. Maddy squirmed out of his arms and fled to her bedroom. He heard a box tip over and toys scatter across the carpet. Following her, he found a box labeled MADDY'S CLOTHES and he soon had her dressed. Annie stood next to Cart, watching her play.

"Do you think we should take her to a hospital?" she whispered. "Get her checked out?"

"I don't know." Cart thought for a minute. "I don't think we want her to be too focused on this. We didn't see anything to suggest he'd mistreated her in any way, and she seems fine. Maybe it was just as Vincent said. Do you think it would be too much for her, upset her? A hospital might be too much for her, but a doctor's visit would be fine. What do you think?"

CHAPTER 6

"It just worries me," said Annie, "but you're right. We should just let it be tonight. He gives me the creeps, the way he acts. He looked so cold standing there like he had no feelings. How does someone as sweet as Kate stay with him?"

"It's hard to say. Some women don't have the strength to leave an abusive relationship because the abuser controls them. They fear what would happen if they left them or called the police. It is sad, though."

"Still, I think I'll call Dr. Jackson in the morning to see what he thinks, just to be safe. He's good at responding on a weekend if something's wrong."

Despite it being a Saturday, the alarm system tech showed up at about 3 p.m. to explain the system to them.

Every door and window, including the six-car garage, had its station; if any station was disturbed, a piercing alarm would sound within one minute, unless someone entered the code into a keypad near each door. If the warning was not disabled, the system would contact the police, who would investigate. They felt much safer knowing it operated correctly and they had control over it.

Sarah had figured out the sound system that linked every room in the home to a central location in the kitchen. With the innate abilities her generation seemed to have been born with, she soon had her favorite satellite station echoing through the house. Cart and Annie laughed, watching Sarah and Maddy happily dance into the kitchen, holding hands and twirling. Cart and Annie soon joined them, and the family laughed together as the darkness of the evening crept over the house.

That night, as Annie slept quietly in their new bedroom, Cart slipped carefully into Maddy's room and silently watched his little girl sleep, her cherubic face lit softly by a Winnie-the-Pooh nightlight beside her bed. Her long eyelashes fluttered, and she smiled faintly, her lips curving upward as she exhaled a puff of breath, sleeping innocently.

She was so perfect and so precious. He reflected momentarily on what could have happened but quickly pushed that away, grateful that she was here and okay.

"Thank you, God," he whispered, lightly kissing his daughter's soft cheek. She rubbed her cheek with her little fist, her nose wrinkling. He returned to his room and crawled into bed, careful not to disturb Annie. Soon, he, too, was sleeping, content in the warmth of their house.

CHAPTER 7

There were some bugs to work out, as with all new houses, but nothing serious. It did mean workers were in the house during the day, but Scott's foreman, Ben, was also present, so that made Annie feel better.

Luckily, the security system had only malfunctioned a few times during the day, or Luke Vincent would have been up in arms. The system tech checked it with the computer diagnostics and fine-tuned it, assuring them it was debugged and functioning correctly. Some of the security cameras weren't working.

Sarah complained about hearing music at night, but a thorough check revealed no malfunction. Perhaps it had been a car passing at night, and a stereo turned too loud, disturbing her sleep.

Things were going relatively well: Sarah was happy at school, and the system they'd come up with to drop her off and pick her up every day ran smoothly, except when Sarah misjudged her time getting ready, and they ran a bit late. Maddy was happy as long as she was fed and warm, had her toys to play with, and had the undivided attention of whoever was around her.

Life was good.

They had a lovely Thanksgiving celebration, part housewarming and part giving thanks. The dinner was perfect. Two of Cart's law firm partners and the Hobarts across the street were there with their four children. They'd left a message inviting the Vincents but had received no response. Annie's family came, too, as did Sam and Cindy, and they laid a feast on the table that would have fed the Pilgrims and their Indigenous friends for at least a month. All in all, the day was a delight.

During the lull between dinner and dessert, Cart's partner, Russell Griffith, asked him to show him his office again. "I'll meet you back there," Griffith said, smiling. "I have something for you in my car, so I'll go get it."

Cart went to his office and waited, sitting at his desk. A few minutes later, Russ walked in, holding a large package nearly five feet long and eighteen inches wide, wrapped in heavy paper. He laid it gently on the desk, smiling at Cart's wondering gaze.

"Well, go ahead. Open it." Russ chuckled.

Cart shook his head and laughed as he tore at the paper, feeling like a little kid at Christmas. "What have we got here?" he said as he glimpsed the gift. He hefted it carefully.

It was a matched set of Scottish claymores used by the Scots from about 1350 AD. Cart had studied Scottish history in school because of his ancestry and loved the design of the swords. A crescent-shaped nut topped the pommel of the longsword, and the distinctive down-sloping cross guard ended in a quatrefoil design, like four connecting circles. There were also two Scottish dirks, the short backup knives Scots strapped to their lower legs for use in close quarters. The aged patina of

CHAPTER 7

the blades was wonderful and gleamed dully in the light from the desk lamp. The edges were sharp, and the only restoration done to them.

Russ grinned broadly, watching the wonder in Cart's eyes. "I thought they'd look good above your fireplace."

Cart carefully laid the sword back on the desk, gripping Russ's hand tightly. "Thanks, Russ. I love them, and they'll look great in there."

Russ broke free and clapped him on the back. "Hey, don't get all mushy with me. I just wanted to get them for you. It's no big deal."

"No big deal, huh?" Cart laughed. "These must have cost a fortune."

"So, I'll take it out of your bonus. What's to worry about?"

Laughing, they went back to the kitchen for pie and whipped cream.

CHAPTER 8

Soon, Annie began preparing the house for Christmas, emptying boxes as she found the perfect spot for each decoration. Annie had hired the landscaping crew to string the great spruces in their yard with thousands of sparkling lights and LED lights permanently hung along the roof line and around windows. The house glowed at night, and driving up each evening delighted Cart. He loved this season, especially when Maddy had met him at the door one night wearing the oversized stockings Annie had hung from the fireplace mantle in the family room when he'd left for work that morning.

"Santa's coming to our house, Daddy!" she exclaimed as she threw her arms around him. Laughing, he scooped her up and hugged her.

"Have you been good today?" he asked her. "Because you know Santa's watching!"

"Yes, I've been really good! I cleaned my room and helped Mommy do the dishes, and I only dropped one!" She kissed him on the cheek and struggled to get down. She ran off with the huge stockings flapping.

Oh, to be a child at Christmas!

The Vincent house remained dark and morose, as though Luke could forestall the spreading of joy in the world by his stubborn actions. They saw Kate Vincent rarely, and then only as she carried groceries into the house. A couple of times when Luke wasn't home, Annie had crossed the boundary between the two homes to deliver a plate of homemade cookies, but the unopened door remained silently unyielding.

The schools were closed for a few weeks during the holiday, and Cart's office was closed between Christmas and New Year, so they decided to go to Hawaii for the week, leaving on the 22nd and returning on January 2nd. It would be a first for the family, and they looked forward to the departure.

Sarah was concerned about finding just the right swimsuit, so Annie had taken her to several stores before finding one she liked. Maddy was just Maddy and couldn't care less about anything except that Santa wouldn't be able to find them if they weren't home. Reassured that Santa would find them anywhere they went, she remained buoyant, living life to the fullest in her tiny world.

* * *

They had just entered the villa after a day of sightseeing when Cart noticed the message light on the room phone blinking. Dialing into the system, he gasped when he heard the message. Annie saw the shock on his face.

"What's the matter?" she asked him after he laid the phone in its cradle. His face had drained of color. He looked to see if the kids were listening, but they were engaged in watching a Disney Channel

CHAPTER 8

show with a bunch of kids running around overacting and frenetically shouting. He nodded toward their bedroom, and they both went in and closed the door.

"Someone broke into the house during the night," he whispered. "They did some serious damage. The alarm didn't go off! I thought the tech had fixed it. Sam went to the house this morning to check on things and saw it. The security cameras showed three guys in ski masks."

Cart told her they'd kicked the basement door open to get in, broken some pipes in the basement, and left faucets running, flooding the basement. They'd kicked in the large-screen TV in the family room and trashed the kitchen. The most disturbing thing was they'd gone into Sarah's room and turned out all the drawers, tipped over her dresser, pulled the comforter and sheets off her bed, and slashed the mattress several times with a knife. Her room was a disaster, holes kicked in the walls and her TV broken. Sam saw no other damage to the house.

"What are we going to do?" she asked quietly. "Do we need to go home?"

Cart shook his head. "Sam called Scott right after he called the police. They were still canvasing the neighborhood, going door-to-door to see if anyone had seen or heard anything. Someone must have gotten cut smashing things in the kitchen, so blood was on the countertop and floor. At least there's DNA to match, if they can. But that was this morning. Scott and his crew cleaned up what they could, draining the basement and hauling out wet and damaged furniture. They'll have to let it dry out before fixing things. The police have been processing everything in the house. It's a cime scene now."

A silent dread filled the room as they both wondered what to do. How could this have happened? Why didn't the expensive alarm system go off?

Cart told her that Sam and Cindy had pulled Sarah's mattress down to the garage and would purchase a new one before they got home.

Cart's lips were thin with anger. "Going home won't do any good, since we only have a few days left. Scott and Sam have it under control, so we might as well stay here."

"I don't want to worry Sarah, either," Annie said. "Maybe we could extend our vacation a few more days to get her room cleaned up."

"What kind of animal would do this?" Cart exclaimed, his mind throbbing with rage and disbelief.

He should be there. Their home was a refuge from the world, and it had been invaded and defiled by some psycho. The alarm company failed to protect their home, and there'd be hell to pay when they returned. Insurance would cover everything, but nothing would make the knowledge that criminals had violated their sanctuary disappear. His attorney's blood screamed for justice, and his father's protective instinct wanted immediate reprisals.

Sam promised to keep him updated on repairs, and Scott had taken full responsibility since his sub-contractor had installed the system.

At 8:30 a.m. the following morning, Sam called. Cart could tell something was wrong with him when he heard his voice. After a few minutes of chatting about their vacation, Cart got him to tell him what was wrong.

CHAPTER 8

Sam confessed that he'd forgotten to turn the alarm system on when he'd left the house the afternoon of the break-in. He was late for a party, and it had slipped his mind. He took full responsibility, which was fine, but the invasion was a massive disaster for them. Cart owned several rental properties and hired Sam to manage them. He trusted Sam to be responsible; it had never been a problem. But this felt like his brother had betrayed him. If Sam had set the alarm, kicking the door in would have triggered the piercing siren, and the creeps would more than likely have been scared away. The only damage would have been to the door.

Cart had learned over the years that dwelling on the past was a useless exercise that wasted time and energy. He'd worry about Sam's feelings when he got home.

Scott quickly repaired the damage to Sarah's room, fixing holes in the wall and repainting and replacing everything where it should be, according to Cindy's memory. They'd explained to Sarah that a pipe had burst and flooded the basement and they wanted everything dry before they got home. They made no mention of the damage in her bedroom.

Cart's partners told him they'd cover things at work, and Annie had Sarah's school email homework so she wouldn't get behind. After complaining about schoolwork on vacation, she settled down and did most of what they'd sent. Nobody was too upset about extending their stay for another week in paradise, falling asleep to the sound of waves on the beach while palm fronds rustled overhead.

Cart was anxious, though, to get home and get their affairs in order. He relaxed his shoulders and uncurled his toes while staring at the ceiling. Eventually, he slept. Some nights he laid awake for hours, speculating on the identity of the person or persons who'd invaded their home.

They landed at Salt Lake City International Airport at 10:30 p.m. on a stormy, snowy Saturday night. Cart drove home carefully, grateful for the four-wheel drive. Maddy was sleeping when they pulled into the garage. Cart carried her to her room, putting her to bed fully clothed, while Annie turned off the alarm. They didn't want a fully awake three-and-a-half-year-old running around the house. Sarah was also tired and went to her room, only carrying what she needed for the night.

CHAPTER 9

After the kids were asleep, Annie and Cart went downstairs to see the damage to the basement, sad and disheartened to see their home in such a state. The hum of fans and dehumidifiers was like a colony of unseen bees.

The flood extended about six inches up the walls, though the height varied somewhat. Scott had ordered replacement baseboards, casings, and doors. The mill had promised to get them there as soon as possible. After everything had dried and the threat of black mold ended, the sheet rockers would replace the bottom four feet of drywall the flood had ruined. All the carpets and padding were at the landfill; James had reordered it, but it would take a month to arrive. The exercise equipment company disassembled and stored the machines in the garage. The insurance underwriter had estimated the repair cost to be nearly $500,000. Scott was footing the bill until the insurance kicked in. Trudging slowly up the stairs, silent in their despondency, they went to bed after setting the alarm.

* * *

Cart woke slowly, like crawling out of cold honey. He'd slept fitfully after a few restless hours, wired from flying and the visual shock of the basement.

A hand gently shook his arm, and Sarah whispered, "Dad?" in his ear.

He rose on one arm, rubbing his eyes. The clock read 2:43 a.m.

"What's wrong? What's the matter?" He was careful not to wake Annie, but she was sleeping soundly.

"It's the music again," Sarah whispered, "only it's louder. I checked to see if the speaker was off, and I think it was, but I could still hear it. It's keeping me awake. Can you come to look at it?" She sounded exhausted.

He pulled his robe on and followed her down the hall to her bedroom. Her lights were on, so he examined the sound system touch pad. It was lifeless and unlit. No sound came from the speakers.

"It's off, Sarah," he said softly, watching the puzzled look on her face. "Can you still hear it?"

She shook her head. "I don't hear anything now." She became a little defensive when she saw the doubtful expression on his face. "I heard the music, Dad. It was keeping me awake."

"Are you sure you weren't sleeping? Sometimes I wake up from a dream and can't tell if I'm awake or still dreaming. Do you think that might be it?"

"No, Dad, I was awake." She scowled. "I was wide awake because the music was keeping me awake. Didn't you hear what I said?"

"Now, hold on there," Cart said evenly, "you don't have to be sarcastic with me. I'm just trying to figure this out. Did you check the

CHAPTER 9

controls in the kitchen to see if they're turned on? Or maybe Maddy's is on, and you heard that?"

"It was coming from my speakers, I think. But I didn't check those things. I'm so tired."

He put his arm around her shoulder and hugged her. "Why don't you hop in bed with your mom while I check this out? I'm awake now, anyway."

She yawned widely. "Yeah, okay. I'm sorry, Dad. I didn't want to wake you, but I didn't know what to do. Where will you sleep?"

"I'll just sleep in your bed, if that's alright. Maybe I can figure it out if it happens again. Now get in bed. You look like you're going to fall over."

She hugged him briefly, then wandered down the hall to her parents' room.

Cart spent a few minutes checking the system, ending up in the kitchen. The central control was off, so there was no way music was coming from the system. He got a drink of water and decided to sleep on the couch in his office, pulling the blanket from the closet up around his head. His eyelids grew heavy, and he fell asleep.

CHAPTER 10

At 11:30 on Monday morning, Cart's secretary buzzed him as he worked through a stack of client files.

"There's a Detective Martina Gregson from the SLPD here for you. Do you want to talk to her?"

"Yeah, I do," Cart said. "I've been waiting for her. I'll be right out."

Detective Martina Gregson was in her mid-thirties, five foot ten or so, and of medium build. She had short hair that was dyed blonde, wore a conservative blue suit, and had a firm handshake. Cart offered her something to drink, and she asked for water. They chatted for a few minutes.

"Anyway," the detective said, answering Cart's comment about her Midwest accent. "I'm originally from Indiana. I moved here a few months back and joined the force. I love the outdoors and couldn't think of a better place to live. I came here once when I was a kid with my parents, and I've never forgotten how beautiful it is. So, when there was an opening, I applied. I haven't looked back."

"Do you have anything to report?" he asked her.

"We haven't had any real breakthrough yet, but we got a lot of fingerprints and DNA from the blood in the kitchen. We'll be checking the prints against everyone who worked at your house. There are no apparent matches yet, but running through the database can take some time.

"We also got good casts from shoe prints in the snow outside your basement door."

"Can you get casts in the snow?" Cart asked, sipping Diet Coke. "I would think it would melt?"

"Actually, we can," said the detective. "We use a commercial dental stone mixture and spray it with wax to hold it together. When the cast sets up, we can pull it and preserve it. Works great."

"Do you know how they got in the backyard?" Cart asked.

"It looks like they jumped the fence from the vacant house west of yours. We followed their tracks to 23rd East, but they stopped there, so someone must have picked them up."

"Have you noticed anything missing? Maybe something your brother or the initial investigation might have overlooked last week?" she asked after drinking some water. "You might want to take an inventory and let me know if anything's gone."

"We're trying to keep what happened from our oldest daughter," Cart said, "especially about her room. She's had a pretty rough time lately, so as far as she's concerned, we had a leak downstairs. My brother and our contractor fixed everything in her room before we returned from our vacation. We want to keep it that way."

"Of course," said Gregson.. "We might have to speak to her to see if she can think of anyone that did this. Kids can do stupid things sometimes."

CHAPTER 10

Cart looked at his watch. "I'm sorry, I'm due in court in about an hour. I've got to get ready."

"Can you think of anyone who might have done this?" Gregson asked as she stood up. "I don't think this was a random break-in; I think it was premeditated. They wanted to do as much damage as possible, very quickly. Anyone off hand you can think of?"

"Oh, yeah," Cart laughed humorlessly, "I can think of a few right off—my neighbor to the east of us, Luke Vincent. He's had a grudge against us and our house since we started building it and has shown a lot of animosity toward us. We've had some confrontations over the past couple of months. Then there's the carpenter who worked for our contractor, a guy named Digger. I don't know his last name, or even his real name but I can get it for you. He made some threats when he was thrown off the job a few months back. I found him talking to Sarah before we moved in."

He walked Gregson to the elevator.

"We checked with your neighbors," she said, "but Vincent wouldn't answer his door. It looks like I need to revisit him. Thanks for meeting with me, Mr. Benson. If I hear of anything else, I'll give you a call. In the meantime, check your house to see if everything is where it should be." The bell dinged, and the door slid open. "I'd also like to see Sarah's room, if possible."

* * *

"I'm glad you reminded me," Annie said when he called her after returning to his office. "Sarah mentioned this morning that she couldn't find her last yearbook or a picture of her and Emma we took at the beach in San Diego last year. She thought she had put the picture on her dresser, but maybe she had forgotten. Should I have her check her room when she gets home later?"

"Yeah, you probably should. Just tell her the moving company found a box without a name. When I get home, we can look more thoroughly. The problem is there are still so many full boxes, and we'd have to empty all of them to be sure. The creeps could have taken boxes, and we'd never know."

"Look, I need to go, but see what you can find out. I've got a huge backlog of cases to go through, but I'll try to slip away early if I can."

He felt uneasy after he hung up. Why would someone take Sarah's yearbook and a picture? And why slash her mattress so savagely? He couldn't imagine his daughter doing anything to provoke such a violent reaction. He drank from his water bottle and tried to concentrate on work.

At home, Sarah couldn't find anything else missing from her room. She'd looked through all the SARAH boxes under her bed and in her closet. She mentioned her drawers seemed organized differently, but Cart and Annie knew that was probably Sam's wife, Cindy, trying to return the scattered clothes the way she thought Sarah might have done it. However, they didn't say anything to her about it.

Annie and Cart spent the evening checking their belongings, but everything looked okay.

* * *

He felt someone shaking his arm, and he lurched up, startled. Sarah was kneeling by the side of his bed.

CHAPTER 10

"Dad, the music is back. . . ." Her eyes looked like dark pits, and her blonde hair hung loosely over her face.

"Oh, for hell's sake," he said. "Are you sure?" He was irritated at being woken up because it was always hard for him to fall back to sleep. "Okay," he sighed, pulling his robe on. "Let's go look."

I'm getting tired of this, he thought.

"I'm sorry, Dad," she mumbled, following on his heels.

"Sarah, the system's off." The sound system touch pad was dark, like he knew it would be. He made no effort to mask his annoyance. "I've had Scott's sound people check it over. It's not broken, and it's not turned on. I can see that. I can't hear anything, can you?" His voice had a sarcastic edge that he rarely used, especially with his children.

She listened for a moment, then shook her head. "I don't hear it, Dad. But I heard it. I know I did."

"Dammit, Sarah," he whispered harshly. "I don't know what's happening with this whole sound system thing. There's nothing wrong with the system; no sound is coming from it. I don't want to hear any more of this. I'm tired of you waking me up in the middle of the night with this nonsense. Now get back into bed and go to sleep."

Her face had grown ashen at the harshness of his voice, and her lower lip was trembling. "I heard it, Dad," she whispered, looking at the floor.

"That's enough, Sarah," he shot back at her. "Get back into bed, now."

She looked up at him, glowering. "Why don't you believe me!?" she shouted, "I heard it, Dad! I'm not stupid, and I'm not hearing things!"

He grabbed her by the shoulders and lightly shook her. "Be quiet!" he hissed. "You'll wake up Maddy and your mom!"

She jerked away from him. "I don't care! You act like I'm stupid or something! I hate this house! I hate you!" Her face had contorted with anger, an ugly parody of her sweetness and beauty. He'd never seen that face before, and it stunned him. Before he could say anything, she flew into her bedroom and slammed the door in his face. He heard the lock click.

He heard Maddy wailing and saw Annie glaring at him from his youngest daughter's door, her face etched in anger, her eyes hard and glittering like blue diamonds reflecting Maddy's nightstand light. He felt shame flood his body.

"Well, that went over nicely. . . ." she said. With a final look of disgust, she turned back into Maddy's room and quietly shut the door.

He stood for a while, leaning against the wall, his heart empty, feeling like the fool he was. He tapped gently on Sarah's door.

"Go away!" she screamed. "I hate you!"

He didn't force the issue. He'd done enough damage for one night.

CHAPTER 11

He had his headphones turned up way too loud.

It was five in the morning, and after a fitful night, he'd abandoned all hope of sleep and went to the nearest twenty-four-hour gym, although he hated the places. His exercise room was a disaster from the flood, and this was the only place to go. It felt good to work out hard, straining against the weight, working until his arms and legs trembled with fatigue. His eyes were closed while he rested on the bench press machine. Maybe the sweat that ran off his body could wash away some of the shame and restlessness he had felt since the episode a few hours ago.

Someone shook him.

"Hey, man." A lean, annoyed face scowled at him. "Your phone's been ringing like crazy. Guess you couldn't hear it, huh?" The man returned to the treadmill, shaking his head.

It was Annie, and her voice was trembling. "Cart, where did she go?"

His blood turned to ice.

"What do you mean?" he whispered.

"She's gone, Cart," Annie said softly. "I went to wake her for breakfast, and her door was locked. She wasn't in her room. I've looked everywhere. Sarah's not here...."

Annie sat alone in the darkened kitchen when Cart entered from the garage, dropping his coat on a chair. Her hair was mussed, and her eyes were red. Cart drew her into his arms and held her while she cried into his shoulder, shaking with grief.

"I'm sure she's fine," he whispered, instinctively rocking her back and forth like he did with the kids when they were small. "She probably went for a walk, or something. Let's not get too excited until we find out what's happening. I'll go out and look for her."

She looked up at him, eyes tormented by the fear that consumed her. "I called the police," she said, her voice husky. "They're sending someone over. That was Mom on the phone just now. She's coming over, too." She began crying again. "Her coat's still in her closet, Cart."

He kissed the top of her head. "I'm going to drive through the neighborhood to see if I can find her. Is Maddy still sleeping?" She nodded, wiping her eyes with a wet tissue. "Will you be okay if I go? Do you want me to wait until your mom gets here?"

"No. You see if you can find Sarah anywhere. I'll feel better knowing you're out and looking for her."

He hugged her and headed for the garage, grabbing his coat off the chair.

God, he thought, *please don't let anything happen to our little girl.*

The streets were empty except for the hardy few who enjoyed walking or running in sub-freezing temperatures. Driving the Porsche up the road through their neighborhood, he felt panic rising and went as fast as he dared, not giving up hope that he'd turn a corner and find her walking, wrapped in her thoughts on the cold morning. Around the block and up and down, every street, tree, and house became a blur in his thoughts.

There was no sign of Sarah.

Desperate, he drove back to their house, his mind racing and his heart breaking, trying to think of any of the reasons for her disappearance except the one reason he couldn't—wouldn't—think of, the one that clung to his mind like a rotten stench. He couldn't shake that fear off, though, and as he pulled into their driveway, it overwhelmed him and he began sobbing; his heart and body racked with terrible lament. He pounded on the steering wheel and rubbed his fists in his eyes, his stomach clenching in despair.

I have to be strong, dear God; help me be strong for Annie.

Then he broke down again, moaning, his heart like lead in his chest, his lungs heaving with anguish, his face drenched with tears and mucus. Slowly, the sobs subsided. He dried his face on his sleeve, took a couple of napkins from the glove box, and blew his nose. He opened the car door and climbed out as a police car pulled behind him, lights flashing. Two officers got out.

"Sir!" said the shorter officer. "Step away from the car and put your hands on your head."

He stared at the men, confused. They both had their hands on the butts of their pistols, still holstered at their sides. Cart stood dumbly as they warily approached.

"Put your hands on your head!" the other officer said firmly.

"But . . ." Cart said, but they were at his side, roughly spinning him around and shoving his face onto the top of his car. One kicked his legs apart while the other patted him down.

"What are you doing here?" the second officer asked brusquely.

Cart's mind returned with a jolt of consciousness and recognition. "What the hell are you doing?" he asked them angrily.

"What are you doing here?" the officer asked again, jerking Cart around to face him. The other cop searched his car, rifled through the glove box and the console, pulled things out carelessly, and looked under the seats.

"I live here," Cart said numbly. "Look, I've got ID right here," he said, reaching for the inside of his jacket to get his wallet, and then he was suddenly face down on the hard, frozen pavers of the driveway, his nostrils filled with the scent of stone and sand, and his arms pulled behind him, a knee on his neck. The freezing grit rubbed his face. A hand pulled his wallet free. There was silence for a few moments; all he heard was someone breathing inches from his ear. Then the officers pulled him from the ground. He leaned back shakily against his car.

The shorter cop handed him back his wallet, and both of them began brushing leaves and frozen sand off him.

"We're sorry, Mr. Benson," the officer said. "We had a report of a possible child abduction at this address and a report of a yellow sports car speeding through the neighborhood. I'm sorry for the mix-up. I'm Officer Walters; this is Officer Ramirez. Are you okay?"

They both seemed genuinely apologetic.

CHAPTER 11

"No, that's okay. I'm fine...." His face itched where the grit had scratched it. He weakly wiped at it with a shaking hand. "I understand. Please, come inside."

He led the way up the cobbled driveway, through the garage, and into the kitchen. Annie was pacing, arms wrapped around herself. She stopped when she saw them.

"Did you find her?" she whispered.

Cart drew her into his arms. "No. I looked all through the neighborhood, honey. I didn't see her."

Her body trembled with anguish. Cart held her tightly, his arms sheltering her, trying to be the strength she needed. A policeman cleared his throat.

"Sir?" Officer Walters said quietly.

Cart let go of Annie and turned to the two men.

"I'm sorry to interrupt you, but the detectives are coming to do the Amber Alert evaluation. They're almost here."

"Yes, of course," Cart said. "I don't know what else could have happened. She wouldn't just leave...."

The sudden realization of what he was saying struck him, and he leaned against the island countertop. The thought of his precious daughter out there somewhere cold and afraid filled his mind, and he couldn't hold back the tears, although he struggled to maintain his composure. Dread and fear washed over him, obliterating his desire to be strong for Annie. He remembered his harsh words from the previous night and wept harder.

Annie pulled him to her, and he sobbed uncontrollably. She hushed him as though he was a child, soothing him with whispered words of Sarah's love for him, of the love of his family, drawing on the instinctive reservoirs of strength within her. He drew upon that strength, hugging her fiercely to him, grateful for the relationship they shared. Her tenderness was like a salve, and he eventually calmed, breathing deeply of her.

The kitchen was quiet now as they held each other, their minds filled with prayers and fear. Officer Ramirez stood silently sentinel by the garage door, quietly respectful.

CHAPTER 12

She woke in darkness, her mind muddy from sleep, sweat plastering her hair against her forehead, her mouth like cotton, and she was so thirsty and tired, more tired than she'd ever felt before. She struggled to raise her head from her pillow and felt a gentle hand on the back of her neck, easing her up gently. Something hard touched her lips, and something wet poured into her mouth. She drank greedily, then lay back on her scratchy pillow. Her bed felt lumpy and uncomfortable. She was hot and itchy; it was too hot. She struggled against the blankets but was too weak to throw them off. The blanket was coarse and scratchy against her cheek. Someone laid a damp cloth on her forehead, and a soothing voice spoke softly, but she couldn't understand the words. She tried to open her eyes, but her eyelids felt like they each weighed a hundred pounds.

"Mom . . ." she whispered.

The hand gently caressed her cheek.

"Ja, ben ik uw moeder."

The words sounded like nonsense to her foggy mind, but she felt soothed by them and the cool cloth, so she let the quiet darkness draw her back down.

The song swelled again, filling her mind like a veil of shadow. She opened her mind to the music, letting it lure her fatigued and muddled thoughts into the engulfing darkness, and she slept.

CHAPTER 13

Cart sat alone in the darkness.

The detectives left a few hours ago, promising to do everything they could to find Sarah. Annie's mom had taken Maddy home with her, and Annie was upstairs trying to get some rest after taking a couple of antihistamines. He might try that later. Right now, he needed the silence and darkness to think.

A solitary policeman sat in his car behind the gates, facing the roadway, a lone guardian against trespassers. Cars and vans crowded the street, and reporters stood by the fence, hoping for information. Satellite dishes aimed skyward, poised, and ready to spread updates parsed from the evening.

Sam had held a hastily called press conference earlier, issuing a plea for privacy on behalf of the family and expressing gratitude for the prayers of the many people offering support. Law enforcement had made no official plan for a search but had posted photos of Sarah on their website and social media accounts. News outlets would also be posting pictures and pleas for her return.

His heart was empty, his thoughts filled with Sarah, his blood like ice in his veins as he contemplated the worst outcome.

He badly wanted the phone to ring, to answer it, and to hear his daughter's voice asking him to pick her up, but it remained mute and uncaring, mocking him in his torment.

His words of the previous night haunted him, clinging to his thoughts, whispering vile recriminations to his soul. If only he could take those words back.

If only...

But that wish was futile. As an attorney, he knew the power of words. Some words could cut like a knife or dog a person's heels for the rest of their life. Words were the tool of his trade and the coin by which he'd bought this good life they lived. He'd cast those words thoughtlessly, heedless of wounding Sarah's sweet and gentle heart. Now he feared he'd never have the chance to ask her forgiveness.

He knew he could never forgive himself.

So he sat, his worst accuser, while reporters' cars rumbled in the street, waiting like vultures for more damnable words.

* * *

Annie slowly regained awareness, rising from the stupor of drug-enhanced sleep.

She laid for a while, watching the gas fireplace flames flicker in her room's darkness. The clock on the nightstand read 11:35 p.m., but it felt like days had passed.

The memory of the night and day flooded her thoughts, and she closed her eyes tightly against the tears that filled them—too many tears, too much heartache.

CHAPTER 13

She had to pull herself together for the sake of Cart, Maddy, and herself; she couldn't give up hope—not yet. Sarah would be found safe. She was somewhere near, somewhere safe. She had to believe that, or she might as well give in to the terrible fear that beckoned her relentlessly.

Despite the blanket and comforter, she was still shivering. Shedding the blankets, she pulled her robe on and sat on the floor before the fireplace, letting the warmth wash over her. She thought of Sarah—their first little angel, her tiny fingers grasping her thumb, the contented sounds as she nursed. Sarah was gone, and she didn't know how to find her. She sat like that for a long time; she didn't know how long. It could have been hours, minutes, or days. She didn't know, and she didn't care.

She just wanted to sit.

It was getting hot, so she shrugged the robe off and leaned against the side of the bed, watching the flames flicker in the fireplace. The tiles surrounding the fireplace drew her attention: figures of people, windmills, and animals. She considered the care and concern she'd put into selecting things for their house. So many hours discussing, looking at samples, and the weekly meetings—and for what?

It all meant nothing without Sarah. She regretted the hours without her. She touched the blank piece of tile that faced her, the missing piece. She suddenly felt cold and lonely, so she crawled back into the bed, pulling the covers over her head, seeking solace in the cocoon of warmth but finding only emptiness.

* * *

A new detective came with Martina Gregson the next day. Will Collins was Black and balding, in his fifties, and built like a linebacker with many years of playing on the field; his shoulders were broad and thick with muscle. His gray suit was a bit rumpled, and his tie was crooked. He was staring at Cart with narrowed eyes.

"I'm sorry," Cart said, "my mind was wandering. What was it you said?"

They sat across from him at the kitchen table. He tried holding Annie's icy hand, trying to rub warmth into it, but she pulled it away and stared at the table.

"I know this is difficult," Collins said, "but we need to ask these questions."

Cart's mind refocused, adjusting like a microscope. Collins glanced at Gregson, who sat sipping from a cup of gas station coffee.

"I was *saying*," Collins said, "we spoke with some of Sarah's friends from the list you gave our colleagues yesterday. None of them have seen her and they don't know where she could've gone." He looked at the notebook in his large hands. "Emma Walsh was her best friend, right?"

Cart nodded. "They've been friends since first grade. They're very close, almost like sisters."

"According to Miss Walsh, you and Sarah haven't been getting along well for some time. She said the two of you argued frequently and that Sarah was unhappy about moving to this house." Collins looked around the kitchen while he spoke, glancing past Cart's shoulders down the hall to his office.

"Well, yes," Cart said, "she was unhappy about moving from the outset. I won't deny that. We did have some arguments about it. Some of them were very heated, but we worked through it. We compromised so she could finish out the year at her old school. I thought she was, if not happy, at least accepting it. As far as I know, she was doing much better.

"Why do you ask? Has this got something to do with her kidnapping?"

Collins laid his notebook on the table. "We don't have any conclusive evidence of that. We aren't sure it's a kidnapping, Mr. Benson. Of course, we're pursuing that possibility; don't get me wrong, we're not dismissing anything. We've got the Amber Alert going, and we're going to her school tomorrow to question the students to see if anyone knows anything. Right now, we have nothing.

"Is it possible she might have run away? Things like that happen constantly: troubles at home, abuse, boyfriends. It's not all that uncommon." Collins cleared his voice. "Was she involved with any boys? Is there a history of drug use?"

Cart felt his hackles rising.

"No, she wasn't into drugs. She's a good girl; she's never been a problem. And she didn't have a boyfriend." He looked at Annie for verification, but she just stared at the table. "Annie? Did Sarah have a boyfriend?"

She looked up at him, a vague look on her face, and shook her head.

Cart looked at her closely for a moment. "I don't like what you're insinuating, detective," he continued. "Someone took Sarah from our home. It would be best to concentrate on that instead of wasting time wondering about boyfriends or nonexistent drug use. If you'd genuinely talked to her friends, you'd know she'd never use drugs. She's a good girl." He was getting angry, fueled by desperation and impatience. Annie laid a hand on his arm, but he shrugged it off and looked at her. "Damn it, Annie, it's true, right?"

She nodded.

"If you're not going to look for her, I am." Cart stood up, pushing his chair back, glaring at the two detectives. "I'm not going to listen to this nonsense."

Gregson was staring at her notebook, but Collin stared at him, one eyebrow raised.

"Have you checked our neighbor, Vincent?" Cart asked, his voice rising. "What about the carpenter that worked at our house, Digger? Have you talked to him?"

Collins met his glare dispassionately. "Please sit down, Mr. Benson," he said calmly. "We're here to help you find your daughter. We check everything out, whether small, insignificant, or uncomfortable. You'd be surprised at what I've heard in my life. Please. Sit down."

Cart sat down, scowling at the two detectives.

"Now," Collins continued, "one more thing I need to ask, and from what I just witnessed, I have to wonder ... Miss Walsh said Sarah told her you had anger issues, that you could fly off the handle sometimes, and that you frightened her when you were like that."

Cart flexed his fists angrily, making his knuckles crack. Now, both detectives were watching him, their eyes like needles pricking him.

"Please, Mr. Benson," said Gregson. "This isn't helping."

Cart was furious. "Look around you. Do you see any indication that my daughter was mistreated in any way? Why don't you two tell me what you think is happening? She has everything she'd ever

CHAPTER 13

want here. I love my daughter! I would never do anything to frighten or abuse her. I don't understand why you're wasting time with these ridiculous questions."

He couldn't help it now. His anger was surging volcanically, with nowhere to go but up and out.

Collins smirked at him, shaking his head. And that was all it took. He wouldn't listen to this anymore or put up with disrespect and innuendos. He shot to his feet, knocking his chair over. He kicked back the chair, and it hit the wall forcefully, leaving a fist-sized hole. "You two get out of my house!" he hissed through clenched teeth. "Get out on the streets and look for my daughter! I don't want to see you if you have nothing substantial to report! Do you understand?"

The detectives were stunned and speechless; Collins's face was grim, his lips a gash. Gregson was wide-eyed, looking almost frightened.

Cart felt Annie's hand on his arm and jerked it away. She wasn't going to stop him this time. No soft voice or gentle touch was going to quench his righteous anger.

"Sit down, Cart," she said flatly.

"No, Annie, not this time!" he said. These two have no right . . ."

"SIT DOWN!" she shouted, her eyes blazing. Tears streaked down her face as she glared at him, her face a mask of anguish and fear for her daughter.

Cart was stunned. He dumbly picked up his chair and sat, staring wordlessly at her. He'd never heard her talk like this, or seen her look like this—her cheeks smudged with tears and anger, her eyes like two pebbles glaring at him from shadowed pits.

Her voice was suddenly quiet, but her eyes were fire, burning him with sudden vehemence. "I'm so tired of your blustering and bullying. My daughter is missing, and you think you can bring her back by throwing your weight around? Everything has to be perfect and orderly, with no deviation. Do you want to know something, Cart? Do you want to know how often she came to me crying because of something you'd said? Or something you'd done? Half the time, you didn't even know you'd hurt her because you're so self-absorbed. She *was* afraid of you sometimes, and the other night . . ." She choked up, and tears swam in her eyes.

"She's gone, Cart." Her voice was like acid, unsubtle and quick, piercing his heart like a knife, digging deep and flailing to do the most damage possible. "My baby's gone, damn you, and all you can do is act like a fool." Then she turned and went up the stairs like a vengeful ghost.

Collins and Gregson stood up and left the kitchen, quietly mumbling apologies, and then they were gone, leaving Cart alone at the table.

After what seemed a lifetime, he rose woodenly and shrugged into his coat. He didn't try to talk to Annie or climb the stairs to try and reason with her.

What was the point? She pretty much said what she had to say. He decided it would be best to leave her alone so she could work through her feelings without him *blustering* and *bullying* her.

He took the keys from the countertop, went into the garage, thumbed the button to open the overhead door, and climbed into the Hummer EV after unplugging it, starting it, and letting it warm

CHAPTER 13

for a few minutes before he backed out and turned toward the gate. He ignored the policeman sitting in his idling car as the gate slowly slid open. He pulled onto the street and headed west toward 23rd East. He saw several reporters pull out to follow him, so he gunned it, accelerating through the red light and turning south, ignoring angry horns and screeching tires. He quickly left everyone behind as the streets and alleys of the city beckoned him.

So many streets.

So little time . . .

CHAPTER 14

Annie laid silent for a long time, watching night seep into their home.

Her eyes were dry and aching, along with her head. She stared at the ceiling, wrapping herself in loneliness, her solitude complete and inescapable. The fireplace was cold and dim; the ceramic logs behind the glass that seemed lifelike when the gas flames danced on them were now just drab illusions, lifeless and gloomy.

Like her heart...

She'd heard him leave the house, and for a few hours, she'd lain motionless on the bed, the ceiling looming darkly over her, holding the weight of the night above her.

Let him go, she thought. *I need him to be gone for now.*

Rousing herself from her catatonic hollowness, she slowly sat up, running a hand through her stringy hair as she ascended from her private hell.

She desperately needed a shower, to feel the hot, purifying water cleanse her body and soul and purge her mind of the anger and dread that consumed it.

Steam filled the shower as she stood under the pulsating head, letting the vigor of the water sluice down her body. She stood for a long time, feeling the tautness of her mind drift into the steam, spiraling down the drain with the accumulated foulness of her spirit.

***

It was dark now, and still, he drove, doggedly calculating which street to go down, which direction to turn. Streetlights emerged from the darkness, and as he approached each cone of light, he searched the shadows cocooning each house, sentinels of life, unlike the empty shell he'd left behind. Leaving the pool of each streetlight, he eagerly sought out the next, following the piercing headlights where they led him, puncturing the night with LED brightness.

Hour after hour, street after street, he drove.

She had to be out here somewhere. He would drive until he found her and brought her home.

***

After dressing in crisp, clean clothes, Annie felt consumed with the desire to clean the bedroom, to scrub away the rage and despair that clung like cobwebs to the walls of her heart. Starting in the bathroom, she scoured the shower and floor with feverish intensity. Her hands ached to cleanse the soul-devouring mood that had settled on her soul.

***

He walked the crowded malls, stalking the walkways like a predator, looking into each store, especially the ones Sarah favored, showing her picture to patrons and salespeople alike until he'd thoroughly foraged

CHAPTER 14

each store. Then he'd feel the pull of the darkened streets, and with the night drawing around him like a cloak, he thrust the Hummer deeper into the city.

* * *

She vacuumed the carpet until it felt lush under her feet. Lastly, she began polishing the fireplace's glass front, perfecting it with unadulterated vitality until it shone back at her. She stared at the doppelganger in the glass. She looked away quickly from the reflection and began to wipe down the blue-and-white tiles encasing it, aware of the delicate nature of each piece.

* * *

He was on State Street at about 7200 South when his cell phone buzzed. He was surprised to see his home number on the screen.

He suddenly thought of Sarah sitting at the kitchen counter, wrapped in a warm blanket and slurping hot soup. Tears spilled from his eyes as relief eased his heart.

"Annie," he almost laughed as he thumbed his phone to life, "is she home?"

A cold and eerie hush answered his question, and his heart plummeted.

"Cart," Annie whispered, barely audible above the rumble of the car's tires, "come home."

Something in her tone made his stomach clench in apprehension. "What's wrong, Annie? What's the matter?"

Her voice sounded spectral when she answered, like a shadow of a glimpse of her real self.

"Just come home. Now..."

* * *

Annie was waiting at the top of the stairs.

The house was dark and silent. Backlit by the glow of their bedroom light, she looked ethereal, her hand resting on the top railing and staring into the gloomy stairwell. The hair on his arms tingled as he neared her, watching her shadowed, unreadable eyes. There was something in the way she stood, still like a pond in a windstorm that didn't ripple.

He touched her hand, but she didn't respond. "Annie," he whispered, "what is it?"

She was like a statue carved in extraordinary relief from marble, her eyes unfocused, motionless but for the rise and fall of her chest as she breathed.

He put his arms around her, but she was stiff and unyielding. He drew her closer, softly whispering her name until she finally looked at him. Then, slowly, she relaxed and melted into his embrace, putting her arms around him and hugging him with surprising strength.

Her hair smelled of shampoo but subtly acrid with an underlying musk he didn't recognize.

Was this the smell of fear?

"Annie, what's wrong?" he asked quietly. "You're scaring me, sweetie. Have you heard anything from Sarah?"

She flinched at the sound of her name, inhaling sharply.

Then she took his face in her hands and looked into his eyes, whispering in a voice so calm he had to strain to hear her. "I've found her."

CHAPTER 15

She led him to the bedroom, her hand like ice.

"Annie, please," he implored, "what do you mean?"

She put a finger to his lips, hushing him as they walked past the bed.

He watched her closely, afraid her sanity had fled in the nightmarish days since Sarah had disappeared. Confused, he allowed her to draw him onto the carpet beside their bed. She looked at the fire, her moist eyes reflecting the golden flames. He took a vagrant strand of hair from her forehead and tucked it behind her ear.

"What are you talking about, Annie?" he asked hesitantly. "What do you mean you found her? Where is she?"

She pointed at the fireplace. "Right there...." Her voice was soft, almost reverential.

He looked at the fireplace, not seeing anything he hadn't seen a hundred times before. "I don't understand," he said. "What are you trying to show me? She's not here, Annie." He was anxious about Annie now. She was looking at the fireplace, her brow smooth. He took her hand and held it tightly. "Sweetie, Sarah's not here."

She turned to him, eyes flaring passionately. "She's right there!" she said firmly, pointing at the fireplace.

Cart spoke gently and quietly, not wanting to upset her or push her over the edge of reason if she hadn't already fallen from it.

"Honey, I don't know what you mean. It's just you and me. How could she be here?"

She put her hand behind his head, pushing it toward the fireplace with considerable strength. Her nails dug into his neck, so he removed her hand and held it to his chest.

"Annie..." he began.

"*LOOK!*" she shouted at him. Then her voice dropped again to a whisper, almost a sigh, and tears filled her eyes, trickling down her cheeks. "Look..."

She pointed at the fireplace and the antique Delft tiles surrounding it. He traced her finger with his eyes.

And there it was.

He stared, trying to understand what he saw, but his mind couldn't comprehend it.

The blank piece of tile, set to replace the broken one, had somehow changed.

It was no longer blank.

The representation of clouds hung in the sky. A girl with long hair tied back by a ribbon walked with a cavorting black dog. Behind her stood a windmill with a lone cow alongside a fence.

The room grew suddenly cold, or maybe his heart was churning ice in his veins. A lump caught in his throat.

CHAPTER 15

"Sarah . . ." he breathed. He reached out a trembling hand and touched the tile. He felt a sharp trickle of energy from it, like touching his tongue to a nine-volt battery, and he jerked it

back. The world shrank abruptly, as though the universe focused on the tile.

The room was silent like a tomb, except for the drumming of his heart.

It thundered in his head as his thoughts reeled.

"No, Annie, no. It can't be. . . . Did the tile guy, Karl, put in the replacement? But when could he have done it?"

He felt desperate for a logical explanation, but he couldn't force himself to cross that line he was so afraid Annie had touched.

"No one's been here since Sarah left," she said raggedly. "It's my baby. I know it is."

"Maybe he came while we were in Hawaii. Maybe he did it before all this." His head ached, trying to process what he was seeing. "Maybe we just didn't notice he'd done it."

"No, Cart. It's Sarah. I know my baby when I see her."

His heart broke at the vulnerability and loss in her voice. He threw his arms around her and pulled her to him. Shudders coursed through her body.

"I don't understand this. I don't . . ." The intense loss they both felt fueled the anguish of their hearts as they clutched each other before the tile with a picture of a girl walking her dog in a long-ago Holland.

* * *

Annie was finally sleeping, her head nestled in Cart's lap. He tenderly stroked her hair, watching her face as she slept, for this brief time calm and peaceful. The dark circles under her eyes saddened him. He traced his finger down her cheek and touched her chin. Pulling carefully away from her, he placed a pillow under her head and covered her with the comforter.

What was he going to do?

As strange as it was, he wasn't sure it was Sarah in the tile, but the contagion of Annie's grief infected him, swallowing up his misgivings. He felt drained, like an empty sieve.

The tile was there, undeniably.

There had to be an explanation, something they didn't know. He'd call Scott and James tomorrow morning to see if they knew anything about it. Maybe the tile contractor had installed it without telling anyone, not wanting to bother them in their distress, but that seemed absurd. Perhaps Annie had been on the phone with her mom, and the tile guy entered unnoticed. But that seemed ridiculous. Scott wouldn't allow anyone in their house without giving them notice.

What would he tell the detectives? *"Thanks for your help, but we found Sarah in a tile. Can you help us get her out?"*

Right. That'd go over well.

He was glad Annie was sleeping so he could focus his logical attorney thinking on solving this, or at least understanding it. But first, he had to put to rest the possibility that the tile had been replaced without their knowledge to rest. It was critical to hold it together for Annie's sake and not let his fear overcome him. He had to exercise

CHAPTER 15

faith in God that his daughter was alive and well somewhere and not in a tile on their fireplace.

He left Annie sleeping before the fireplace and went to the family room. He'd rest on the sofa until morning, only a few long hours away.

* * *

Scott was immediately concerned for them. He'd stopped all repairs on the basement earlier that week but assured Cart that the tile hadn't arrived yet. Installation wouldn't take place until everything was back to normal. He thanked Scott for the caring and kind man he was.

James's secretary started crying when she heard his voice. She was an older woman in her late sixties, a friend of James's mother. Barely able to speak, she offered him her prayers for Sarah and the two of them, then connected him to James's office.

"I wanted to call you," James said, his usual cheery voice subdued. "I've been heart sick about this. Is there any word on Sarah?"

"No, nothing's changed," Cart said. "I'm sure the police are doing all they can. We need a lot of faith right now." He paused for a moment. "I have a question for you about the replacement tile for our fireplace. Has it come in yet?"

James was silent for a long time. Cart heard him breathing.

"James?" he asked when he didn't answer. "Are you still there?"

"Uh . . . no, Cart," James said slowly. "The last time I checked, my source in Germany said it'd be at least a month before it'd be shipped. He assured me he'd get it to us ASAP when it arrives. I told Annie the last time I talked to her that I'd keep her updated." He paused for a moment. "Forgive me for asking, but are you okay, Cart? I don't usually get involved with clients' personal lives, but this situation with Sarah has hit us all. We consider you and Annie friends, and I have to ask because I'm concerned about you. The tile seems so unimportant, considering what's going on with you. I don't want to offend you, but why are you worrying about this now?"

He let James hang for a few seconds before he answered. "I think you need to come over here, James. I need your advice on something. Can you break away for a few minutes?"

"I think I could," he answered. "I was just heading out to meet a client, but I could swing by your place on the way back to my office, say, around eleven?"

"Thanks, James," said Cart. "I can explain things when you get here."

He hung up and leaned back in his chair, hands behind his head, gazing at the Scottish claymores above the fireplace.

It's too bad things were so different these days. Buckling on one of those swords and mounting a warhorse to look for Sarah would feel good.

He frowned. Maybe his mind was slipping.

He didn't know how to ride a horse or use a sword.

CHAPTER 16

James's eyes were wary when Cart opened the door to him. A chill wind swirled behind him, and Cart hurriedly closed the door. He shook James's hand as he took his coat and hung it on a coat tree in the foyer.

"Thanks for coming, James. This means a lot to me."

"Of course," said James. "I'd do anything for you guys, especially now." He looked out the window next to the door. "It's quite a circus out there. Do they ever leave?"

"I don't think so," Cart said, shaking his head. "They're doing their job, I guess. It does make us feel trapped, though. If I even step outside, they're at the gate, shouting questions at me. It gets annoying, but if it helps us get Sarah home, it's worth it."

He led James to the kitchen, offering him a muffin from a plate a neighbor had dropped off, and a glass of orange juice. James refused the muffin but took the orange juice.

When James was seated comfortably, Cart excused himself. "I need to see if Annie's awake. Would you mind waiting a minute?"

He felt James's eye on him as he left the kitchen and walked upstairs.

The bedroom was dark and gloomy, despite the sun rising several hours earlier. The room was stuffy and smelled stale. He drew back the curtains and opened the door a bit. The room filled with light, and some cold air came in.

Annie was awake, sitting on the floor with her back against the side of the bed, staring at the tile. Sleep had left her hair snarled and her clothes wrinkled. She didn't look at him as he sat down next to her.

"I'm a mess, Cart," she said when he told her James was sitting at the kitchen table. "I don't want any visitors right now. I'm too tired to think."

Her voice was flat and emotionless, like her eyes. He put his arm around her and pulled her to him. She laid her head on his shoulder. Her breath was sour from sleep and not eating. Brushing his hand through her hair, loosening the knots, he pulled the freed strands back from her face.

"I know this is hard, sweetie, but I didn't know what else to do. Something strange is happening here, and I'm hoping James might have some ideas we can't see or think of. We have to figure this out and deal with it. I honestly don't know where else to turn."

She continued looking at the tile before finally sitting up and pulling her head off his shoulder.

"Okay," she said, struggling to rise. "At least give me time to change my clothes and brush my hair," she said as she faded into the bathroom.

Faded....

He thought that was the only way to describe her as he watched her close the bathroom door.

CHAPTER 16

She was fading; a sad ghost of herself replaced her lively attitude and cheerful demeanor. Yet how could he blame her? He felt like he was losing it himself. He needed to focus and sink his mind into something substantial that could draw them from the terrible future that lay before them.

Maybe trying to understand this tile would help him gain mastery over his thoughts and emotions before he slipped into the dark recesses of his mind, never to return.

* * *

James knelt speechless before the fireplace, his tie and collar loosened. Sweat trickled down his face from under his blond hair. He visibly shook as he reached out to touch the tile, jerking his hand back and staring at Cart.

"You felt it, too, then?" Cart asked.

"What is it?" James asked. "What the hell is going on?"

"We don't know," Cart said. "We were hoping you might have some ideas."

James stood, running his hands through this hair, and began pacing in front of the fireplace, stopping to stare wildly at the tile every few seconds. "I don't believe this. It just can't be. Can it?"

Annie came out of the bathroom and sat on the edge of the bed, watching him. She'd brushed her hair and put a little makeup on. James's eyes softened when he saw her. Over the months of designing and building the house, he'd grown fond of Annie. She was like the sister he'd never had. He sat beside her on the bed, his back drenched with sweat.

"Annie," he said, "I'm sorry, I don't understand. I don't get what happened with the tile. It can't be Sarah, and it's just an old tile. Where did it come from? I don't know what to say, what to think." He took a handkerchief from his pocket and wiped the sweat from his face.

Suddenly, he stood and grabbed his jacket from the chair where he'd draped it earlier.

"Look, I've got to go," he muttered as he shrugged it on. "I can't be here; I can't be in the room with this." Panic had seized his voice. "I need to get back to the office; I have a lot of work to do. I've got to get out of here...." His voice was trembling as he headed for the door.

"Please don't go," Cart said quietly.

James stopped at the door, his back to them.

"We need your help, James," Cart said. "We don't know who to turn to."

He saw James trembling where he stood.

"What can I do?" James asked softly. "I'm just a designer. I can't do anything for you."

"You're our friend, James."

He turned and looked at the two of them, his eyes filled with despair.

Cart stood by Annie now, his arm around her shoulder. "You've become ingrained with our family. I've watched you over the months while Scott built our house. I've seen how you are with Annie and our kids," Cart said as he walked over to him. "You're a kind man, a good man." He put his hand on James's shoulder. "Annie thinks the world of you. She trusts you. That's good enough for me."

James's lip was trembling. A tear slid from an eye.

CHAPTER 16

"I'm proud to call you a friend. . . ." Cart said.

James hadn't expected this. He grabbed Cart in a fierce bear hug. Cart hugged him back and let him work through his feelings. Annie joined them and put her arms around both of them.

* * *

They sat at the kitchen table, a plate of muffins between them.

"I can't tell you how much this means to me," James said as he took a bite of a banana nut muffin. "You're right; I do care about your family. I don't usually allow myself to feel this way. I've had a pretty rough life since I was a kid. I've had harsh treatment from some people and clients who would treat me one way to my face, and then I'd find out what they really thought of me. When I came out, many friends and family distanced themselves from me. It hurt pretty bad, but I got through it. It's easier to keep things as a strict business relationship."

He looked at them across the table. "I've seen how you are with each other and your kids. I don't know if I'll ever have kids or a family, but if I do, I'd want it to be like yours."

Annie squeezed his hand.

"What can I do to help?" he asked.

"I think the first thing we need to do is talk to your contact in Haarlem," Cart said, "see what information you can get from him. Maybe he can tell us something about these tiles and their story. You said you got a pretty good deal when you bought them. Is that unusual, given the unique design of the tiles?"

James was nodding. "I didn't think much of it when I first talked to him. I was excited about what a reasonable price it was. In hindsight, it was unusual. More often than not, they try to take you for as much as they can. Some dealers have taken me for a ride a few times, I can tell you. It's night in Holland, but I'll try calling him when I return to my office. He sometimes stays late in his shop. Otherwise, I'll have to call him in the morning. What else can I do for you?"

Cart considered this. "We lead kind of an insulated life, James. We have our friends at church, at work, and our families. We don't have what you'd call a worldly outlook on life. I know nothing about this except what I read or see in movies. I always thought anything like this was for entertainment purposes only. I never imagined this would be true in my wildest dreams." He sipped his orange juice, feeling his hand tremble. "We have to get Sarah back somehow. I feel foolish even thinking this, but do you know anyone that has had experience with—*supernatural*—things?" He laughed bitterly. "I can't believe I'm saying this."

James watched them, his head cocked to one side, chewing on his lower lip.

"I did a house remodel for a couple of old ladies a few years back," he said, "sisters that were very into the occult: seances, tarot cards, that sort of stuff." He paused, considering them. "Charlotte, the older sister, is a psychic and gives people readings. She does pretty well, actually. Everyone's searching for something to give meaning to their lives and answers to questions about life and death. You've found answers in religion, but not everyone believes as you do, so they look for different explanations. Do you want me to talk to her?"

Cart thought for a moment. "I don't like the idea of getting involved in this kind of stuff. It seems too closely aligned with Ouija

CHAPTER 16

boards and evil spirits. Just because I'm an adult and an attorney doesn't mean I don't believe these things can influence people's lives."

"I went to a sleepover when I was thirteen," Annie said. "One of the girls had a Ouija board, only she called it a spirit board. We started using it, asking questions we probably shouldn't have. A bad feeling came into the room, and some girls started freaking out. Pretty soon, most of them were crying, wanting their parents to come and get them. Some parents came and talked about casting evil spirits out. My friend's mom came downstairs and angrily sent everyone home, calling it all nonsense. I've never forgotten that feeling, though, like pure evil."

Cart sighed. "I don't see where we have any choice, though. We have to look into everything, no matter how bizarre. There has to be a reason Sarah disappeared and this tile appeared." He looked at James, his eyes narrowing. "I don't want any of this getting out, though. They'd turn this into an even bigger circus if reporters learned about it. Can this old woman be discreet about what you tell her?"

"I'm sure of it." James nodded. "She takes herself quite seriously. If she can help you, she will." He leaned over and looked into Cart's eyes. "I'll do whatever I can to help, Cart. You need to know that."

* * *

Annie had a rough night.

She hardly slept, if at all. She was sitting before the flickering fireplace in their darkened room, keening the loss of Sarah, a heart-breaking lament that sent Cart staggering from the room, helpless to offer consolation. She'd rejected his offerings of comfort, wrapping a blanket around herself like a shroud as she wept.

He wandered the house, haunting it like a sad apparition, voiceless and restless, before finally collapsing on Sarah's bed, empty and alone. He fell into a fitful sleep, filled with voices he didn't understand.

CHAPTER 17

Will Collins sat across the table from him, notebook open. Detective Gregson was at the high school again today, questioning students.

Cart explained that Annie was still sleeping and wouldn't join them today. He felt Collins' eyes on him, like itchy bugs on his nerves, while he poured juice for the detective. Not having showered yet, Cart's hair was sticking up like a porcupine. He was unshaven and unkempt, and he didn't care. He was exhausted.

Collins looked like every bad guy's worst nightmare. His shirt and tie loosened, flexing his huge hands impatiently, waiting for Cart to talk. He stared at Cart, unblinking.

"Look, I'm sorry for the other day," Cart said. "There's no excuse for how I acted. I guess the strain of all this is getting to me. Please forgive me."

Collins's eyes softened a bit, but his face remained impassive.

"No problem," he said, his voice a low rumble. "I'm sure the pressure is immense."

"Do you have any children, Detective?" Cart asked suddenly.

The big man looked at him, eyes narrowing, nostrils flaring. "I don't talk about my private life," he grumbled.

"Please," Cart said, "I want to know."

Collins's eyes bore into him, and then he sighed.

"Three," he said, "I have three. Two boys and a girl."

"Are they still living at home?"

Collins glared at him. "I don't see . . . ."

"Please, Detective."

"My boys are married; my daughter is still in high school."

"Do you love them?" Cart asked.

"Of course I love them," Collins said through clenched teeth. "What father wouldn't? I'm not going to talk about my family. It's none of your business and has no bearing on this case."

"I only ask," Cart said quietly, "if you could put yourself in my place. Do you know what it's like to have a child missing, to wonder if you'll ever see them again? I can't stop thinking about her, hoping to hear her voice."

The room was quiet except for their breathing and the rustle of snow against the window.

"Every time I sit across from a grieving parent, I try to understand what they're going through," Collins said, staring at the table, "what they're feeling. But then I think: I don't want to feel that pain. I don't want to walk that dark path. It's too awful to contemplate.

"I've seen too many parents lose hope and faith when that happens. I want so badly to help them, and I want to bring their child home safely." His eyes had filled with pain. "Too often I've had to leave a home with a parent's grief echoing in my mind. . . . I've spent too many

CHAPTER 17

nights staring at the bedroom ceiling, trying to sleep, haunted by the loss those people feel." He looked at Cart, his dark brown eyes soft. "I can never understand your feelings, but I can empathize with you. And I can promise you I'll do everything I can to bring Sarah back to you."

There was an awkward moment of silence at the table. Cart felt a sudden surge of friendship for the big man. It probably took a lot for him to tell Cart what he did.

The doorbell rang.

Cart opened the door to find Detective Gregson standing on the porch.

She came into the kitchen and sat next to Collins.

Collins cleared his throat. "You remember we were going to meet with the kids at her school yesterday?" he asked.

"Yes. How did that go?" Cart replied.

Gregson put her briefcase on the table and opened it.

"Very well, actually," she said as she pulled some papers out. "The principal set up a room for us next to his office to interview students. It went slow most of the day until just as we cleaned up to leave. A student came in and wanted to talk to us." She looked at a piece of paper she'd removed from the briefcase. "His name is Tyson Mayer. He's a senior at the school."

They heard a gasp from the stairway. Annie was standing at the bottom of the stairs, a hand to her mouth. They all stood, and Cart went to her, taking her hand and leading her to the table, aware of the detective's startled looks when they saw her. He was surprised, as well, and frightened by her appearance. She looked like a disheveled scarecrow; her face was gaunt and haggard, her eyes like marbles sunk into pale clay. She'd lost weight over the past week, subsiding on nothing substantial, despite Cart's pleas for her to eat. She emanated grief, and his heart broke further at the sight of her, the messy hair and rumpled clothing hanging from her thin body.

Collins looked deeply affected by her, sympathy filling his eyes.

"Does that name mean something to you, Mrs. Benson?" he asked gently.

Annie nodded briefly. "He asked her to a dance last fall." Her voice sounded weary. "She turned him down. He was pushy and obnoxious. She didn't want anything to do with him. She said he got angry with her, sent nasty texts to her, and said rude things at school."

"Why didn't you tell me about it?" Cart asked, surprised that she'd keep something like that from him.

"She said she could handle it." She shrugged. "There was no reason to involve you."

"Obviously, she couldn't," Cart said, annoyed at being left out of an incident that had produced such drastic consequences. "Is he the one that broke in?" he asked Gregson.

"Yeah, he was," she said. "He named two more boys that were involved—one a senior, the other a junior. But he was the instigator. The other boys got caught up in it and went along with him, afraid to back down once they started smashing things.

"Tyson came to us worried he'd be charged for her disappearance once word got out about their little adventure. Tyson's eighteen, so we arrested him and booked him into the county jail. We released his buddies to their parents yesterday.

CHAPTER 17

"Tyson's in serious trouble, facing several felonies, considering the monetary damage done. He's not a happy boy right now."

"Why hasn't he been released?" Cart asked. "I'm sure they could post bail."

"He's been getting into a lot of trouble lately. His parents are tired of bailing him out. They hope to teach him a lesson while he cools off in jail," Gregson said.

"We didn't get any leads, though, on Sarah's disappearance," Collins interjected. "A lot of the kids were pretty traumatized by the whole thing. So, the school district brought in counselors to help them deal with it. Several girls left school worrying they'd be next."

"They don't have to worry...." Annie whispered.

Cart stiffened. Now wasn't the time for this.

Collins shifted his gaze to Annie, but she seemed oblivious to him. "I'm sorry, Mrs. Benson. What was that?"

"I said they don't have to worry," she murmured. "They aren't going where she is."

Collins looked at her with narrowed eyes. "What do you mean?" he asked. "Where is she?"

"Far away," she said, her voice vague. "My baby is far away...."

Cart stood, taking hold of Annie's arm and trying to get her to stand. "My wife's exhausted. I'm going to take her upstairs and put her to bed."

"No," she protested weakly, pushing his hand away. "You know where she is, Cart. You know. Why can't you bring her home?" Her eyes filled with tears that then spilled down her cheeks. "I want my baby...."

He had to get her upstairs now and away from these detectives before it was too late. "Come on, sweetie, let's get you upstairs."

She finally relented to his urging and slowly stood, eyes staring vacantly.

"I'll be right back," he said to the detectives. Annie could barely stand as he approached the stairs. Her strength failed her as she tried to step up. He gathered her frail body and carried her up the stairs to the bedroom. He gave her two sleeping pills and pulled the comforter to her chin, nestling her head into her pillow.

"Hold me," she whispered. "I'm so cold. . . ."

He touched her cheek gently, his heart saddened, wishing he could do just that. "Go to sleep, Annie. I have to go back downstairs."

"Sarah . . ." she whispered, her voice so soft, he could barely hear her. He looked at her, his throat thick with heartache. And then she was asleep.

She looked so tiny and helpless, the dark circles under her eyes accentuating the ethereal pallor of her skin.

He felt like he was losing her, as well. The very essence of her, her sweetness and joy for life, was slipping away, evaporating like snow in August.

Sarah was gone; Maddy was at her grandmother's. Now Annie.

He'd never felt so alone.

He quietly closed the bedroom door and went back downstairs.

CHAPTER 18

The detectives were in the foyer, heads together, whispering. They looked up when Cart came down the stairs, studying him.

"I'm sorry," Cart said, "my wife is not doing well. She hardly sleeps and rarely eats. I'm really worried about her."

"Anything we can do?" Collins asked.

"Not really, but thanks for asking; we just need to get Sarah home somehow."

"What did your wife mean when she said you knew where Sarah was?" asked Collins, his eyes hard like obsidian.

"I have no idea," Cart lied. "I wish I did. I don't know what to do for her. I should get some counseling for her."

"That might be a good idea," Collins said, zipping up his parka. "Lots of hard things are going on for her right now.

"One more thing," he continued. "You're not planning on going anywhere, are you? Like a business trip or anything?"

"Of course not," Cart said. "I'm not going anywhere until my daughter is safe at home." He paused, looking at the detective. "Why would you ask me that? What kind of man would leave his family at a time like this?" Realization dawned on him. "Are you saying I'm a suspect? Is that what you're thinking? Where did this come from?" he asked, but he thought he knew the answer.

"I'm just saying, is all," Collins said. "In case we have more questions, you know."

Cart's blood went cold. *I don't need this right now.*

"Look," he said, opening the door, letting the cold winter in, flakes of snow slithering past his feet, "we had a rough night. I'm going to join my wife in bed. You know where to find me," he said as he closed the door on the two detectives.

He leaned back against the door, breathing hard, his heart pounding.

Her comment focused their attention on him because she was confused and troubled. Why hadn't she stayed upstairs, as he asked her? She'd said too much, things that were impossible to explain. Now the detectives were suspicious of him, and why wouldn't they be? It was their job to be suspicious. They'd probably spend excessive time looking for evidence to support their suspicions. He knew they were already wary of him because of his temper and his explosive rage the other day.

It's not like he could drag them upstairs and show them the tile. They'd think he was crazy. He was beginning to believe that himself. It was all incredible to him, even after seeing the tile. He didn't know what to do or where to turn. And he hadn't heard back from James yet. He was exhausted from all the worry and stress. He was glad Maddy wasn't here to see her parents like this.

He went upstairs, undressed, and laid down beside Annie in bed. She was snoring softly. He was glad she was sleeping. He sensed the

CHAPTER 18

silence of the snow outside in the waning afternoon. The fireplace glowed, low flames dancing on fake logs. He could tell sleep wasn't going to come easy tonight. His mind wouldn't stop.

Each day was getting harder to face as his and Annie's sorrow affected him. He'd never allowed himself pity or self-doubt. Sometimes, he'd been accused of overconfidence and arrogance, but it wasn't that. Every day before Sarah's disappearance was another day to get up and work; each day was a new opportunity to create as he wanted. It was how he'd accomplished so much in his life. He'd always known what he'd wanted, even as a child, and set about to achieve it, no matter the cost. He'd been the master of his life.

But now...

It was like the playing field suddenly shifted, tilting upward on one end, becoming a slippery slope of hopelessness. He felt he was losing his footing, afraid he would plunge recklessly down that slope, careening into a chasm of despair. He couldn't let that happen now, not while so much was at stake. For the sake of his family, he had to keep fighting, trying to stay afloat as a whirlpool of desperation sucked him down its yawning mouth.

Twenty years ago, fresh out of law school and determined to scramble to the top—pushing his way past the chaos of thousands of other attorneys graduating from different schools across the country—he'd sacrificed much to further his career, especially during those early years. He'd spent much time away from his young family, working late hours and weekends. Annie stayed home, raising the children virtually alone, more concerned for their comfort than hers. She'd always been selfless with her family.

He regretted those lost years, knowing they were irretrievably gone. Rechanneling the energy and focus that was his gift, maybe he could take their lives back and bring Sarah home. That was the only way to get his family back from the brink of destruction.

* * *

Following a worthless workout the next morning, he ate a breakfast of grapefruit. After Annie had refused breakfast, he'd left a banana and juice on the nightstand for her, hoping she'd eat it later. She was still in bed now, refusing to rise from her sorrow, subsisting on oxygen and the scant reserves of her body. She would get ill if she didn't care for her basic needs.

The phone rang as he rinsed his bowl in the sink.

James Phillips's Design glowed on the caller ID. He snatched the phone up.

"James!" he said excitedly. "Did you get any information?"

"Hey, Cart," James said, "how're things today?"

"Another rough night, I'm afraid. Annie's not doing well at all. I might have to take her to our doctor if it continues." He sighed. "Did you get any information from your Holland friend?"

"Well," James said, "I've been on the phone with him for an hour. I rescheduled my appointments so I could deal with this."

"Thank you, James," Cart said, "I appreciate it."

"Before you get too excited, he wasn't forthcoming about the tiles. At first, we just chatted about our lives like we usually do. I didn't want him to get suspicious right off the bat, so I took it slowly," James said. "We go back quite a few years, so there's always something to discuss.

CHAPTER 18

"Anyway, I started asking him about the replica tile since he's the one taking care of that. He told me the craftsman was doing a lot of research to ensure it was perfect. Then I asked him about the bedroom tiles: where they came from, and their history, you know, its provenance. He was getting evasive and ambiguous about them; it got to the point where he kept trying to get off the phone. Finally, he told me he had customers in the shop, and hung up on me. I tried calling back, but it just went to voicemail.

"He's hiding something. I could practically smell his sweat over the phone. It was very odd," James said.

Cart thought about what he'd just heard. There was a connection between the shop in Holland and Sarah's disappearance, just as they'd expected. Otherwise, James's friend in Haarlem wouldn't have been so guarded. Cart felt his attorney genes kicking in, the buzz of his brain as the wheels started turning.

"Cart," James said, "are you still there?"

"Yeah, I'm still here, just thinking. What do you think we should do? Should I try to talk to this guy? I could get a flight out of here tomorrow."

James was quiet for a moment. "You can't do that right now, can you? It sounds like Annie is pretty fragile. I don't know if leaving her would help with that. You've got a lot riding on you."

Cart told him about what happened with the police and Annie yesterday.

"Now I'm even more against you doing this," James said. "Don't you think it would make them more suspicious of you if you left the country? Doing that is definitely not a good idea." He paused. "There's something else you need to know.

"Last night at dinner, Ron and I overheard a couple talking in the booth next to us, discussing Sarah's 'kidnapping,' as they called it. They think you had something to do with it."

"*What?!*" Cart exclaimed. "How could someone think that??" His voice rose, and he felt sweat itching up from the pores in his head.

"It's just people talking, Cart. You know, I heard from a friend, who heard from a friend. I wouldn't worry about it, although it does mean you are under close public scrutiny. People are always looking for something wrong with people in the spotlight—especially someone like you who is successful and well-to-do. That's why you have to be careful. You need to focus on getting Sarah back and not letting this stuff get to you, or you'll go crazy. It won't go away until Sarah's home, or . . ." James let the unsaid words hang.

Cart felt speechless. He knew the police suspected him, thanks to yesterday, but he had no idea the general public would think such a thing.

"What can I do, James?" he asked. "I've got to do something, or I'll go crazy."

"That's another reason I called," James said. "I spoke to Charlotte Delcanto yesterday, the psychic I was telling you about. She wants to see your tile."

"I thought I told you—" Cart began.

"No, don't worry," James reassured him. "I didn't tell her anything specific, just that I had a friend who might need help. She has a good heart, despite being a bit odd."

CHAPTER 18

Cart thought this over. "I don't know. I'll have to talk with Annie about this. I don't want this to become a bigger circus than it already is. Do you trust her?"

"I do. It can't hurt. Charlotte couldn't have gotten the clientele she has without being discreet."

"I guess you're right." Cart sighed. "What time do you want to come over?"

"After dark, say about seven? That way, there's less chance those reporters will see who she is."

"Let's plan on it, then. I'll get Annie prepared."

* * *

Annie was hesitant, of course.

She'd finally showered and put on clean clothes and a little makeup. She'd eaten the banana and drank the juice, so it was a good start. Now, she was eating a bowl of oatmeal in the kitchen when Cart brought up the conversation with James.

"I don't know how much more of this I can take," she said. "Sometimes I feel like I'm losing my mind, like it's all a bad dream, and I'll wake up, and she'll be here. And I can touch her and hold her. It's so heavy, I feel like it will smother or crush me. When I sleep, it's all darkness, like there's no life left in the world, just a big empty sky full of black. There's a big hole in my heart, and it's getting bigger. . . ."

He put his arms around her, trying to give her warmth, letting her feed off his love. It was like holding a cold, lifeless mannequin.

"We have to do whatever we can to bring her back, sweetie," he said, "even if it means talking to someone like Charlotte. There's always the possibility she can do something. If we lose faith, we'll dry up and blow away."

"I guess," she said. "I just don't want a bunch of mumbo jumbo going on. We have enough right now without that." She laid her head on his shoulder. "Thank you for being strong for me. You're always the strong one. I love you."

His eyes watered, hearing her say that.

"I love you, too," he whispered.

* * *

Sam dropped by midafternoon, and after hugging Cart fiercely, he told him what had been happening outside in the world he was ignoring. He was grateful for his older brother, who had taken the role of spokesman for the family, having it thrust on him by the past week's events. Cart had come to rely on his quiet strength and natural, calm demeanor.

He knew it wasn't easy for Sam. He'd always been uncomfortable around people he didn't know, carefully avoiding the spotlight—unlike himself, who loved to plunge headlong into conversations with people he'd never met. Cart knew Sam felt inadequate because he hadn't finished college and never pursued higher learning after his freshman year. He knew this was nonsense, but could never convince Sam otherwise. Sam was a good man, honest and reliable, devoted to his family and friends.

When he told Sam what James said about the overheard conversation, Sam looked at the snow piled on the patio.

"Yeah." He sighed. "I've heard people whispering at press conferences, like background noise. I heard one guy ask a lady next to him

CHAPTER 18

if you'd taken a lie detector test, and that he'd heard from a 'source' in the SLPD that you were a 'person of interest.' I walked over to him after and asked what he meant by that, but he wouldn't answer me. I told him to keep his mouth shut if he had nothing constructive to say."

Cart's heart went cold. "Why haven't you told me this?"

"It's just people talking. He left after I called him on it."

"Do you think I should?"

"Take the test? I don't know, Cart. You're the lawyer. I don't see what good it would do, anyway. Give the police time to do their job before you do anything. If you start pushing this, people will think the worst, like you're trying to hide something. Just keep a low profile, like you've been doing. Let me take care of it. I'll handle the reporters and everyone else."

When he was leaving, Sam put a hand on Cart's shoulder. "We'll get Sarah back, brother, no matter where she is."

You have no idea, Cart thought as he walked him to the door.

CHAPTER 19

A few minutes past seven that evening, James buzzed from the gate saying he had a visitor with him.

Cart opened the gate from the security touchscreen, then opened the garage so James could pull into the empty spot next to the Hummer. As the door closed, he saw reporters lining the fence like starlings on a telephone wire, squawking questions at them. Cart shook his head in disgust, wondering when it would all end.

James emerged, waving at him, and then went to the passenger door to help the woman climb from the car. Cart couldn't see much of her, except she was wearing a blue coat. James took her gloved hand as she climbed from his car.

He took her hand to help her into the house and the mudroom, where they stood, shrugging off their coats. Her parka looked huge, and she had a scarf wrapped around her head like a turban. Over the scarf, she wore a stocking cap and earmuffs, so he could only see a pair of bright eyes peering out of the warmth of her blue cocoon, looking at him intently. James helped her unwrap, hanging her coat, hat, and earmuffs on the peg next to his jacket while she unwound her scarf.

"Cart," he said smiling, "I'd like you to meet Charlotte Delcanto."

She smiled at him, crystal green eyes set in a thin, wrinkled face etched by the years. At first, he thought she'd been heavier, but a thinner woman emerged as she shed her coats. He saw she wore a light windbreaker over a cream-colored sweater as he took her hand. Her hair was dyed red and drawn back into a ponytail hanging to her waist. She'd shaved off her eyebrows and penciled on new ones, arching dramatically over her eyes; 1940s red lipstick covered her thin lips, flowing outside the natural line of her mouth to make them appear fuller.

"I'm Cart Benson." He smiled as he carefully took her deeply veined and age-spotted hand, afraid he would crush her fingers. "I'm pleased to meet you."

"No, you're not," said the woman in a thin voice. She stared at him, and he felt himself being measured by her and coming up short. She looked away from him, tracing the line of the stairs up to the second floor.

"So much sadness here. . . ." she whispered, her voice like leaves rustling across an empty street. "Can I see your daughter?" she asked suddenly.

He sucked in a breath and looked at James, who shrugged and mouthed, *I didn't say anything!*

"Um, she's at her grandmother's house," he said.

The woman's eyes darted back to him. "Not the little one. Please don't play games with me, Mr. Benson. My time is too precious to waste playing games." Her eyes pierced him, and he had to look away, ashamed. He felt naked under the gaze of those eyes.

"You're right," he said stupidly, embarrassed. "I'm sorry." The back of his neck was burning. It made him feel like he was twelve again,

CHAPTER 19

getting caught smoking one of his dad's stolen cigarettes at the side of the house.

"Cart," he heard Annie call from the stairs, and he looked at her, grateful to be out from under that knife-like gaze.

It broke his heart to see Annie's shadow standing at the bottom of the stairs, dressed nicely for their visitor. If it wasn't for the gauntness of her figure and the dark smudges under her eyes, she could look like the woman he'd fallen in love with all those years ago.

He heard a gasp from Charlotte and turned to see her rush to Annie and throw her arms around her. Cart and James followed, both of them puzzled.

"Oh, you dear mother," she said as she hugged Annie. "You dear, sweet mother..."

Annie was startled but hugged her back, stiffly holding her head from the old cheek. Charlotte began softly crooning something barely audible into Annie's ear. With a start, Cart realized it was the lullaby Annie had sung to Sarah and Maddy when they were small, contentedly falling asleep in their mother's arms.

"Up, up in the sky
Where the little birds fly,
Down, down in their nest
Where the little birds rest,
With a wing on the left
And a wing on the right,
Now, all the dear birdies
Sleep all the long night."

Charlotte was swaying gently back and forth, almost like she was rocking Annie, who'd been startled at the song's first words, her eyes wide as Charlotte softly sang the beloved song.

Then, as Cart watched, Annie's eyes rolled back and closed as she laid her head tiredly on the woman's shoulder, swaying with her as she murmured the song. His eyes watered as he listened, remembering.

My little girls . . .

So many years had flown by with him too busy to help put them to bed or spend a Saturday with them instead of playing golf with clients. Again, the loss of those years weighed heavily on him, knowing time was a flowing river with branches heading off in different directions to alternate lives he could have—should have—lived. Other lives where he was present for his whole family: Annie, Sarah, and Maddy, the little girl he hardly knew. He hoped those other Carts were doing better than he was at being a father and husband. But alternate universes were things for fantasy and movies. If he could go back and row up a different river to a better life, he would, without hesitation. But this was the reality of their lives. There was no changing that. The only thing he could do now was try to be better at the things that were of real worth.

He would never again allow his job to interfere with his family or his desire to be with them. If they got Sarah back, things would be different.

If . . .

And if they didn't get Sarah back, he would still be there for his family. He had a family he loved, and he needed them as much if not more than they needed him. He was suddenly filled with a new,

CHAPTER 19

wondrous sense of purpose, making the old Cart seem like a sad and lonely man.

Charlotte disengaged from Annie, then began walking up the stairs, suddenly stopping at the bedroom door, leaning against the frame, a hand to her mouth. "Oh..." she whispered. Cart wasn't sure he'd heard her correctly.

Annie was at her side, a hand on Charlotte's arm. "Charlotte, are you okay?" she asked.

Charlotte was visibly trembling, her eyes wide beneath her painted, furrowed brow. Her face was wan, the network of wrinkles tightly drawn. Running a thin hand through her hair, she looked at them all standing protectively around her. James had an arm around her.

"So strong..." her voice was quiet and indistinct. "Can you feel it?" She peered past James into the darkened bedroom. "It's so *strong.*"

Cart leaned over and flipped the lights on in the bedroom.

Charlotte flinched, covering her eyes with her arm.

"No lights! Please turn them off!" she exclaimed, recoiling into James's arms. "I can't see with the lights."

Annie turned them off, plunging the room into darkness, except for the dull glow of the fireplace.

"I'm sorry if I startled all of you," Charlotte said softly, gesturing into the room with trembling hands. "I can't see things like this with normal vision. I don't use my eyes for this kind of sight. I've never felt anything like this before. To be honest, I don't know what to make of it. I don't know if I can go into the room.... I'm frightened."

The hairs on the back of Cart's neck prickled, and his stomach had a strange tickle in it, like when he was a kid at church, and his friends had dared him to go into a dark bathroom alone and stare into the darkened mirror, while rubbing his cheeks and saying, *"Ouija Queen, please appear..."* over and over again until he'd fled the bathroom in a panic, sure he'd seen the beginning of a ghostly face stirring in the depths of the mirror. He'd felt foolish after as his friends laughed at him, but it was years before he would go into a darkened restroom.

Charlotte regained her composure, dabbing at her face with a lace handkerchief. Sweat tinged her hairline.

"What is it, Charlotte?" Annie asked her. "What do you feel?"

"It's hard to explain," Charlotte said, "but it's like a stone wall, thick like a stone wall, and so tall I can't see the top of it, built of power and strength as I've never felt before. It's so strong, it's almost tangible. None of you have felt it?" She looked at them.

"All I feel is sadness in there," Annie replied, "like my heart will break whenever I walk in the room. But I have to go in there because I feel close to Sarah, yet so far away."

"You do feel it, then." Charlotte nodded. "I feel it more intensely because I'm attuned to these things, but sadness is a big part of what's in the room. It's the mortar that holds the great walls together." She shook her head and sighed deeply. "I know the only way to understand better is to confront it in that room. But I am frightened. I'm eighty years old, and I've been helping people with my abilities my whole life, but *this*—I feel like a child compared to what's in there.... No, not a child, a baby, a newborn—actually, like I haven't even been conceived yet."

"We're all here, Charlotte," James said. "We'll all be with you."

"And that does help." She smiled weakly. "Even though you three aren't involved in the psychic arts, your auras strengthen me. And I

CHAPTER 19

do have to try, for your daughter's sake." She looked at Cart, raising an eyebrow. "You cannot disbelieve, Mr. Benson. It's essential to present a united front. If you're skeptical, you must stay out of the room. Do you understand?"

He promised to do this because he was desperate to get Sarah back. He'd have to suspend his skepticism and see what happened. He saw that she believed what she was saying—almost zealously.

"Alright, I can do that," he said.

Annie squeezed his hand.

"Thank you. Having you as Sarah's father in there will help immensely." She squared her shoulders and took a deep breath. "Well, then. Let's get started."

Cart and James each took an arm for support, and she leaned heavily on them. Her fingers were like ice, even through Cart's shirt sleeve. She was shivering, and he felt an instant fondness for the woman. She was sacrificing a lot by doing this.

She stopped just inside the door, letting her eyes roam the room before focusing on the fireplace. "It's there," she said in a tiny, frightened voice. "The fireplace. We have to go to the fireplace."

They carefully helped her around the foot of the bed; she seemed so weak now, they were almost carrying her. Her legs gave out, and they lowered her to the carpet in front of the flickering flames. She stared at the glowing logs for a long moment, her legs curling to her side. She traced the outline of the fireplace in the air with a finger, careful not to touch it. She gasped and jerked her hand back, massaging it with her other hand.

"My, you *are* a strong one, aren't you?" she murmured, struggling to rise to her knees. She reached out to touch the tile with Sarah's picture on it.

There was a sudden burst of white light and a crackling sound like the echo of thunder. Charlotte flew back with such force she arced onto the bed, rolling over it to fall off the opposite side onto the floor. The smell of singed human hair filled the room.

Annie screamed and scrambled to her side, Cart and James beside her, stunned by what happened. Charlotte's eyes had rolled to the back of her head, her mouth was open, and a thin stream of saliva dribbled from her lips. Her chest was rising and falling rapidly, though she was so weak it was barely noticeable. James felt for a pulse.

"It's there but very weak," he said. "I think she might be going into shock!"

Cart grabbed a blanket from the bed and covered Charlotte while James put pillows under her feet. Annie rubbed her hand while Cart took the other one. James caressed her forehead, whispering to her, "Charlotte, you're okay, you're going to be okay. . . ."

Cart desperately wondered if he should call 911 when Charlotte suddenly drew a great shuddering breath, letting it out slowly before drawing another. Her eyelids fluttered, and she began breathing normally. They were relieved when she opened her eyes briefly, then closed and reopened them again. Charlotte saw James's concerned face close to hers and said weakly, "James . . ."

"Yes, Charlotte," he said, tears in his eyes, "what is it?"

"You're kneeling on my arm," she said.

James leaped back, startled as she struggled to sit.

CHAPTER 19

"You need to rest," Annie told her. "Just lay back and relax."

'No," she said feebly, "I've got to leave this room. Now. It's too strong for me, and I can't take much more of it; it feels like it's eating me alive. Please help me up...."

CHAPTER 20

Annie made herbal tea while Charlotte laid on the couch wrapped in a blanket. Charlotte looked much better than she had earlier, though still pale and exhausted. Her hand hadn't burned black like Cart feared but only looked like a mild sunburn. Cart had been worried she'd die and bring more suspicion down on him, but that had been a selfish thought, and he discarded it immediately. He was glad she was alive.

The soothing smell of chamomile and lavender drifted from the kitchen as Annie brought a tray into the family room holding cups, saucers, spoons, milk, and sugar. James helped Charlotte sit up so she could drink her tea. She gripped her cup tightly, breathing the scent deeply, her hair loose around her face.

Cart, who'd never liked the taste of tea, dumped a massive amount of sugar in it, stirring vigorously.

"You shouldn't use so much sugar," Charlotte said, "it's not good for you."

What is it with this woman? he wondered. She'd flown halfway across their bedroom like a rag doll yet could still find a reason to rip on him.

"I like it sweet," he said defensively.

James smiled at him, shaking his head.

"What happened, Charlotte?" Annie asked. "What did you see?"

She took her time answering, sipping her tea and rolling it around in her mouth before swallowing. She gazed intently at the fireplace, watching the flames dance on ceramic logs.

"It was old," she said, her voice still raw, "old like the stars and just as cold." She shivered, pulling the blanket around her shoulders. "It was old when the earth was young and powerful. It has the power of the stars and everything between them. I've never felt anything like it before."

Annie stared at her, wide-eyed, Cart's arm around her.

"You've got to get her back," Charlotte said. "You've got to get her out of there."

"Is she there?" Cart asked. "Was Sarah there?" He'd tried to remain objective through this whole evening, but he felt himself slipping into Charlotte's world, despite his best efforts to avoid it.

"There was innocence there," Charlotte continued. "I felt sweetness—tenderness, too, but faint and hidden deeply, like remembering what honey tastes like when you haven't had it for years." Her eyes became distracted, looking somewhere beyond their sight. Then she jerked suddenly and looked at Cart, her eyes wide. "It's like that; it feels like that. I can almost see her, but I can't tell where she is, like she's far away, too far to touch; then in the next second, she's so close I can almost feel her. It's like she's an intangible and unreachable light in the darkness."

"Is she safe?" Annie whispered as a tear leaked down her cheek.

CHAPTER 20

Cart's hands were clenched fists, knuckles white with tension.

"I don't know," Charlotte answered. "I caught that glimpse of light that felt like her, similar to the shadow of her aura in your home, but it wasn't aware, or wasn't—*awake*, I guess you could say. You have to understand, I don't see these things like we usually would; I don't see faces, people, or things. I see differing shades of light and shadow. I have to feel my way through like a blind person; only that blindness strengthens my other sight." She paused, considering. "I don't *feel* danger, though, nor evil. Not evil. It's more like a great, irresistible, overpowering sense of self-confidence. Whatever has Sarah in its web or net can't be destroyed—that much I'm sure of. It's too strong."

Annie held on tightly to Cart, her nails digging into the flesh of his hand. "How can we get her back?" she asked. "It seems so hopeless."

Charlotte put her head back and rolled her neck around. They heard cracks as she loosened her tension.

"I don't know," she said, looking at them with intense green eyes. "But you have to try."

* * *

After she put her coats on, Charlotte hugged Annie, then stood momentarily looking at both of them. Then, without a word of farewell, she was gone. They stood on the side porch, watching James and Charlotte pull out of the driveway.

Cart drew Annie from the cold night, holding her close to him in the silent house. They stood like that for a while, neither speaking. He buried his face in her hair, smelling her shampoo.

The fear and uncertainty of the evening filled his thoughts. He honestly didn't understand what had happened. He remained unconvinced of its authenticity, even after what he'd seen. It was so far out of his area of belief as to border on insanity. But there was no denying what he'd seen and felt. Old women don't fly across rooms of their own accord unless they were much more agile than Charlotte appeared to be. Or unless she was a witch. If it was all bogus, it was quite an act.

"What do we do now?" Annie asked, her head on his shoulder. "What does it all mean?"

"It means I can't go and bring her back," Cart said. "It means she might as well be on the moon. As hard as it is to say, if I believe this whole thing, I've still failed her; I can't get her back, so she might as well be dead. But I can't think that while there's still hope."

Suddenly, Annie hugged him fiercely. "We'll get her back, Cart. I know we will."

I don't know how to get her back.

They tiredly climbed the stairs, but he couldn't drift off after Annie fell asleep. He'd always had a solid belief system, and that system didn't allow what happened tonight to happen. His mind was full of uncertainty and questions, so he sprawled on the family room couch.

He almost wished he hadn't told James about the tile because all he felt now was a mass of confusion. He wanted to be like Annie and believe Sarah was alive and well and living in some strange, unreachable place, but he couldn't see how that was possible.

He felt a deep sadness. Lying on the couch under the quilt his mother had made for them, watching the flames dance on the logs,

CHAPTER 20

filled him with loneliness, and he wondered why he'd ever let Charlotte inside his house. All it'd done was make things feel worse.

CHAPTER 21

The morning was like a glorious rebirth. The storm had fled during the night, and the clouds had disappeared. The sky arched like a brilliant blue bowl overhead. The sun rising above the Wasatch mountains reflected like a billion diamonds off the fresh snow.

Sitting in the kitchen sipping a Diet Coke, the sun felt good on Cart's face. It gave him a sense of well-being and a small glimmer of hope, if only momentarily. As impossible as this situation seemed, maybe there would be a way to figure something out. He had to have hope, or his life would be a pile of emptiness.

Annie had changed overnight, her eyes regaining the faded joy, and seemed imbued with a new, refreshing sense of optimism. She'd been cheerful when she came down for breakfast, and it gladdened his heart to see her smile and eat something substantial. He felt hope while Annie sat with him, but after eating and leaving him with a kiss, she returned upstairs to be "with Sarah." She seemed renewed while he'd sunken further into despair.

Being with Annie was all he ever wanted from the first time he met her. This last week, with Annie wrapped in her blanket of sorrow, had been the worst of his life. He'd felt like a solitary man facing a bleak future without the comfort of her strong and reassuring love.

It seemed he'd received a reprieve from the sad possibility. Annie was almost happy, sitting in front of the fireplace, talking to Sarah, telling her of their love for her, and whispering sweet urgings of faith that she'd soon be home, as though she was listening.

Maybe Sarah *was* listening. Perhaps she heard her mother's encouragement, and maybe she was listening as Annie softly sang to her. Maybe...

His phone rang.

James Phillip's Design

He wasn't ready to talk to anyone this morning. He certainly didn't want to talk to James about last night. He was enjoying the sun on the snow and the spark of hope he was feeling. But James was trying to be supportive and help them, and he felt gratitude for that. It wouldn't hurt to at least say hello.

* * *

Annie was sitting with her back to the bed, singing softly to Sarah a song from church about how fresh the earth was after rain, a song about cleansing and forgiveness, rainbows, and hope. Cart stared down at her, wishing with all his heart that he could make this horrific world they'd been thrust into new again and rinse it clean of the filth that consumed it. His heart felt like a stone in his chest, heavy and lifeless like the iron core at the earth's center.

Annie finished her song and smiled at him, her eyes filled with the glowing day, then stopped when she saw his face.

CHAPTER 21

"What's wrong, Cart?" she asked. "What's the matter?"

Why do I have to do this? Dear God, how much more can we take? "James's office just called," he said. "James is dead. They found him at his office this morning. Someone shot him."

Annie stared at him, uncomprehending, her mind slow at processing what he'd told her. He dumbly watched as her eyes filled with tears and she wept for the loss of their friend, his mind dull from the never-ending question: Why?

* * *

The day of James's funeral had been depressing and gray, the clouds hanging halfway down the mountains, threatening rain. A beautiful dark bronze casket glowing in the light of a single overhead fixture was closed and covered with some of the many flowers delivered earlier. A light breeze moaned around the eaves of the small stone chapel in the middle of the cemetery, a lament for James.

The service was by invitation only, but the chapel was packed. James' mother sat by Ron on the front row, dabbing at her eyes with a white handkerchief and clutching Ron's arm. James' staff sat on either side of them. Charlotte and another woman they assumed was her sister sat just behind Ron and James's mother, and a few rows ahead of Annie and him. James smiled from a large portrait on an easel to the left of the casket. Another picture of James and Ron stood on the right. A spray of dark roses and greenery with the words *Beloved Friend* sent by Cart and Annie stood beside the picture of the two.

They'd arrived a half-hour before the service to express their condolences to Ron. When he saw the two of them, he hugged them both.

"I hope you know he loved you guys. . . ." he'd told them, which made Annie cry.

Ron looked awful, his eyes red-rimmed and sorrowful, his black suit hanging from his thin frame, trying to be brave but failing miserably. James's mom greeted them warmly, grasping Ron's arm with a slender white hand.

As the service progressed, Cart realized James's impact on people's lives as a son, partner, friend, and client. Many people would deeply miss him. James's personal touch was in the interiors he'd designed with great care, but more so in the hearts of those he'd befriended over the years, including theirs.

Cart was surprised by the affection he felt for James. He'd known some gay guys but couldn't comprehend them and hadn't tried. Seeing the grief on Ron's face in the chapel, he realized that James and Ron shared a deep and loving relationship just as he and Annie did. That realization had been a long time coming, and he was ashamed it took James's death to see it. He'd be devastated if he lost Annie, but it was best not to think of that now. Ron's tragic loss consumed him, and Cart wished there was a way to console him.

James was buried that afternoon as the threatening clouds finally released their moisture.

As they returned to their car, Charlotte Delconto stopped them, umbrella sprouting from a gloved hand, and introduced her sister, Amelia, who graciously offered her hand. Charlotte leaned toward them.

"About the other night . . ." she said, but Cart interrupted her.

CHAPTER 21

"I don't think it's the appropriate time for this, Charlotte," Cart said. "We've had enough grief for one day."

Annie gripped his arm tightly.

Charlotte stiffened. "I dreamed about Sarah the other night," she said, eyes flashing. "I think I know how to get her back."

Cart laughed grimly, looking at Annie. "I told you it would come to this." He glared at Charlotte. "How much is it going to cost? I have my checkbook, or we can go to an ATM if you prefer cash. Or do you take American Express?" He smirked at her.

"I don't want your money, you arrogant fool!" she said. "I want to help get your daughter back. If you're too blind to see that, I pity you. Your money won't return her, and neither will your stupidity. You'll have to go to the source and find the key. That's the only way. I won't bother you again, and I won't send you a bill. I did it because James asked me to, and for Annie and Sarah.

"You, on the other hand," she finished, "can go straight to hell!"

Cart's neck was burning. Charlotte turned to Annie, taking her hand. "I'm sorry for you, Annie." Then she turned and walked away with her sister.

Annie was silent during the ride home, staring at the dreary gray streets, rain distorting her view. Cart glared at the road in front of their car.

He felt livid and humiliated. Charlotte had treated him like an imbecile since stepping into their home that night, and today capped that off very well. It was natural for him to want to lash out, but he was driving erratically in his anger. After Annie yelled at him for running a red light and almost hitting a minivan driven by a woman with several children in it, he realized he needed to get a grip on himself. Slowing down and taking deep breaths, he completed the trip in dismal silence.

CHAPTER 22

Detective Will Collins returned the following day without Detective Gregson. She'd been assigned to a different case since they'd solved the break-in. After offering Collins a drink at the table, Cart sat in his usual place. Annie had gone to her mother's house to be with Maddy, who missed her mother.

Collins told him that James had been shot with a .22 magnum. Despite its small size, it did a lot of damage, bouncing around inside his skull. There hadn't been a lot of blood from the shooting; only a slight amount leaked from the entrance wound. It was quick and quiet. Most of the blood came from the beating just before he was shot. It made Cart sick to his stomach. He vowed not to tell Annie the details.

"Was it a robbery?" Cart asked, "or some gang thing?"

"We don't know yet," Collins said. "It was execution-style, though. He'd been forced to kneel, then shot. The place was a mess, papers and trash scattered everywhere, furniture tipped over, and lamps and ceramics smashed. We have no idea who did it, or why."

"It's just awful," Cart said. "I feel bad for his partner and his mother, not to mention the people who worked for him. But why are you telling me these things? I assume you didn't come here to tell me how James died. Is there something else on your mind?"

"Can't fool you, can I?" Collins smiled humorlessly, "you being a lawyer and all."

"Look, Detective," Cart said, trying to control his anger, "I don't have to sit in my house and be insulted by you. If you have something to say, say it. Or you can leave right now." He stared back at the big detective.

Nobody flinched.

"Tell me, Mr. Benson," Collins said, "do you like coconut?"

The question surprised Cart, coming from left field as it had. "What does coconut have to do with anything?"

"Just answer the question, please." Collins wasn't smiling, so it must not be a joke.

Cart shrugged. "I guess so. Why?"

"Whoever killed James left a coconut on his desk, sitting on a very expensive piece of Delftware. It wasn't there when the ladies in his office left for the day, and we know James didn't bring it with him because there wasn't any trace of it on his hands or clothing. He's allergic to coconut, too. This may strike you as silly, but it's important."

"Silly?" Cart said. "It sounds strange, to be honest. What has a coconut at his office to do with me?"

Collins drained his orange juice and set the glass back on the table. Hard black eyes stared at him. "Can you tell me where you were last night from five p.m. to two a.m.?"

"Of course I can," Cart said. Collins's questions were getting ridiculous. "I was here at home with Annie. Where else would I be?"

CHAPTER 22

"Can Mrs. Benson verify you were here?"

"She can," said Cart. "Look, what makes you suspect me in this? James was our friend. We miss him terribly. Why don't you tell me what's bothering you so we can move on? You know I didn't do this. It's not like I can leave without your officer in the driveway and about a thousand reporters noticing."

Collins sighed, standing and walking to the patio's sliding glass door. The sun shone on his face. He leaned his head back and closed his eyes. Sunlight reflecting off the puddles flickered on his face.

"Yeah, I know," he said. "Nice tight alibi you've got there. You understand I have to ask these questions. It's part of my job, if only to clear you as a suspect." He turned and leaned against the door. "Along with the coconut, there was a note on his desk. It said: 'Cart-evil. Don't go to Haarlem.' Now, why would he leave a note like that? What business do you have in New York? What was he warning you against? Do you know, Mr. Benson?"

Cart's mind started churning. "It's Haarlem in the Netherlands. . . ." he said absently.

"Right. What is evil in Haarlem in the Netherlands? Is that why he was killed? And why would Haarlem in the Netherlands be important to both of you? Or is he saying *you* are evil?"

The blood drained from Cart's face. Why would James warn him about Haarlem? He had seriously thought about flying there earlier in the week when he and James had discussed the tile over the phone.

He thought about Charlotte at the funeral, what she said about going to the source to free her, to find the key to her world. Of course, it was clear to him now that he thought about it. The source of the tile was Haarlem. That was where he had to go. He decided he had to talk to Charlotte, though he'd treated her poorly at the funeral. He had to get Collins out of the house so he could speak to her.

He rose shakily to his feet, leaning on the table.

"Are you okay, Mr. Benson?" Collins asked. "You don't look so good."

"I'm not sure," Cart said. "Look, I don't know why he left that message, and I didn't leave a coconut on his desk. I can't help you with this, and you're right, I'm not feeling well. It's been a rough week. I need to lie down. Would you mind seeing yourself out?"

"I'd rather stay and talk with you," Collins said. "I have a lot of unanswered questions. You seemed fine when you first let me in, and now you're all nervous about something. Did you know you're sweating?"

Cart touched his temple, feeling the wetness. His mind was racing. *Why won't this man leave? I have to call Charlotte, get going, keep moving.*

"I have to admit, I think you're guilty as hell, Mr. Benson, in both the disappearance of your daughter and the death of Phillips, although I have no evidence of either." He walked toward the table, eyeing Cart. "You're hiding something from me. I can taste it. I can smell it on you like the stench of a landfill." He was a foot from Cart, leaning into him, staring at him with those hard, obsidian eyes. His breath was humid and smelled faintly of garlic. "I will take you down, Mr. Benson; I promise you that. And I always, *always* keep my promises."

Cart surrendered right then. There was no point trying to go on like this. There was nowhere to turn; he couldn't run off to Haarlem

CHAPTER 22

with Collins dogging his every step. He looked at Collins, making his decision. He felt his heart rate go down.

"You're right, Detective Collins," he said evenly, "I am hiding something."

The detective's face hovering near his went blank. "You are?" he asked, stunned.

Cart nodded, relieved to have someone to share this with, whatever the consequences. Despite the man's natural cynicism, Cart felt he was honest and sincere. He had to trust him. He had no choice.

"Sit down, Will," he said quietly. "I have something to tell you...."

CHAPTER 23

Annie had come home, joining them as they climbed the stairs. They watched as Collins inspected the tile.

Of course, he didn't believe them, insinuating they were either making it up to cover the actual situation, or they were crazy. Why would anyone believe such a ridiculous tale? Cart didn't blame him.

When Collins touched the tile, he'd jerked his hand back and stared at the blue-and-white tile. He thought it was an electrical short behind the wall, telegraphing through the tile. He was sure there had to be a reasonable explanation.

"You're sure no one put this in? Like, when you weren't here?" he asked. He maintained his disbelief even after reassuring Collins they hadn't gone anywhere since James's funeral.

In the end, it was Annie who convinced him.

He slowly moved toward the bedroom door, carefully trying to extract himself from them without offending them. Annie stopped him, looking into his dark, disbelieving eyes.

"Have you ever lost someone close to you?" she asked softly.

He shifted his gaze from the sun glaring on the snow outside. "I don't talk about my private life," he said, his voice a deep rumble.

"When Sarah was born," she continued, ignoring his reluctance, "I thought nothing was more beautiful in the world; her tiny nose and eyebrows, the way she just knew how to nurse, learned how to sleep. Everything about her was like a little angel wrapped herself around my world. When she grasped my finger in her little hand, I knew everything I'd ever wanted was true. She was my baby, my little angel. I swore right then I'd do anything to protect her. I'd even die for her if I had to.

"Do you remember when your first was born?"

He continued staring out the window, but Cart saw him clenching his fists, his shoulders bunching.

"When Sarah disappeared, I thought I was going to die. My baby was gone. I thought I'd never see her again. My heart was breaking, and I wanted to die. I was so sad. Then we saw this...." She looked at the tile, shining eyes reflecting the fire's glow. "She was near me the whole time, but we didn't know it.

"If there's any chance, *any* chance at all, that we can bring her home, we have to try. We have to *try*."

Collins turned his face to her as she spoke and stared into Annie's eyes, his brow furrowed like a fist over his dark eyes.

"Wouldn't you do the same?" she asked.

Collins bent and traced the outline of the tile, careful not to touch it. He was silent for a long time, just looking.

He stood and looked at Annie.

"What can I do to help?" he asked gently.

* * *

CHAPTER 23

Sitting around the table, they decided the most important thing was to get Cart to the airport without anyone noticing. They didn't need a parade or reporters in cars and vans following them. Getting into the airport would be a problem, as well.

"What about James's warning?" Collins asked. "Aren't you worried about that?"

Cart had thought a lot about that note. "I don't know what he meant by that," he said. "James never got a chance to tell me what else he may have found out besides what he'd told me earlier. I just know I have to go to Haarlem. I don't know the name of the antique shop there, but we can probably find some receipts with it. Before I go, I need to talk to Charlotte Delconto to see if she can tell me more. And I need to do some research about where I'm going." He looked at Collins. "What about the investigation?"

"I'll take care of that," he said. "I can stall things for a few days while you're gone. When do you want to do this?"

"I'd like to leave tomorrow if I can," Cart said. "The sooner I get there, the better. Annie can start looking for the name for the shop while I see if Charlotte will talk to me."

"Well," Collins said, and chuckled, "I have to say, I never thought I'd be conspiring to get someone out of town under the cloak of darkness. I feel like Nick Fury, only fatter."

They all laughed.

Collins put his coat on, pausing to look at Annie. "We'll get her back, Annie," he said, squeezing her shoulder.

Cart waited for him under the dimmed glow of the chandelier in the foyer.

"You know," Collins said as he stood by him, "I'm not entirely convinced of this whole thing, although I don't doubt *some*thing is happening with that tile. I'm willing to give you the benefit of the doubt. I want you to get your daughter back; that's the whole purpose of my job, hard as it is sometimes—that and give justice to victims." He eyed Cart. "If that means having you go to Holland to find some magic key, that's what it'll take." He looked out the narrow side window next to the door. "If you don't return with your girl, I'll look you up again. I'm giving you this chance because your wife believes it, even if I don't fully. You need to know that. So, go and do your best."

Cart stuck out his hand, and Collins took it in a grip that could have broken Cart's fingers had he wanted to.

"Thank you, Will. That's all I ask."

CHAPTER 24

Cart shouldered his way past the reporter, grumbling as he ignored the man's questions. It was hard to ditch the reporters who followed him. But he'd left them all behind, except for the one that followed him to the florist's door. Climbing back into his car after his purchase, he noticed the reporter following him at a respectful distance.

Twenty minutes later, he pulled in front of a house in the lower avenues of the foothills on the city's north side, below the state capitol building. It was a small, white-and-blue Craftsman-style bungalow, neat and well cared for, with winter-bared hedges and rose bushes lining the front of the home. A small sign in the front yard read:

PSYCHIC
Tarot cards - Readings - Spiritualist

Her phone number and website were listed below, so she must be reasonably modern.

As he got out of the car, he noticed the reporter sitting in his car up the street, holding a camera to his eye. Shaking his head, Cart walked onto the wooden porch and rang the doorbell, feeling nervous like a jittery sixteen-year-old arriving to pick up his first date. He heard footsteps on a hardwood floor, then the jangle of a key in a lock. The door cracked a few inches, and Charlotte's sister, Amelia, peered out at him through a pair of red-rimmed reading glasses.

"Yes?" she asked. "How may I help you?" Then she recognized him and opened the door wide.

"Mr. Benson, please come in, come in...." She seemed genuinely pleased to see him. "I don't suppose those are for me?" she smiled, eyeing the roses.

"Um, hi. Is Charlotte available?" he asked nervously.

She led him into a small sitting room just off the entryway, ensuring he was comfortable on the floral couch. She bent and whispered in his ear. "She wants to see you. Don't let her fool you!" Then she was gone, the faint scent of lilacs lingering in the room.

The room was spotless; the walls were a subtle shade of powder blue, if he remembered James's color samples correctly. Beautiful tiger oak trimmed the door and windows, and the baseboards were also oak.

Handmade Persian rugs laid on the hardwood floor, with unique patterns that drew his eye, but he had to look away from the faces he kept seeing in the patterns. The room smelled of wood polish, and the woodwork gleamed in the sunlight streaming through the window.

Footsteps approached from the hallway, and Charlotte entered the room. She had her long hair pulled into a ponytail and wore a long-sleeved beige shirt with the sleeves rolled to her elbows, a pair of old denim jeans, and some worn slippers. She wore no makeup except for the painted-on eyebrows, one of which raised as she looked at him skeptically. He immediately stood and was surprised at how different

CHAPTER 24

she looked today. He'd only seen her in less than favorable conditions at home and at the funeral.

"Uh, these are for you," he said awkwardly, holding out the roses.

"Why?" she asked.

He cleared his throat. *Why did he always feel so uncomfortable with Charlotte?*

"I wanted to apologize," he said, "about how I treated you at James's funeral. I can be pretty pig-headed sometimes. It was wrong of me, but I was reacting to your treatment of me. It seems you don't like me very much."

"It's not that I don't like you," she said, "it's that you're an enigma to me. You're a man who has everything he could want. You take things for granted, like you deserve them. I know you've earned it all through hard work. I know it couldn't have been easy. But somewhere along the way, you lost some of your humanity.

"We're all here by the grace of God," she said firmly. "I know the bitterness of loneliness and loss, through no fault of my own, but it's a valuable aspect of my life that helped shape who I am today. Your loneliness is self-imposed, though. Being self-absorbed to the point of arrogance, you fail to see the goodness and beauty in your life."

"I've heard all this before," he mumbled, looking at the floor.

"No doubt," she said, "but you fail to act on it. You keep blundering through life, like a bull in a china shop, to borrow an over-used but apt cliché. I think you're a good and decent man. You've just forgotten that you are."

"These past few weeks have taught me a lot," he said, "and I'm sorry about the conversation we had at James's funeral."

"Conversation? Is that what that was?" She laughed. Her eyes softened. "I know this is hard. Things like this are never easy for you. You don't like to lose control of a situation or feel like a fool." She sat beside him, taking the roses and smelling them. "Well, then, apology accepted. Thank you. These are beautiful, Cart. Let me put them in some water, and I'll be right back." She left him speechless on the couch. He amazed at how good he felt now.

"When are you leaving?" she asked when she returned.

"I was hoping tomorrow," he said. "I need to get back home to book a flight. I don't know what to do once I get there. I wanted to talk to you before I leave to see if you have more information. What you said at the funeral was rather cryptic, to say the least."

"It wasn't the place to talk about it, you were right." She settled back onto the couch. "I wanted to tell you the depth of my dream, so I'm glad you came here today. It wasn't a dream as you'd expect. It was more like a jumble of feelings and urges. It's like looking through a keyhole from inside a dark closet—very brief glimpses of things and a narrow view. I can't open the door, but if I rattle the doorknob, it changes my perspective, altering my insight.

"An ancient power surrounds Sarah, and it won't give her up easily. It holds the lock to its world, and finding the key is the only way to bring her back." She took a drink of water. "These tiles were made in Holland in the seventeenth century, correct?"

Cart nodded. "Mid-century sometime, we think."

"That's where you need to start. Try to find precisely where the tile was made and by whom. I'm sorry. I don't know enough about Dutch history to help you. That's all I can tell you, I'm afraid."

CHAPTER 24

"I'll research as much as possible when I get home. I'm unsure how much I'll find, but I've got to try."

Charlotte stood, her bones creaking. "You'd best get on your way so you can get started." She hugged him at the door. "Good luck. Be careful. Bring Sarah home."

CHAPTER 25

Annie got Cart a flight out of Salt Lake at 5:15 a.m., with a two-hour layover in New York. He'd land in Amsterdam about 7:30 a.m., Dutch time, or about 11:30 p.m. here at home. He knew he'd be exhausted by the flight over, so he'd try to sleep as much as he could in the air.

Collins would pick him up at home at 3:30 a.m. and have him lie on the car floor while driving out of the gate. Nobody would follow Collins. The policeman in the car and any reporters would think he had some business with the Bensons that couldn't wait. Collins wasn't a story to the reporters, so they ignored him.

Annie had found the shop's name in a file of receipts in her office: *"Aniek uit de Gouden Eeuw,"* or "Golden Age Antiques," as the translated version said. The shop was on the Grote Houtstraat, a street leading to the center of the Old City.

In his office, he entered "Haarlem History" in the search engine and got nearly a million hits.

He discovered that Haarlem had a rich and varied history, beginning in pre-medieval times as an agricultural center for peat. He remembered from history class that most medieval countries drank beer or whey to avoid sickness from the water. In the 1400s, beer production became an institution until the canals became too polluted for use, shutting down most of the breweries until a cleaner water source was found. By the 1600s, the Dutch Republic of the Netherlands was the most powerful country on Earth due to the trading and wealth of the Dutch East India Company, which controlled the trade routes to the Far East, especially Indonesia, which meant immense wealth for a relative few. The Dutch navy was the most powerful on Earth then, which he hadn't known.

During this time, Holland's "Golden Age" flourished, with the wealthy demanding the finest in art and riches, and produced many famous artists, including Franz Hal and Rembrandt. The Dutch economy collapsed in the late 1600s, and Haarlem became one of the poorest Dutch states, never recovering like the rest of the nation. It is mainly known now for pharmaceutical companies and tulips.

There was an interesting sidenote about tulips.

During the Golden Age, tulips became quite a fad, and bidding wars amongst wealthy speculators raised the price of tulip bulbs to ridiculous heights.

The source said that one single "Semper Augustus" bulb sold at the time for 10,000 Florins, the monetary equivalent of roughly twenty-three tons of cheese, or enough to fill a house back then. It didn't specify what kind of cheese, but Cart had tasted enough cheese to be glad their home wasn't filled with it. Not only would it stink, but there would also be no place to sleep.

The city celebrated its 775th anniversary in 2022.

Next, he plugged in the History of Delft Blue Tile.

CHAPTER 25

Although pottery had been made for hundreds of years in Europe, it wasn't until the late 1500s that the Dutch became fascinated by the beautiful porcelain imported from China. Being the industrious people they were, they set about copying it.

From the mid-1500s to the late 1600s, as many as thirty factories produced distinctive blue-on-white tiles. Builders used the tile in kitchens, around fireplaces, baseboards, and for waterproofing, among many other uses. The city of Delft, from which the tile took its name, was the most famous of the towns, and a few original factories survived, still producing tile in much the same way as in the early days.

Thanks to the Internet, he knew much more now than before. At least it was something to start with.

He printed out the information he needed and went to show Annie.

* * *

Collins was there at 3:30 a.m., waiting in his car with the garage door closed. They all thought having him park in the closed garage would be better then having Cart walk out to his car in clear view of any reporters who might be out at this time. The night was clear and cold, hovering near twelve degrees Fahrenheit.

Annie held him tightly, trying to be strong. She was afraid—afraid for him and herself to be without him. He whispered strength to her, reminding her of her courage and independence. He also took resolve from her, depending on her to keep herself and Maddy safe while he was gone. They knew he had to go, but it didn't make it any easier.

She gave him one last fierce hug and let him go, standing by the door while he stashed his bag in the trunk and climbed into the backseat, blowing her a kiss before lying on the floor. Collins smiled encouragingly at her, giving her a thumbs up.

She opened the garage door, and they pulled out, leaving her alone in the house.

* * *

The house was empty now except for herself—as quiet as a tomb. She saw Cart's cereal bowl in the dimmed kitchen light by the sink. She leaned against the fridge, fighting the tears swimming in her eyes.

She was terrified not by the darkness or the lonely stillness, but more that it would remain that way forever. Having him leave her at a time like this was the hardest thing she'd ever done. If he didn't come back with Sarah, or if *he* didn't come back . . .

But that was too much to consider. Annie knew she couldn't live here with the silence gnawing at her thoughts. She'd decided to stay at her mother's house while he was gone, missing Maddy's exuberance and loving personality. She also knew she was obsessed with the tile. It would be good to get away from it and the house. She turned out the light and went upstairs, knowing she'd cry when she got there.

* * *

"Morning," Collins said when Cart climbed into the car. "Keep your head down and put that blanket over you until I say to sit up. I have to talk to my guy before I leave."

Cart drew the blanket tighter around himself, careful not to make a sound. Collins backed out of the garage, waiting to make sure it closed,

CHAPTER 25

and turned toward the gate, then paused and rolled his window down. Cold air crept in, flowing down the door panel.

"How's it going, Hamblin?" Collins asked.

"Doing okay, sir," a muffled voice answered. "Quiet and cold. Same old, same old. Everything okay inside?"

"Yeah," Collins said, "just having a rough night, is all. That coffee keeping you warm?"

"Sure is," the officer said. "Thanks for bringing it."

"Hey, anything I can do to help, you know. Well, keep your heater running. I gotta go."

"Thanks, Detective," Hamblin said. "See you later."

The window rolled up, and Collins pulled onto the street.

"Stay down for a while yet," Collins said. "There's only one news van out here, but I'll pull over as soon as possible so you can get in front."

The ride to the airport was uneventful. Collins asked Cart how he and Annie met, then shared the same regarding his wife.

"We met in high school up in Boise," he said. "At first, she didn't like me because I was a jock. She was smart, taking AP classes; Alicia's way smarter than I am. Her dad's a minister, and her mom's a psychologist. They frowned on their little girl getting mixed up with a dumb football player. We got married after we graduated. She was eighteen, and I was nineteen. We went to school down here at the Uiversity of Utah. She got her degree in physical therapy, and I got mine in criminal psychology, which endeared me to her mom. Not sure her dad ever approved."

"You bucked the odds, though, didn't you? Most early marriages don't last."

"Yeah," Collins said, "we've had our problems over the years, but nothing we couldn't overcome. She's always been my best friend. I can't imagine life without her."

"I feel the same about Annie," Cart said. His throat tightened at the thought of her alone in the house.

They spent the rest of the drive in silence.

He took his bag from the trunk when Collins pulled into the drop-off zone at the airport, and they both got out. He shook hands with the big detective.

"Thanks, Will," Cart said. "We'll never forget your help with this."

Collins seemed embarrassed by this. "Hey, just glad I could help. You be careful, Cart. And get your daughter back. Don't worry about your family. I'll keep an eye on them while you're gone. See you around." Collins started climbing back into the car, but Cart hugged him awkwardly.

"Thank you, my friend," he said.

He watched the car pull away from the curb, feeling a surge of affection for the man. He was going out on a limb for them, possibly jeopardizing his career. Yet, here he was all the same. Cart wondered if he'd do the same.

The airport was surprisingly busy at this hour, but he sailed through security with his first-class status. The security guard at the first checkpoint looked at his passport and license, then eyed him curiously. He said nothing, so Cart walked past him to the next checkpoint.

While waiting to board the plane, he called Annie, knowing she couldn't sleep. He could tell she'd been crying, so he told her again how

CHAPTER 25

much he loved her. She'd cleaned the house to stay busy. He smiled, knowing that she would be doing just that.

They called for first class to board the plane, so he clicked off with reassurances of love and concern. He entered the breezeway leading into the aircraft and the long flight to Amsterdam.

CHAPTER 26

Sarah

She woke with a horrible headache, and the sunlight stabbed into her closed eyes. She remembered being sick when it was so cold during the night. It must have been because she was so angry at her dad. What an awful night that was! She'd never screamed at him like that before, and she regretted it. He was probably at work now, so she'd have to call to apologize to him or wait until he got home. Then she remembered her bedroom window faced north so there'd be no sunlight in her room.

She opened her eyes but shielded them with her hand because it was so bright. She stared at the wall across from her. It wasn't the wall in her bedroom, but an ugly, bumpy white wall with an old wooden chair next to a table in front of it. There was no desk and no closet.

This was not her room.

She tried sitting up, but pain lanced her head, and she laid back down. She wasn't in her bed, but a lumpy, straw-filled thing. The blanket was rough and scratchy, and the pillow was bumpy and smelly. She threw them as far from her as she could, drawing her legs up to her chest, wrapping her arms around them, and looking around the room.

The room had only one window, and it was all wavy, looking like it had melted. The wooden table sat under the window, and a pitcher and bowl with blue-and-white designs sat on it. The floor was wood, not the soft carpet in her room. There weren't painted boards along the bottom of the walls but pieces of blue-and-white tile like the ones around her parents' fireplace, only without cracks or chips. The door was heavy wood and was closed.

This room looked like it belonged to some old pioneer house, like the ones they visited at the heritage park by the zoo, where there were a bunch of old houses, and people dressed up like pioneers pretending they lived there.

Where was she, and why had her parents brought her here? And if they had, it had been snowing last night, so why wasn't it cold now? Her chest tightened as she began to panic. Her tongue felt dry, and she was thirsty. Was it a joke? Because if it was, it was definitely *not* funny!

She looked around for clothes, but there weren't any, just the lounging pants and tee shirt she wore as pajamas that her dad had given her after he had run a 10K race. If she could find her clothes, she'd put them on and get out of this room because if they thought they would punish her for last night by leaving her here, they were wrong!

"Mom? Dad?' she shouted. No one answered her, so she repeated it louder. Still no answer.

She cautiously put a foot out onto the wooden floor, feeling the rough surface on her bare feet. When she stood fully, she had to put a hand on her head because the pain was bad. She was dizzy, so she

CHAPTER 26

leaned back against the bed. It improved after a minute, and then she quietly walked toward the window. The floor was cold, unlike at home, where all the floors had built-in heat.

There was no crank to open the window, and she couldn't see how to open it. She pulled up on the bottom section of the window, and it moved slightly. She pulled harder, and it slid up a few inches more, then stopped.

She knelt and put her nose next to the space and felt a cool draft coming in. She heard sounds, too, animal sounds—was that a cow mooing? She heard little bells jingling and the baa of goats or sheep.

Shapes appeared distorted through the wavy window, like trying to look through a window with rain on it. Peeking through the space at the bottom, she saw she was on the second floor of whatever this place was. The ground was flat as a wooden floor, not on a hill like the heritage park they'd visited. There was a dirt road in front of the building and a slow-moving river next to the road. A wooden bridge about as wide as a car crossed the river, and on the opposite side was an enormous field of flowers growing as far as she could see. In the distance was a clump of trees, tall and green, and some trees along the river on this side, too. There was another building to the left, but she couldn't see much of it, except that it was tall.

Everything was green, like some park—greener than anything she'd ever seen. The sky was blue like springtime, and there wasn't any snow.

She heard a low rumble of voices below her—downstairs? It was probably her mom and dad laughing about the joke they played on her. They could laugh all they wanted because she would tell them how mad she was when she got downstairs, even if it made *them* angry.

She swung the door open quickly, noiselessly, revealing a narrow hallway. There were a couple of doors, but they were both shut, and there were no windows, so it was not very bright. Stairs going down were at the end of the hall.

She stepped carefully into the hallway, listening. The voices were louder now, but she still couldn't understand them. It was a man and a woman talking, and the closer to the stairs she got, the angrier she became.

They were in for a big surprise if they thought she was upset last night!

Halfway down the stairs, she froze. It was not her parents talking; it was someone else, and they weren't speaking English.

She slid quietly to the wall, putting her back against it, her heart beating so fast, it felt like it would jump out of her. What was going on? Where had her parents taken her? And what language were the people speaking? It sounded like gibberish to her, all throaty and thick like they were gargling.

She moved slowly down a few more steps until she was at the bottom, slowly leaning to peek around the corner when she heard a baby cry out. She listened to the woman make cooing and shushing sounds, and the baby stopped fussing. She rested against the wall. She took a big breath and did the bravest thing she'd ever done. She stepped into the room.

Sitting at a wooden table in what must have been a kitchen sat a woman nursing a baby, and a little boy about six or so eating something from a plate. There was an assortment of dishes and a pitcher on the table, made of the same blue-and-white pottery as upstairs. A

CHAPTER 26

large fireplace covered with the same blue-and-white tiles around the upstairs floor held a fire burning, and a man stood beside it with his foot on a stool, smoking a long, skinny pipe.

They were all dressed in weird clothes, like from a play, because she'd never seen anything like them, really old fashioned, so this must be a heritage park of some sort, like she thought, except it wasn't the pioneer one by their house.

A large, black dog lying next to the table stood up, staring intently at her, ears pricked forward.

"Where are my mom and dad?" she asked nervously.

The woman covered herself and stood up, smiling at her. Everyone in the room stopped what they were doing and stared. The little boy stared wide-eyed at her, wooden spoon frozen halfway to his mouth.

"*U bent wakker, dochter,*" the woman said, walking toward her. "*Hoe voel je je?*"

Her head swam. "What?" she asked, puzzled. "What are you saying? Where are my parents?" She saw the door standing open to the outside, beckoning her. She bolted for the door, but the man was very fast and caught her firmly. She screamed and tried to pull away, struggling against him, but he was too strong. She kicked his shin while she resisted, but he jerked her tighter and growled, "*Stop dit. Je maakt de kinderen bang!*"

The little boy was cowering behind the woman's skirts, and the baby was crying. The woman gave the baby to the boy, who went and sat by the fireplace, intensely watching them. The woman approached Sarah and gently ran a hand through her hair. She tried to pull away from her touch but couldn't.

"*Shh, kind,*" the woman said softly, her eyes tender. "*Shh, je zult je snel beter vorlen, shh. . . .*"

Sarah felt like screaming at the top of her lungs for someone to help her, maybe people outside touring the park or insane asylum or whatever this place was. She opened her mouth to do just that, but the man clamped his hand over it. She bit his hand, and he jerked it away with what sounded like a curse. "*Genoeg van deze onzin!*" he said, shaking her lightly. "*Eindig nu of ik sluit je in op in de slaapkamer!*" His white teeth were clenched through his goatee, his black brows bristling.

"*Echtgenoot, ze is bang!*" the woman said crossly to him. "*Zacht ben!*" Sarah stared wildly at the woman, trying to make sense of everything. She looked kindly at Sarah, her long, blonde hair tucked under her white cap, smiling with white teeth and gentle blue eyes.

"*Laat me Haar nemen,*" the woman said to the man. "*Ze wil haar moeder.*" The man looked at Sarah, frowning, and then back at the woman, his dark eyes softening as he looked at her.

"*Zeer goed.*" His grip loosened on Sarah, and she stepped back from him, rubbing her arm.

"*Als ze weer schreeuwt, bring ik haar naar naar slaapkamer.*" The woman put a protective arm around Sarah, drawing her away from him, taking her to the table, pulling out a chair, and gesturing for her to sit down. The boy looked anxiously at them, holding the baby tightly.

Sarah hugged herself similarly tightly, ready to start crying. Maybe if she cried they'd get scared about holding her captive and let her go. The man stayed by the door, arms folded while he watched her, blocking that route, so escaping that way was out of the question.

CHAPTER 26

"*Heb je honger, kind?*" the woman asked, placing a plate of fish and cheese in front of her, a large hunk of brown bread hanging off the side. Sarah pushed the dish away, shaking her head. Her eyes were watering, and a huge lump formed in her throat. The last thing she wanted to do was eat, especially fish, and especially fish that smelled like this.

"Where's my mom and dad?" she asked as a tear rolled down her cheek. The woman sat down next to her, hugging her. "Why don't you speak English?" Sarah asked her. "I can't understand you. I want to go home...."

The woman rocked her gently back and forth, humming a tune she didn't recognize. She seemed gentle and kind, but why was she doing this if she was? Why wouldn't she let her leave so she could go home? She thought of her mom, dad, and Maddy and began to cry in earnest, sobbing uncontrollably while the woman rocked her, crooning some unintelligible song.

"*Ze kan onze woorden niet begripjen. Kun jij haar helpen ons te begrijpen?*" the woman asked the man, Sarah's head on her shoulder. Then Sarah she sat up. She could almost understand some words. But there were too many consonants, like it was a joke language they'd made up to confuse her.

She had started to panic again, wondering how she could get out of there, make them stop babbling, when the man walked over to her, licking his forefinger and pushing it wetly against her forehead, rocking her back a little. It felt wet and sticky, and she rubbed at it with her arm.

"Ewww! Why did you do that?" she demanded. The man laughed as he returned to the door.

"It's not funny!" she shouted. "How would you like it if I wiped spit on you?"

"Come and try it," the man said. "You won't get far!"

The woman laughed.

"It's going to make my forehead stink," she began. She stopped and stared at the man. "Wait, what did you say?"

"I said come and try it." He bent over, pointing at his forehead. "Here it is!"

"Why are you speaking English now?" she asked, her eyes narrowed. "Why didn't you speak it earlier?"

"I'm not speaking English," the man said. "Why would I speak that filthy tongue?" His teeth were white and perfectly straight, like the woman's.

"I don't understand...." she said.

"Do I need to wipe spit on you again?" he asked.

"No!" she said sternly. "I don't think it'll ever wash off as it is!"

The man laughed again, and the boy joined in.

The woman smiled.

Sarah whirled on the boy. "What's so funny?" she said, eyes blazing.

"You are," said the boy. "You're funny when you're angry!"

"Who are you people?" Sarah demanded, glaring at all of them. "Where is my family? You don't have any right to keep me here. I have to go to school! I have to go home!" She stood abruptly, knocking her chair over loudly, and backed to the fireplace where she could see all of them. The dog trotted to the woman, standing before her and growling.

"No, Nico," said the woman, pointing at the floor. "Down." Nico laid down but kept his head up watching Sarah.

CHAPTER 26

"Woman," said the man, "control your daughter before I have to." His face and voice were stern.

For the first time, Sarah noticed his eyes: They were completely black, shiny like a beetle carapace, with no whites or pupils. It frightened her.

The woman hurried to her side. "Please," she said soothingly. "I know you don't understand what's happening, but please calm down. You'll feel better in a while." She reached for her, but Sarah batted her arms away, scurrying from her touch.

"No!" she shouted. "Are you all insane? Let me go! I won't tell anyone! Please let me go!" she pleaded, sobbing again, terror clawing at her thoughts with cold hands. "I want my mom and dad!"

Sarah shoved the woman away, seizing the bread knife, and waving it at her.

"Stay away from me!" she screamed. "Stay away!" The woman was almost within reach, her blue eyes concerned. Sarah thrust the knife at the woman through blinding tears, but the kitchen blurred and tilted; her mind was spinning wildly. Then she was back in the room she woke up in, alone and without the knife.

She ran to the door, but it wouldn't open, though she tried with all her might. The window wouldn't open, either, so she took the pitcher from the table and hit the window as hard as she could. The broken glass and shattered pitcher fell to the table and floor. Heedless of the sharp, jagged edges of the glass, she stuck her head out the window and tried to scream, but she couldn't make a sound, not even a grunt.

She climbed up on the table, breaking the remaining shards of glass out, leaving a smear of blood from a cut she received, and put one leg outside it. When the room tipped suddenly, she thought she would fall out. Then she was in bed, the scratchy blanket over her, unable to move or scream. She was so tired, and she couldn't keep her eyes open. . . .

CHAPTER 27

Thunder rumbled outside, shaking the house. Rain clattered on the roof and slapped against the windows. Lightning suddenly flashed outside the window, startling Sarah, followed quickly by the crack of thunder. She was still unable to move, lying in the lumpy bed with the scratchy blanket pulled to her chin, and someone had plumped a pillow under her head.

Although she couldn't move even her fingers, her mind worked just fine. She could also move her eyes. Looking around as best she could, she saw someone had fixed the broken window, so they must have had a repairman in while she slept. And a new pitcher and bowl like the broken ones sat on the table.

Why was this happening to her? She couldn't think of anything she'd done that would have made her parents abandon her here. She wanted to go home. A tear trickled down her temple.

The bedroom door opened, and the woman came in carrying a neatly folded pile of clothes. When she saw Sarah looking at her, she smiled, laying the clothes on the bed and moving the chair near her, where she sat on it and tenderly touched Sarah's cheek.

"He told me you were awake," she said kindly, her blue eyes shining. "I wanted to come up earlier, but he wanted you to sleep so you could adjust to your new surroundings. I know this is hard to understand, daughter; I know how that feels."

Sarah was concerned about the word "daughter." What was this woman talking about? They must have somehow taken her from her house, but how had they gotten in? They all must be crazy: the man, the woman, the boy, and maybe even the baby and the dog! They had a security system, and nobody but their family knew the passcode. Anyway, her dad would have heard them and stopped them, unless he had been the one who brought her here. She'd heard of places where parents dropped off troubled teens, lockdown places where the kids supposedly got help with their problems. But those places were modern, like a school, not an old house in some kind of park. Was that where she was? That would explain a lot. Make her shape up for screaming at her dad? That didn't seem like a bad enough offense to leave her here. They had a lot of explaining to do, if she ever saw them again.

The woman ran her fingers gently through Sarah's hair. Sarah tried to pull from her touch but couldn't.

The woman poured water from the pitcher into the bowl, took a white cloth from a pocket in her apron, and put it in the bowl. Wringing it out, she returned and gently wiped off Sarah's face. The cloth was cool against her skin. She closed her eyes, feeling the delicate touch relax her.

"I know you have many questions," the woman said while wiping off Sarah's tears. "I'll try to answer as many as possible as best I can.

CHAPTER 27

What happened to you isn't very clear, and I know this because I had the same questions." She glanced at the door. "If you promise to behave yourself, I'll have him Unbind you so you can talk and move. But you have to promise. If you threaten me in any way or try to hurt yourself, he'll Bind you again. Do you understand?"

Of course, Sarah couldn't answer, so she quickly blinked a few times to let the woman know she understood. The woman seemed content with that because she smiled broadly, nodding, then stared at the door for a few seconds.

"Very well, then," the woman said, looking at her again. "Are you feeling ill?"

"No," Sarah said automatically, startled that she could talk. She moved her arms and legs, her hands, and her head. It felt normal, not numb, as if they'd been asleep. She cast off the blanket and sat up, leaning against the wall behind her. She felt sweaty, like she'd had a bad dream, hair plastered to her head.

"Where am I?" she asked the woman.

"You are here," she replied.

"I know that, but where is 'here'?"

"This is where we live," said the woman. "This is where you live."

"I don't live here," Sarah said, puzzled. "I live in Salt Lake."

Now the woman looked puzzled. "Salt Lake? What is Salt Lake?"

Was this woman stupid or something?

"Salt Lake City, Utah," Sarah said, growing frustrated. "You know, here."

"This is not Salt Lake City, Utah, whatever that is," the woman frowned. "I haven't heard of that place. Is that where he took you from?"

"Where who took me from?" Sarah was getting more confused.

"My husband. Your father," she replied.

"Is this a sick joke? Why am I here? Are we in a park of some kind? Are you guys actors? Why did you take me from my home? My father is a lawyer, and you will so be in trouble when he finds out what you did. He's the best lawyer there is."

The woman seemed unconcerned. "He can't find you here. No one can."

"Oh, you don't know my dad!"

The woman looked at her, eyes narrowed. "What year is this?" she suddenly asked.

Sarah frowned. The woman didn't seem stupid, and she talked with intelligence. She told her the year.

She stared at Sarah, blue eyes wide. Her hand was at her mouth, tears welling in her eyes. "How can that be?" she whispered. "Dear Lord, it can't have been that long...." A tear slid down her face.

"What's wrong?" Sarah asked hesitantly. "What do you mean?"

The woman walked to the window, gazing out the distorted panes. Sarah didn't understand how the woman saw anything through the mixture of rain and wavy glass. She was upset; Sarah saw her chest heaving as she tried to control her emotions.

Sarah walked over to her, the wood cool on her feet. Why was the woman acting like this? Sarah felt concerned for her, even if she was

CHAPTER 27

part of the group that brought her here. The woman had been nothing but kind to her. Maybe she could talk the woman into letting her go?

"What's the matter?" Sarah asked. "Can I help you somehow?"

The woman faced her. Her eyes looked haunted and distant. "We've been here for nearly four hundred years...."

Now Sarah knew for sure these people were crazy.

She was stuck in a weird house with lunatics, with no way out or to call home. She'd heard about people like this and seen movies about people who thought they were someone else, or lived in the woods like a pack of dogs. But this woman seemed so—*normal*—that she couldn't comprehend her saying this. She seemed gentle and caring, like her mom. But if she was, why was she making her stay here, and why was she talking like a crazy person? Now, more than ever, she had to leave before they used her as a sacrifice—or something worse.

The woman stirred, her breath misting the window.

"We were celebrating our new home," the woman began. "We had a large celebration; many people came. It was exciting with so many people I didn't even know laughing and enjoying themselves. But then they were gone, leaving my husband and me alone. The children were in bed, and the house was quiet. The dog whined like she was frightened, scratching at our bedroom door. My husband was snoring drunkenly and didn't hear a thing. I got up to see what was wrong with the dog when the room suddenly shifted and tipped like a ship in a storm. I thought I was going to fall, and I was so dizzy. My head spun like I had drunk too much, but I hadn't. I finally swooned, trying to catch the door as I fell. Then I fainted and knew nothing."

Sarah listened, frozen. The room had darkened as the storm suddenly increased its fury. Lightning flashed, startling her and throwing harsh shadows around the room, casting the woman in silhouette. Thunder boomed, raising the hair on Sarah's neck, but the woman didn't move or even step away from the window.

"When I awakened," she continued, "I was much like you were, disoriented and very ill. My children were in the room with the dog and me, and all of us were ill. He came and cared for us, kept us warm and clean, and fed us. I was confused and frightened like you.

"He calmed me, assured me of his goodwill. We eventually came to accept him. My other husband was cruel and wicked. He did things best left unsaid. We were safe and free here from my former husband's cruelty and brutality. My husband is kind to us. I know he would not harm us—or you, for that matter. I know he cares for us. In time, I came to love him. For all intents and purposes, he is my husband now."

Sarah was captivated by the woman's story, true or not. "So, if what you say is true, where are we?"

"He brought us from a city called Haarlem in the Netherlands. Do you know of it?"

Sarah shook her head.

"It is a beautiful city, near the sea, with lovely buildings and a beautiful church on the town square. There are fields and fields of tulips in the springtime. And the smell of the tulips in bloom is wonderful. This place is like Holland but is not Holland."

Sarah wasn't sure what to believe. "What is it, then?" she asked. "If it isn't Holland, and it's not Salt Lake, what is it?" The more the woman talked, the less sense she made.

CHAPTER 27

"I don't know how to explain it. I know this isn't easy to believe; it isn't for me, even after all this time. You see, this is a place, yet not a place. My husband made this place, patterned after the memories of my home as a child. He wanted us to be happy here with him. I don't know how he did it, or where he came from. He is who he is."

"What are you saying?" Sarah asked, thoughts swirling. "This place is, like, make-believe, like a pretend Holland?"

"Oh, no," the woman replied, and smiled, "this place is as real as he wants it to be. It rains, like it is now, to water the fields and remind me of my home. When it is time for the rain to stop, it will stop. It is never cold here, like in Holland when winter comes. We never suffer."

"So, why am I here, then?" Sarah asked. "I don't come from Holland."

The woman looked out the rain-smeared window. When she looked back at Sarah, she had tears in her eyes. "When we first came here, I had a lovely daughter with beautiful long hair and a sweet smile. She was a joy to me." She tried to touch Sarah's face, but she flinched away. "She was much like you, strong-willed and self-confident, until my other husband broke her, but she flourished here."

"Where is she?" Sarah whispered.

"We were having our midday meal downstairs around the table. My daughter looked at me strangely, like she was getting ill. 'Mother . . .' she said, and then she disappeared as if she'd never existed. I reached for her, but it was too late.

"I was inconsolable. My precious daughter was gone. He searched for her in ways I don't understand, but she did not return. Our home seemed cold and empty without her. He knew I could never be happy here without her. I need to be a mother, to care for my children, and to nourish and teach them. He knew that, so he went fishing."

"Fishing?" Sarah asked. "What has that got to do with your daughter?"

"That is what he does. That is what he is: the Fisherman. That is how he found you, casting his net about, searching. You were unhappy, resentful, and angry. He saw you, cast his net, and took you, knowing that as he'd made me happy, he could do the same for you.

"You are our daughter now, to replace the one I lost."

She stepped back from the woman. "I'm not your daughter!" she shouted. "Why are you telling me these things? You're all crazy! I'm going home, and you can't stop me!" She lunged for the open door and then stopped, suddenly falling to the floor, landing on her side. She couldn't move or speak again.

"He does not allow shouting or disrespect," the woman said calmly. "You must learn to control yourself, and everything will be fine. You must understand something; the sooner you do, the better off you'll be, and the sooner he'll release you from the Binding: You are never going home to your Salt Lake. This place is your home until there are no tomorrows. I've been here for nearly four hundred years, apparently. Today is just the beginning for you.

"When he does Unbind you, get dressed, and come downstairs. I'll need your help with the children while I prepare the evening meal."

She left Sarah alone on the floor. The only part of her she could move were her eyes, blinking as tears flowed.

The rain stopped suddenly, and sunlight lit the room through the window.

CHAPTER 28

The clothing was hard to figure out.

There were several layers to the yellow corn-colored dress that made it fuller. The same colored blouse—or top, or whatever it was called—came to Sarah's throat and was topped by a white lace collar. The dress didn't have zippers or buttons but hooks that took a few minutes to understand. She also had a blue apron tied around her waist. Her stockings were wool and itched like crazy. Her shoes were wooden, shaped like boats with pointed toes, and decorated with bright colors. There was a scarf she didn't know what to do with that she gathered up and took with her. What else could she do? She clomped down the stairs in her uncomfortable wooden boat shoes.

She was starving. Her stomach had been growling for a while. She hoped they didn't have fish for lunch.

Maybe if she played along with them, she'd figure out how to get away. Maybe she could convince them to let her go. After her talk with the woman, she didn't know what to expect.

She was afraid of the man, the Fisherman. How had he paralyzed her as he'd done without touching her? Maybe he was like a witch doctor or something like that? Perhaps he had a little doll that looked like her that he carried with him and could cast spells or stick pins in it. She would have to be very careful around him.

The kitchen was warm and smelled like a campfire. A fire blazed in the fireplace, with hooks in the walls holding various sizes of black pots. The table had several familiar things to Sarah: wooden spoons, knives, blue-and-white bowls, plates, and pitchers. A loaf of dark brown bread sat on a wooden tray next to a circular wheel of cheese about the size of a dinner plate.

The baby sat on a blanket spread on the stone floor, playing with a little rag doll and some small wooden animals. The woman had her back to her, bent over something she was working on. She wore a blue scarf holding her hair away from her face, food, or both. The man and boy and the black dog were not in the room. The door stood open.

With the man and dog gone, she might sneak out, run away, or hide outside until dark. Or until someone walked past the house that would help her. Then she remembered the helpless feeling when she was "Bound," and it seemed like the man knew what was going on all the time, whether he was in the room or not, so that probably wouldn't work. She decided to wait until she had a better opportunity to maybe escape this loony bin, if she had patience. She cleared her throat, and the woman turned around, smiling.

"Are you feeling well, daughter?" the woman asked as she walked over to Sarah, drying her hands on her apron.

"I guess," Sarah said. "Where is everyone?"

"Your Father and Jacobus went to fetch wood. They should be back soon." She took something from her apron pocket. "Let me help you

CHAPTER 28

with your hair." The woman pinned Sarah's hair on top of her head, then wrapped the scarf around it so it looked like hers.

"What's your name?" Sarah asked. "What do I call you?"

"Well, my name is Katharina, but you may call me Mother." The woman smiled broadly.

Sarah frowned. "But..."

"You may call me Mother," the woman said, "and only Mother. Please do not argue about this. It will do you no good. My proper name is only for your Father to use. It is simple and easily remembered. I am Mother, and he is Father." She turned back to her meal preparation. "Now, please, Sophiia, take Willem while I finish our meal. He loves goats. Take him out to see them."

Sarah stood silently, glaring at the woman's back. "My name is—"

"NO!" the woman shouted, rounding on Sarah, who stepped back from her vehemence. "Your name is Sophiia, and you are my daughter. Do not forget that! Do you understand?"

Sarah stared open-mouthed at the woman.

"Do you understand?" the woman asked again.

Sarah was stunned by the woman's anger. From what she understood about insane people from movies and TV shows, you had to treat them carefully so they didn't kill you. The woman seemed very friendly earlier and had just changed to someone completely different. Sarah was getting more frightened now.

"Yes," Sarah said, carefully watching the woman.

"Yes, what?" the woman asked, anger still etched on her features.

Sarah had to think for a minute about how to respond. "Yes—Mother?"

"That is right," Mother said. "I'm glad we understand each other. Now, please take Willem outside."

Without another word, Mother went back to work. Sarah picked up the baby, who gurgled sweetly.

"Yes, Mother," Sarah said and obediently took him outside.

The sun was bright, and the sky was clear and blue like a robin's egg. The sun felt good on her face. It was good to be out of the stifling house with all the craziness that filled it. It also allowed her to look around the house and see things she couldn't see from the crack below her window.

Across from the house next to the river, a windmill stood. The big arms moved slowly around, the sails catching the wind that blew across the fields. She'd seen pictures of windmills in books and movies before, but never in person. She was amazed by how it worked. She wanted to go inside and watch the workings of it. Maybe another time when she didn't have the baby. The rhythmic creaking was soothing, along with the wind in her face.

She looked up the river to the right. In the distance, almost too far to see, was another house and windmill. Light smoke drifted from the house's chimney, and trees towered over the buildings. So there were other people here. That was a good thing. If the other people weren't part of this group and lived here, maybe she could run up there and ask for help. Her dad was rich, so perhaps if she promised them money, they'd help her. He'd be happy to pay to get her back.

Looking to the left down the road, she saw another house and windmill surrounded by many trees. She heard a dog barking in the distance. She was relieved that other people lived here. The man must

CHAPTER 28

have brought them here—oh, *Father*, she remembered. She had to be sure to call both of them by their proper names, as hard as that would be. She didn't want to feel threatened again.

Willem squirmed and grabbed her nose, tugging on it. She smiled, thinking of the many times Maddy had done that to her, and then she got sad thinking about her little sister. Would she ever see her again?

The animal pens were amazingly clean. One had several sheep, another had a couple of goats, and a cow gazed at them with big brown eyes in the last one. Willem was excited to see the animals, laughing and pointing at them. Willem loved touching them when they rubbed against the fence, probably hoping for a treat.

The cow was white with dark blue splotches on it. It was kind of cute, with long lashes around its big eyes, although its tongue was huge and green, slobber dripping from its mouth as it chewed. There were no flies, which Sarah thought was odd, and no bad smell. At her friend Emma's uncle's house, flies were everywhere, crawling on their faces and trying to get in her and the cow's eyes. But there were none here, which meant no drone from the buzzing flies, either.

"Sophiia!"

She turned to see "Father" and the little boy, Jacobus, walking toward her from the bridge. They each carried a load of wood, Jacobus struggling to hold his. The little boy watched her pensively as they drew near her.

"Are you enjoying the beautiful day?" the man asked. "How is my little Willem?" He didn't mention the Binding or apologize for placing her under it. He bent to kiss the baby on the top of his curly haired head. Willem giggled and reached for him.

"Not now, little one!" he said. "My hands are full!" He looked at Sarah. "Is Mother finished with our meal?"

The entirely black eyes creeped her out. Father must be so high on drugs that his dilated pupils swallowed all the color.

"Um, I don't know," she said. "I've been showing Willem the animals." She felt like his eyes were drilling into her brain.

"He does love animals!" Father laughed. "Well, let's go see, shall we? I'm so hungry I could eat the cow!"

The cow mooed and turned from the fence, walking to the back of the pen, where it stood staring at them.

It was strange enough that everyone had supposedly lived for almost 400 years in this fake Holland, so the idea that the cow could probably understand Father's desire to eat it didn't seem so peculiar. Sarah had begun to think nothing could surprise her here.

She followed Father and Jacobus to the house, removed her wooden shoes while they stacked the wood by the door, and then removed theirs. Sarah was unsure why she knew to do this, but accepted it as part of this new life.

She was surprised at how nice the kitchen looked. A cream-colored tablecloth covered the wooden tabletop. On it sat the oddest vase she'd ever seen. It was the same blue-and-white design as every piece of pottery in the house, but instead of just one large hole on top, it had several circular extensions at varying heights on the sides of it. It looked oriental, like different floors in a house, with two extensions on each of the four sides, each holding one tulip. A few tulips also extended from the top hole. It was pretty, and the scent of the tulips was pleasant. There were also candles lit around the room.

CHAPTER 28

Mother had set four plates at the table, with a small porcelain cup next to each. She took Willem from Sarah and put him in a highchair beside the table. Mother, Father, and Jacobus stood behind their chairs, looking expectantly at Sarah. She felt uncomfortable standing alone by the door with all of them staring at her, so she stood behind the chair Father indicated.

Father took the pitcher and poured a yellowish liquid into each cup, then picked his up and held it at arm's length. Mother and Jacobus did the same, looking at her expectantly. Apparently, she was supposed to do the same thing, so she did, feeling foolish.

"We have missed you, dear Sophiia," Father said, "and welcome you back to hearth and home. After a long absence, our daughter has come back." Sarah lowered her cup in protest, but Mother raised Sarah's elbow. The other three took a long drink from their cups, but Sarah didn't want to. What was the point of toasting their daughter, pretending Sarah was her? Father was staring at her with his shiny black eyes. She knew if she didn't drink, she'd find herself back in her bedroom, Bound. She took a swallow, almost gagging. It was warm and sour, with an odd, cheesy taste that stuck to her tongue and felt thick in her throat like a butter milkshake. Jacobus smiled at her with a yellow mustache.

Everyone except her drained their cups and took their seats. Sarah sat, looking hungrily at the food on the table: platters of cheese, more brown bread, odd little apples, and steaming sausages. A fish stared passively back at her.

She hadn't had anything to eat since she got here. She dove hungrily into her plate of food, minus the fish, grateful for the meal. The salad was pretty good, made with cabbage and sprinkled with raisins, celery, some kind of sausage, and cheese. The sausage was spicy, she thought, and the bread dried out her mouth. She was thirsty but didn't want to drink the horrible yellow stuff.

"Could I have some water, please?" she asked. They all looked at her oddly.

"We don't drink water, Fytie," Mother said. "It will make you ill."

Fytie, Sarah wondered. *Who is Fytie? I thought I was supposed to be Sophiia.*

"But I can't drink this," she said, pushing her cup away. "It's disgusting...."

"It is what we drink," Mother said. "You loved it before you went away."

"I've never tasted buttermilk, except in pancakes, so I don't know what you're talking about," she said, getting angry. "My name isn't Sophiia, Fytie, or whatever else you make up. My name is Sarah, and I only got here yesterday, and I don't know any of you."

Father was staring at her, his mouth in a grim line. She stared defiantly back at him, ready to say more. The hairs on the back of her neck prickled as she met his gaze. Father raised an eyebrow.

She picked up her cup and drained it. She wanted to puke right there on the table.

"Thank you," she mumbled. "It's delicious." She ate the rest of her meal silently, the taste of buttermilk sour in her mouth, brooding while everyone else talked and laughed.

For dessert, Mother had made a cake with nuts and dried fruit sprinkled on top of it, with a sort of honey glaze covering it and drip-

CHAPTER 28

ping down the sides. Sarah could have eaten the whole thing; it was so good and sweet.

Sarah helped clear the table when they finished eating, scraping any leftovers into a wooden bucket Jacobus showed her. Mother cut slivers from a brown chunk of something that must be soap, tossed it into the pot, and stirred it with a wooden spoon. Father had hung the large black pot from an iron peg above the fire. When it was steaming, Mother took the pot and sat it on the stone floor..

"There you go, children," Mother said, wrapping a shawl she'd taken from a peg around her shoulders. "Your Father and I are going for a walk. We won't be long." She left the door open to cool the kitchen when she walked out with Father.

A cool breeze wafted in the door as Sarah walked to look out of it. The sun was setting, and the immense sea of flowers across the canal glowed like a sea of color lit by the last rays of the sun. It was breathtaking: the golden ball of the sun, the sky ablaze with purple, orange, and magenta, like a reflection of the tulip field. The breeze stirred the flowers in the waning light, setting them nodding.

"It's beautiful," she whispered. "I've never seen anything like it." At home, the mountains to the west blocked the light of the fading day, and though the sky could be a brilliant mix of colors at times, it was nothing like this. She felt a tug on her sleeve and saw Jacobus looking at her.

"We need to wash up before they return, or Father will be angry," he said, drawing her from the door. He showed her where the brush was for scrubbing the dishes and pots, helping her clean and dry them. He was looking at her with nervous eyes.

"What?" she asked impatiently. She was getting tired of being stared at.

"Are you real?" Jacobus asked.

"Of course I'm real," she grumbled. "Are you?" She hadn't meant it to be so sarcastic and immediately regretted it. The little boy's eyes filled with tears.

"You're not Sophiia, are you?" he asked. "Not really." He stared at the floor, sniffing and rubbing his eyes.

She felt terrible about being mean to him. He didn't deserve to be treated like this. It wasn't his fault he was living with crazy people. And where was Sophiia, anyway? She must have upset Father and was probably buried somewhere out in the flowers. Sarah knelt and hugged Jacobus, feeling his thin arms wrap around her.

"You miss her, don't you?" she asked him. He nodded, and she could tell he was trying hard not to cry. Her whole attitude toward him changed right then.

"Do you want me to pretend I'm Sophiia, like your Mother and Father are doing? Would that make you feel better?" she asked, raising his chin to look into his eyes.

"Yes...." he whispered.

"Okay, then," she said. "My name is Sophiia, and I'm your big sister. You are my little brother, Jacobus, and we have a baby brother named Willem. We live in a house in Holland surrounded by big fields of flowers. Does that sound better?"

He was smiling broadly now, his eyes shining. Sarah noticed his two front teeth were missing. She hadn't noticed that before and felt affection for the little boy. If she could get away from here, she'd send

CHAPTER 28

someone back to rescue him so he wouldn't have to live with these crazy people anymore.

CHAPTER 29

The sky to the east was barely beginning to lighten when she quietly closed the door. Standing on the step, she listened for any sound indicating someone was awake. The house was silent. She feared Nico, the dog, would wake up and bark, but he remained silent. She'd taken a big hunk of brown bread and a piece of the sweet cake to eat on the way, wrapping them in a clean cloth and tucking them in her apron pocket. Her wooden shoes sat where she'd left them by the door last night, so she slipped them on. There wasn't enough light to see the other house yet, but there was no denying she'd seen it yesterday. She just had to walk down the road to get there.

Taking a deep breath, she started.

She'd only gotten a few hours of sleep because her mind had been racing as she planned her escape. Would the people at the other farm be ordinary? Would they know about the craziness going on here? If they did, why did they ignore it? They should have done something long ago. The police should have arrested the parents and taken the kids away. It wasn't safe for them to be living with obviously deranged people.

The still morning air scented with flowers felt cool on her face. Far to the east, across another immense field of flowers, the sun had begun to rise as the night retreated, as though a velvet curtain had been pulled back. The goats rustled along the fence, probably expecting a treat, but they didn't make a sound, thank goodness.

The canal whispered to her left, endlessly flowing to wherever it went. The day was swiftly growing lighter. With no mountains to block it, the sun rose with surprising speed, like a vast balloon inflating below the horizon, taking to the air in majesty. In this new day, she saw the distant house. She quickened her pace as she breathed the cool, crisp air. She felt exhilarated knowing she'd be home soon.

She'd been walking for quite a while as the day grew increasingly warm. She stopped to rest, eating some of the stolen bread and cake, and quenching her thirst by sipping carefully from the canal. It didn't taste bad, and the water was so cool and clean, she could see the bottom several feet below the surface. She didn't worry about what Mother had said about it making her sick. The woman was a crazy liar, anyway. Why should she believe anything she said?

The size of the tulip fields amazed her! Even with all the walking, she hadn't reached their edge, and it still spread before her like an enormous multicolored quilt. No one was working in the fields, but she didn't know anything about growing tulips, so she didn't know if that was odd. She'd run into the field and ask for help if she saw a worker.

The other farm grew slowly closer yet remained in the distance, enticing her with the thought and hope of freedom. The buildings were a bit clearer now, a thin line of smoke curling from the house's chimney. At least the people living there were awake.

CHAPTER 29

The sun was past noon now, and she was hot and tired.

She'd rested again in the shade of a tree, drinking her fill of the canal, always at her side. She took her wooden shoes off and cooled her feet in the waterway. A sizeable blister had formed on her right foot from the ill-fitting shoes. She left them there, knowing she'd never wear them again when she was free.

She thought it would only take another hour of limping to reach the house, or at least no more than two. Yet it remained just beyond her reach. She figured her perception was off because of the flatness of the terrain. Still, it seemed to take much longer than she thought it would when she started.

The clouds gathered swiftly like an old silent movie in fast motion, gray clouds filling the sky with alarming rapidity, roiling and boiling like a stirred pot. Then, suddenly, it began raining hard, falling like pebbles from the sky. Thunder boomed overhead, and lightning creased the sky. She didn't dare seek shelter under a tree, fearing the lightning. The downpour drenched her in seconds, her hair hanging in her face, clothes clinging to her body. Rain streamed down her face, and it felt like she was breathing water. She kept plodding along, feet squishing in the mud that sucked greedily at her every step, exhausting her.

It was raining so hard, she couldn't see the tulip fields, let alone the farm ahead of her. She feared she'd walk past the house, not seeing it through the sheets of rain pummeling her. She felt lost in a world of water, a drowning figure stumbling across a vast ocean of rain with nowhere to turn and nowhere to go.

The rain stopped with a suddenness that staggered her, bent and struggling as she'd been, clouds whisking away like mist in the sun, the ground drying beneath her as quickly as it had turned to mud.

The sun was lowering to the west beyond the tulip fields. The cake and bread were long gone, and her bare feet were aching. The road ran straight and true with monotonous regularity like a string pulled tight on the ground with neither twist nor turn. Her shadow reached toward the unseen horizon like a crack in the earth.

The sun was gone so quickly, it took her breath away. She walked faster in the waning light, praying to reach the farm before night fell completely. Her fickle shadow mingled with the growing darkness and was lost, leaving her alone on the road. It was getting colder as the evening became complete.

It had been dark for a long time when she was suddenly there, passing the windmill on her left, silent in the windless evening. She heard a dog barking, and a black shadow burst from the open door of the windmill. It raced toward her, barking ferociously. It stopped, growling as it walked around her, sniffing. She stood frozen in the road, afraid to move so the dog wouldn't attack her.

"Good doggy," she said, slowly extending her hand. "Good boy..."

The dog smelled her hand and licked it, dropping to its rump in the dirt, its tail thumping the ground happily. She bent down, petting the dog while it licked her face. She usually avoided dog spit like poison, but touching something warm and alive felt good. The dog abruptly stood, ears pricking as the door to the house opened. A man stood in the doorway, silhouetted by the light streaming from the room behind

CHAPTER 29

him. He held a lantern above his head as he peered into the night. He stepped into the darkness, closing the door before walking toward her.

Finally, she would be free! This man would help her; she was sure of that! Soon, she'd be home with Mom and Dad and Maddy! She began crying with relief as he drew near her.

"Please help me," she sobbed through tears. "I need to get home to my parents. I need to go home." The lantern's light and her tears blinded her as the man studied her. He laid a heavy arm around her shoulder as he knelt beside her.

"You *are* home, Fytie," Father said. "Come inside where it's warm."

CHAPTER 30

She woke with the sun on her face, wondering how she'd gotten into bed. It was all a blur with the movement around her and the voices muffled. Her head ached horribly. Her dress was freshly laundered and draped over her chair. She stared at it, her mind confused, despite sleeping all night and part of the day. She was exhausted and wanted to stay in her bed.

What happened yesterday?

She's walked farther than she'd ever walked in her life. None of it made any sense to her. She must have gotten turned around during the rainstorm, bewildered by the downpour. But that didn't explain why the canal was on her left the entire journey. She was getting ready to roll over with the blanket covering her head when the door opened, and Jacobus was standing in her doorway, looking nervous. He cautiously walked to her bed.

"Fytie, are you ill?" he asked. "Mother sent me to fetch you. She needs your help."

"I don't want to," she mumbled, pulling the blanket over herself and turning from him. "Go away."

"Please, Fytie," he pleaded. "Please come and help her. If you don't come down, Father will be angry. It frightens me when he's angry."

"Why do you keep calling me 'Fytie'?" she asked from the itchy depths. "I thought my name was Sophiia?"

"That's your short name, like mine is Jaap, and Willem's is Wilm. It means they love you," he said softly. "It means *I* love you."

Throwing the blanket off her, she rolled over and looked at him. He seemed so small and sincere, shyly standing by her bed. Sighing, she made him leave the room while she dressed. She felt terrible for Jacobus, having to live with these two maniacs. She was the only normal person he knew.

If these crazy things kept happening to her, it wouldn't be long before she would be a girl named Sophiia living in a fake Holland, babbling about how pleasant the weather was, and oh my, aren't the tulips beautiful today? And every day after, forever and ever.

It didn't seem like a good idea to fight it right now, so she finished dressing and went downstairs.

After putting their shoes on, Mother took her by the hand and led her from the house. Sarah's shoes were spotless, with no dust or mud from yesterday's walk. She silently followed Mother as she walked to the middle of the road, where Mother took Sarah by the shoulders and looked into her eyes.

"You need to listen to me now," she said sternly. "My husband allowed you to take your little journey yesterday to teach you a lesson. You aren't helping yourself with this stubbornness and disrespect, and it upsets the whole family. He knows you want to leave; he knows

CHAPTER 30

you're unhappy here. It makes him sad because he wants you to be happy like the rest of us."

Sarah jerked free from her, walking away a few steps before turning on her. "Are you happy, *Mother*?" she said, sarcasm filling her words. "You claim you've been here almost four hundred years, which I *don't* believe. If that's true, look at you and the boys: Jacobus hasn't changed in all those years; he'll never grow up, have friends or a family, and never be anything but a six-year-old boy with no front teeth. Willem is still a baby; you're still nursing him after four hundred years. Do you call that happiness? I call that hell!"

Mother recoiled as though Sarah had slapped her, staring open-mouthed at her, eyes brimming with tears. Then her face changed, becoming a mask of anger, her blue eyes like cold flame.

"Don't you think I know that?" she said viciously through gritted teeth. She grasped Sarah's shoulders and jerked her around to face the direction she'd walked yesterday. Her hand was tight like a claw. Sarah gasped from the pain and tried to pull away, but Mother was too strong.

"Do you see what is up there?" she hissed in her ear. "Do you see what you walked to?"

In the distance, Sarah saw the buildings surrounded by trees, smoke rising from the far-off chimney. She turned Sarah to look up the opposite way on the road. She saw distant buildings, trees, and smoke rising from a far-off chimney.

"Do you see them?" Mother asked, her voice harsh and cold like ice.

"Yes," Sarah whispered, trying to make sense of it.

Mother spun her to face their house. "And since you are so *brilliant*, I suppose you see that, too?"

What was this woman talking about? Had she truly lost her mind? Sarah was frightened.

The woman's features were twisted into a mask of fury, her lips a spittle-covered gash. She roughly turned Sarah to look the other way up the road, her fingers digging into her shoulder. "You are there!" she screamed, pointing at the remote buildings. She dragged her around to face the opposite way on the road, pointing those buildings out. "You are there!" Her voice was harsh, like a shrieking crow. Then she spun Sarah to face their farmhouse again, releasing her to sprawl in the dirt, where she sat rubbing her shoulder and fighting back tears.

"And you are here!" Mother dropped to her knees in the road, facing Sarah, her anger suddenly gone, disappearing like the gale from yesterday. She gently took Sarah's chin, tenderly turning to look intently into her eyes.

"Don't you see?" she asked. "Don't you understand?" Her voice was like the calm after yesterday's storm. "Don't you think I've tried to walk to those places after all this time? It is always the same. When I get there, I am here. When I am here, I am there. I wanted friends, someone to laugh with and gossip with. It's all the same. These places are all one place; no matter how far you walk, you always return here. Or there. I don't understand any of it. I know it's useless to try to leave.

"He controls it all. He directs the weather, the sun, and the flow of time, so the years are nothing to us, never changing. I know our circumstances better than you. I know Willem will forever be a baby,

CHAPTER 30

Jacobus will never grow older, and I will never leave here. I will never die."

Her face had grown morose, her brows creased with sadness. She looked at Sarah.

"There is no escape, Sarah. Yes, I know your true name. I know who you are and where you came from. Knowing how terribly I missed her, he brought you here to replace Sophiia. But she is gone now forever. I thank God every day she is free from this place." She stared at the field of flowers. She slowly stood, brushed dirt from her face, and wiped her eyes with a dusty hand, smudging mud on her cheek.

"I will never be free. . . ." Facing the house, she sighed. "I have no choice but to be happy for the sake of my children. They are here through no choice of their own. They are fed and cared for, and they are safe and warm. They know no fear or cruelty like with my other husband. What more could a mother ask?"

She left Sarah on the road, the sun hot on her back.

Sarah stood, looking back and forth between the distant farms. She didn't understand any of it, but understood her helplessness and the despair that flooded her.

She would never leave this place or see her parents or Maddy again. She would be here for a hundred million years, maybe until the sun burned out and withered. There was no escape and no hope.

Sarah wondered if they remembered her back at home. When Father took her, did she cease to exist there? Was the memory of her erased from their minds and thoughts? Did anyone care or miss her? Or was it like she had never been there? She walked slowly back to the house, her heart heavy like a stone in her chest, pausing to place her shoes on the flat rock by the door before entering the cool shadows of the house and closing the door on the bright, sun-lit day.

CHAPTER 31

Cart

Rain pummeled the plane as it descended through a storm into Amsterdam, distorting the view of the cloud-shrouded city. It had been a long flight from Salt Lake, with a two-hour layover in New York. Cart felt prepared for any weather unless there was a blizzard. Annie had packed plenty of rain gear for him, including waterproof shoes. His umbrella was in his carry-on.

He'd tried sleeping on the flight but couldn't get his mind to shut down long enough to rest. He missed Annie and Maddy. It was tough to leave Annie alone to deal with everything, but hopefully, her mother and Sam could shield her from the worst.

Schiphol Airport was extremely busy; people were everywhere. The remarkable train system of Holland had a train station right in the airport, making it easy for travelers to head to destinations in a matter of a few minutes. The trains and the country's bus system enabled people to travel anywhere without a car. He'd decided to rent a car, but no one was manning the rental desk, so he took a minute to call Annie.

Her mother was annoyed that he would leave Annie at such a terrible time but knew better than to say too much without crossing the line between concerned mother and skeptical mother-in-law.

Maddy was happy to see her mom but wondered where her daddy was. It was good for Annie to see her little girl, who covered her in hugs and kisses. Sam had called Annie, wondering why Cart wasn't answering his phone and asking why he'd gone to a psychic. Apparently, it was all over the media: *Distraught Father Turns to Psychic for Answers! More at 10!*

She'd convinced Sam that the woman was one of Cart's clients and he needed her signature on a document, and that he was trying to stay busy, turning off his phone to avoid distractions. Cart told Annie to let Sam know what was going on. Detective Collins had called to let her know he was around if she needed anything. She was grateful the big man had been positive about this whole thing and told him so. Cart told her he loved her and would be back with Sarah soon.

He wished he felt that positive.

* * *

The BMW was comfortable, with heated leather seats, which was great on this cold and windy day. After plugging the Haarlem's hotel address into the car's GPS, he allowed the kind "British lady" to take over the navigation as he ventured into the rainy and unfamiliar country.

The A9 led him from the busy city into the countryside, which was similar to Utah, except there were no mountains. The terrain seemed perfectly flat. Oh, and there were windmills dotting the landscape. He was surprised at the modern buildings and the smooth freeway. He

CHAPTER 31

didn't know why he thought that. He knew Holland was as contemporary as the US and not a medieval or third-world country.

Before long, the British lady announced his exit. He slowed down, merging off the A9 onto city streets. He had to listen intently to the GPS. There were a lot of one-way streets and quick turns to the right or left. It was difficult not to slow down to see the passing architecture slowly change from modern to older styles. He drove over a canal on a narrow bridge, which excited him. Suddenly, the buildings began to look much older, and the roads became narrower. The GPS directed him down the narrowest street yet, not much more than a single lane lined with old shops and taverns. Red-brick cobbles covered the lane, and his was the only car anywhere. A sign appeared to request a permit, but there wasn't a gate. He drove over the boundary between the modern and ancient, like going through a time machine, thumping over cobbles, and trying not to hit the flocks of pedestrians and bicycle riders. Everyone glared at him like he'd committed a faux pas, but no one stopped him.

Old buildings with various shops lined the narrow lane: cafés, taverns, antique stores, and candle shops. He turned left past a leather shop and was suddenly in a great, open space like a plaza. A massive church loomed to the right, its vast bulk rising like some tremendous old ship from a sea of cobblestones, dwarfing the buildings lining the square.

It was one of the most impressive sights he'd ever seen. The rounded uppermost tower stretched like the finger of Adam reaching for God's touch. Rain poured out of gargoyles' mouths high on the flanks of the church. He sat momentarily gawking at the sight while pedestrians and bicycles flowed around him.

"You have arrived at your destination!" the British lady said. He looked around the square, trying to see the hotel. Frustrated he couldn't see it, he got out of the car and slowly turned, eyeing the old, narrow buildings. Then he saw it just across the square, a few buildings from the narrow road converging on it: the Hotel Mozart. He pulled the car as close to the building as he could.

The hotel manager kindly explained that the square he'd parked on was the Grote Markt, or the Large Market, and was for pedestrians only to lessen the impact of vehicles on the medieval buildings and atmosphere of the square, leaving the open space for shoppers and tourists. The streets converging on the town square, mainly dating from the 1500s, were also pedestrian only, except for deliveries on certain days. That explained the glares he'd gotten from the people he'd driven past.

The hotel manager explained how to exit the square so he could park outside the bounds of the car-free zone. Leaving his luggage at the desk, feeling like he'd just fallen from the tulip truck, he headed into the confusing warren of streets. He was grateful to find a parking space almost immediately, not far from the Mozart.

Exhausted from the long flight and the stress of trying to find the hotel, he threw his clothes on a chair, collapsed on the bed, and fell asleep as soon as his head hit the pillow.

A few hours later, after a deep, uninterrupted sleep, he took a long, hot shower, washing the weariness from his mind and body. The hot water relaxed his shoulders and back.

After dressing, he drew back the dark blue velvet curtains and sat on the edge of the bed as he surveyed his surroundings. His room was

CHAPTER 31

on the hotel's third level. But since the bottom level of the building was a café, the second level was the hotel's first level. So, from his perch on the third floor of the building, he faced the Grote Markt.

He was astounded by the number of people on bicycles, hundreds in different varieties. Many bikes had little platforms built on the front, holding benches for children to sit on or seats fixed to the handlebars or seats in the rear. Little children sat calmly on these contraptions, seemingly without fear. Whole families rode past, older children keeping abreast or following their parents on their own bikes.

There were a great many pedestrians, as well. He was surprised at how carefully everyone meshed and flowed effortlessly around one another, as though they were born to do this. He gasped a few times as he watched, sure a collision between pedestrian and biker was imminent, but at the last second, one or both would gracefully shift to the right or left, moving on without concern. As far as he could tell, there were no angry comments or gestures following the near misses, just an easy flow of traffic making its courteous way across the Grote Markt.

It was a charming Old-World city. He could have sat for hours watching the shoppers' or bike riders' ebb and flow. Most traffic gushed from the street opposite the hotel, passing a McDonald's occupying the corner building.

A McDonald's?

No Golden Arches here, though. The building that housed the fast-food restaurant reflected Dutch architecture, preserving the charming aspect of the city. In most cities worldwide, there was a McDonald's, the one constant that could comfort travelers in a strange city. He knew nothing of the county's culinary tastes, except for their love of seafood, as any coastal country would be. At least he knew he could fall back on the tried and true if he had to.

He fought the urge to go sightseeing. He wasn't here as a tourist but to rescue his daughter from wherever she was. Although the city looked exciting and inviting to a newcomer, he found he didn't really care. He looked at the map and saw that the Grote Houtstraat was just a few streets from the Mozart. He headed that way and turned down the street.

He passed several shops, bakeries, leather shops, and mobile phone vendors, calmly passing the many people who flowed past and around him. Most seemed kind and smiled at him, though some were grumpy and in a hurry.

Then he saw it:

Antiek uit de ouden Eeuw

Golden Age Antiques

Fredrik Snabel

Proprietor

It was printed on a small sign in the window. Slender stained glass windows were on each side of a darkwooden door. A bewildering variety of goods were displayed for sale, everything from old doorknobs to aged yellow sheet music, stuffed animals, and toys. He saw shelves holding Delft tiles and pottery inside the store—pitchers and platters in distinctive blue-and-white designs.

Here, at last, was the shop he'd flown halfway around the world to find, this small insignificant shop among so many others, the shop where he hoped he'd find the answer to get Sarah back.

CHAPTER 31

A small brass bell above the door jingled when he entered, appropriate to the Old-World ambiance. The shop smelled old and musty, although it appeared spotless. Several chairs and tables held stacks of old newspapers and magazines. There was an eclectic collection of items for sale, almost too much to see in a single day. Old desks, tables, chairs, and highboys filled the shop, holding other antique items for sale. He heard movement from the rear of the shop.

"Ik kom zo bij je!" a voice said from beyond the counter at the rear.

Of course, he couldn't understand anything, so he looked around while he waited. He was looking at an old book in German from 1783 when he heard a man say: *"Hallo. Hoe kan ok u helpen?"* Cart could almost understand what he said. It was apparent that English and Dutch had common Old Germanic roots. Given enough time and resources, he could probably come to understand the language.

He put the book back on the shelf and smiled at the shopkeeper. The man was about five-foot-six, with graying black hair sprouting from the sides of his balding head. His mustache was pencil-thin and graying, as well. He had a little pot belly like a loaf of bread under his white shirt. His suit was dark blue, with a red vest and tie, and he wore small, gold-framed glasses perched on his thin nose, which bristled with untrimmed hairs.

"I'm sorry, Cart said, "I don't understand. . . ."

"Ah," smiled the man, revealing crooked brown teeth. "You are American?" His accent was heavy, reminding Cart of old war movies where German soldiers spoke English with a German accent rather than using subtitles.

"Yes, I am," Cart said, "I just got in this morning."

"And how was your flight?"

"It was okay, thank you, but very tiring."

The shopkeeper nodded. "Are you here for business or pleasure? Are you staying nearby?"

"I've got a room in the Mozart on the square."

"Yes, yes," the man said, "I know it well. It's nice being right on the square like that, in the middle of everything. How are you liking it?"

"It's nice," Cart said. "A little austere but comfortable. I'm sure I'll enjoy it when I have time."

"Welcome to Haarlem," the man said, spreading his arms. "How may I help you?"

Cart thought momentarily, trying to decide how best to approach the subject. He decided on a circuitous route rather than a direct confrontation. He didn't want to alarm the guy, but if he knew something about all of this, Cart had to know what it was. Too much depended on it. The man didn't seem to be an evil person who participated in his daughter's disappearance, but looks could be deceiving. The devil wouldn't appear with horns and cloven feet, after all.

"I'm interested in your collection of Delft Blue products," Cart said as he walked to the display. "May I take one down?"

"Of course," the man said. "Here, let me help you." He took down a beautiful pitcher with scenes of boats and windmills painted on it, heavily covered with representations of flowers and trees overhanging a lake or pond. It was in excellent condition, except for a small chip on the bottom edge. Even that was amazing, given that it was nearly 400 years old.

CHAPTER 31

"Holland is famous for our Delft Blue," the shopkeeper said as he took down a matching platter. Do you know anything about it?"

It was a beautiful set, and he immediately considered buying it for Annie. It would look nice in the kitchen. It might also put the man at ease if he bought something.

"I'd heard about it and looked it up online before I came over. I was hoping to see some samples." He held up the pitcher. "How much is this?"

"The pitcher and platter are a set, actually," the shopkeeper said, quoting a price that made Cart blink. He offered a lower price, and the man quickly countered.

"I'll take it," Cart said. "Can you wrap it so it doesn't break on the way home?"

"I can certainly do better than that!" the man said. "I can ship it directly to your home if you'd prefer. That way, you won't have to worry about it getting damaged in your suitcase."

"That would be fine." Cart smiled as he handed over his credit card. "Thank you."

The little man took the set behind the counter and, turning to lay them on a wooden countertop behind him, began wrapping them in bubble wrap while he waited for the card to clear. Cart studied the man, hoping to see a strange tattoo on his neck or some other indication of evil machinations, but he seemed like an ordinary man.

"I have a few questions about the tiles," he ventured. "Do you sell many of them?"

"Oh, yes," the man answered, his back to Cart as he wrapped. "They're very trendy right now."

"We had some installed in our new house. Our interior designer loved them."

"Oh?" Cart heard tape ripping from a roll.

"I believe you may know him," he said, closely watching the man. "His name was James Phillips." The man hesitated for a second, fumbling slightly with the dispenser. His shoulders hunched ever so slightly.

The shopkeeper cleared his throat and turned around, leaving the pitcher and platter on the worktop. Cart saw a nervous twitch around the man's eyes. His narrow mouth was taut as he chewed his lower lip. As an attorney, Cart was good at this sort of thing. He could read this guy like a book; the man definitely knew something.

"My good friend, James," said the man, looking out the window beyond Cart's shoulders. A bead of sweat ran down his temple. "How is he?"

"He's dead," Cart said flatly.

The guy put on a pretty good show of looking shocked, but it was a little too dramatic for Cart's tastes. The man drew a shaking hand to his mouth, widening his eyes, leaning back against the worktable. Sweat ran profusely down his face now. "Oh, my dear James! How did it happen?"

"Someone shot him," Cart said, his eyes on the man's face.

"God in de hemel!" the man cried. "Why would someone do this?" His hands shook as he removed his glasses and wiped sweat from his face. His eyes watered, but Cart didn't think it was from grief.

"He bought some Delft tiles from you for our new house," Cart said, leaning casually on the countertop by the cash register, picking up his credit card and receipt. "According to James, they were exceptional.

CHAPTER 31

Quite unusual, as he put it: a set of tiles based on a fisherman and his family. I believe he talked to you right before someone killed him. Do you remember the tiles?"

The man visibly shook, loosening his tie and wiping his face again.

"So, tell me," Cart asked casually, "where did you get them?"

The shopkeeper fumbled with his glasses, replacing them crookedly on his nose. "Why, at an estate sale, or—no, I don't remember!" He was backing very slowly toward a hallway leading to the rear of the shop. "I may have bought them from a contractor demolishing a house." He was almost in the hallway. "I buy a lot of tiles from various vendors and places. I can't remember them all!" He suddenly lunged for the hall.

Cart reached across the counter and grabbed him by the lapels, pulling him toward him until his loaf-of-bread stomach strained against the glass countertop, Cart's face inches from the man's. His breath smelled of rotten sausage mixed with sour beer and old fish. A dish in the counter display tipped over, striking a glass bowl next to it.

"I'm going to ask again." Cart put as much threat as he could into his voice so that it was heavy with the quiet promise of violence. He didn't want the man to question his sincerity. "Where did you get them?"

"I don't remember!" the man croaked. His eyes bulged, his face purpling from Cart's hand at his throat. His glasses slipped from his nose and clattered to the wooden floor. Sweat dripped from his head onto Cart's hands. "I swear to God, I don't!"

"Try harder," Cart hissed.

"No, please, I don't!" the shopkeeper spluttered.

Cart suddenly shoved him back. He staggered against the wooden worktop, shriveling with fear.

"I know you're lying," Cart said, "I make my living watching people lie. I would advise you to think very hard about where you got them. I didn't fly clear over here to listen to you lie." He picked up a crystal clock next to the register. "This is nice. . . ." He let it fall to the floor, where it shattered.

"No, please, stop!" the little man squeaked. A lovely platter painted in a dazzling theme was next, the multicolored shards adding to the shards of the clock. He ground them under his foot.

"If you don't remember where you got them, remember this: I'll be back in the morning, so you'd better be more forthcoming by then. I'm not leaving Haarlem until I know."

The bell tinkled as he left the shop, accompaniment to the whimpering of the shopkeeper.

CHAPTER 32

Cart leaned against a brick wall several buildings from the shop, hands on his knees, taking deep breaths.

As soon as he was out the door, the adrenaline that had sustained his anger drained from his veins, and he began shaking. His legs felt like Jell-O, and he feared passing out.

He'd never done anything like that before. He saw the headlines now: *Father Suspected in the Disappearance of His Daughter Flees Country, Arrested for Assault in Holland.* He'd be held for trial and probably disbarred back home.

He could hammer someone as far as the judge would allow in court, but confronting someone in such a threatening way was wholly out of character. He briefly considered returning to apologize and pay for the broken merchandise, but thought better of it as he remembered the man's reaction. The shopkeeper knew more than he was saying and lied about what he did know. The life of his daughter was at stake. He couldn't dally about, trying to soothe a weasel shopkeeper. He didn't have time to be kind. Maybe he'd have to break more tomorrow.

Sick with worry and apprehension, he returned to his room, stopping to grab a Big Mac, fries, and a Coca-Cola Light (the Dutch version of Diet Coke) to eat while watching TV.

He talked to Annie while he ate. Her mother was becoming increasingly annoyed and unpleasant by Cart's absence, continually questioning Annie about it. Annie finally had to tell her to stop and mind her own business, which only made matters worse. Annie finally had to return home with Maddy in tow. She couldn't stay there any longer. Detective Collins called her every day to check on them. Annie said Sam was concerned about Sarah's story and wondered how going to Holland would help.

He talked with Maddy for a few minutes and choked up when he heard her voice. He missed his family and wanted them all back together. He spent the rest of the day in his room, sad and tired.

When his room phone rang, he was watching a Dutch-language comedy on TV, trying to figure out what was so funny. He glanced at his watch: 11:15 p.m.

"Yes?" he answered.

"Is this Carter Benson?" a deep voice asked in heavily accented French.

"I'm Cart Benson," he said. "Who is this?"

"I understand you are looking for the source of some Delft tiles. Is this correct?" The man's accent was difficult to understand.

"I am," he said. "Do you know something about them?"

"I know a little," the man replied. "Now, listen to me. Tomorrow is market day in the square. When you wake up in the morning, many long booths will have been installed overnight. Look out your win-

CHAPTER 32

dow and memorize the location of the central medallion. Find the medallion's center or as close as possible at thirteen hundred hours. It will be very crowded. It won't be easy to find with all the booths and people. I will meet you there and take you to the source of the tile."

Cart was sitting on the edge of the bed, holding aside the heavy drape to survey the square.

"How will I know you?" he asked the man.

"No need to worry," the Frenchman said. "We know you." He hung up, leaving Cart holding the dead phone and staring at the medallion in the middle of the square.

* * *

He woke to laughing and rattling noises from outside at about two in the morning. He looked out to see several trucks and vans parked in the square. Men were erecting skeletal pipes, long and peaked in the middle, strapping white canvas or tarps on them to form tents. He was too tired to watch, so he stuffed in some ear plugs and pulled the spare pillow over his head.

* * *

It was like tent-making elves had been out all-night working magic. Long, tented booths filled the square, stall after stall selling anything imaginable—a tent city of commerce, like a flea market back home but classier. The lanes between the booths were wide enough for a car to pass through, but shoppers and the ubiquitous bicycles filled the spaces instead. There were people of every age and gender, hundreds carrying plastic bags of purchases, strolling among the booths. The smell of fish and pastries hung heavy in the air. Old men sat on the perimeter of the square, smoking and talking with old friends. Many families were drifting among the booths, and kids were chasing each other and laughing like kids everywhere do.

At about 12:50, he found the medallion's location covered by a booth. He was standing as close as he could to it—watching a man sell apples to a lady with an old, wrinkled face, her hair covered by a black scarf—when he felt an arm around his shoulder.

"Pretend we are friends, Monsieur Benson," a harsh voice dripping with a Gallic accent whispered in his ear. Cart caught a glimpse of an acne-scarred face below a thatch of black hair. The man held his arm firmly, hand hard like iron.

"Do not look at me!" the man hissed. "If you make the trouble, you will be dead in seconds."

Cart had no choice but to accompany him. They merged effortlessly with the crowd, and with the man's arm around his shoulder, they looked like two close friends wandering the square.

"We are going to a white van that is to be found by the town hall. When we get there, you will climb into the back of the van. I have friends in the van who will explain to you the tiles. Do not cause us concern, Monsieur Benson. Do as we instruct, and you will soon be free."

After walking a few hundred feet, Cart saw the van parked near the steps of the Stadhuis. When they got to the back of the truck, his guide turned to Cart. The man was about six-foot-four, heavily muscled, wearing a black leather jacket and blue jeans. He had a cruel, narrow face, a two-day stubble of black whiskers prickling his features. His

CHAPTER 32

eyes looked as cold as granite under thick brows, hard and unyielding. He smirked at Cart as he opened the van's back door.

"Thank you for your cooperation," he said. "Now get in the van." He shoved Cart toward the open door. Cart struck his shin on the bumper, eliciting a groan. The man picked him up, threw him bodily into the van, and slammed the doors.

Two men were squatting on the deck of the van: a blond guy wearing old, gray sweats, the other bald, heavyset, and clothed in black jeans and a tee shirt. The bald guy grabbed him and shoved a dirty rag in his mouth before he could react. Startled, he pulled away from the men, trying to push out the back door but finding it locked tightly. The bald guy forced Cart onto his stomach on the deck of the van, kneeling on his neck while holding his arms. Cart heard tape ripping from a roll. He panicked and began thrashing around, kicking and struggling.

The blond guy wrapped tape around Cart's ankles and wrists, and placed a strip over his mouth. The van started and pulled from the square, tires rumbling on the cobbled street.

Cart watched helplessly as the blond man pulled a hypodermic needle from a case, adjusted the plunger, and tapped the barrel. He struggled frantically, but the heavyset bald guy held him tight, sitting on him now. The needle felt like a bee sting as it plunged into his neck. A warm sensation flooded him, and his thoughts grew fuzzy.

"Goodnight, mon ami," the driver said. "Sweet dreams!"

The three men laughed, but it was like a strange echo that had no source, ringing in Cart's ear as though he was in a lead pipe. His vision blurred, narrowing to a pinpoint, and then he was gone.

CHAPTER 33

Sarah

Of all her chores, making cheese was probably her least favorite. The whole process, from milking the cow and the smell of the animal, then the smell of the milk warming on the fire, sticking her hands in the congealing mixture, all combined to make it a less than pleasurable experience. But she was getting accustomed to it, like many things here.

What choice did she have?

It was either do things willingly or be Bound, which she didn't like above all things—the feeling of hopeless surrender and helplessness.

She hadn't been Bound for a long time and had free run of the farm and the tulip fields. She enjoyed her morning walks picking fresh flowers for the vases in the house. She would make cheese daily if it meant not having Father Bind her again. So, she put on her happy face and made cheese.

She decided it was like being in chemistry, trying to make the best of it. The mixing of critical components, the watchful waiting, hoping for good results. How many of her friends could say they made cheese?

Probably, like, none.

The cheese she made was different than what she was used to. This cheese was always white, not orange as she'd had in her Other Life. (She had begun thinking of her life before she came here like that: her *Other Life*, with capital letters, when she thought of it at all. Mostly, she tried not to think about it because it hurt too much.)

Depending on what Father wanted, the cheese sometimes had a different consistency—occasionally soft, almost like cottage cheese, or hard, almost like a rock, taken from the shelves of the cheese house wrapped in a cloth and made long before she got here, with a pungent smell and a sharp, bitter taste. It was one of many new experiences she'd had here, like eating fish at almost every meal.

Ugh . . .

And like milking the cow.

Of course, she'd always known milk came from cows. But to actually milk one? The feel of the warm, spongy teat as she squeezed, pulled, squeezed, and pulled, learning the rhythm that worked. The stream of white milk squirting into the wooden bucket had become like second nature to her.

At first, the smell of the cow almost sent her gagging out of the pen, but with Mother and Jacobus watching, she would not do that. So, she learned to do it well. It was her job now twice a day: morning and evening.

She'd grown fond of Truida, the solemn-eyed, spotted cow that patiently submitted to her ministrations, relieved to unload the swollen udder at each milking.

CHAPTER 33

One morning, not long ago, as Truida stood chewing her cud as Sarah milked her, she was hit with a sudden thought. Here, in the confines of the cow pen, she made one of the most profound and life-changing decisions in all of her sixteen years. She decided to be like Truida, never complaining and just doing her job day in and day out. It had taken a simple cow to make her see and understand how best to deal with a man like Father—if he was a man.

What kind of man had the power to do the things he did: making it rain on a whim; keeping the temperature of the place at the most pleasant temperature; *Binding?*

While other girls her age back in her Other Life were busy texting and hanging out with friends, idolizing one pop star after another, her own idol—the thing that would save her over the long months or years—would be a cow. She would pattern her life after Truida. Being efficient and docile was the best way to avoid being Bound.

And so, she became Fytie, the little cow, never complaining, always helpful, day after day.

It made life much easier for her.

She also knew it would be harder for her if she continued thinking of herself as Sarah, the girl from the Other Place. It would be less confusing for everyone and help her accept who and where she was now. She would never return to her old life or be Sarah Benson again. She was Fytie or Sophiia, but she would never again hear her real name spoken by her family.

* * *

The next cheese day, she rose earlier than usual while the sun was below the horizon and lit a fire in the cheese house before milking Truida.

With the fire warming the cheese house, she skimmed the cream from the milk, saving it in a pot to use later to make waffles or butter. She poured the milk into the copper cooking pot and stirred it for a while, adding a cup of buttermilk and letting the banked fire slowly warm it. Then she pulled the heavy pot from the hook over the fire and placed it on the scarred wooden tabletop, careful not to spill it. Putting the lid on the container, she closed the door and left it for the day.

As she passed Truida on the way back to the house, the cow sauntered to the fence, her huge, slobbery tongue wrapped around a mouthful of grass. She stood and rubbed the cow's nose, gently whispering to her, "Thank you, Truida," before kissing the cow's forehead.

Startled, she stood back. *I wouldn't have done that in a million years back home! Where did that come from?*

But thinking of her home in her Other Life made her sad, so she didn't think of it anymore and returned to the house for breakfast.

CHAPTER 34

Early the following day, after milking Truida, she opened the copper pot waiting in the cheese house, freeing the smell of sour milk. Skimming off the little cream that had risen, she picked up the strange piece of meat Father had left on the table. It was rubbery and smelled a bit like grass, only with a rotten smell. Neither Mother nor Father would tell her what it was, just that it came from a cow, but not Truida, and that it would make the milk mixture thicken. She cut it into small pieces and dropped them in the pot.

As she was stirring the pot, she heard footsteps behind her. Looking up, she saw Father standing in the doorway, smiling at her.

"Hello, Father," she said, bowing slightly in respect.

"Good morning, Fytie," he said, "and how is the cheese coming along?"

"Fine, Father," she said, looking into the pot. "It will be ready to separate in a few hours."

"Excellent," Father said. "You're a fine daughter, Fytie. You've come a long way in learning your place here, and because you've done so well, I have a surprise for you!"

"What would that be, Father?" she asked him. He'd never offered her much praise and certainly no prospect for a surprise.

"I'm taking you fishing with me! You've learned how our farm works, and now it is time to learn what your father does during his day." He smiled expansively, showing his perfect, white teeth. His black eyes glistened in the firelight like two shiny beetles peering from their hiding place.

She didn't dare think anything but what he expected her to. She'd learned from experience that he knew what she was thinking. It was always best to be the dutiful daughter and show gratitude. She had to be Fytie, the little cow.

"But what about the cheese, Father? I can't be gone when it's ready, or it will spoil. It would be a waste."

"You needn't be worried about the cheese," he said. "It'll be ready when we get back. Now, gather your scarf and shawl. It can be cold out on the water. Hurry, little cow; I'm ready to go."

She flushed with embarrassment, realizing he'd read her thought.

He turned and left the cheese house, whistling.

Mother was waiting for her at the door to the house, Sophiia's scarf and shawl in her hand.

"Your Father is excited to take you with him. You should feel honored. I've never gone fishing with him." She helped wrap the scarf around her neck and onto her head.

"One thing you need to remember," she said as she placed the shawl on her shoulders, "be careful to show him the respect he deserves. He is the kindest man I've ever known, but he is quick to anger."

CHAPTER 34

"Yes, Mother," Fytie said. Sarah was a person she hardly knew anymore. She was Fytie now.

"If you anger him," Mother said, her blue eyes watching her intently, "If you anger him, you will suffer the consequences."

"Yes, Mother. I know only too well." She thought of being Bound and quickly thrust it from her thoughts. *Fytie, the little cow* . . .

Mother hugged her. Her hair smelled of bread dough and Willem.

"Well, do as he asks," Mother said, "and have a good time with him!"

"Yes, Mother."

* * *

Father untied the boat and pushed off from the canal bank, loosening the sail as it caught the current and drifted away toward the other place she'd walked to so long ago. (Or had she returned from it? It was hard to understand.) She sat in the front of the boat, watching the fields of tulips slide by. A sudden breeze filled the sail, and they began moving faster.

They passed the house far down the canal she'd walked to. Jacobus waved at them from the shore. They sailed farther. To her amazement, the canal banks fell away, and they entered a lake with calm water reflecting the sun like a smooth mirror.

Father, his strong hand on the tiller at the rear of the boat, pursed his lips and blew into the sail.

The boat sped across the water, barely making a wave.

"Here we are," said Father. "I like this spot. Now, hold tight!"

The boat stopped as though it had hit a stone wall.

Fytie lurched forward from her bench, almost falling overboard. She felt Father's strong arms around her, placing her back on the bench. She turned to thank him and was surprised to see him still at the back of the boat, smiling at her.

"Be careful," he said. "Mother will be angry if I bring you back looking like a soaked rat!" He stood and stretched his muscles. "Ah, what a beautiful day, don't you think, daughter?" he began pulling down the sail and lashing it at the crossmember. "I couldn't have asked for a better day if I made it myself." He laughed, drawing a canvas bag and some baskets from under his bench. "I love the sun on the water, the smell of freshness in the air. It makes my mind sing, and my thoughts soar. This is my true love: the sun on my back and the water before me, the life of a Fisherman."

He unrolled the net and cast it into the water, careful not to hit her. Satisfied with the cast, he sat on his bench and opened a basket with their noon meal. He handed her an apple, some bread, and cheese (cheese she had made!). The bread was wonderful, as was her cheese. She bit the apple, and sweet juice filled her mouth and dripped down her chin. She wiped it off with the shawl.

Suddenly, Father jumped up, dropping his meal from his lap, and began pulling in the net, his back and shoulder muscles bunching from the effort.

Why doesn't he just command it to rise? she wondered. *It would be easier.*

"Because I like to work," he said, looking down at her. "It is what I do. I am the Fisherman."

CHAPTER 34

She shook her head, angry at herself. But she got up and helped pull the net in. Soon, the deck of the boat was covered in silvery, flopping fish. They gathered the fish in empty buckets and stowed them in a basket by the mast. Collecting the net, he cast it again.

She watched him and saw the contentment and joy he found in this simple task. She gathered courage, despite Mother's warning.

"May I ask you a question, Father?" she asked, looking into his black eyes.

"Of course, Fytie," he said as he chewed his bread. "What would you like to know?"

She steeled herself. "Where did you learn to fish?"

He stopped chewing, gazing at her, his fathomless eyes dark like a moonless night.

"Why . . . I've always fished. I am the Fisherman."

"But someone must have taught you," she pressed. "I mean, how can you just know how to fish? I didn't know how to milk a cow until Mother showed me. Now it's easy. You and Mother have taught me a lot." She paused, taking a breath. "Did your father teach you?"

Clouds began forming in the sky—dark gray like dirty snow, scuttling in from the west. The wind stiffened, moaning around the mast. The boat rocked, waves lapping at its sides. He was staring past her shoulder, his mouth grim.

White foam lashed her face. It was getting colder as the wind grew. She drew her shawl tighter around herself.

"I have no father," he grumbled.

"But you must have a father," she insisted. "Everyone has a father."

He rose sternly, grasping the net and hauled at it, his hands corded with strength. She sat carefully in the wildly lurching boat, the wind steadily moaning. He silently ignored her, eyes like flint.

"Where did you come from?" she suddenly asked. Then she knew she'd crossed a line.

The dark sky exploded with a blinding light so bright, she threw her arms around her head and fell back onto the boat deck. Thunder crashed and rolled through the sky, deafening her. She cowered in the front of the boat, wrapped in the shawl as lighting and thunder slammed like giant fists drumming in the roiling sky, pounding her with raw intensity.

Father stood alight in the brightness, angrily pulling the sail up, heedless of the fury that lashed the sky. Then he was at the tiller, one hand gripping it tightly. The sail snapped like a gunshot with the force of the gale, and the boat shot across the water faster and faster, the cold waves drenching her. The sail ripped and tore loose from the mast, fluttering into the darkness like a pale, ragged ghost. The boat hurled across the surging waves, rising and falling, cresting wave after wild wave.

Then hail struck her once, twice, then thousands and thousands of hard balls of ice that clattered and stung her like tiny hammers.

"*I* am my father!" he shouted into the wind like a clap of thunder, rumbling in her chest. "There were none before me!" His voice rang out across the tortured sky and filled her mind. "My breath is the wind!"

The boat flew up the face of monstrous waves, a speck of flotsam against the wild rage of the sea, cresting them and falling like a rock as it

CHAPTER 34

careened down the opposite side with breakneck speed. Then they were on the open sea, swiftly leaving the coast behind like a dark shadow.

She cringed in the boat's hull, grasping the mast with feverish terror, fearing the greedy depths of the sea. She was choking on the waves, gagging at the salty flood that drenched her.

"My will is the earth, and my eyes are the sun and the moon!"

He stood at the back of the boat, the broken tiller waving in his hand as he shook it at the storm, screaming into the wild and furious wind. His eyes were glowing red, like fiery coals stoked by the wind, specks of flame that burnt the night. His hair was a corona of fire that whipped and flared in the shrieking night.

The boat soared up the next wave, cresting and rising like a kite. Then it plummeted like a stone down the other side, flipping over and flinging Fytie from the boat into the hurricane of wind, sea, and thunder.

The freezing water hit her like a sledgehammer, forcing the air from her lungs in a sudden gasp. She flailed her arms, trying to swim, but it was useless. Her heavy clothes pulled at her like grasping hands, and she sank into the sea, helpless against the vast, cold darkness. Her arms felt like they weighed a thousand pounds each, and her clothes seemed a ton even as she fought. She sank farther, then when her lungs were empty, she breathed in a great mouthful of water, bitter and cold, and she wept tears of salt mixed with the sea.

She was drowning. That last thing she thought was of her true family: her mother, father, and her little sister.

Darkness bloomed in her thoughts, and then she died.

* * *

Father sat on his bench beside the tiller, chewing on a hunk of brown bread. He smiled as he watched her, his eyes like black stones. She gasped at the warm air, filling her lungs with its sweet taste. She was warm and dry. Tears coursed down her cheeks as she cringed away from him.

"Would you like some bread?" he asked her casually.

Suddenly, she was sick, leaning over the side of the boat and vomiting breakfast and apple. She saw herself reflected in the sun brightened water. Her reflection wore a dress of seaweed, cloying and sickly green. Her skin was in tatters, ribbons of flesh hanging loose in the water, her hands skeletal, bone fingers clutching her shawl around her bony shoulders. A school of fish surrounded her, feeding on her.

Empty sockets gazed back at her in somber detachment, fleshless lips revealing a toothless leer. One thin, bony hand pulled loose by the feeding fish floated up toward her, waving slowly in the current, skinless fingers like white twigs. Then her point of view abruptly changed, and she was under the water gazing back at herself, hanging wide-eyed and frightened over the edge of the boat.

She felt nothing—neither the cold water nor the beat of her heart. It was curious not to feel anything, but she didn't care. All she wanted to do was sleep, to descend into the lonely, silent darkness. Her bone arm came loose from her shawl, and she waved goodbye to herself.

Then she was back in her natural body, trembling with fear. Her pitiful twin sank from her view into the waiting depths, bidding a solemn farewell.

CHAPTER 35

Cart

He woke slowly, with effort. Pain lanced through his head as he tried to move. It felt like someone had stuffed a watermelon into it and then plunged a dagger into his eye. Nausea roiled through him, and his stomach flipped a few times. He fought the urge to vomit. He breathed deeply, trying to stifle the disorienting sensation. He opened his eyes to the painful glare of sunlight filling the room from a tall window to his right. The delicate scent of roses filled his nostrils, subtle and soft.

He was in a soft bed with a silk sheet pulled to his chin. Someone had strapped his arms and legs to the sides of the bed with leather straps. He looked around the room as best he could—slowly so he didn't lose whatever was in his stomach.

There were two windows, one on each parallel wall perpendicular to his bed. Rosewood crown molding encased the ceiling, with matching rosewood baseboards and door trim. Pale roses on a cream background papered the walls. Dust motes floated lazily in the pillars of sunlight slanting from the window to his left. A small rosewood table below one window held a vase filled with blood-colored roses.

So, this must be the rose room, he thought humorlessly. *Where am I, and why am I here?* He struggled briefly against his bonds, but pain and nausea quickly ended that.

"Please, try not to move, Mr. Benson," a pleasant voice said to his left and beyond his point of view. "I think you'll find it worsens the pain."

A slender man walked into his line of sight. White hair fell to his shoulders, and thick white brows crowned his blue eyes. A crimson rose sprouted from the lapel in his blue pin-striped suit, a white handkerchief folded neatly in his breast pocket. He didn't sound European but American and highly educated.

"Where am I?" Cart asked. "Why am I here? And why am I strapped down?"

"My, aren't you inquisitive?" The man laughed. "It's good to be curious, though, don't you think? It lends so much to the experience of life. Someone will answer your questions soon, so please be patient. I can answer your three questions, however.

"Number one: You are in the beautiful Belgian countryside in one of the many guest rooms in our chateau.

"Number two: You are here because you have something we want.

"And, lastly, number three: We have restrained you so you don't harm yourself or do anything foolish, like trying to kill me. I assure you you'd die if you attempted that, which brings us back to not allowing you to harm yourself."

CHAPTER 35

"I don't understand," Cart said. "What could I possibly have that you want?"

The man walked to the vase and withdrew a rose, smelling it as he sat on the bed next to Cart. "Now, now, all in due time, as I said. I love the smell of roses, don't you, Mr. Benson? So sweet, so fragile . . ." He held the rose under Cart's nose. "Now, isn't that delightful?"

Cart turned his head away. "I prefer carnations."

The man smiled. "The one thing I dislike about roses is these pesky thorns." He touched a finger to one. A bead of blood welled from the wound. The man licked it off, watching Cart's expression with amusement. He abruptly dragged the thorn down Cart's cheek, ripping painfully through his skin. Cart jerked his face away.

"What the hell?" Cart exclaimed. "Why did you do that?"

"Oh, just having a little fun," the man said. "My, you need to control yourself! That's nothing compared to what's waiting for you." He dropped the rose on Cart's chest. "I'll leave you alone now so you can ponder your future. Try to enjoy yourself, won't you?" He left the room chuckling, leaving the door open long enough for Cart to see the long hallway outside the room and the two armed guards standing by the door.

* * *

It was getting dark; shadows of trees fell across the window to his right. Cart had to use the bathroom badly and was concentrating on holding it when a woman entered the room, followed by a guard with a hand on the grip of a holstered sidearm. The other guard stood watchfully outside the door.

"Sorry about the wait," the woman said with a light Irish accent. She appeared to be in her thirties, dressed in a gray pantsuit with a rose embroidered on the breast pocket. Her brown hair was shoulder length, and a faint blush of freckles dusted her cheeks and nose. She carried a black medical bag.

"We've been discussing you," she said as she drew a stethoscope, a blood pressure cuff from the bag, and a digital thermometer from the bag. She proceeded to quietly check Cart's vitals.

"You seem fine," she said, undoing the straps holding him down. "Now, remember, don't make a fuss when these straps are off. We don't want to create a scene here." She smiled as Cart massaged his wrists. "I assume you need to use the facilities?"

"Uh, yeah . . ." Cart said as he slowly stood. The guard watched unblinkingly. "What is going on here? Why am I being treated like this?" he asked as he entered the bathroom.

"I believe my friend said you'll have answers soon," she said. "Now, please, hurry. I need you fed before the Mistress returns. Get cleaned up, and I'll wait out here."

The walls of the bathroom were two-foot polished Carrara marble, delicate gray veins running through the stone. Marble crown moldings topped the ten-foot walls, and marble base pieces lined the one-inch hexagon marble floor. The ceiling was twelve-inch marble set diagonally. There was a six-inch wide stripe of rose-colored stone in a pattern of Celtic knots above marble chair rail pieces.

A mirror covered the wall above the countertop, and Cart was startled by the man staring back at him. His face was dark with stubble; dark smudges underlined his eyes. A scarlet gash ran down his cheek,

CHAPTER 35

dried blood caked where the wound had oozed. His hair looked like a rat's nest, sticking out at all angles.

There were towels, washcloths, and a shaver on the countertop. Cart turned on the shower and let it run while he undressed.

The bathroom was the most opulent he'd ever seen—and he'd seen some nice ones, including his own. This place must have cost a fortune.

What is it with the roses? he wondered. *Someone must have an obsession....*

The hot water refreshed him, sluicing the dirt and sweat from his body. He let it run over him for a long time.

The woman rapped on the door while he was drying off. "Everything okay in there?" she asked.

"Yeah," he answered, "I'll be out in a minute after I shave and dress."

"I've left clothes out here for you. Please put them on, and we'll discard your old ones. I'll wait in the hallway while you finish."

The clothes fit like they were tailored specifically for him. The white shirt was impeccably starched and pressed, the suit crisp and clean. There was a blood-red rose in the lapel, which he discarded, and he didn't put on the rose-embroidered silk tie.

He decided he'd rebel by not wearing any rose accessories.

After a brief discussion with him, the woman, aided and abetted by the guard aiming a gun at his head, waited while Cart put the tie on and placed the rose back in the lapel.

So much for rebelling....

She silently refused to answer his questions, stoically leading him down hallways covered with old, rose-colored carpet. "Can you at least tell me your name?" he asked.

"Elizabeth," she replied, not slowing her brisk pace.

The paintings he walked past were all original masterpieces from the Renaissance or earlier. He'd taken an art history class at university and was stunned by what he saw.

There were early Egyptian statues and symbols everywhere they walked: statues of Anubis, the jackal-headed Guardian of the Scales, who decided by the weight of a deceased person's heart where he'd end up in the afterlife; Pharaonic masks of scarlet and gold; chunks of recovered masonry with remnants of Egyptian paintings clinging precariously to all surfaces; and much more.

The windows he passed revealed expansive grounds darkening in the failing day, leading to shadowy forests of dark green pine and naked hardwoods, skeletal branches thrusting like imploring penitents into the winter chill. Snow clung tenaciously to the gloomy darkness among the trees.

They finally entered a large hall with exquisite panels of rosewood rising to the high ceiling. Lowboys and tables lined the room, displaying a variety of vases, all of which held bouquets of crimson roses. There was one long table in the hall, covered by a tablecloth of rose-colored lace, and in the middle of the table was a centerpiece of—what else?—roses. All the roses he'd seen in the house were bloodred—not a single white, yellow, or any other color.

Whoever owns this house must spend a fortune on florists.

Elizabeth pulled out a chair at one end of the table, looking expectantly at him. He sat.

An older woman dressed in black slacks and a white shirt embroidered with a red rose brought a platter of food through a door and

CHAPTER 35

placed it before him, pouring water into a crystal tumbler. The water was cold and sweet. He thirstily drained the glass.

His meal consisted of a tender, bacon-wrapped filet mignon that almost melted in his mouth, steamed vegetables, garlic mashed potatoes, and a hard-crusted roll.

"I hope you haven't poisoned this meal," he said after swallowing a mouthful of steak.

"Mr. Benson," Elizabeth said, smiling, "if we wanted you dead, you would have died long ago."

"Who was that guy in my room?" Cart asked, pointing at his face. "The one that gave me this?"

"Oh, that was Roland," she said. "He gets a little overenthused sometimes. I was supposed to be with you when you woke but was busy with other things." She looked at her watch. "Finish your dinner, and I'll be back shortly." She left him alone, the two guards watching him emotionlessly.

"And who are you two?"

The guards answered him with stony faces.

He raised his glass. "Well, cheers, then. Here's to our lasting friendship."

CHAPTER 36

Cart was finishing his dessert, a rich pasty with cream filling, when the door opened and Roland walked in, still impeccably dressed and smiling.

"Mr. Benson," he said. "Feeling better?"

"A bit. My face hurts, though."

"I'm very sorry about that," Roland said. "I was having a rough day, and I took it out on you. But it will heal in time, as all things do. We're all excited to visit with you."

"What are we going to visit with me about?" Cart asked, wiping his mouth on a silk napkin.

"Please be patient, Mr. Benson," Roland said, "you must be more flexible. As you'll soon see, it will go much easier for you." He indicated the door that Elizabeth had exited through. "Now, if you'll accompany me." He pulled Cart's chair out as he stood.

"I thought Elizabeth was coming for me," Cart said. "Where is she?"

"She was unavoidably detained. No fears, though. You'll see her soon enough."

The grounds looked desolate in the cold afternoon, broad lawns brown from winter, and the dark forest surrounding the chateau seemed thick and impenetrable. Roland led Cart down a hallway he hadn't been in yet, more richly decorated than any he'd passed through. The walls were all paneled floor to ceiling in rosewood, with more old master paintings and Egyptian decorations. Spotless windows looking onto the rear of the chateau revealed an Olympic-sized swimming pool, empty for the winter, surrounded by marble Grecian statues and pillars. The landscaping would have been lush during warmer months, but now winter-bared trees and bushes lined the walkways.

"Who owns this place?" Cart asked.

Roland answered with a silent smirk.

They drew up to a set of double doors, and Roland tapped on one with a knuckle.

"Come," a woman answered from within. Roland opened the door, gesturing for Cart to enter before himself.

This must be the library.

Hundreds of books lined the paneled walls, shelf after shelf of books; the musty scent of old leather and paper filled the room. Cart wished he could look at some of them. The bindings bore a mixture of languages, most of which he didn't recognize. Rolls of parchment and loose sheets of yellowed paper were also stacked on the shelves. This wasn't just a library but a history repository of tomes in various sizes and shapes. On one wall was an ancient map with what appeared to be a continent west of Africa and the Strait of Gibraltar in the Atlantic Ocean. Atlantis? A day in this room looking at things would be fantastic.

CHAPTER 36

He heard a cough.

At an ornate desk behind him sat a woman in what he guessed to be her early sixties, hair the color of steel drawn back into a severe bun so tight, it distorted her eyes and face. Her face had harsh lines of authority sculpted into it. She looked tiny behind the massive desk—a small woman no taller than five feet. Her eyes were the color of an old, dead tree and hard as iron, appraising him, thin lips pursed. A pair of glasses hung from a golden chain around her neck, reminding Cart of the librarian at his high school, a stern, frowning woman who tolerated neither nonsense nor noise. The ubiquitous red rose adorned the lapel of her black suit. They were silent as the woman sized him up. Cart was beginning to grow uncomfortable. Didn't this woman blink?

Hanging on the wall behind her was a large, ancient painting of a white cross, a sizeable bloodred rose at the center of the crossbar. A crown of gold radiated from the top of the cross. *Was this a Christian organization? They seemed a little intense and offensive if they were. If they weren't, why the cross?*

The woman looked at Roland, who immediately took a chair from near the window for Cart to sit in, which he did. She continued gazing at him before finally speaking.

"I'm going to get right to the point, Mr. Benson," she said in a harsh, firm English accent. "We don't appreciate how you mishandled poor Fredrik in Haarlem. He's just a shopkeeper caught up in things beyond his ken. It was entirely uncalled for, and rude on top of that."

"You drugged me and dragged me clear to Belgium just to scold me for roughing up 'poor Fredrik'?" he asked. "He had information I needed and wasn't forthcoming with it."

"As I said, Fredrik is a shopkeeper," she said, eyeing him. "What sort of information could he possibly have for you to frighten him so badly? The poor man soiled himself."

Cart smiled humorlessly. "Now you're trying to make me feel guilty. It won't work. You're not my mother."

The woman sat forward, leaning across the desk. "If I were your mother, you wouldn't have such atrocious manners. I'd have seen to that."

"And if you were my mother, I wouldn't be here visiting you since she's dead. I have other, more important business to be concerned with. If that's all you wanted me for, you could have saved the expense—and your breath." Cart started to rise, but Roland's hand was firm on his shoulder. "I need to go. You have no right to keep me here."

"Actually, we can do whatever we like, Mr. Benson." She smiled, showing small, gray teeth. "No one knows you're here except our staff, and I can assure you they won't be forthcoming, either."

Roland chuckled.

"Now, let's skip the niceties and get down to business, shall we? I don't have the time or desire to bandy about with one of your wits." She stood and walked around the desk, leaning against it while she gazed down at Cart. "You see," she said, "we know about the tiles."

Cart's heart skipped a few beats. *Finally, and hopefully, some answers.*

"Did you think we wouldn't hear about your little confrontation? When Fredrik called us, we decided it would be best to bring you here before anyone noted your poor interrogation attempt. And you being such a famous attorney? I'm sure your lovely wife, Annie, would be

CHAPTER 36

disappointed in you. We thought it best to let you rest during your trip here. It was simply a matter of convenience on our part—less of a chance for you to cause more problems by bringing more attention to yourself."

"Why are you even concerned about this?" Cart asked. "They're just a bunch of old tiles."

"Come now, Mr. Benson," she said, "we both know they are much more than just some old tiles. Our organization has been searching for those tiles for centuries, and I can assure you that we're not the only ones."

Cart was speechless, his mind churning, trying to understand what she was saying. "I don't understand...."

"Of course you don't. Not many people in the world would." She stared down at him. "We know you're aware of these tiles because of your treatment of poor Fredrik. The question is, why are you so interested in them?"

It was apparent she knew more than she was letting on.

"Why are *you* so interested in them? And how do you know my wife's name? There's too much going on here that I don't know about. I need some answers before I tell you anything. Those tiles have been in Haarlem for hundreds of years. Why didn't you want them until now?"

"We know all about you and your family, Mr. Benson," she said. "We have methods to find things out. We mean no harm to either you or your family. This organization has long had an interest in these tiles. Their unusual characteristics have kept them hidden from us all these years. Now that we know you have them, we want them. Now, please tell us what you know. The sooner we deal with this, the sooner you return to your family."

Cart sighed, knowing he had no choice but to tell her what was happening back home. Maybe she could help get Sarah back.

"We had the tiles installed in our new home."

"*What?*" the woman said, standing away from her desk, hands to her mouth. "This is terrible news! Don't you realize the situation you've put yourself in?"

"We didn't know," Cart said, stunned by the woman's reaction. "But I have a pretty good idea now. Please tell me what's going on."

She began pacing, walking to the window and back to the desk, muttering, and running her hands through her hair.

"Madame Locksley," said Roland from behind Cart, "are you okay?"

She whirled on Roland. "Of course I'm not okay! How could I be? Knowing this changes everything, don't you see? We'll have to move quickly before all is lost." She turned to Cart, eyes fierce. "How much do you know about these tiles?"

"Not much," he said, watching her closely. "Only that they were made in Holland about four hundred years ago. What more can you tell me?"

Ignoring him, she gestured to Roland, and he followed her to the corner of the room, where they conversed in whispers, occasionally glancing at Cart with furrowed brows.

Cart was growing more concerned as he watched them, wondering what was happening here. But if they knew so much about the tile, he could only hope they could help get Sarah back.

CHAPTER 36

The sun waned in golden fire when they finally stopped conversing, staring at Cart. Roland nodded, and the woman sighed.

"You're right, of course," she said. "He needs to know before we make any rash decisions." She returned to sit at her desk, resignation firmly on her face.

"Please forgive my previous harshness, Mr. Benson," she said. "I didn't realize how serious this was until you told me you'd installed those tiles in your house. It explains why you've been poking around Haarlem. We're sure you must be gravely troubled to have traveled so far to find out the nature of the tiles. I can understand your anger over our treatment of you, but we didn't know your connection to them, and we certainly had no idea of the seriousness of the situation. Hopefully, we can make amends. Would you like something to drink—a coffee, perhaps?"

"No, thank you. Water would be nice, though." Cart was startled by the change in her demeanor. "Can you please tell me what's going on?"

There was a tap at the door, and Roland let a man into the room bearing a silver tray with a carafe of coffee, two cups, cream and sugar, and a bottle of mineral water with a glass of ice. Setting the tray on the desk, the man bowed slightly to the woman and left the room. The woman and Roland filled their cups with coffee, the rich aroma filling the room. The ice crackled when Cart poured his water into the glass.

"Despite my rudeness, I am a kind woman," she said, "but the responsibility I bear tends to make me forget that. First, my name is Bryna Locksley. I'm from England but have lived in this chateau since becoming the leader of our organization.

"The tiles were made in Delft, Holland, in 1654 by a man named Pieter Jacobszoon. He was a prosperous artist then, a contemporary of Franz Hals and Rembrandt during the Dutch Golden Age when the country was tremendously wealthy because of its trade routes to the East Indies.

"He was also a prominent member of a forbidden society, a group of intellectuals dedicated to promoting the teachings of a German knight named Christian Rosenkreuz, who traveled to the Middle East in the fifteenth century, immersing himself in the esoteric teachings of mystics, even drawing upon the ancient learning of the Egyptians, and the belief that the universe contains far more knowledge than exists in the minds of mere mortals. Combining all he'd learned, he returned to Germany, wrote several treatises explaining his beliefs, and dedicated his life to teaching these ancient powers for the benefit of mankind."

She'd been sipping her coffee, carefully watching Cart.

"Problems arose when these beliefs came into conflict with the rigid monotheistic doctrines of the Church. You must understand that the Church wielded great power at this time, maintaining its greedy hold on the minds of the ignorant masses with violence and terror. I'm sure you're aware of the Inquisition?"

"Of course," Cart answered. "It was a terrible time."

Madame Locksley nodded. "Far beyond terrible, I'm afraid. It's difficult to imagine the scope of atrocities during this time merely to keep ancient beliefs from promulgating. The Society had to stay underground for centuries to nurture their truths carefully.

"At any rate, this Pieter Jacobszoon, who went by the name of Piscator, Latin for Fisherman, was an Adept in this society, a remark-

CHAPTER 36

able intellectual and leader. He also traveled to the East, studying the same esoteric knowledge that Rosenkreuz had and learning from Rosenkreuz's writings.

"The Society offered a better way of life for all people, one free from the iron fist of the Church and world governments at the time. They provided a plan of unity among men and women, where any person could freely learn and grow regardless of their station in life—a society of equals, where no person is greater than another. There were endless wars and conflicts between the childish and greedy leaders of the world.

"The Church, of course, had no choice but to root out the true believers. They couldn't allow such ideas to prosper. They had to maintain their hold on the people's lives at all costs. To do otherwise would appear weak, which they, indeed, were not.

"Piscator was arrested, tried illegally by a wicked judge and prosecutor, and convicted on many false charges. Then he was tortured in the most heinous way, trying to get a confession from him. He was left a broken man in both body and spirit. When I think of what he went through merely because he believed in the universal possibilities of the human mind, it makes me weep.

"After his torture, he was sent to a pottery factory in Delft to paint pictures on tiles. Can you imagine this? He was a Master, the equal of Rembrandt and Hals, forced to paint tiles for room and board. They took his home from him and forced him to watch while they burned his paintings in the town square, unable to move because of the intensity of his torture. He lost everything—everything! It's inconceivable to me. He had so much to offer mankind."

She grew silent as the shadows lengthened in the dark room. Roland flipped on a small light, insufficient to chase the accumulated shadows from the room.

"What happened to him?" Cart asked, stirring Madame Locksley from her thoughts. "Is he the one that created our tiles?"

"Oh, indeed, Piscator was the creator." Her brown eyes were muddy in the weak light. "When he discovered that the prosecutor of his case, the author of his destruction, had taken his home and that Piscator was going to paint tiles for the remodel of his former home for this terrible man, he exacted his revenge upon the man in a way that is beyond our understanding to this day.

"Drawing upon the abilities learned in the East and from the Society—abilities lost over the centuries—Piscator the Martyr imbued the tiles with an ancient power, old as the universe, creating an object of unbelievable potency.

"The Martyr died shortly after the creation of the tiles, following the installation in his former home, on October 12, 1654. A massive explosion occurred when a powder magazine in a building next to the pottery factory caught fire. It destroyed much of Delft, injuring over a thousand and killing at least a hundred. It has become known in history books as 'The Delft Thunderclap.' When he died, his knowledge died with him. Despite numerous attempts, no one has accomplished what he had."

Cart sat dumbfounded. Was he dealing with an insane woman fixated on something that may not have happened? How could he know? It was like listening to an old horror story, like something Orson Welles would have broadcast on Halloween in the '30s. He wanted to

CHAPTER 36

stand up and say, "I don't believe this nonsense" and leave the room. But he was very much a captive audience.

"What has all this to do with the tiles in my house?" he asked.

"Are you saying a demon possesses the tiles? Is that what you're trying to say?"

She shook her head. "The *tile* possesses the demon, if that's what you want to call it. This thing is far beyond a demon. The closest word I can think of to describe it is a god, a deity." She saw Cart looking skeptically at her.

"These are things so far beyond your limited knowledge of the universe, it would take the rest of your life to comprehend it, so before you insult my intelligence further, hear me out."

He sat rigidly. *Who was insulting whom?*

"Before I tell you more," she said, "I need to know how these tiles have affected you. That will help me to understand what is going on."

Cart sat silently, looking at the woman. How could he trust her or anyone right now? There was so much at stake. How could he put his daughter's life into this woman's hands? But maybe she could help; maybe she would know how to get Sarah back. Perhaps this woman knew where he could find the key to Sarah's world. She was obviously very knowledgeable about the history of the tiles. That was why he'd gone to Holland, after all. He decided he had no choice. He didn't know where else to turn.

"When the tiles arrived from Holland," he said, "there was a broken tile. It was a picture of a girl and it was beyond repair. Our designer was ecstatic about finding these tiles because they represented a family life in Holland when they were made."

"That would be James Phillips?" she asked.

"Yes." Cart frowned. "How do you know that?"

"Fredrik told us," she said. "Please, continue."

"James was trying to get the tile replicated when he was murdered," he said, getting angry. "Did you know that, too?"

"We only know what Fredrik told us," she said impatiently. "I'll explain after I hear your story."

"What else do you know that you're not telling me?" He started to stand, but Roland's hand gripped his shoulder.

"Mr. Benson," she said, "if you don't control yourself, I'll have you taken back to your room and drugged again. This situation is too vital for your personal feelings to get in the way."

"My personal feelings?" he spat. "The bastard took my daughter!"

Madame Locksley's face went ashen, ghostlike, as the color drained from her face. Her eyes widened in surprise. "What did you say?" she whispered.

"This thing took my daughter. We had a blank tile installed while we waited for the replacement. One night, our daughter disappeared. We thought she'd been kidnapped." His voice was becoming thick with emotion as he thought of Sarah.

"One day, her image appeared on the tile. My daughter is in that tile, or whatever is happening with it. That's why I came to Haarlem in the first place. Do you understand what I'm saying? I need to get her back and bring her home."

He was stunned when he saw a tear roll down her pale face, her eyes softening.

CHAPTER 36

"I'm so sorry to hear this, Mr. Benson," she said softly. "This is dreadful news." She turned to Roland. "It's what we feared, Roland. There can be no doubt, now.

"He's back...."

CHAPTER 37

Night had long since fallen; the forest's dark shadows crept to the windows, freed by the constraints of the day. A watchful silence pressed against the glass, heavy and intent. Cart almost felt the weight of the night hovering in the darkness.

"Why are you so interested in these tiles?" Cart asked. "How do you know so much about them?"

Madame Locksley had regained her composure, looking at him with red-rimmed eyes.

"As I told you, Piscator was a secret society member. When he died, we discovered that a separate group had been hunting the Society for hundreds of years. They sought the tile for themselves and were behind the conviction, horrific torture, and end of the Martyr's life.

"Four hundred years ago, we were forced into hiding here deep in the Ardennes forest, fearing not only death but also that this group would find the tile before we did and release the demon to wreak havoc on the face of the Earth with their desire to dominate the world.

"We are the true heirs of the Martyr, Mr. Benson. We cannot allow them to gain control of the tile. For that reason, we must destroy the tile ourselves. That is the only way to ensure we no longer live in fear and isolation and save the world from destruction."

"But you can't do that!" Cart exploded out of his chair. "If you do that, my daughter will be gone forever, like the Dutch girl in the broken tile!"

"Just the opposite, I assure you," said Madame Locksley quietly. "That is the *only* way to free her. When the tile is destroyed, she will be freed from the place where the power within the tile took her."

"That doesn't make sense." Cart was shaking with fury. "When the original tile was broken, this . . . *thing* . . . took my daughter to replace the girl in the tile. If that girl wasn't gone, why did it take my daughter? Whoever that girl was must have *died* or something when the tile broke."

"Please, sit down, Mr. Benson," she said. "Your display of fatherly concern is admirable, but you really have no idea what you're talking about. We know what we must do. We have the knowledge and ability to do this. We have spent the last four hundred years studying the mystic arts that made this tile possible.

"Your daughter will be returned to you."

Cart collapsed into the chair. He didn't know these people. How could he trust his daughter's life to people he didn't know or trust? All of this was too much to comprehend.

"I don't believe you. . . ." he whispered.

"Of course you don't," she said. "I don't expect you to. The difference between the girl in the tile and your daughter is the principle of family and home, which I'm pretty sure you do understand.

CHAPTER 37

"It's simply this: The home where the tiles were initially placed has been vacant for many years, and that home had no family living in it, no cohesive power to hold her to the rest of the tiles. When the house was demolished, the energy that held the girl diminished. When that tile was broken, there was nowhere for her to go, so she went... *elsewhere*.

"Your daughter, on the other hand, has a loving family waiting for her, like a magnet that will draw her back to you when we destroy the tile. She will be free, and you will have her back with you."

His mind was fuzzy with doubt. How could he know this was true? At the same time, he didn't know what he was dealing with—this woman did, or sounded like she did. He wanted Sarah back so badly, he couldn't stand it. To see her again, to hear her voice, to hug her....

"How?" he asked quietly. "How can I get Sarah back?"

Madame Locksley visibly relaxed. "It's quite simple, really. As the owner of the house where these tiles have been installed, you have within your power to allow the proper disposal of the tiles. All you have to do is sign a legally binding contract transferring the tiles to our ownership. That makes us the legal owners of the tile. Then we can rid the world of this evil power and free your daughter from its clutches. Sarah will be home again."

"That's it?" he asked. "You just take the tiles?"

"That's all there is to it," she said. "When it comes to dealing with these sorts of things, it's all a matter of ownership. It's the nature of the beast, so to speak."

Roland chuckled.

Cart stood and began pacing the room. He had to think and make sure this was the right thing to do. As an attorney, he understood the validity of contracts. He dealt with them daily. But what if they were wrong? What if she died when they destroyed the tiles? How would he live with himself if he allowed that to happen? This situation was so far from what he thought possible that it seemed like insanity. He needed time to think. He needed to talk to Annie.

"Do I have to do this right now, tonight?" he asked. "I'd like to talk with my wife about this, and I have a friend back home who's a psychic. I want her advice, as well. I don't want to lose my daughter. . . ." He felt sweat on his forehead.

"A psychic?" Madam Locksley laughed. "A little child playing in the mud? They're all charlatans standing on the shoulders of true mystics like us! She wouldn't have any idea what we're talking about." Then her demeanor changed, and she frowned.

"I must say you disappoint me, Mr. Benson. I had hoped you'd understand the critical nature of our conversation. Still, I guess it's waited these long years. A day or two more won't hurt, I suppose." She looked at Roland. "Let's take him downstairs," she said to him. "Let's take him on a little tour and show him our facilities."

Roland left the room and closed the door behind him.

Madame Locksley smiled at Cart, exposing her gray teeth. "I understand your reluctance, Mr. Benson, I genuinely do. But there is more at stake here than your child."

The door opened, and Roland entered, accompanied by the two guards, pistols drawn.

"Let's go for a walk, shall we, Mr. Benson?" she said as she stood.

* * *

CHAPTER 37

Exiting a very slow antique elevator, they entered a large, windowless room. Where the main level of the chateau was ostentatious to the extreme, this floor was its opposite. It had white painted walls and a concrete floor. Desks and computers filled the room, screens glowing in the subdued overhead lighting. Sitting at the computers were men and women of every age and ethnicity, busily working until the elevator door opened. The workers turned to watch the procession walking across the floor.

"Get back to work!" Madam Locksley snapped at them. "It's not like you've never seen this before!" Cart noticed several workers glance at each other before lowering their heads to their tasks.

At the far end of the room, on the wall the workers faced was a large screen on which a world map glowed, with political borders lit in yellow. The capital of each nation burned red, several blinking. In front of the screen was a podium with a microphone attached.

"What is this place?" Cart asked. "What do you people do?"

Nobody answered him, which didn't surprise him. He was getting nervous, knowing he could not escape this situation, especially with two guns pointed at him. Why wouldn't they answer him? How could he contact Annie to let her know what was going on?

They entered a long hallway, their feet echoing dully on the concrete floor. Fluorescent lights hummed overhead. At the end of the corridor was an old iron door, rusted and chained closed with a massive lock. Roland took a key from his pocket and unlocked the chain, which clanked heavily to the floor. He pushed on the door, but it only moved an inch, rusty hinges screaming like a wounded animal.

Gesturing to the two guards to help Roland, Locksley took a gun from one and aimed it at Cart while the two joined Roland. Pushing, grunting, grimacing, and clenching their teeth, they leaned into the door. It moved a foot and stopped.

Locksley waved the gun at Cart. "Help them," she ordered.

"No," Cart said.

Her hand moved quickly, lashing at him with the gun barrel. It caught him on the cheekbone below his left eye, and he stumbled back, pain lancing his face. Blood ran from the wound into his mouth and dripped off his chin.

"What the hell?" he shouted angrily. "Why did you do that?" He spat a mouthful of blood onto the floor.

"Don't be foolish, Benson," said the woman. "Now get over there and help push." Her words were hard like steel. Wiping his face on his jacket sleeve, he glared at her as he joined the three men at the door. Slowly, with a final groan, the door swung fully open under its ponderous weight.

Darkness oozed up from the stone steps leading down to a lower level, and the smell of mold and mildew filled the air, thick and cloying. Roland pulled a thin, metallic flashlight from his jacket pocket and thumbed it on, aiming it into the blackness below. The gloomy recess swallowed the brilliant beam, reluctant to submit to the light. Roland looked at Locksley and nodded.

"Very well, then," she said merrily, "down you go, Benson."

Cart eyed the dank gloom. He was not going down there, no matter what happened. The dark portal made his stomach churn in trepidation.

CHAPTER 37

"I don't think so...." he said.

Someone pushed him. Cart stumbled forward, his head striking the stone wall at the door's threshold. A guard struck him on the back of his head with the butt of his pistol. He sagged to the floor, vision blurring as he clenched his teeth against the pain.

"What the hell is wrong with you people?" he groaned. "Why are you doing this?"

"Oh, don't be such a whiner," Locksley said, nudging him with her toe. "Now get up. We have a special surprise planned for you."

"What is it?" he asked, gritting his teeth. The pain in his head throbbed down his neck and into his shoulder. A guard took him under the arms and dragged him to his feet. He jerked free from the man and leaned against the wall, breathing deeply to ease the pain.

Locksley laughed. "If we told you, it wouldn't be a surprise, would it?" The group joined in her laughter. "We are going down those stairs now. You can go on your own, we can carry you down, or we can push you. It's your decision."

"No," Cart said.

There was a sudden flurry of movement as the guards grabbed him. He fought desperately with them, thrusting, hitting, kicking, and scratching them. But they were all over him, relentless, and soon he was pinioned against the wall, breathing in ragged gasps above the head of a guard holding him. They were all sweating profusely. It was useless fighting them; they were well-trained and Cart wasn't.

Even if he could escape, where would he go? How far would he have to run to be safe? He didn't even know where he was.

He gave up, soaked with sweat, and frightened.

"That's better," said Locksley. "This will be much easier on you." She nodded at the guards. "Let's go," she said, taking the flashlight from Roland and aiming down the yawning entrance, stepping over the threshold, the light playing against the stone walls.

The guards shoved Cart into the opening, following him, Roland taking up the rear.

The smell of the old, moldy stone was overwhelming. The stone walls were sweaty with moisture, and black mold darkened the steps and walls. The stairwell reeked of age, like the breath of a dying man, ancient beyond years. Cart reached out and touched the rough-cut stone. His finger came away damp.

The steps wound around a cylindrical wall with no railing to hold onto. Locksley's light seemed dim and pathetic as they descended, the gloom swallowing the light like a hungering creature. The dim light revealed dark-stained walls, and he heard a constant water drip over the sound of shuffling feet.

There were no windows to chase the darkness, and it felt oppressive and claustrophobic, like he was in a small closet, the ceiling brushing his head. He was finding it hard to breathe; the air was moist and thick, like a tropical atmosphere but without the palm trees, sun, and warmth. It got colder the farther they went, as though the winter outside leached freely through the walls. They finally reached the bottom of the steps where Locksley waited for them. A room opposite the stairs had a thick, wooden door hanging limply from one hinge. She aimed the flashlight at the doorway; the darkness was unyielding to the weak light.

CHAPTER 37

Locksley gestured to Roland with the flashlight. "Let's shed some light on this, shall we?"

Roland took a stick from a bucket at the bottom of the stairs. It had a solid mass of rags at the end of it, and it smelled of kerosene. Roland flicked a lighter on, and the torch *whooshed* to life. The flames lit the room with eerie cascades of light dancing on the stone walls. Roland handed the torch off to a guard and lit the second one.

Their faces looked ghastly in the torchlight, shadows surging and retreating from their features. Locksley looked particularly evil, her mud-brown eyes glowing amber. Wordlessly, she turned and entered the ink-black room. They followed her, ducking under the low doorway, a guard pushing Cart ahead of him.

"Sorry about the lights," Locksley said as they drew near her.

"We haven't got around to updating this level of the chateau. We rarely come down here, anyway, and then only for our most special guests, like you." Her voice was dull in the stone room, swallowed by the dank walls. The air was much worse here, like no one had breathed it for hundreds of years.

"We much prefer the character of this room for what we have planned. The ambiance is so exquisite here, don't you think? It adds so much to the experience! Electric lights would only detract from its unique intent."

Cart looked sharply at her. "Which is?"

Her eyes sparkled brightly in the torchlight. "Oh, come now, Carter, surely even a dull-witted American like you can see what this room—or, rather, this chamber—was used for. Look around you, for heaven's sake. All the finest chateaus have them!" She gestured grandly around the room.

Cart looked around the chamber and noticed rusted chains hanging limply like dead snakes from the walls. Various sizes of iron rings hung suspended from the walls and ceiling, along with several on the floor. Empty cages, cylindrical with inward pointing spikes, also dangled from the ceiling. A long table behind Locksley held a spoked wheel attached to it. Tools of damage hung from the walls: prongs, shackles, brands, and pointed objects that made Cart's heart feel like lead in his chest, all iron and red with rust or long-dried blood.

Locksley chuckled. "I can almost see the light bulb come on over your head. It is a torture chamber, Carter, as you've deduced, and quite a fine one. We're lucky to have one in such fine shape, with all the equipment of that fine old craft still here. They may be a little rusty, but I assure you they function as well as the day they were first put in here." She smiled gray teeth like pebbles at him.

"Would you like to try them out?"

Cart felt the cold of winter pumping through his veins, chilling his heart and soul. "You can't be serious. . . ." he whispered.

"Oh, I'm very serious, Carter," said Locksley. "We've given you every chance to sign that contract with us. However, we will have that signature despite you."

"Why don't you just take the tiles if you want them so badly?" he said. "It seems like it would be much easier."

"As I told you in my office," she said, "we can't do that. The tiles are 'Bound' to your house because of your legal ownership. You have a contract with the tiles, so to speak, though you weren't aware of it.

CHAPTER 37

No one can own them but you. If we tried to take them by force, it would destroy them, the god within rendered useless. We can't have that now, can we?

"All you have to do is sign that contract. You can go your way, and we can take the tiles and all the power that comes with them."

Cart glared at the woman. "And my daughter?"

"Collateral damage, Carter. Sorry."

"Then go to hell." He spat on the floor.

"Well, then," she said, "you give us no choice, do you? Please remove your clothes."

"I'm a happily married man," he sneered.

"You're so clever, aren't you?" She glanced at the guards. "Let's see how amusing you are in ten minutes." The guards held him while Roland removed his clothing. He was too exhausted to fight them. Ultimately, he stood in his underwear on the damp floor, trembling with cold and fear, while the guards tied his hands behind his back. Locksley stood watching. Her face was garish in the flicker of the torches.

"One last chance before we start," she said. "Will you sign the contract conveying ownership of the tiles to us?"

"I already told you: Go to hell!"

She shook her head and snapped her fingers.

The guards dragged him over to iron rings set in the stone floor and put his feet through each one. He tried kicking at them, but he had no strength. He was sweating despite the cold, and his heart was racing. One guard took a stout rope lying on the table, threw it through a ring hanging from the ceiling, tied one end to Cart's hands and the other to the spoked wheel, and turned the wheel, tightening the rope. Cat felt his arms pull up behind his back, forcing him to begin bending over.

"You know," said Locksley, touching him gently on his cheek. "I must admit, you're much more defiant knowing your fate than your friend, James. I understand he cried like a baby before he died."

Cart wrenched his head up, sending pain through his shoulders and arms.

"You killed James?"

"Oh, good heavens, no!" She laughed. "I would never sully my hands with such an awful act. I have people for that sort of thing." Cart smelled her sour breath.

Anger welled up in him, and he wanted to lash out at her, but he could do nothing. "Why did you kill him? He never hurt anyone."

"He was a meddlesome nuisance," she said, "prying into things that didn't concern him. He was getting close to discovering us. We couldn't have him blabbing about what he'd learned of us, could we? Besides, like all deviants, he was a waste of human flesh." She looked closely at Cart. "Stop worrying about your dead friend. If I were you, I'd be more worried about your own future, which portends nothing good." She circled behind him.

She tugged the rope, and he groaned. "This is the same method they used on the Martyr Piscator. Did you know that?" She was speaking softly, almost absently. "He suffered tremendously at the hands of his tormentors . . . as will you. If I were to reel this rope in as tight as it can go, it would wrench your joints out of their sockets, starting with your shoulders. Gentlemen," she said to the guards, "please show Mr. Benson what I'm talking about."

CHAPTER 37

The two grabbed the wheel and began slowly turning it, tightening the rope. Cart's arms painfully pulled up behind his back, bending him farther forward at his waist.

"Why in God's name are you doing this to me?" His voice was harsh with pain.

"God's name?" she asked. "What God would that be?"

"*The* God." Pain lanced his arms and shoulders. He felt like screaming.

"Oh, I see," she smiled. "You mean the weakling Jewish God? The locust eater? The bread-breaker? The desert god?" She laughed. "No, our gods are the gods of darkness, from the Dark Lands; gods that wandered the shadows of men's earliest nightmares. They don't eat locusts or bread...."

It seemed to get colder as she spoke.

"They eat souls."

CHAPTER 38

He hung helplessly dangling from the ceiling ring, sweat dripping from his face, powerless to relieve the pain that consumed his whole being. They'd left him on the edge of destruction, the rope taut enough to exact immeasurable pain from the pressure of joints pulling against joints, yet not strong enough to finish the dreadful task of pulling those joints loose, allowing him to pass out.

The darkness he hung in was absolute, like being lost in a cave with no lights. No matter how bright they were, there could be no true light where such evil had occurred. It would be a mockery of light. It felt like the room had never been light, even when the torches blazed.

He heard water dripping, *drip, drip, drip,* from somewhere in the darkness, and then that was all he heard. It dripped in time with the beating of his heart, a metronome of pain, and he focused on that, trying to distract himself from the throbbing fire in his body.

He heard rustling from behind him, furtive movement slithering along the floor. Something tickled his foot, and he jerked, but the rings held his feet tight. He felt something nip the big toe on his right foot. A rat? It must have been. He spat at his feet, hoping to chase the creature away, but it kept nibbling him. He howled helplessly, screaming in agony as his movements sent pain ripping through his body. He stopped struggling and began cursing himself, Locksley, Roland, his parents for giving him birth, and whoever else came to mind.

The endless night went on and on. He thought he saw flickers of light in the corners of his eyes, little flares of red and yellow, but he knew it was his brain firing unanswered synapses. He thought he had slept. How else would he hear Annie whispering in his ear, her hand soft on his chest? Phantom voices laughed, mocking him. He heard screams echoing in the chamber but realized it was himself, pleading for release. More nips at his feet, thrashing, cries, then whispers, in an endless repetition of agony. It seemed he'd dangle from the ring for eternity.

Then merciful exhaustion embraced him, and he left his body dangling in hell.

* * *

Movement. A brief flash of light. Voices. Had more demons come to mock his agony? A light in his face, blinding, and spasms of pain in his brain.

Suddenly, his arms were free, and he screamed as he squirmed on the damp floor—his shoulders ablaze with pain, his arms flopping uselessly, rough hands rubbing his muscles, his throbbing limbs. Then, he felt a sting in his arm. Rats were crawling on him ... biting his arm? He tried to brush them off, but his arms wouldn't work.

No. Not rats, a needle.

He passed out. Whispers in the dark ...

* * *

CHAPTER 38

Finally, he was warm, wrapped in a blanket. The pain had lessened, occasionally echoing in his shoulders. Roland offered him some water.

Why? What is going on? Nothing made sense.

Cart couldn't hear what they said. Footsteps echoed in the chamber, and Roland's face came into view.

"Are you okay?" Roland asked. "Can you stand?"

"I don't know," Cart mumbled. "What's going on?" He struggled to sit, and Roland put an arm under him and raised him to a sitting position.

"We need to get you out of here," Roland said grimly. "We don't have much time." He turned away. "David, help me get him up."

Strong arms grasped him from behind, around his chest, and effortlessly lifted him to his feet. Cart felt woozy, but the pain wasn't nearly as bad. His stomach suddenly surged, and he vomited on the floor, heaving and gagging until nothing else came up. Roland gave him a handkerchief. Cart wiped his mouth, spitting the foul taste on the floor.

"Keep it," Roland said when he tried to return it.

"Thanks," Cart muttered.

"The painkiller will do that," Roland said. "We'll go as slowly as possible, but David will have to carry you if you can't keep up."

Cart looked at the man standing behind Roland and was startled by the severe visage looking back at him. Cart stepped away, fleeting fragments of his pain-haunted dreams scrabbling up from his thoughts.

David was tall, probably six-foot-five, with broad shoulders and massive arms, his coal black hair tied in a tight bun on the top of his head. But his face . . .

It took him a moment to realize David's face was heavily tattooed, with a swirling dark design covering his neck and chin, wrapping around his eyes, and onto his forehead. He looked fierce and gigantic, like an angry Polynesian god. Then David smiled gently at him, his white teeth gleaming in the glow of Roland's flashlight.

"Sorry," Cart said, "you startled me."

"No problem," said David. "I have that effect on people. The tats are a history of my family, our strength, and our commitment, but it mostly scares kids and enemies."

"He's really a big stuffed animal." Roland chuckled, handing Cart a bundle of clothes, including a jacket and warm gloves. Clothes never felt so good. Both men helped Cart get dressed, since his arms still weren't working well.

Roland led them quietly from the room. Cart was relieved to leave this awful room behind. He fought back another swell of nausea and followed Roland into the antechamber, David close behind.

"What are you doing?" a woman asked.

A flashlight flicked on, backlighting a slender form standing across the chamber near the stairs.

Roland turned his flashlight on her. "Lizzy," he said quietly, "go back upstairs."

It was Elizabeth, dressed in sweat clothes under a down jacket, her hair pulled back into a ponytail, and she wore no makeup. Her face was stern, eyes brittle with anger.

"No, Roland, what are you doing?" she asked him again.

"I'm getting him out of here before she kills him." His voice was a whisper. "Please, Lizzy, go back upstairs."

CHAPTER 38

She walked toward them, slowly circling to the left. Cart saw she had a pistol in her free hand, the muzzle pointed at Roland's chest.

"You know I can't do that." She smiled ruefully. "Madam Locksley's not going to be pleased. She's been waiting her whole life for this. I'm not going to stand here and let him slip away. There's too much at stake."

Roland moved closer to her. David stepped to his right, a slow dance on the stone floor.

"I don't know who you are, big guy," she said, easing the pistol in David's direction, "but I suggest you stay where you are. I'll shoot you with no hesitation whatsoever."

David stopped, his big fists clenching.

"You don't believe her nonsense, Lizzy, surely you don't." Roland moved slowly, step by step, closer to her. "She's insane. You know that."

Lizzy moved away from him, keeping her distance. "Is she, Roland?" she asked. "I've known her my whole life. I don't think she's insane. A little obsessive, maybe, but not insane." She gestured with the pistol toward the door into the torture chamber that gaped like a broken tooth into the torture chamber.

"Now, let's get him back in there before Mother wakes, shall we?"

Roland stopped moving. "Mother?"

Elizabeth laughed, cold like the air. "Of course. Why do you think I'm so devoted to her?"

Roland's eyes were wide. 'I thought you were just a member of the Brotherhood."

"Well, I am that. Mum's made sure of it." She smiled. "She's an excellent teacher, actually. If you'd paid closer attention in our meetings, we probably wouldn't be having this conversation right now."

"Oh, I think we would have eventually." Roland narrowed his eyes, curling his lip in scorn. "I've never been much of a believer in world domination."

Cart saw a slight movement at the top of the stairs, white against black.

"I'm sorry to hear that," she said. "I truly am." She cocked her head slightly, and a sad smile touched her lips. "I guess you didn't know Mother had chosen you to be my husband. You were all she ever wanted for me: rugged, handsome, intelligent, and devoted to the cause. It seems such a shame. I did enjoy our little encounters, Roland. You were so . . . *enthusiastic*."

The movement became a shape, cautiously moving down the steps on white-sneakered feet, silent as the room in the chamber was dark.

"Come with us, Lizzy!" Roland said suddenly, stepping closer to her and extending his hand—a diversion. "It's not too late. We can still be together, just not here."

"Stay where you are!" she hissed, stepping away from him and toward the stairs. "I'll shoot you where you stand, damn you! If you think I'll let you waltz out of here with Mother's prize, you're sadly mistaken—as I apparently was. . . ."

The sneakers became legs, and Cart saw a slender man easing down behind Elizabeth. How could someone move so quietly?

The man tapped Elizabeth's shoulder while simultaneously dropping to her side. Elizabeth spun, the gun snarling in her hand like it

CHAPTER 38

had a life of its own. The explosion of the gun was deafening in the stone antechamber. Cart threw his hands over his ears and stumbled back, falling weakly to the floor.

David leaped forward quickly for a man his size and grabbed her gun hand fiercely while Roland eased the weapon from her grasp. She gasped, resisting David's big hands. The slender man took both of her hands, tying them behind her back as she struggled, kicking and squirming.

"We've got to get out of here," the slender man said. "That gunshot will bring guards soon."

Roland grabbed Elizabeth's shoulders, staring intently into her smoldering eyes. She glared back at him, her body trembling with rage.

"Come with us, Lizzy," he whispered, "Please, you don't have to stay here. We can start a new life, far away from this madness. Please . . ."

She spat full in his face.

Roland let go of her, wiping his face on his sleeve. He stared at her briefly, his face emotionless.

"Tie her up. Gag her." His voice was flat. "Leave her here."

"But—" David began.

"LEAVE HER!" Roland shouted, rounding on the big Māori. Then he softened, clasping David on the shoulder. "Leave her . . ."

David and the new guy tied her hands to her ankles and gently laid her on the floor, putting Cart's blanket over her and stuffing a clean cloth in her mouth.

She glowered at them.

Roland kissed her gently on the forehead. "I'm sorry, Lizzy," he said. "More than you could possibly know." Then he turned and disappeared down the corridor to the left, farther into the blackness leading from the antechamber.

David stood her flashlight standing upright near her.

"You are one dumb *wahine*, lady," he said.

She growled ineffectively.

"This might keep the rats away; it won't matter much longer, anyway." He stood and took the slender man's flashlight.

"Let's go."

They followed the Māori—Cart behind him, uneasy on his feet, the slender man trailing them both.

Cart heard an inhuman whining from behind them, then silence.

CHAPTER 39

"Where are we going?" Cart asked. The flashlight offered little in the way of illumination besides what the narrow beam revealed. As near as he could tell, they were going deeper into the bowels of the chateau, padding through doorless openings and high stone arches. They had to skirt several puddles of greasy-looking water before finally finding an aluminum ladder leading up to a good-sized hole near the ceiling.

"You okay?" David asked Roland.

"Don't have much of a choice, do I? Let's get out of here and on our way," Roland said, indicating the ladder. "You go on, Mr. Benson, and Warren and I will follow.

David grasped the ladder's rungs, which appeared too flimsy to support his weight, but he swung nimbly up, disappearing into the hole. He stuck his head out a few seconds later and gave a thumbs-up.

"Can you do this?" Roland asked Cart.

"I'll try. My arms still feel weak," he answered. "Where are you taking me?"

"Somewhere safe. I'll be right behind you, so if you need help, let me know."

Cart grasped the ladder, swung his foot onto the first rung, and then pulled with his arms, testing his strength.

"I think I'll be okay," he said, although his joints still hurt. He was unsteady climbing but soon felt David's strong hands pulling him through the hole. He was in a garage or a storage shed, the flashlight exposing garden tools and hoses of various lengths. A snowplow was attached to a tractor, and the smell of oil and gasoline was strong.

Roland and the slender man, Warren, soon kneeled beside him. David handed out coats and gloves from a box stashed under a worktable. Warren stole off to the right, amazingly silent like in the antechamber below. There was a rasping noise, and David took Cart by the arm, leading him past the tractor and some ATVs and out a man door in the side of the building.

The night was bitterly cold and silent, stars a billion pinpricks in the moonless, velvet sky. Cart's lungs stung as he breathed the chill air. He was wondering why they hadn't provided balaclavas when David tapped his shoulder and handed him a black one, smiling. It was much better wearing that.

They crept silently from the building, walking single file down a gravel walkway lined by winter-bare trees, then climbed a fence and ran into the deep woods surrounding the chateau. They stopped and looked back at the great building, well-lit by ground spotlights and lampposts. It looked like a fairy castle, far more extensive than Cart had imagined, with lightless windows peering out on the night. So far, the area was silent, and Cart saw no movement inside the chateau.

The moonless night gave the forest a deep darkness, making Cart's anxiety skyrocket. It was nearly as dark as the chamber he'd hung in. If

CHAPTER 39

it weren't for the flashlights the three men carried, he would have given up trying to find his way in the thick pine forest. He'd never been in woods with so many trees; it was so closely grown, it felt claustrophobic as they hurried away from the building.

The three men didn't hesitate as they dodged trees and boulders, so they must have known where they were going. They didn't talk or confer with each other, but hurried through the forest.

Cart decided he had to trust the men, whoever they were. If they'd meant to harm him, they could have easily done it at any time, or simply left him dangling in the chamber.

He had turned briefly to look back at the chateau, surprised that it had disappeared so quickly from view, when he suddenly fell. He landed heavily on his side, a harsh curse escaping his lips. A flashlight lit him, and he saw he was in a hole about five feet wide, three feet across, and a couple of feet deep. The pit had forest litter in it: small branches, twigs, pine needles, and what appeared to be several small pieces of rusted metal. He stood, brushing himself off. Puzzled, he looked around him. Roland had stopped about ten feet away, leaning against a tree and peering into the darkness.

"What is this?" Cart asked. "It looks like someone was digging here. Were they prospecting?"

"It's a foxhole," David whispered, extending a gloved hand to him and pulling him out.

"Why is there a foxhole here?" he asked. David was nudging him in Roland's direction.

"Benson!" Roland hissed angrily. "We don't have time for this! Are you going to stand there playing twenty questions while they come looking for us, or do you want to get away from here?"

Roland turned and disappeared into the forest, his flashlight bobbing like a disembodied spirit weaving among the darkened boughs.

"He's sacrificing a lot to get you out of here," David whispered. "We'll explain it to you later. Let's try to keep up, okay?" He gently shoved Cart toward the vanishing light, and then they moved as quickly as Cart could through the encompassing darkness.

When they caught up with them, Roland and Warren were standing by a narrow dirt road, cut like a slashing wound through the forest. They stood within the trees, watching the darkened lane in each direction.

Roland turned to face them, his face taut and grim. Then he dropped to the ground next to Warren. David pulled Cart down and covered him.

There was a sudden flash of brightness behind them, lighting the trees in stark relief. Then the sound hit them, shaking the trees like a great wind, thunder rolling across the sky as more flashes and explosions rocked the night, echoing across the forest like a New Year's celebration from hell. Pine needles rained on them as one last brilliant burst creased the night. The shock wave and explosion from the blast were the greatest of all. Trees groaned and swayed, littering the ground with dead branches and needles. An immense cloud of dust rolled across the forest like a thick fog, choking and dense.

Cart was on the ground. Arms over his head, screaming, his ears ringing from the explosions.

CHAPTER 39

Then, there was silence, so deep and still that it seemed the world had ended.

The darkness was absolute—clogged blackness he could taste, thick and gritty. He spat a mouthful of the night on the ground and rose slowly to his elbows.

He looked around frantically, but the clotted air made it hard to see. Flashlights stabbed ineffectively at the cloud of filth. It was hard to breathe. Dust clung like flour to his face and his clothes. He felt a hand on his arm, pulling him up.

David stood in the roiling darkness, face gray with dirt and dust. He looked like a Māori ghost, tall and backlit by his flashlight.

"Are you okay?" he asked Cart. His voice sounded far away, but Cart knew it was because of the deafening explosions.

"What the hell was that?" he shouted. His voice sounded tinny and weak in his head.

"Something blew up," David said, heading toward Roland's coughing figure. Cart grabbed his arm, which was as solid as granite. David turned back to look down at him with eyes the color of night. He shrugged Cart off and headed to Roland and Warren.

Cart stared after, mind racing along with his heart. He stumbled after the big man.

"What are you saying?" he shouted. "Did you blow up the chateau?" The thought made his mind reel. *No, no . . . It's too awful to contemplate.*

"All those people . . ." He whispered, staring wide-eyed at the three men. "What have you done?"

Roland rounded on him, fists clenched.

"We did what we needed to do! Do you remember what Locksley said your daughter would be? Collateral damage. Well, that's what *they* were!" Then he was in Cart's face, grasping the collar of his jacket and pulling him close. "Would you rather be hanging in the dark still, rats eating you bit by bit? Would you rather they took that tile and destroyed your daughter? This is a war, Benson. Bad things happen in a war." He pushed him away, and Cart stumbled back and would have fallen had it not been for David's iron grip.

"Of course not!" he shouted as he shoved away from the Māori. "Wasn't there some other way? Couldn't you have spared them?"

Cart struggled to grasp the reality of what had happened. All those lives were gone. How many had died? A hundred? Two hundred? More?

All because of him...

He felt tears stinging his eyes, muddy rivulets forming on his cheeks. He tried to see Roland, but he was just a figure lit by vagrant light beams.

Roland spun back on him. "Would you just shut the hell up?" He glared at him. "You're making me wish you were still back in the chateau. If it weren't for your daughter, you would be. We don't need you for what we still have to do, except for your signature. But we aren't that way. We're not like them." He pointed with his chin toward the chateau. "We've got to get out of here before everyone in the province is breathing down our necks." He turned away from Cart. "Warren?"

"Yeah?" Warren's voice came from behind Cart.

"Which way?"

CHAPTER 39

A green glow lit the dark, lighting Warren's face a sickly hue. He looked at the small screen on his wrist. He pointed off to the left, across the road. At least that's where Cart thought the road was. He'd gotten turned around in all the confusion.

"That way," Warren said calmly.

David's hand was on Cart's arm again, pulling him in the direction Warren had indicated. He followed, stumbling away from the road into the forest-shrouded night. A garish, orange-yellow glow fitfully lit the night behind them like strobe lights in the roiling dust. The smell of smoke mingled with the cloying night. He heard a siren wailing in the distance as another, smaller explosion rang through the night, like a far-away echo of the earlier devastating blasts. The night ahead was abruptly filled with a thrumming sound like a large angry wasp, growing louder as they dashed through the trees.

Suddenly, they were out of the forest, standing in a large clearing, like a field or a meadow. The thrumming was louder now, almost deafening. He followed the gaze of the others into the night and saw flashing red lights slowly descending from the darkness. He covered his ears as the black helicopter settled on the ground. He saw helmeted men at the controls, lit by the glow of instruments. A door in the side slid open, and a man gestured for them to hurry.

The three men ran across the intervening space, instinctively ducking the rotating blades. Cart pulled from David's grasp and stood watching them, wondering if he should run back into the forest, find his way to a town, and make his way home.

Roland stopped and turned around, looking at him. He said something to the other two, who climbed into the helicopter. He ran back to Cart and took his arm. "We have to go!" he shouted above the helicopter's roar. "You can't stay here!"

Cart looked back at Roland. "Are you any better than they were?" he shouted.

Roland's face softened. Then he pushed Cart toward the helicopter. "I guess you'll have to see for yourself!" he shouted as he followed Cart into the helping hands of Warren and David. The door slid shut as they lifted off, swirling the clouds of dust and dirt dizzyingly.

As they cleared the treetops, Cart looked back at the flames that scoured the night. The clouds of dust and debris had begun to settle, but black smoke poured from the raging flames that surged with greedy, grasping tongues into the night. In the distance, he saw flashing red and blue lights, minuscule against the distant hills. They were far too late, of course.

Nothing could have survived such tremendous destruction.

Someone handed him a headset with padded ear cups to protect against the screaming engine and rotating blades. He switched off the intercom so he wouldn't have to talk to anyone. He turned away from the window, hugging his jacket tightly around him and pulling his balaclava over his eyes as the helicopter cut through the night.

So many lives . . .

CHAPTER 40

"What the hell is going on?"

They were in an office in a private hangar at an airport in Antwerp, a map of Belgium on the single desk in the room. It was cold in the room, despite the small space heater at their feet. Roland had been trying to pinpoint where the chateau was, but Cart had his arms folded stubbornly. He finally looked at the map.

He showed him a heavily forested area between Liège and Bastogne, explaining where the last big battle of World War II had occurred, The Battle of the Bulge.

"Those foxholes we saw in the forest last night? They were from the battle, but I don't know if they were Allied or German. It was Hitler's last-ditch effort to stop the Allied advance and salvage what he could from the defeat." He stopped and looked at Cart. "Look, I know you don't understand what's happening, but you'll have to trust me. My great-grandfather died in the Bulge. He was massacred by the SS near Malmedy, along with about ninety other unarmed soldiers. It seemed fitting to do my part in the same area."

He put his hands on the desk and leaned towards Cart, his eyes fierce. "We're still fighting a battle, maybe not as big and fierce as World

War II, but a battle, nonetheless. It's still about good versus evil, right versus wrong. Those people are intent on ruling the world. They already have people embedded in most of the world's governments, like a virus waiting to strike when conditions are perfect.

"They'll do whatever it takes to implement their plans and achieve their goal. That's why the tile is so important to them. With that tile and their knowledge, they can unleash the demon within it and force it to do their bidding. They'd have a world full of slaves at their feet."

Roland had grown more intense as he spoke and had not blinked since he started talking. He may not be telling Cart the truth, but he sure believed what he was saying.

"Why should I believe you, Roland?" Cart asked. "Yesterday, you were part of them, cruel and insensitive. How do I know this isn't another ploy by them? You said they'd do anything to achieve their goals. Maybe that means blowing up the chateau and having you conveniently there to take me away and lead you directly to the tile. I don't know if anyone was even there when it blew up."

Roland smiled sadly, shaking his head.

"Oh, I can guarantee people were in the chateau last night," he said quietly. He stood up, seeming to shake himself free of the memory.

"I had to stay in character," he said. "It's taken me years to get into this organization. They're very secretive and wary. They watch everyone closely, twenty-four seven. Constant video surveillance is everywhere. I had to have a ruthless reputation with them. When we get where we're going, maybe you'll understand."

CHAPTER 40

"Where are we going?" Cart asked, somewhat mollified. "I need to get home. If they're as willful and strong as you say, blowing up the chateau isn't stopping them."

"Well, you're right about that. It won't stop the organization completely. But it will slow them down some. It'll take them some time to get reorganized, and we'll take that time to get you and your daughter home safely. As far as the rest of the organization is concerned, we died in that explosion, too."

Cart was watching him closely as he spoke. *Was he playing his part?* "How do I know you don't want the tile for yourself?" he asked. "Maybe you want to be the sole dictator."

"You're going to have to trust me in this, Cart," he said. "Believe it or not, our only focus is to get your daughter back safe and sound and destroy that tile. We should have destroyed it long ago, but we lost track of it. It holds a monstrous power within it, which would boggle your mind if you knew the full extent of its power. *We* don't even know the extent of its power. I can't explain it any more right now.

"You'll have to wait until we get to St. Lucia for more answers."

"*St. Lucia?!*" Cart exploded out of his seat. "You mean St. Lucia in the Caribbean? I don't have time to lay on a beach and go snorkeling. I can't go traipsing around the world. I've got to get home. My wife and little girl may be in danger!"

Cart's mind was reeling with anger and uncertainty. He couldn't follow these guys around the world. He'd have to get the first flight home as soon as they landed.

"There's no question about that," Roland said, watching him. "They are in grave danger. And so are you. But we have to take this window of opportunity to help prepare for what we need to do. That can only be done in St. Lucia. So it would be best to calm down and let us help you. We're the only ones who can."

Cart fumed, waiting while the ground crew fueled the jet and prepped it.

Roland told him the jet was a Bombardier Challenger 3500. It could fly at 637 miles per hour at over 40,000 feet. He impatiently looked through it while they waited. He'd never seen anything so luxurious, so comfortable, fit for a king, or at least a president.

It was all cream-colored leather and carpeting, with big oval windows and granite tops in the galley. Large-screen TVs hung from the ceiling, although nothing was on the screens.

Where on Earth did these people get their money? First, the chateau in Belgium, then the black helicopter, and now a private jet. He was evidently in the wrong business. Still, he'd rather be an attorney than seek world domination.

David sat in one recliner, listening to an audiobook, and Warren reclined his chair back and fell asleep, snoring softly. Roland allowed him one call to Annie. She'd been apprehensive when she couldn't contact him, but he explained he had left his phone in a café in Haarlem, and it took a while to find it.

Roland told him Annie didn't know anything about Belgium or St. Lucia, and it was best for her not to know what was happening. Cart agreed.

"What she doesn't know won't hurt her, especially now," Roland said. "She needs to stay with her mother until this is over."

CHAPTER 40

"How did you know she was at her mother's?" Cart asked, eyeing Roland suspiciously. "I didn't tell you she was there."

Roland shrugged. "I just know."

CHAPTER 41

Fytie

Despite the harrowing experience in the boat, she still had to do chores.

She'd avoided Father's eyes as they sailed back to the farm. She'd lain against the inside of the boat, shaking like she'd been ill. She kept seeing herself, a horrific apparition bleakly sinking away from herself like a *thing* from a nightmare.

Father sang while they returned as though nothing unusual had happened. When he tied the boat off and helped her onto the bank, he thanked her for going with him.

"I think we have learned an important lesson today, Fytie. Let us not forget." Then he left her on the canal bank while he went into the house, whistling.

Hugging herself, she went to the cheese house to finish her duty there.

Her finger came out of the milk mixture relatively clean, leaving a cut in the gelled milk, so she took the long, wooden blade from the wall and began cutting the curd that had formed. She rotated the pot and cut the curd four times.

She had now seen Father's strength and suspected it was just a fraction of what he could do. He was an absolute ruler here, and she would never get back home. Even if she found a way to escape, Father would know about it, just like that day long ago when she walked to the "other" farm. Then she would be Bound again, or worse, go fishing.

She might as well face the fact that she would be milking the cow and making cheese forever and ever. The thought made her feel like sitting on the cold stone floor and crying until her eyes fell out. What was the point of this miserable existence? How much cheese and fish could one family eat? Apparently, tons of it, judging by how much cheese she'd made since she'd come here.

That was another thing. Despite eating three times a day and drinking gallons of buttermilk or whey, she never gained weight or, more importantly, neither she nor the rest of them ever had to use a bathroom. Ever. When she asked Mother about it, Mother just smiled and said, "Yes! Isn't that wonderful?"

Forever was a long time to milk a cow and make cheese; she'd never envisioned pulling on a cow's teat for eternity.

After cutting the curds, she poured the excess whey into a smaller pot to save for later.

While the big pot sat over a low fire, she stuck her bare, clean hands into the warming mixture and began stirring the curds and adding salt. Why she had to wash her hands, she didn't know. It's not like they'd get sick and die from the germs. But Mother insisted.

CHAPTER 41

She stirred and stirred, breaking up the larger curds as she found them. When the curds felt just the right size and temperature, she pulled the pot from the fire, sat it on the table, and covered it with a clean cloth. She didn't have to worry about flies contaminating the curds. Father didn't allow flies here, or any other insects. How the tulips got pollinated, she didn't know, because she'd never seen a bee here, despite having as much honey as they wanted.

After cutting and separating the curds, she went outside for a few minutes while the mixture rested, relishing the cool breeze redolent with the smell of tulips. The sky was a rich blue, brighter and more expansive than back at the Other Place, cloudless and fresh, which it always was unless Father decided it was time for rain.

Neco nudged her leg, wagging his tail furiously and holding a stick in his mouth. She stroked the dog, scratching behind his ears.

She threw the slobbery stick into the field next to the house as far as possible. Neco bolted from her, tail up as he ran after the stick, pouncing on it and excitedly running back to drop it at her feet, intently staring at it. She rubbed the dog's neck and threw it again. This time, he brought back a different stick.

"Couldn't find it, huh?" She laughed, threw it again, and walked back to finish the cheese, Neco staring at her in disappointment.

She scrubbed her hands with a bucket of water and Mother's harsh brown soap until her hands were bright red. She might not get sick from germs, but she wouldn't eat cheese with dog spit in it.

Sitting on the wooden bench outside the door after she'd finished, she wiped the sweat from her head with a handkerchief from the pocket on her apron. Staring at the stone wall opposite her, she bleakly realized she was no different than Neco. Like Truida, the cow, he was content to do dog things forever, always grinning and wagging his tail. Why was it that the only living things she could pattern her life after were animals? Did that mean, in Father's eyes, she was no more than an animal, here to please him and Mother? Because that's what she felt like—an animal that would spend an eternity milking Truida and making cheese until the whole world was covered with cheese.

Thinking of that made her want to bawl like a baby, but she couldn't find the strength. She'd already reached the depths of sorrow and loss, so she sat tiredly, waiting for the cheese to harden, which was about as exciting as watching tulips grow.

CHAPTER 42

Cart

Stepping off the plane onto the airport tarmac in Castries, the capital of St. Lucia, was like stepping out of a refrigerator into a steam bath. The humidity had to be in the ninety-percentile range, with the temperature in the eighties. Although he'd taken the opportunity to shower during the long flight from Belgium, changing into the clean clothes Roland had given him, he was sweating profusely after five minutes. The air was stifling and heavy, like breathing green-scented steam.

Nearing the island on the final approach, he'd been impressed by the abundant greenery and the volcanic nature of its terrain: steep mountains and jumbled tropical forest-covered hillsides. According to Roland's brochure, the two massive volcanic mountains—like inverted green ice cream cones jutting from the sea—were called the Gros Piton and the Petit Piton, the Big Peak and the Small Peak.

Roland said the population of St. Lucia, like most of the Caribbean Islands, was predominantly black, descendants of slaves brought from Africa to work on the many plantations on the island. Initially colonized by France in 1660, after fourteen wars fought by the French and

England over possession of the island, Great Britain finally took complete control in 1814. It was now a member of the British Parliament.

The hangar office was comfortably air-conditioned, and Cart was glad to be out of the heat and humidity. Roland used the office phone while Cart sat quietly at a table drinking a Diet Coke. David and Warren casually leaned against a black Range Rover in the hangar, quietly talking.

Warren fetched a cigarette from a package in his pocket and lit up, sighing as the smoke drifted from his nostrils. David gave him a disgusted look.

"Why do you have to smoke those things, man? You know what they're doing to you, right?" he said. "Why don't you quit?"

Warren drew smoke languidly into his lungs, eyes closed and leaning back. "'Course I do," he said. "They're good for me. They put hair on my chest."

"I don't get you...." David shook his head, pushed away from the truck, got a beverage from the machine, and walked out of the hangar, popping the tab and taking a long drink.

Roland replaced the phone in its cradle and stood up. "Okay, he's ready for you. It's time to go," he said, leaving the office with Cart behind him. "David, Warren, let's go."

David looked at the cold drink in his hand, shrugged and threw it in a trash can as he trotted to the Range Rover. Warren dropped his cigarette and crushed it with his foot, then climbed into the driver's seat. David settled in the front passenger seat while Roland and Cart sat in the back. Everyone buckled up as Warren started the car, pulled out of the hangar onto the tarmac, and then sped across the fenced-in

CHAPTER 42

area toward a guarded gate, slowly sliding aside as they approached. The guard saluted them as they drove out.

"Where are we going?" Cart asked. "Who am I meeting?"

"Someone important," Roland replied but would say no more, so Cart watched the scenery out the window.

The streets were narrow and rough, potholes jarring them as they drove through the town, passing an assortment of businesses of stucco and metal. Leaving the industrial area of Castries, they entered a residential area of dilapidated homes and shacks crowding the hillsides, shoeless children staring at them wide-eyed as they passed by. Dogs and chickens scattered from the car's wheels, and a couple of malnourished cows chewing their cuds in the middle of the road were almost hit by the car as they rounded a blind corner.

"Slow down, man," David muttered. "You're going to get us killed."

Warren chuckled and stepped on the accelerator.

They'd left behind the glitz and façade of the resorts near the beaches, and the island's impoverished majority lay exposed in all the helpless, hopeless filth and degradation of people experiencing poverty, trying to eke out a hardscrabble living as best they could.

It was times like this that made Cart appreciate the wealth and cleanliness of the USA. He knew there were poor people in America, but it wasn't as prevalent or open as here. It made him sad to see little children playing in the dirt and garbage, and he promised himself he'd try to do something about it. Wealth and prestige meant nothing when people lived like this.

The road steadily climbed, becoming worse the higher they drove. They zigzagged through little villages surrounded by dense forest crowding the road with coconut plantations and minor fields of crops somehow stolen from the rainforest, worked by solitary black men and women eyeing them suspiciously as they passed.

Warren pulled onto a narrow road, not much more than an overgrown path at times, as it climbed and descended steep hillsides. There were hair-raising drop-offs with no guardrails, barely wide enough for the Rover to squeak around tight corners, only to be met on the other side by old, beat-up transports belching blue smoke and demanding right-of-way by sheer size, overloaded with people and crates of chickens or pigs.

Warren remained impassive the whole time as he backed up to horrific pullouts on the outer side of the road, seeming to teeter on the very edge, while David covered his eyes and prayed. Cart clenched Roland's arm and braced himself against the door, trying not to look down into the depths of the yawning canyon. Sweat broke out on his forehead, and he joined David in fervent prayer.

"Are you going to be okay?" Roland asked, smiling.

Cart shook his head. "I don't think we're going to live through this...."

Roland laughed. "Just think of it as the Indiana Jones ride at Disneyland, without the giant rolling boulder. Although that could be a definite possibility."

Cart groaned.

A rough hour later, they drove through the rainforest, towering hardwoods and ferns choking the sunlight with emerald ferocity. Vines hung like thick cobwebs from the tree branches, and what they could see of the ground was covered with a litter of branches and leaves.

CHAPTER 42

Warren slowed as they rounded a curve and suddenly veered to the right, bouncing onto a deeply rutted track that led them deeper into the forest.

The Rover twisted and turned around trees and undergrowth, making a slow, tortuous journey through what seemed to be a claustrophobic green tunnel. Branches scraped the sides of the Rover, sounding like fingernails on a chalkboard, setting Cart's teeth on edge. Brightly colored parrots rose squawking from trees, rainbows of color stark against the forest's gloom.

Warren slowed the Rover to a crawl, then to a complete stop when they came upon a thick tree that had fallen across the path. It was too big to move, and the jungle was too dense to drive around it.

"Well, I guess this is where we get out," Roland said, climbing from the Rover. "We'll have to walk the rest of the way." David and Warren slid from the Rover to stand beside Roland, staring into the foliage. Cart shut his door quietly, astonished by the variety of plant life surrounding them: hundreds of different plants jumbled together in a slow-moving frenzy to reach the canopy-dimmed sunlight.

Flowers hung lazily from vine-choked branches, and vividly colored birds flitted around them, eating hordes of humming insects. Cart slapped at a sting on his neck, leaving a blood smear on his hand. It was so hot and humid in the rainforest, the air felt wet when he breathed.

This is going to be fun....

"How far do we have to go?" Cart asked, waving a hand in front of his face, vainly trying to disperse a cloud of mosquitoes hovering around him.

"I don't think it's too far," Roland grunted as he opened the back hatch of the Rover and handed out pith helmets with mosquito netting attached to cover their faces, along with cans of heavy-duty insect repellent. "This will at least keep the buggers out of your eyes and ears."

He sprayed himself well with bug repellent and passed it on.

Warren had been fiddling with his GPS watch as David watched him.

"Which way?" David asked.

Warren pointed to the right. "That way." He sighed. "You ready?"

Roland took some machetes from the hatch and gave them to the two men. "We are now!" he smiled.

Warren groaned.

David smiled gleefully, black eyes gleaming in his tattooed face, and began chopping at the growth. Warren gave him a few minutes, then followed, hacking at leftovers. Roland soon ducked into the tunnel they'd excavated, the sound of grunts mixing with the drone of insects.

It was hard going for a while, Roland and Cart cleaning the debris from the path as they followed. The undergrowth began to thin out a bit, and they saw sunlight ahead through the mass of trees. Small lizards flicked across their trail, sudden movements that startled Cart more than once. Another time, he heard a heavy rustling on the thickly covered floor to their left, more substantial than a bird or lizard.

"Probably an iguana," Roland said. "They can get up to six feet long, but that's mostly the tail. Good eating, though."

Cart looked at him to see if he was joking, but if he was, he hid it well.

CHAPTER 42

The ground began to rise slightly, and beyond the canopy of trees he saw a rainforest-covered hillside looming like a pea-green mound. It was growing lighter with each whack of a machete. They suddenly burst into a clearing, the sunlight briefly blinding them.

About twenty feet in front of them was a meager shack slapped together with old, corrugated steel like something a kid would build with odds and ends pilfered from a construction site. Great hardwoods leaned wearily over it, offering scant relief from the pounding sun. Layers of giant leaves and palm fronds thatched the roof, at least a foot thick, and Cart soon found out why.

Before they could reach the door, it began to rain, suddenly and with ferocity, the sky no longer able to contain the weight of the humid air, releasing giant drops that fell straight down and hit hard like pebbles. David reached the door first and wrenched it open to allow Roland and Cart to stumble in, drenched to the skin. Warren closed the door after himself.

The inside of the shack looked much like Cart thought it would: poorly constructed walls that leaned against one another as if offering solace for a long-lived life under the tropical skies. Two windows on walls perpendicular to the door offered little light and were covered only with mosquito netting.

The ceiling was tree branches holding up the thatched roof, with pillars of tree trunks bracing the whole thing up. The floor was hard-packed with dirt, but a few rugs laid on it. In one corner was a single cot with a thin mattress and blanket, draped with mosquito netting. There was a table in the room with two chairs around it, old and looking weak.

The oldest black man Cart had ever seen sat in one of the chairs, dark face lit by a single candle, next to a small picture easel holding a plaque with a square red cross on a white background.

CHAPTER 43

Annie

Although she'd grown up in the modest home nestled in the foothills of Bountiful, she felt out of place. She had good and bad childhood memories, but now it was no longer her home. She was a grown woman with a home of her own. She'd been with Cart longer than she'd lived here. Her father was still the same good-natured, quiet man he'd always been—a reassuring, stalwart figure she could always count on.

Her mother, while caring and nurturing, had never lost the ability to make Annie feel like a child. She believed her mother's doubting and cutting remarks were caused by a lifetime of insecurity about her immigrant parents and an underprivileged upbringing. She was unbearable to be around sometimes, and Annie would retreat to the bedroom she'd shared with her sister as a child. It had always been easier to ignore her remarks or find something else to do.

Then she would get angry at herself for being manipulated by the woman and climb the stairs, reminding herself she was forty-two years old.

Last night was the worst. Missing Cart and worried for Sarah, she'd told her mother how lonely she was.

Big mistake...

Following two hours of belittling remarks and sarcasm about Cart's sudden disappearance and his general lack of manly behavior by abandoning his family in their time of need, Annie decided she'd had enough. Turning on her mother, she threw words back at her like daggers, sharp and slashing, shielding herself and her love for Cart.

Her mother retreated from the unexpected onslaught, open-mouthed and wordless for the first time in Annie's memory. Her father, who usually withdrew silently into his office to be spared the woman's tongue, entered the kitchen frowning.

"What's going on?" he asked quietly, eyes burning into her mother's.

Her mother snapped out of her shocked muteness, eyes narrowing with displeasure as fire leaked back into them.

"I don't need to be talked to like this!" she said. "I'm her mother. If she can't show respect, she'll have to return home or go to a hotel until her loser of a husband comes home from wherever he is."

The room felt hot and suffocating, like a wool blanket on a hot summer night.

Her father looked at Annie, his old blue eyes softening.

"I don't think so," he said softly. He put his hand on Annie's arm, and she felt love and warmth from his age-spotted touch.

"Annie, why don't you check on Maddy to see if she's still sleeping after all this."

She slipped from the room, leaving behind the stifling kitchen.

CHAPTER 43

Upstairs, Maddy was sleeping, her little mouth twitching, her blonde hair tousled. Filled with loneliness and despair, she quietly laid by her daughter, hugging her gently, trying not to wake the precious little girl. Annie began weeping softly as the dam of hopelessness flooded her. Maddy squirmed, grunting, and Annie realized she was hugging her too tightly.

Maddy slowly opened her eyes, focusing on Annie. "Don't cry, Mommy," she whispered sleepily, her little hand touching Annie's cheek. "I'm still here."

Annie hugged her and wept harder, basking in the innocent concern of her younger daughter.

* * *

The following day, she rose early and went back to their house.

Maddy ran to her bedroom and flung herself at her toys with reckless abandon while Annie walked through the silent rooms, checking the state of the house.

How did something that seemed so alive feel so dead now? She was haunted by the dreadful silence, reminding her of a tomb. She'd put months of her life and energy into the house and now wished she'd never seen it. She would gladly trade it all for one more hug from Sarah, one day of happiness. She feared she'd never feel joy again or the warmth of a family living and loving together.

The house was a bleak and forlorn shadow of itself, as devoid of life and purpose as some fire-ravaged ruin. She felt like a refugee, wandering the desolate landscape where only sorrow reigned. This was not her dream house but an unrelenting nightmare from which she'd never wake.

She wandered into Cart's office and sat in the leather chair at his desk, closing her eyes and laying her head on his desk. *Dear God,* she thought tiredly, *please give me strength, if only for Maddy's sake.*

She could almost feel Cart's presence standing by her. She longed to feel his hand on her shoulder.

After several days of silence, he'd finally called her that morning, assuring her he was fine and would be home in a few days. When she asked him if he'd found out anything, he said they'd talk about it when he got home.

She missed him with a palpable ache and wondered what it would feel like if she never saw him again. She immediately thrust that from her thoughts.

Down that road lay madness....

A thought suddenly entered her mind, jarring her from her solemn brooding. She turned to the fireplace, questioning the sanity of her thoughts. She ignored the multi-colored Delft tiles surrounding the glass front. They weren't the same as the tiles in their bedroom. These were dead and silent. Above the mantle, the Scottish claymore swords hung silent and foreboding in the cold morning light pouring in from the window across from the door to the den. But it wasn't the swords whispering to her.

The Scottish dirks, the matched set of daggers, hung below the swords. She rose from the chair, hesitantly took one of the dirks from its place, and slipped it from its sheath, slowly turning it in her hand,

CHAPTER 43

feeling the power of it, the balance of weight and length. It felt comfortable. That was the word.

Comfortable....

She wondered if this blade had killed anyone and who'd wielded it, if it'd ever slipped through ribs and entered a beating heart....

She gasped at the thought, appalled by the horrific vision that entered her mind unbidden: the dagger protruding from a heaving back, just below the shoulder blade, blood issuing from the wound. She heard the echo of a scream, or thought she did, as though from a vast distance.

Annie....

She dropped the dagger, which landed point down into the hardwood floor, stuck upright and vibrating slightly.

She stared at the dagger embedded in the wood.

What had she seen and heard? She felt faint, queasy at what she'd glimpsed. She had never—*ever*—had a thought like that. She'd seen her share of violent movies, death and mayhem scattered across the screen like so much useless waste, but she didn't like violent movies the way Cart did. He loved the revenge-type movies where "someone got their butts kicked," as he put it. They agreed that he had to see a chick flick for every action-adventure she watched, which usually made him fall asleep or leave the room.

But movies were fiction, actors with fake wounds and blood. The lights came on, and you went home. But this had seemed so natural and real.

The blade stood at her feet, waiting. She looked at it, frowning at the memory of the pierced, bleeding back strong in her mind. She plucked it from the floor. It instantly conformed to her grasp, warming in her hand.

Comfortable and comforting.

She replaced it in the sheath and slid it into her bag.

CHAPTER 44

Fytie

Little Willem sat on a blanket on the stone floor, playing with a few odds and ends Mother had given him: a spoon, a small brass bowl, and a ball of yarn. It didn't take much to entertain him. He laughed when she took the little ball and tossed it against his chest so it would bounce onto the floor in front of him. She loved the little boy with shining eyes and tiny white baby teeth.

She was getting used to being his big sister.

She took him for a walk outside every day, letting him touch the goats or the cow. They'd sit by the canal while Jaap threw stones into the slow-moving water. Willem tried, but his eye-hand coordination wasn't good enough to do more than accidentally let it go somewhere between picking it up and attempting to throw it. More often than not, it would just fall out of his hand and roll to his feet.

It made her sad to think he'd never be able to do much more than that. He'd never grow, so his bones and muscles would never progress to support his weight. He would always be like this: a helpless baby, unable to function like a growing boy.

He was cute and cheerful, except when he was hungry or tired. Luckily, he never had to have his diaper changed, except when it was dirty from playing on the ground. It was fun to watch him playing with things everyday. But she wondered what was going on in his little brain, if the ability to grow and develop typically was even in him, struggling to waken and bring about the change from infant to toddler to adult. Or had Father taken it from him, wiping it out like deleting something from a computer? Maybe it was just gone when he brought them here, like the ability to die. She'd have to think about that.

In the meantime, she'd enjoy him as he was: a bright, shining part of her otherwise drab existence. After all, this was the closest she'd ever be to having a child of her own.

That night, around the table, as they ate the evening meal, Mother told them about growing up in Haarlem, the canals and the market square, and the Great Church in the middle of town. They laughed when she told them about her father pushing a barrow full of apples and hitting a loose paving stone, and the whole thing, including her father, falling into the canal. Jacobus laughed so hard, buttermilk came out of his nose, which made everyone else laugh harder.

It was a good meal, with syrup waffles for dessert, dried fruit, and tea for the late meal. Sarah went to bed smiling, hugging Jaap as he went quietly into his room so as not to wake Wilm. The night was cool, and a light breeze ruffled the curtains. She snuggled under the blankets and slept soundly for the first time since coming here.

The days floated by like a leaf in the slow canal. Fytie lost track of how many times the sun rose and set and how many times she milked

CHAPTER 44

the cow. Each day was like the one before and the one after. She grew content, knowing she was safe, fed, and loved.

* * *

Today was cheese day, and she was looking forward to it. It made her feel good to contribute to the needs of the family. She worked hard and did her best at everything.

Father was more jovial and complimented her on how well she'd prepared the fish and how wonderful the cheese tasted. It took a few months for the cheese to ripen to Father's taste, and he'd said the last batch was as good as any he'd eaten! She felt good when he told her things like that.

After cleaning up the noon meal Father and Mother went for a walk along the canal, leaving Fytie to care for the children. She loved to play with them.

Wilm sat on his blanket under the big tree while she and Jaap played tag, running around the house, into the cheese house and cold house, behind trees, and into the windmill, carefully avoiding the moving and grinding wheels.

After a while, they stopped, relaxing in the shade of the tree, letting the gentle breeze cool their sweat, sitting by Wilm on his blanket while eating leftover waffles and drinking cooled whey from the cold house. She noticed Jacobus looking at her closely.

"Are you happy?" he asked, "because you seem happier now than when you first came here."

She had to think momentarily, looking at the boy next to her. She loved Jaap. He could be fun-loving and mischievous one minute and serious and intent the next.

"I guess I am, Jaap," she said. "I didn't think I ever would be, but I decided that since I had no choice about being here, I might as well be happy. Being with you and Wilm makes it easier. I know Mother and Father love me. It's better than being miserable."

Jacobus's blue eyes studied her.

"What?" she asked him, smiling at his apparent hesitation.

"What was it like there?" he asked.

"Where?"

"Where you came from. What was it like?"

She sat for a moment, puzzled by his question.

It hit her like a stick to the side of the head. Her stomach was suddenly sick.

She hadn't thought about home for a long time—her natural home in the Other Place, about her life back there. She began to panic, realizing she couldn't remember what Maddy looked like and had only a vague recollection of her parents' faces.

What had happened? How could she have forgotten these things? Her heart felt like a cold stone in her chest as she tried to remember her family and friends at school and church. It was like trying to look through a foggy or filthy window. She would catch a glimpse of something or someone familiar, only to have it fade like a waking dream.

She couldn't understand how anything so precious to her could be gone, like it never existed. It was like she stood on a boat heading out to sea while back on shore, her family watching her sail away. The

CHAPTER 44

farther she sailed, the less she saw them, until they finally went beyond the horizon forever. She would completely forget her life and family in the Other Place. Sarah would be gone, as well, and she would be Sophiia forever and forever.

"Fytie?" Jacobus asked nervously, "are you alright? You don't look like you feel good."

She looked down at the little boy and saw the concern in his eyes. Willem was beginning to fuss. She picked the infant up, avoiding Jaap's eyes. "I'm fine. I just got too hot."

She took the baby into the house, Jaap silent at her heels. She fed Willem some of Mother's milk, rocked him until he slept, and then took him to his cradle. When she returned downstairs, Jacobus was still sitting in his chair, staring at the floor.

"Come on, Jaap," she said, extending her hand. "Let's go play hide-and-seek while Wilm sleeps. You count first, and I'll hide." Her enthusiasm sounded false to her, but Jacobus didn't notice, jumping from his chair and grabbing her hand.

While Jaap counted in the cheese house, she left the yard and entered the windmill, carefully climbing the steep wooden stairs until she was as high as she could go, up among the rafters where she knew Jaap was afraid to go alone. The view from the narrow window looked out over the endless tulip fields, where never a bee buzzed nor a fly annoyed.

She sat beneath the window, her back against the rough wooden wall, where the constant groan and creak of the enormous machinery drowned out all sound. She cried for the first time in what must have been months, sobbing until her chest heaved and her face and the front of her dress were drenched in tears, grieving for the family she'd lost.

Exhausted, she slowly descended the stairs, one level at a time, until she walked out the door into the sunlight of the yard. Jacobus was running around, feverishly calling her name, shouting for her. She heard the fear in his voice and saw the tears running down his face. He'd probably never been alone his whole long life. When he saw her, he ran and hugged her fiercely, his thin arms like steel bands.

"I couldn't find you! I couldn't find you!" he sobbed into her apron.

She hugged him to her, bending down to wipe his tears with her apron, tenderly kissing his forehead. "I'm sorry, Jaap," she said, "I fell asleep. Do you want to play some more or go in and rest?"

"Could you count this time?" he asked. "I don't want to...."

"Well, come on, then," she said, taking his hand, which still trembled slightly. "Let's go start over."

Together, hand in hand, they walked to the cheese house, where she went inside the cool darkness to count, and her little brother ran to hide somewhere in the yard.

CHAPTER 45

Cart

The old man had been reading a book on the table before him, a thin blanket draped over his shoulders. When they entered the shack, he put a marker on the page, closed the stained leather cover, and looked up at them, eyes shining in the glow of the candle. A single red rose stood in a crystal vase on the table.

His hair was white and thin, closely cropped like a scattering of frost above a face seemingly carved from old mahogany. Roughly hewn wrinkles furrowed his features, laid by years of grief and toil. There were also laugh lines radiating from around his eyes and mouth. He smiled at them with unrestrained joy. There were only a few teeth the color of old ivory left in that old smile, but his eyes drew Cart's gaze. They were old and partially clouded by cataracts but steady and focused. From where Cart stood four or five feet away from the man, Cart saw the strength and intelligence filling them. He instantly felt at ease with this man, felt the warmth in his friendly gaze.

"Ah, you are finally here," the man said.

His voice was soft and quiet, and Cart had to strain to hear him. He had a soft French accent and a mild Caribbean *patois* that reminded Cart of a pirate movie. The tropical rain thundered outside as the man put his book aside and stood slowly, bones settling into place with audible creaks and snaps. He extended a hand that looked like a gnarled bole of wood. His arthritic fingers were bent nearly sideways to a palm the color of creamed coffee. Cart took the offered hand carefully, afraid he'd hurt him.

"Yes, Master Alain," Roland said respectfully. "We got here as quickly as we could. We had to walk the last bit. A tree in the road delayed us."

"We'll have to see to that!" The man chuckled, his eyes nearly swallowed by swaddling wrinkles. "I am truly sorry for that. I will see to it soon!"

There's no way this old man could cut up that tree and move it, Cart thought. *He looks like he couldn't make it to the bed.*

"This is Carter Benson, Master," Roland said. "He's anxious to speak with you about his daughter."

The old man put his hand over Cart's and squeezed gently, yellow eyes brimming with concern. Even that minor movement must have been excruciating to those crooked fingers.

"I am so sorry for your daughter, Monsieur Benson. Truly, I am sorry," the man said. "I hope we can be of help to you. Roland has told me much about you, and I've been waiting for you. Please sit, my friend." He indicated the chair across from him. The old man carefully lowered himself into his own chair.

CHAPTER 45

Cart sat at the table, wondering what this was all about. Why had they made the long trip to this poor shack in the middle of a rainforest? It seemed so incongruous compared to the luxury of the aircraft that brought them here. Who was this man who earned such respect from these men? And why didn't they fly him directly home so he could deal with the tile himself? It seemed like answers were in short supply lately, but perhaps he'd get some now.

"Welcome to my humble abode, Monsieur Benson," the man said, "or may I call you Carter?"

"Please call me Cart," he answered. "All my friends do."

"And," Master Alain smiled. "You may call me Alain. And I assure you all my friends do, as well." The smile quickly faded from his face. "But we have much to discuss before you leave here. It will get dark soon, and we must get you home to Utah as quickly as possible. There are things you must understand and explanations that you richly deserve that can only be discussed here, in my home.

"Please, Cart, tell me what you know about the Templars."

"Templars? The Knight Templars?" Cart was confused. "They were disbanded in the 1300s." He'd taken a Medieval History class at the U. "They were tortured and burned at the stake in France. But that's about all I know. What does that have to do with the tiles and my daughter?"

"All in good time, Cart," Alain said. "It is a long story, but I'll be as brief as possible. Roland tells me you heard from our Belgian friends the origin of the tiles, yes? I believe Madam Locksley somewhat explained her organization seeking this tile?"

Cart nodded to both questions.

"The Templars, or the Poor Fellow Soldiers of Christ and of the Temple of Solomon—also known as the Order of Solomon's Temple, the Knights Templar, or simply Templars—were organized in 1119 in France and commissioned by Pope Innocent II for the protection of pilgrims to the Holy Land during the Crusades. Although Jerusalem was reasonably safe under Christian control, the rest of the area was not. Many Pilgrims were slaughtered or robbed on the long, dangerous road.

"These first Knights were very poor and needed donations to survive, but that changed over the years. Many wealthy kingdoms in Europe had sons who wanted to join and donated land and gold to the Knights. They became rich, with vast landholdings and many castles. They even owned the island of Cyprus at one time.

"But the story is long, and we would be here for many hours while I talk until my voice is gone. When you get home and this is all finished, I suggest you research them. It is sufficient to say they were distrusted by King Louis V of France, who was jealous of their wealth and owed them much money from loans they had given him to support his war against England. He used false charges and collusion with Pope Clement to arrest the Templars in France and seize their wealth and properties there.

"The arrested Templars were tortured to make false confessions and were burned at the stake as punishment. But that was only those Templars in France. After the Pope officially disbanded the organization, many Templars held to their oath. They went underground, fleeing to many nations to continue their God-given duty of protection to those needing it. Over the centuries, many Knights have died in

CHAPTER 45

their commitment to their oath, but they never failed. Marriages took place, and sons followed fathers into knighthood, son after son, until now. I am the son of a Templar, my line going back to the early days of our brotherhood. My own sons are Knights now, serving throughout the world."

Cart was stunned by what he was hearing. The Templars still exist?

"But how can this be?" he asked. "I mean, I know they're legendary, and books and movies about them have been made, but I thought that's what they were: legend. Why aren't they more well-known?"

"We are a secret organization, Cart, and we find that works best for our purposes. Initially, we were shock troops in the battles with Muslims in the Middle East during the Second Crusade. We would swoop down on foes and destroy them or die ourselves. We never surrendered and never will."

"How did you stay hidden?" asked Cart. "I can't understand how no one ever reported your existence. Surely, someone must have noticed you."

Alain smiled. "We have been doing this for nearly one thousand years. We know what we are doing.

"Our organization has evolved over the centuries. Initially, we were an organization of warrior-monks dedicated to the Pope and the Church, and pilgrims traveling to the Holy Land. After the betrayal by Pope Clement, we branched out into other areas of protection. We now protect any who need us, regardless of religious affiliation or ethnicity. We also investigate and watch other secret organizations that may be invested in the destruction of society, such as those over which Madam Locksley governed.

"We've been aware of this tile since the 1600s; indeed, Roland's ancestor testified at the trial of Pieter Jacobszoon, although he was neither part of the scheme to convict him, nor part of the torture following the trial. As a Templar, he was investigating Jacobszoon. His name was Roland de Hastings."

Cart glanced at Roland, standing by the door, who nodded. "I'm a direct descendant of that Knight. I'm honored to be in his line. I was tasked with infiltrating the Brotherhood and keeping watch for when they discovered the tile.

"It took me two decades to gain their trust. I had to do things I'm not proud of to get to this point. It was time for me to act when I knew they'd brought you from Haarlem. David and Warren are sergeants within our organization but aren't Knights. They are my friends and my responsibility. They, and I, are willing to die to retrieve your daughter and protect your family."

Cart was touched by Roland's words and didn't doubt his sincerity. He wanted to ask so many questions, but there was only one question he wanted them to answer.

"How can we get Sarah back?"

Master Alain looked deeply at Cart, his eyes moist. "You and your family are under our protection, Cart, and I'm happy to explain what we need to do.

"When this artist, Pieter Jacobszoon, created this tile, I don't believe he understood what he had drawn from the darkness. I'm amazed he could summon this creature from wherever it languished and capture it within the bounds of a piece of tile. Fortunately, the knowledge of how to do that died with him, thank God. But I do not judge the

CHAPTER 45

man, for to do so, I would have to stand in his shoes and undergo the pains and suffering he experienced. I am only a man, yes? However, I can hope he's found forgiveness through the blood of Christ, and we can try to right the wrong that has been done. Are you prepared to do whatever it takes to get your daughter back from this creature who has taken her?"

"Of course," Cart said. "I would die for her."

Alain nodded. "I believe you. What I tell you comes from a lifetime of studying the works of evil, and most especially this Brotherhood. As with the life of our Master, Jesus Christ, all good comes from sacrifice. As He told the rich young man, sell all you own and give to the poor, then follow Him. This young man couldn't give up his precious possessions and lost what would have been the most precious.

"I liken you to this young man in some ways. You are wealthy and have many possessions, including a wonderful family. You must consider your life and decide what to sacrifice to get Sarah back. This is how we receive blessings from God. It is also the way to defeat evil in all its forms. Christ offered Himself to allow us all to gain eternal life and forgiveness for our sins.

"By retrieving her, we can simultaneously banish this unspeakable being back to the darkness from whence it came, but you must commit yourself to do this. You, out of all the billions in this world, are the only one that can do it. It won't be easy, and it won't be safe. But you must do what must be done, or you will never see your daughter again, and this creature will be free to run rampant over this world. Are you willing to listen to me and learn?"

Cart suddenly felt the world's weight fall on his shoulders and was filled with a great weariness. The sweltering shack suddenly felt cold, like the winter in Europe had followed them here, but maybe it was the cold he felt in his heart. How could he save the world from this creature and get his daughter back? He imagined never seeing his family again, never giving Sarah a hug. He sighed deeply and looked at the old man. A sudden fire filled him.

"Yes," he whispered, "I would give my life for Sarah. Tell me what to do."

The master smiled widely, his eyes lost again in the wrinkles of his face. "That is what I wanted to hear, Cart. I know your heart and your desire. This will take great sacrifice on your part, although I pray it will not require your life. It must be done with great care, or Sarah will be irretrievably lost and great evil will be unleashed on the world. I cannot tell you what to sacrifice, for I am me, and you are you; you have your own passions and dreams, your own path in this world. As you return home, think about this, then act swiftly.

"Our friends in Belgium also want this tile and will do anything to get it, with regard for no one. They are reeling from losing their headquarters and those in the chateau. It will take them some time to regroup. But be assured they will regroup, then turn the full strength of their organization and focus it on you."

He paused for a moment, looking intently into Cart's eyes.

"This much I can tell you: Do not break the tile! Whatever you do, do not break the tile! Your daughter will be lost forever, and the demon will be free to wreak havoc under the control of the Brotherhood. Do you understand these things?"

CHAPTER 45

"Some things I do, but not all. I'll have to trust what you say is true. But I'll do whatever I have to."

The old man nodded.

"Sacrifice, Carter. Remember that word." Alain struggled to stand. "Ah, I am weary of my own voice, Cart. I haven't talked this much since I was a much younger man. I am worn to the bones and an old man."

Cart jumped to his feet and reached to help him. The old man took the offered arm and pulled Cart to him, hugging him tightly.

"Good luck, my friend," he whispered into Cart's ear. "My thoughts will be with you, though I cannot leave this place. Follow your heart and do what you know is best."

"I will, sir," Cart said. "Thank you."

"No, I am simply Alain, a tired old man. Now I must rest." He smiled weakly, his eyes buttery soft. "Will you help me to my bed? It is time for a nap, I think!"

As he left the table, he took the rose from the vase. "Please, give this to Sarah when you get her back. It is my gift to her." His gap-toothed smile warmed Cart's heart. He took the rose from Alain, helped him to the cot, and gently lowered him onto it, drawing the sheet over the old, crooked body, bent and distorted by age and arthritis.

The old man took Cart's hand in his own gnarled one. "Goodbye, Carter Benson. Good luck, and God be with you." Then in moments, he was asleep, and Cart laid the old hand on his softly rising and falling chest. He reached out and quietly touched the man's cheek.

He felt a hand on his shoulder. "It's time to go, Cart," Roland whispered. "We need to get you home."

A Jeep was waiting outside the shack, engine idling. Cart was puzzled about how the SUV got there. The three men smiled, and Roland clapped him on the shoulder.

"You didn't think Master Alain lived here alone, did you?" he asked.

"I guess I did," Cart answered. "It never occurred to me that he didn't."

"That's the idea. The Master appears to be a lone old man living in the forest."

Puzzled, Cart nodded.

"Then I would say our ruse works well, don't you think?"

Cart looked dumbly at Roland, who laughed. "The hill that the shack is built into," Roland said, "is filled with the same sort of installation the Belgians had: offices, computers, satellite communications, housing, and a couple of hundred people working twenty-four seven, including bodyguards for Master Alain. To the outside world, he's just an old man living alone in a hut in the rainforest. He is never alone and never unprotected. That is how important he is to our work."

* * *

Cart sat silently on the return trip to Castries, thinking about all he had heard and learned.

David and Warren stayed behind in St. Lucia, and after shaking Cart's hand, David swept him up in his massive arms, Cart's feet dangling off the floor.

"Be careful, man," the big Māori said. "Get your girl back safe." When he lowered Cart to the ground, Cart saw tears in the man's

CHAPTER 45

eyes. Warren had shyly taken his hand, shaking it silently. Cart was deeply touched by both of them. He'd come to feel close to them all over the past few days.

Alain had sent Roland with Cart to assist him and function as a bodyguard, and he was grateful for the man's presence. He had come to appreciate the stalwart man and his willingness to sacrifice so much to get Sarah back.

* * *

The low rumble of the jet was soothing background noise as it flew northwest through the dying day, chasing the sunset.

"Roland, what was it with the roses?" he asked Roland. "Back at the chateau in Belgium, what were the roses about? There were so many, it seemed obsessive, yet Alain had only one rose with him. What's the deal with them?" Cart was looking at the rose Alain had given him, now in a white vase on the table between them.

Roland smiled. "Master Alain keeps a rose on his table to remind himself of the Sacrifice of Christ and our devotion to Him. For you to understand the Endless Rose Brotherhood, I need to explain its roots. I'm sure you'd like to hear that, wouldn't you?"

"Absolutely, I do," Cart said, "You're not going to kill me afterward, are you?"

Roland laughed. "You've seen too many movies, Cart. Movies, books, and video games sometimes portray Templars as evil, money-grubbing, murderous thieves, but we aren't. We aren't part of their Rose Brotherhood, just observers and warriors willing to defend our world from their actions. I don't care if you know about them. The more people who know the truth will help shed light on their existence, which has been shadowy and evil. We've learned a lot about them through the years.

"They use the symbol of a white cross with a red rose at its center in mockery of the Blood and Death of Christ, whom we serve. They say their cross represents the human body, and the rose represents the opening consciousness. But really, their cross is a phallic symbol, the most base and evil part of mankind, and a symbol of their depravity.

"Do you recall what Locksley told you about the origin of their society?"

"Well," Cart said, "I don't remember names, but she said it was founded in the 1500s by some German guy that traveled in the Middle East."

"We honestly don't know what's true and what isn't regarding them," Roland said. "They claim this guy, Christian Rosenkreuz, who, by the way, may or may not be an actual person, wrote several discourses about alchemy and things he'd learned from mystics, couching things in obscure, mysterious terms they claimed they got from ancient Egyptians gods and the secret society that the Masons supposedly formed from.

"Some modern societies claim to be the true descendants of the Rose Brotherhood, but that is purely speculative. Some believe other secret societies have ties to the early Rose Brotherhood, including the Freemasons, the Illuminati, and the Templars, which is absolute nonsense. Some modern groups call themselves Templar, but they are only people trying to dress like us, making false oaths, and walking in parades. Silly stuff, really. Although they say imitation is the sincerest

CHAPTER 45

form of flattery, in this case, it's a mockery of who we truly are, bordering on blasphemy. The same is true of the modern Masons."

"Masons?" Cart asked. "You mean like the stone masons that built the pyramids? I've read that the Masons also claim to have begun in Egypt."

"I guess it depends on what you want to believe," Roland said. "Masons may have adopted some of the Rose Brotherhood's beliefs, but that hasn't been proven, at least not to my belief. That was a strange time in the history of the Earth. There was a lot of unrest among people. Many, intellects mostly, were searching for something to give purpose to their lives. They were tired of being told what to do and how to live by those in authority."

"Like the Church?" Cart asked.

"Yes, exactly, and various governments. Different philosophers and scientists claimed to be able to make gold from lead or what they called alchemy, and occult beliefs were propagated among the various sects supposedly drawn from the ancient gods of Egypt."

"I read somewhere that alchemy really meant changing a person through learning or spiritual growth," Cart said. "Anything that makes them better."

"That's right," Roland agreed, "but some people weren't content with that simple explanation. They wanted something—*more*—that made them feel essential or unique among the filthy humans they lived with. They talked about the need for equality among all the Earth's inhabitants, but when it came down to it, they actually wanted to have power over mankind. Unfortunately, they couched their ideas in attractive ways to those who felt downtrodden.

"That's where our friends in Belgium entered the picture. They may have begun by trying to better the world but became so intrigued by the darker aspects of the beliefs and esoteric nonsense that they lost their way. They gained great power from their magics, incantations, initiations, and filthy rites."

Cart stared at Roland. "You mean they are magicians? Witches? Wizards?"

"Whatever they call themselves makes no difference. They are evil and will not stop until they subjugate the whole world and crush any resistance beneath their feet. You saw how little Sarah's life mattered to them. They will do whatever it takes to accomplish their goal: to rule over all mankind. When that creature within the tile is released, they can do that.

"And that's where we, as Templars, come in." Roland's face was grave, etched in resolve. "We also will not stop until the Endless Rose Brotherhood is destroyed. Part of our original oath was to never leave a battlefield until we emerged victorious or were carried off the field in death. As long as our standard stood, we would fight."

He looked intently at Cart. *"Non-Nobis Domine, Non-Nobis, Sed Nominituo Da Gloriam,"* he said. "'Not in Our Name, Lord, Not in Our Name, But in the Name of Your Glory.' That is our motto and the Rule of Life. We do not take this oath lightly. I would die to protect you and your family and to return Sarah to you."

Cart felt tears forming in the corners of his eyes. He found it hard to speak. Here was a man so devoted to his Order and Christ, as the Lord, that nothing else could overcome his beliefs and oath. He felt small next to Roland—not because Roland's size made him feel that

CHAPTER 45

way, but because Cart thought of his weaknesses as a father and a husband. He vowed that if he and his family survived this, he would be different: calmer, understanding, and more—*there*—for them.

"Thank you, Roland," he said. "I believe you."

"Then let's get some sleep. We have a lot to do when we get to Salt Lake."

Roland dimmed the lights and reclined his seat, quickly sleeping.

Sleeping took Cart longer, but he eventually drifted off, wondering if he could ever prove himself worthy of the name Templar.

CHAPTER 46

Fytie

One early morning, while making cheese, Sarah heard a persistent whining sound that seemed familiar, but she couldn't figure out what it was. Her hand was deep in the copper pot, stirring the warm curds, breaking them up when she first noticed the sound. It would whine and stop, whine and stop, in irregular patterns, over and over again.

It was very annoying!

It seemed to come from different areas in the cheese house: first by the door, then the fireplace, the window, and now over the drained bucket of whey. She couldn't see anything when she looked at a particular area where the whine was, which puzzled her.

She knew what the noise was but couldn't put a name to it. She tried to ignore it, but that was impossible. The constant whine was seriously getting on her nerves.

She was washing her hands when she felt a tickle on her arm.

She looked at it and saw a black—thing—crawling on her arm just above her elbow. It crawled slowly down onto her forearm, irritating the tiny hairs on her skin. It had two wings on either side of its black body, and as she watched, it raised two front arms.

She was suddenly repulsed by it and instinctively swatted it with her other hand without even thinking. Pulling her hand away, she saw it was flattened and unmoving, with a syrupy red substance like jam smeared all over it. Fighting the impulse to gag, she wiped it off her arm with her handkerchief, but carefully so she could show Father.

He would know what it was.

Fytie stopped Father as he walked from his boat, a bucket of fish in each hand and Jacobus at his side.

"Good day, daughter! What have you been doing?" he asked in his usual cheery voice.

"Just making cheese, Father," she answered, "but this was also in the cheese house." She showed him the glob in her handkerchief.

He stared at it for a while, unmoving, before taking it from her. "Was this the only one?" he asked quietly.

"Yes, Father."

"What is it?" Jaap asked, standing on tiptoes to see what the handkerchief held.

"It's nothing," Father said, folding the cloth and shoving it into his pocket. Take one of the fish buckets to your mother while Fytie and I go to the cheese house."

Jaap picked up one of the buckets and waddled toward the house, the bucket swinging heavily between his legs.

Father led the way to the cheese house. The cow stared dumbly at them, swishing her tail as they passed. Fytie saw more of the black

CHAPTER 46

things flying around Truida. Father opened the cheese door, and she hurried to follow.

Father stood inside the door, head cocked to one side as he listened. He walked back to the cow pen, staring at Truida, his black brows furrowed. The cow wandered to the far side of the pen, eyeing them nervously while she constantly swished her tail, slapping her back and ears.

"What is wrong, Father?" she asked him. He ignored her and walked to the goat pen, leaning on the fence and watching the animals as he listened.

He went to the middle of the road in front of their home and stood silently gazing out at the tulip fields. His face was like a stone, his black eyes troubled as he turned from her and walked to the windmill, staring at the ground.

Why should he be so worried about a fly? she wondered, watching him. Then her eyes widened in shock.

A fly! It was a fly!

Why couldn't she remember that earlier when she first saw it? It was just a fly. She must have seen thousands of them in her lifetime. She began walking swiftly to Father, eager to share her insight. Then she stopped as she processed what she'd discovered. She'd never seen a fly here before—not in this world, not even running through the tulip fields or cleaning fish with Mother. Not once.

"It's a fly!" she called to Father as he opened the windmill door. He stopped and looked back at her, his great shoulders sagging, his brows clenched over his black eyes.

"It's a fly," she said softly.

"I know," he said before disappearing into the darkness of the windmill.

Fytie was dumbstruck on the road as her mind churned.

It was a fly....

CHAPTER 47

Cart

It was shortly after 3 a.m. when they landed in Salt Lake City. The air was clear and cold, like frozen crystal. The stars that weren't washed out by city lights sparkled in the velvet bowl of the sky. It must have stormed recently for the air to be this clear.

It was cold, standing on the tarmac of the private hangar, waiting for the group's Land Rover to warm up. To go from the tropical humidity of St. Lucia to this bone-numbing cold shocked his system, like returning home after the Christmas vacation to Hawaii. That reminded Cart of Sarah, and his heart suddenly ached for her.

"Are you okay?" Roland asked, standing near him, bundled in a parka and woolen hat, his white hair bristling around the edges. they climbed in the Rover, Roland taking the driver seat.

"Just thinking," Cart said. "Nervous, too, I guess. This is it, isn't it? I'm almost home and still haven't decided what to do. My mind is a mass of confusion. I don't want to make any mistakes with this. I'm scared, Roland, to be honest. This is my daughter and my last hope to get her home."

Roland patted his arm. "Just keep thinking, Cart. I'm here to help however I can, but it has to be your decision."

Cart left a message on Annie's phone, letting her know he was back in town, heading to the house, and telling her to stay away until he called her.

Terminating the call, he stared morosely out the window as Roland headed north out of the parking lot to get on the freeway. To the north, Cart saw the oil refineries that filled the space between Salt Lake and North Salt Lake, west of I-15. The fires of many waste stacks lit the ugly, treeless mountain to the east in a garish glow, like the smoky fires of hell. Staring at the flames against the night sky, his mind clicked into place. He suddenly knew what he had to do.

Cart told Roland what he planned on the drive along the cold, nearly empty freeway.

Roland nodded. "I think that's what Master Alain had intended all along," he said. "I was just waiting for you to make the right choice, although I would have helped you, no matter your decision."

* * *

Now they were sitting in the long, circular driveway of the vacant house directly west of his own, headlights out, car turned off. Cart's nerves were on edge, tingling with anticipation.

He led Roland across the frozen, snow-covered driveway, carefully opening the gate to the home's backyard. Creeping in the snow was difficult, their shoes crunching with every step. He hoped the many overgrown bushes and trees would muffle any sound. Luckily, no dogs barked.

CHAPTER 47

Roland grabbed a discarded garbage can as they crept and upended it at the wood fence dividing the two properties, probably the same spot the hooligans had used to break into his home over Christmas. Roland and Cart took turns scrambling over the fence, landing softly on the piled snow that had built up.

It felt odd standing at the side of his house in the bitter cold darkness like a thief, especially with what he planned to do. He saw Maddy's play set in the backyard. The playhouse swings and slide looked like an alpine chalet. The tennis court was covered with snow, the net long stored away.

He looked at the roofline high above him, looming heavily overhead. He dropped his keys twice as he tried to unlock the basement door with shaking hands.

What am I doing? he asked himself. *This is our house, our home.* Then he thought of Sarah and unlocked the door leading to the gloomy hallway. The alarm keypad by the door beeped as he closed it, beginning the silent countdown, and he quickly entered the passcode that would disable the system before the alarm started shrieking and the police were summoned. He stood momentarily, breathing deeply, trying to slow his racing heart, and listened.

The house was like a tomb. No sounds emanated from its depths, just the somber loneliness of a deserted house. He shed his coat, gloves, and hat as Roland went around the outside of the house toward the front yard. He headed for the common area in the basement, carefully threading his way around buckets of paint, lacquer thinner, ladders, and wood trim left by the workmen repairing their home before Sarah disappeared, using his phone's flashlight to find his way.

He heard the basement door close softly and saw Roland come toward him, quiet as a ghost. "We don't have to worry about the cop," he whispered to Cart when he stood beside him.

Cart stared at him. "You didn't . . ."

"No." Roland chuckled at the expression on Cart's face. "I didn't kill him. He just got really sleepy all of a sudden. He'll be fine, just a mild headache. I even left his car running so he wouldn't freeze."

"Nice guy," Cart said, and shook his head. He led Roland down a short hallway to the mechanical room door. He unlocked the door and pushed it open. The overhead light came on automatically. Roland squeezed past him into the concrete space.

Tiny, multicolored lights glowed on various machines. The boiler, the snow-melt system in the driveway, the water softener, air purifier, backup furnace, and everything else that made their home comfortable in all seasons. Metal panels hid wires, switches, knobs, and electrical breakers.

He knew next to nothing about the workings of this mysterious room. All he knew was that when everything was working correctly, they were safe and warm, safe and cool, or just safe, thanks to the alarm system. There was also a sprinkler system throughout the house in case of a fire. Roland seemed to understand what everything was for, though, and quickly began opening panels, scanning each section before moving on to the next.

"Ah," Roland said, "I found what I needed. This won't take long, so you better go upstairs and get started while I disable the alarms and other systems we need off."

CHAPTER 47

Cart left him in the mechanical room and headed for the stairs, pausing to pick up a heavy, five-gallon bucket of lacquer thinner.

* * *

The house was silent except for the refrigerator compressor. The kitchen was bathed in darkness, except for the backyard light they kept lit at all times. He thought about turning it off but decided against it. If a neighbor noticed it was suddenly off, it might alert them. It was best to leave things as normal as possible. It wouldn't matter in a while, anyway.

He slid a drawer open and took the box out. Hefting the can of thinner, he stole through the silent shadows to the great room on the opposite side of the house. Quickly surveying the room, he began taking books off shelves and throwing them into a pile in the middle of the room, on top of the expensive Persian rug that covered a section of the hand-chiseled wood floor. He added the antique chairs, coffee table, and side tables to the pile.

Twisting the lid off the can of thinner, he dumped some onto the pile, reeling at the overwhelming smell. He was growing dizzy from the chemicals, so he quickly splashed some on the wood-paneled walls and across the wood floor.

Satisfied, he took the box from his pocket and drew a slender wooden stick from it. Striking the match against the side of the box, it flared to life.

It's now or never, he thought. *This is for Sarah....*

He stepped back several feet and threw the match on the pile of expensive tinder.

The fire burst into life with a resounding *fwumph* like a miniature explosion. The flames were voracious, greedily spreading across the floor and up the walls; dry wood popped and crackled, and books smoldered and burned as the fire ate into them.

Cart picked up the thinner and ran from the room, worried about the highly flammable liquid sloshing inside. He didn't want to become a screaming human torch. The garish glow danced and surged along the walls as he went to the bedrooms on this level. He left them in flames.

He heard a pop from the basement and smiled, knowing Roland was busy down there.

The kitchen and family room were next, so he splashed the remaining lacquer thinner through those rooms. Satisfied that the thinner was doing its terrible job, he threw the empty can to the side and headed for the stairs to the basement. Hopefully, Roland had the fire alarm disabled now because it would soon be shrieking in protest at the flames greedily devouring the house.

Hastily running down the stairs, he wondered if he should get a fire going down there, as well, but he needed to get Roland and himself out of there.

"Roland!" he shouted as he crossed the floor. "You about finished in there?"

No answer. Roland must have the door shut.

He rounded the corner to the hallway and saw the door was closed. Roland must be working on something behind the door, and he wouldn't have heard him with it closed.

CHAPTER 47

He tapped lightly on the door to warn Roland so he wouldn't get hit when the door swung open. Cracking the door open and saying Roland's name, he saw the room was darkened.

Why had he turned out the light? Maybe the pop he heard earlier were some electrical breakers tripping? He stumbled over something on the floor as he entered the room. He swiveled his phone light down.

Roland laid prone at his feet, lifeless eyes staring at him indifferently. A small hole in his temple fed a growing puddle of blood on the concrete floor. Cart dropped to his knees and held Roland to his chest, feeling his shirt dampening from his blood.

"Roland . . ." he whispered, panic surging in him. What had happened? What could he do now, knowing his friend was dead and he was alone in the burning house? Roland . . .

He felt something hard and cold press against the back of his head.

"Sorry about your friend, Mr. Benson," a familiar voice said. "These things happen, you know."

CHAPTER 48

Sarah

There were flies everywhere now.

The constant drone of what seemed like a billion tiny wings was deafening. Fytie's head throbbed from the vibration. It felt like her bones were quivering with the tone enveloping their world.

She remembered an old movie they'd watched every Easter back home in the Other Place: *The Ten Commandments*. That's what this was like. A plague sent by God to punish Father and Mother for not letting her go.

Let me go! she shouted in her mind as the flies crawled all over her.

She couldn't make the cheese because of the flies. They drowned in the warm milk, floating in thick black clumps on the white surface as more flies crawled over the dead ones. The room whined around her maddeningly. She spat out flies trying to creep into her mouth, closed her eyes, and frantically slashed her arms around her head to ward off the insects. When she could take it no longer, she fled the cheese house.

Truida stood forlornly in the corner of her pen, covered by a surging mass of black flies, tail uselessly flicking back and forth. Flies crept into her eyes, nose, and mouth. The mounds of stinking poop looked alive as flies assailed the pungent masses. Father had never allowed poop or bad smells here.

Mother had the doors and windows shut tight, trying to keep the hordes of flies at bay. That, too, was hopeless. They found their way down the chimney and through minute cracks around windows and doors. Mother covered Wilm with a light blanket to shield him, but it was too hot. He cried, trying to fling the blanket off.

That was another thing, the days were hotter now, and the nights frigid. Before, the temperature was constant, a perfect temperature at all times. Now the sun blazed like an angry god, and Sarah had to wear all her clothes at night, shivering under her blankets, waiting for the sun to rise and bring warmth and the plague of flies again.

Sweat poured off Mother's face, dripping into the bread dough she was kneading. She looked exhausted, her brow furrowed on her lovely face, the circles under her eyes like charcoal smudges. Jacobus must be outside somewhere.

Sarah hadn't seen Father for days. Wait … Sarah? She realized she wasn't thinking of herself as Fytie or Sophiia anymore. She knew her name was Sarah. Sarah Benson. It awakened her desire to leave this horrible place and return to her family. But how? She didn't know.

When she asked Mother where Father was, she only shrugged and answered with a tired, ragged voice: "Gone to find out what is going on. I don't know where Father is. He's gone to wherever he goes."

If Father had so much control over this world, why had things changed so much? Was he losing control? Were they all going to be eaten by swarming hordes of flies and maggots?

CHAPTER 48

She tried to help Mother as best she could, holding Wilm, cooing to him, and playing with him, but in the end, she laid Wilm in his cradle and fled to the bridge over the canal leading to the tulip fields, staring down the canal to see if Father was returning. Flies crawled up the back of her dress, in her hair, and on her face. She didn't bother to shoo them away. What was the point? They just returned with more flies.

She looked out at the grove of trees in the field, looking for Jacobus, startled by what she saw.

The tulips were dying.

CHAPTER 49

Cart

"Stand up slowly and keep your hands where I can see them. And don't turn around. I don't want to kill you, not just yet, but don't think I won't."

Cart gently laid Roland down on the concrete and slowly stood. He knew he was a finger twitch from death.

The light flicked on overhead, his eyes recoiling from the sudden brightness. The sight of Roland's lifeless body broke his heart. Ultimately, Roland had become a friend and had tried to help get Sarah back.

"Put your hands on your head and turn around slowly."

Cart complied.

Detective Martina Gregson stood by the door, the barrel of her pistol staring like a cyclopean eye at Cart's chest. Her hair was mussed, and she wore no makeup.

"Did you have to kill him?" Cart asked.

He suddenly felt tired and hopeless, like the optimism Master Alain and Roland had instilled in him was draining away. And now it was all over. All the days of searching, travel, and knowledge he'd gained were replaced by empty desperation.

"Actually, I did," she said, her teeth gleaming in the light. "I didn't need Roland's self-righteous interference—not right now. He would have died eventually, anyway. It's the way things work. He knew too much, and besides, he was the enemy."

"He was a friend," Cart said numbly, "and a good man."

"When I was sent here to find the tile, Madam Locksley told me it would probably end like this: mano a mano or 'mano a womano,' I guess you could say, with a Templar. I've been waiting for this a long time, Cart. You remember you asked me to call you Cart, don't you? Back at lunch the first time we met."

Cart stared at her, hatred filling his heart and flooding his mind. Then he smelled smoke.

"Cat got your tongue?" she smirked. "I thought we had a real connection going there, didn't you? A real friendship."

Cart's eyes burned with anger, like the burning house above them.

"Guess not, huh?" she said. "Well, we have work to do upstairs, old friend, before the fire reaches your bedroom. I should shoot you now, but unfortunately, I need your help with the tile." She gestured with the gun toward the door.

"Come on, time to go upstairs."

She stood to the side of the door to allow Cart to pass, keeping the gun pointed at him.

He walked slowly, with a last glimpse at Roland. When he reached the door, he lunged at Gregson, pushing her back into the room. She tripped over Roland and fell, the gun exploding in her hand, the bullet

CHAPTER 49

driving into the wall next to Cart. He slammed the door shut and ran for the stairs, dodging construction debris littering the floor.

Adrenaline flooded him, and he ran up the stairs two steps at a time, listening to Gregson screaming and cursing. She was coming up the stairs. The rooms beyond the kitchen were burning hot, smokey, the flames devouring them voraciously.

He needed to protect the tile and any possibility of rescuing Sarah. He ran blindly up the stairs to the bedroom, choking on the smoke. He heard Gregson cursing in the kitchen, thinking Cart had gone to his office.

Then she began calling up the stairs. "Carrterr! Oh, Carrrtteeerrr!" Gregson's sing-song voice was a chilling parody of a child's hide-and-seek game. "Where are you?"

CHAPTER 50

Sarah

The tulips were withered and dead—every single one, as far as she could see.

Walking among the desiccated husks, flies flailing her unmercifully, the ground crunching under her feet, she shouted Jacobus's name above the drone of the flies. He wasn't in the windmill or any other outbuilding. That left the trees in the dead tulip field.

The bridge was behind her, and she was headed for the grove where he loved to climb and play an adventurer. Her voice was harsh from shouting, and the flies drove her insane. She'd wrapped a cloth around her face to shield her mouth and nose from the unrelenting hordes, but they still crawled all over her, thick like black fog.

The grove was near now, and she saw that the leaves were all dead, brown, and stiff. The trees were dying, as well.

Jacobus sat hunched on a thick branch about ten feet above her, clinging to the trunk and hiding his face in his arms, a black cloud around him.

"Jaap, didn't you hear me?" she called. "Please come down. Mother needs you. She misses you. Wilm misses you. I miss you."

Jacobus stared at her with pale eyes, his face pallid against the swarm of flies.

"Remember the first day I came here?" she asked him, standing next to the tree and grasping the lowest branch. "I was so scared and lonely...." She began to climb, speaking as gently as possible, but loud enough to be heard above the flies. "I didn't know what to do, how to get home. I missed my family, friends, and life back in my world."

She climbed higher, careful not to slip on the squashed remnants of flies, and then she was next to him, sitting on the branch. It swayed with her added weight. She put her arm around him and drew him close, brushing the flies from his face.

"You made me feel like I was your real big sister, the most important thing in the world."

He laid his face on her chest. She felt him lean into her, letting the fear seep from his small body.

"You are the reason I stayed here, Jaap. You made me strong."

He looked up at her, tears welling in his blue eyes. He drew a deep breath and sobbed, his tears wetting the front of her dress.

"You are my little brother, Jacobus. I love you."

Then she was crying, too. They held each other in the tree's embrace, swaying gently to an unsung lullaby.

She smelled smoke and looked up, scanning the fields around them. On the western horizon, she saw coils of black smoke rising and the first flickers of flame against the blue sky.

CHAPTER 51

Cart

Gregson noticed movement as she slowly walked into the bedroom, and was reflexively swinging her gun toward Cart when he struck her heavily, throwing the whole weight of his body into the attack. The mass of the two bodies and the brutish force of the tackle flung them both back against the bookcase. Books fell around them, white pages flapping like wounded birds.

Gregson took the force of the blow on her upper back. Breath burst from her lungs. Her head struck a corner of the bookcase, and she fell heavily to the floor, groaning. Then Cart was on top of her, straining to reach her gun. He hammered at her hand. She brought the weapon down hard toward Cart's head, but his adrenaline-fueled reflexes helped him beat it aside, and the gun flew from Gregson's grasp. It bounced across the floor and came to rest against the bed's leg. Cart pushed her back and dived at the pistol. Then she was all over him, arms and legs scrabbling with him. She pulled at Cart's legs frantically to keep him from getting the gun. He kicked at her blindly, belly crawling across the floor.

Gregson fell on his back and clawed at him hysterically, screaming and cursing, frenzied like a wild animal, hands and arms all over his neck and head, her breath hot on his neck. Cart threw his head back and struck Gregson violently on the bridge of her nose. He felt a satisfying crunch of cartilage smashing, and Gregson's scream filled his ears. It felt like someone hit his head with a hammer. His vision swam for a few seconds, hot blood covering the back of his head.

Gregson rolled off him, groaning and sobbing. The gun was within Cart's reach, so he grabbed it and rolled onto his back to aim at Gregson. But she was faster. Recovering from the blow, she shrieked and clawed at him, her face a bizarre mask of rage and blood, raining blows with incredible strength. Cart flailed clumsily back at her, his own blows largely ineffective against the ferocious attack. She was in his face screaming, bloody spittle spraying his cheeks. He was quickly tiring as his adrenaline-fueled speed and strength lessened.

He had to end this now, or Sarah was gone forever. The thought of his trapped daughter filled him with rage and ferocity. His body suddenly flooded with anger and intensity, filling him with a fire hotter than the flames devouring his house.

He kicked back at Gregson, then attacked with heavy blows and slaps, forcing her backward. They rolled across the floor, grunting and cursing, sweat flying. She had Cart's hand in her own, slamming it against the bed frame, trying to dislodge the gun. Then she bit down on his hand, teeth sinking into his palm. He screamed and dropped the pistol as blood welled from the wound, torn flesh hanging. Gregson grabbed the gun and scuttled from him to the wall opposite the fireplace.

CHAPTER 51

Cart struggled to stand, holding his wounded right hand, pain filling his arm.

Gregson stood slowly, pistol aimed at Cart, who had crawled to the fireplace. They were both exhausted, panting in huge gulps of air.

"Stand up, Carter," she said through blood and sweat, her broken nose flattened, her face a bruised and bloody mess. "Let's get this over with."

CHAPTER 52

Sarah

The fire was coming fast, racing across the dead, tinder-dry fields, filling the entire horizon with leaping flames and curling smoke, which enveloped them, faintly at first, then thick and choking as the fire raged toward them.

They ran as fast as possible toward the bridge's safety and the canal's firebreak. Sarah matched her speed to Jacobus, despite her inclination to run as fast as she could. He struggled and stumbled a few times, choking on the smoke and ashes billowing around them.

The flies had all disappeared, but this new affliction was much worse.

Their world was burning.

Sarah stopped on the far side of the bridge, gasping for breath. Jaap leaned against her, crying and coughing. The fire was at the canal's edge, its aggressive approach halted by the expanse of the water. The fire raged, flames belching and bursting. Sarah felt her eyebrows singeing, so she pulled Jaap toward the house.

The bridge began to smolder. Soon, the fire would crawl across the wooden structure and be on this side. What would they do then? Frantically, she looked down the canal toward the lake where Father fished. Should they run that way and wade out into the lake? They had to do something or they would burn to death.

In the billowing vales of smoke, she saw a flutter of white moving their way. Father was returning at last!

She picked up Jaap and ran toward the house to get Mother and Wilm. They would be safe now. Father would take them to the lake in his boat.

Then she stopped, staring dumbly at the flames approaching the rear of the house, out in the dry tulip fields beyond the cheese house.

CHAPTER 53

Cart

Cart slumped against the fireplace, wiping his face with his shirt sleeve. He was exhausted, his legs were trembling, and his head hurt from hitting Gregson's nose. He watched her standing on the other side of the bed, grinning wickedly at him, her face a bloody mask, eyes hard as stone. She'd unfolded the contract and laid it on the bed, along with a pen.

"Well," she said, "here we are at the end of the game. You know I can't leave here without that tile. You also know I can't take it until you tell me to. You sign this, I'll take the tile and leave you and your family alone. And you know you won't get Sarah back. As Madame Locksley said, she is collateral damage, unfortunately."

"Then just go," Cart said. "Leave here and go wherever it is you want to go, but it won't be with the tile. I want my daughter back, but I can't allow you to take the tile and loose that creature on the world."

"Oh, Cart," she said, "you can't be that naive. You know that's not how this will end. I wish my sister was here with me so she could see that I was always stronger than she was. She could never have killed Roland. Elizabeth was always too soft."

Sister?

"Elizabeth was your sister?" he asked.

"Stepsister, actually. Not that it matters now. What's done is done. I'm now the leader of the Rose Brotherhood since Roland and his merry band destroyed the chateau. Luckily, I was working here to fulfill my duties. It's been wonderful getting to know your family. And meeting James. He was a decent designer. I love what he's done to your house."

James?

"How do you know James? I mean, besides as a fake cop?" He thought of the many times this woman had been in their house.

"Poor, poor James." She smiled through her mask of blood. "He whined like a baby before I shot him. I didn't even care. Not a second thought. He didn't deserve to live, anyway. He was a disgusting, deviated, dysfunctional Sodomite. Absolutely disgusting."

"You killed him?" Cart asked, barely suppressing his rage. "He never harmed anyone. He was my friend."

"Oh, a friend?" she sneered. "Did you partake of his proclivities, too? The two of you? That makes sense now that I think of it. That would explain why you were so close."

"Stop! I'm done with your idiocy. I loved him, yes, but as a *friend*. He didn't have many, but I was one. Now, get the hell out of my house. You're not taking the tile. I'll die before I let you!" Smoke was circling around the ceiling. He heard flames crackling somewhere in the stairwell.

"Oh, Carter," she said, "that was always the plan."

CHAPTER 53

And then she shot him.

CHAPTER 54

Sarah

Father climbed wearily from the boat, his face a mask of sweat and ashes.

"Get your mother out here," he ordered Sarah, "quickly, while we have time."

She ran for the door, leaving a wide-eyed and frightened Jacobus clutching his father's big hand.

Mother was nursing Willem, sitting in the rocker, and humming a soft lullaby. Wilm made soothing sucking sounds as he gazed at his mother's face. Mother was staring vacantly at the fireplace, rocking back and forth.

"Mother?" Sarah said carefully. "We have to get out of here. It's all burning."

Mother looked up at her, and Sarah saw streaks of tears on her cheeks.

"Father's back."

"He's back?" Mother's eyes brightened. "I thought he deserted us."

She tried to stand with her free arm, supporting the baby against her breast with the other. Sarah helped her stand, and Mother pulled Wilm away with a popping sound and covered herself.

"Help me gather our things," Mother said dumbly, staring around the room.

"Mother, we don't have time for that!" Sarah urged, pulling her toward the door. "We have to get out now! The fire is almost to our back door!"

Mother let Sarah steer her to the front door but then hesitated at the threshold. "This is my home," she whispered. "It's all I have."

Sarah was pulling at her frantically, trying to move her. "You have Jacobus and Willem. And you have me and Father. He's waiting to take us away in his boat. We can have another home somewhere else. Father can do that. You know he can!"

Mother reached back and pulled the door shut. "You're right," she said, her eyes finally clear and lucid.

***

Father stood with Jacobus in the middle of the road, flames roaring across the fully engulfed bridge like an angry beast. Mother gave Wilm to Sarah and ran to Father, throwing her arms around him. He hugged her fiercely, burying his face in her golden hair. There was a loud crashing sound behind them. Startled, they all turned to see the house in flames. The roof had collapsed, sending fire and sparks bursting explosively into the smoke-filled sky.

CHAPTER 54

Willem began squirming in Sarah's arms, fighting against her, struggling with surprising strength, his eyes wide and terrified. Mother took him from Sarah, holding him tightly to calm him.

And then he was abruptly gone, Mother clutching empty air.

Mother began to scream.

CHAPTER 55

Cart

He'd seen her hand twitch, and he reflexively covered the tile with his right hand. She wasn't going to take Sarah. His hand exploded in a burst of flesh, bone, and blood. The tile shattered, covered in Cart's blood, and fell to the floor.

Cart slumped to the floor, agony filling him, squirming in pain. Then Gregson was standing over him, smiling grimly through her horrible mask. He clutched his hand to his chest, trying to staunch the blood flow from the jagged stump. She aimed the pistol at his head.

"Goodbye, Cart," she said. "I've had a great time. Your blood on the contract is all I need."

His mind was consumed with pain and fear, but he thought he saw quick movement behind her in the hallway.

Gregson's eyes flew open wide. Her scream was sudden and piercing, like a siren's wail in Cart's ears. He moaned, covering his ears, blood flowing down his face.

She clawed at her back, flailing and shrieking. She spun around and lashed out behind her. There was an explosion, and the side of her head burst. She collapsed to the floor, the handle of Cart's Scottish dirk sprouting like a bloody flower from her back. Annie stood over Gregson, glaring at the woman dead at her feet.

CHAPTER 56

Sarah

Father howled to the skies, his voice like thunder echoing around them, drowning out the fury of the flames. Mother was hysterical, clutching at him as she screamed, "My baby, my baby!" but it barely registered with Sarah.

Panicked, she reached for Jacobus, who stood staring at Mother and Father, eyes round with confusion and fear. She hugged him tightly against her, whispering in his ear: "I love you, Jaap, I love you, Jaap," over and over, his face plastered into her apron, thin shoulders convulsing. Suddenly, he pushed back from her with eyes wide and his mouth open.

"I love you, Jaap."

Then he was gone, like a shadow in the glare of a midday sun.

She knelt in the dirt and ash, emptiness filling her arms and heart as tears streamed down her face. Father's wail enveloped her like a wave, knocking her back on the dirt and taking the breath from her lungs. Mother sobbed in anguish as the sky rumbled. Lightning lashed the earth as rain began to pour from the heavens.

"Damn you, damn you, bring my babies back!" She pounded on his chest as he tried to console her, holding him to her as she flailed ineffectually. "Bring them back! I want them back!"

The rain hissed and spattered in the mud and ash. The fire still raged, although hot steam rose in billows from the fields and the remains of the house, enveloping the three of them in moist heat. Father took her hands in his great, calloused ones, his face a mask of sorrow.

"I can't, my love, I can't. I'm sorry. I don't know what is happening; I can't stop it."

Sarah could barely hear him above the clash of thunder and the torrential downpour, but there was no mistaking the sorrow in his voice. As she watched, Mother suddenly stiffened and looked up wildly into Father's eyes, then hugged him with so much force, he stumbled back. Then she, too, was gone like a whiff of silent thought.

Father's pain was like a living thing, visibly coiling and thrashing in the storm-racked sky like a headless snake, snapping whip-like around and above her, striking the mud with incredible force. She cowered from it, afraid it would destroy her. He fell on his face in the muck and clawed at the ground, mud and ashes like black clay in his grasping hands. He tore at his hair and clothes in anguish, covered in the mud like a golem brought to life.

Sarah carefully crawled to him, keenly aware of the power and agony roiling out of him like waves thrashing against a beach, falling to the ground protectively as it surged over her, raising her hair like static electricity.

She knelt over him, her heart aching with loss.

CHAPTER 56

This—*thing*—had ripped her from her family, taking her from the loving embrace of her home, and somehow brought her to this awful, unchanging place. How long had she been here? Months? Years? She couldn't count the number of times she'd milked the cow and made cheese or helped Mother clean the house. Her heart ached for Jacobus and Willem, knowing they were gone and she'd never see them again.

She thought of her family back home: her mom, her dad, and Maddy. She'd never been able to tell them how much she loved them before she came here. She'd been a prideful, spoiled brat then. But everything was ending now, and this world would soon be gone. She would go to whatever dark place the others had disappeared to. She was okay with that, although seeing her family again would be nice so she could apologize and tell them she loved them.

She had thought Father was an all-powerful being, like an ancient god who could create and obliterate with the wave of a hand.

Yet here he was, covered in mud and weeping like a disconsolate child. She unexpectedly pitied him, although she didn't know why she should feel that way after all he'd done to her. She'd been a prisoner here, mourning the loss of her home and family until she finally understood things wouldn't change. He had been kind to her, in his way, after forcing her to obey. He'd treated the others with love and concern. She touched his shoulder.

"Am I going to die?" she whispered, tears filling her eyes. She was filled with an immense sadness that almost overwhelmed her, grieving the loss of Jacobus and Willem and the loss of Maddy and her parents.

What would happen now? Would it hurt? She wanted her mom and dad and missed their comforting embrace.

He put a muddy hand to her cheek, softly touching it, then slid it to her chin and raised her eyes to his. "No..." he whispered so quietly she could barely hear him.

She felt a strange clenching in her stomach, like a turning, flapping bird. Her vision began to blur, and she panicked. Tears were running down his cheeks.

She touched his face, wondering.

"Goodbye, Sarah," he murmured. His voice had a strange echo as though from a distance. "I'm sorry."

Her mind was filled with a dizzying roar, and she fell into a great darkness that spun and sucked her into it like a black hole.

Then she, too, was gone.

CHAPTER 57

Cart

Annie was kneeling beside Cart, holding his bloody wrist against her chest, trying to staunch the bleeding with her jacket. His thoughts were growing muddy, the loss of blood taking its toll. He struggled to make sense of what he was seeing.

"Annie..." Even to himself, his voice sounded like a croak. Where had she come from? "Did God send you?"

Then Collins was there, shoving his pistol into his shoulder holster as he dropped to Annie's side, tearing the tie from around his neck and tying it tightly above the shattered hand. Cart groaned in pain.

"We've got to get him out of here!" Collins shouted like a great cannon echoing off the cliffs of Cart's mind. "Help me get him up!"

Smoke curled around them. Annie helped Cart stand, got some hand towels from the bathroom, and drenched them in water. They tied them around their faces.

Strong hands grasped him, and he was lifted, Annie at his side like a vision from heaven, a halo of fire around her golden hair. The flames were everywhere, and he floated through it on a cloud of smoke. No.

Collins was carrying him, stumbling toward the stairs. Bright lights seemed to beckon him, urging him like the hand of God, but it was the fire devouring their house. Wailing filled his mind, strident and piercing like the lamentation of angels.

Sirens...

Then cold air was on his face, and the smoke lessened, the fierce heat gone. He was floating in the cold night air on the wings of angels, Annie herself white and radiant at his side, droplets of ice on her cheeks. Then he was on the hard, frozen ground, and he saw his house in flames, the glow reflected in Annie's blue, blue eyes. Sirens howled, lights flashed red and blue, and the trees around the house were lit with garish strobes. Strange people were running and shouting, dragging hoses. Then, to his wonder, Sarah was kneeling by her mother, wearing a strange white and yellow dress, and Annie was hugging her, and Sarah was hugging her back, and they were both bawling like babies. Collins stared at them with wonder in his eyes, mouth open.

"Sarah..." Cart whispered, reaching for her with his good left hand.

His daughter leaned over him, her beautiful face so much like her mother's. She took his hand into her own and held it to her cheek.

"My Sarah. You've come home." His voice was fading, becoming insubstantial. Was he only thinking those words?

Sarah bent and kissed his cheek. "Yes, Dad, I'm home."

His heart flared like the sun in his chest, and tears stung the corners of his eyes. "My little girl... I love you...." His voice failed him. His vision dimmed. The lights in the darkness faded, and he was lost in shadows.

CHAPTER 57

In the far distance, where he couldn't see, he heard a blur of voices urging him home.

CHAPTER 58

The Fisherman

His boat, tied to a stone and bobbing in the current, waited for him. He stood looking at the smoking ruin of his home, stark against the sky's great blue bowl. He knew it was time to leave, but couldn't pull himself away.

Maybe he would heal someday. He didn't know for sure because he'd never known such feelings and that he was capable of such love until he'd come here, lured by the Song still holding him.

I will leave this place now, *he thought.* I will never again know such love and happiness. I never deserved it, anyway.

He heard a different Song now, one of his own making, a beautiful melody about Katharina of the Golden Hair, whispering in the breeze that ruffled his hair and stirred the ashes at his feet. He would never again listen to another's Song.

He sighed and climbed into his boat, unlashing it and loosening the sail. It spread like a great wing above him as the wind grew at his call, stirring the boat on the water's surface. He breathed into the billowing sail, and the boat began moving down the canal, leaving behind the silent home and the echo of a life he never thought he'd have.

The boat moved faster, skimming the surface of the water like a bird past the burned tulip fields and the devastated world he'd created, faster and faster, the wind in his face, and then he burst from the canal and was on the open sea, the sail whipping in the wind that carried him, froth and salt stinging his face.

Then he was above the thrashing waves, and the smell of salt and water faded as he followed the Song, urging him onwards, pulling him from his grief. The clouds and fog enveloped him, a comforting cloak, and opened for him like immense curtains, and he was gone. . . .

Katharina of the Golden hair,
Eyes of blue and skin so fair...

EPILOGUE

Waves lapped at the boat as he stood in the bow, watching the Laughing Gulls wheel and sail in the sky above him, raucous cries a sharp contrast to the grace and beauty of their flight. The cloudless sky was glorious; the sun was warm on his shoulders. The children were playing happily on the beach, running from the surf as it rushed toward them, happy to be together again. He smiled as the gulls landed and approached them, hoping to scavenge a morsel of food before launching into the air when they got too close. He breathed the warm, humid air deeply. It was a beautiful day.

The boat rocked as Annie climbed aboard from the beach, a flowery sarong wrapped around her, a straw hat and sunglasses perched on her head. Her blonde hair had lightened significantly in the Caribbean sun, almost white.

She smiled as she drew next to him and put her arm around his waist, hugging him to her. She smelled like coconut and lime. Cart kissed the top of her head and pulled her close, wishing he could caress her hair simultaneously.

Sometimes, he felt his hand where it used to be, what doctors called phantom feeling, the plascticity of the brain's synapses firing at the end of his wrist, trying vainly to move nonexistent fingers. He didn't think he'd ever get used to losing his hand, but what choice did he have? He was thinking about a prosthetic, but that was a ways off.

Sarah was healing, as well.

At first, it was hard for her to adjust to everyday life. She missed Jacobus and Willem, the little boys from her other life. Cart worried for her. Sometimes, she would have to be alone to grieve, and he would hear her crying in her room. But for the most part, she threw herself into life with a joy and vigor that amazed and gratified him.

She spent every spare moment with Maddy, and of course, Maddy took advantage of the extra attention as only Maddy could. He feared Maddy's demands for Sarah's attention would annoy his oldest daughter, but to his surprise, she seemed to be thriving on the focus of her younger sister.

So far, so good...

While Cart was healing, Master Alain invited them to Scotland to attend the memorial service for Roland on a private estate the Templars owned: hundreds of Knights dressed in resplendent white robes with the square red cross over their left breast, swords hanging from their sides, lining the grounds of the castle. It was amazing and touching to see. Row after row of Knights standing at attention, honoring their friend. David and Warren, as sergeants, held the banner of the Poor Knights of Christ and the Temple of Solomon aloft on a castle wall next to Master Alain and Cart and his family. A line of bagpipes and drums played "Amazing Grace," its strains echoing over the highlands.

Master Alain also offered some remote Order-owned property on the mild west coast of St. Lucia with a long private beach and magnif-

EPILOGUE

icent isolation for the family to spend some time alone. They could leave whenever they wanted to tour the island or shop, but preferred to stay in the modest house provided for them among the tall palms and deep forest, watching the sun sink like a great golden ball into the sea, and lying in the darkness listening to the whisper of the surf at night.

David and Warren visited occasionally.

The big, happy Māori taught the girls some of his island dances, laughing as Maddy danced the Haka, trying to look fierce and angry, sticking out her tongue and opening her eyes wide.

The girls loved the guys.

Warren, ever the quiet one, played chess with Cart or Annie at the table under the palms in front of the house or simply sat with them and watched the waves stroke the beach, telling them about Roland. They missed their friend and captain.

Every morning, there was a fresh rose in the small wooden vase on the table in the kitchen.

Sarah loved helping her mother prepare meals and had even offered to make cheese for them someday.

He chuckled at that. *Sarah making cheese.*

After healing from his surgery enough to make plans for the future, he resigned from the law firm to focus on his family. He could never bring back those long hours and days spent working, but he would try his best to make up for it.

They had enough in their savings and retirement to keep them for some time if they were careful. Their rental properties still generated good income each month, so Cart gave Sam the deeds to half of the properties for all his efforts during Sarah's disappearance.

Their insurance company approved rebuilding the house, but that decision had been put on hold for another day. What was the rush? They had their whole lives to worry about that.

Someday, they might return to the long winters and four seasons in Utah, but right now, the sun, surf, and beach were all they needed.

And, of course, each other...

* * *

It turned out Martina Gregson was a rogue cop, stalking Sarah after she'd been assigned to the Christmas break-in, kidnapping her, and forcing her to live chained in the basement of a rental house. She'd come to their home that night to destroy any evidence of her crime, leaving Sarah tied up in the back seat of her car while she went inside to start the fires that destroyed their home.

Despite great effort, the body found in the basement mechanical room had remained unidentified. It was presumed to be a homeless man who had tried to help and had gotten caught up in the nightmare of Gregson's insanity.

Or at least that was how Detective Will Collins explained it.

Cart and Annie paid for Roland's memorial and burial, and a nice monument with the words "UNKNOWN HERO" carved into the stone. He was buried on a hillside overlooking the city and the lake in the west. The sunsets were superb.

When the long days of summer were over, and autumn's gold and scarlet leaves crackled underfoot, and if they returned home, Sarah would be back in school, one student among hundreds in her high school.

EPILOGUE

Just trying to fit in . . .

THE END